D0855813

THE
BEACHED
ONES

THE BEACHED ONES

ONES

Colleen M. Story

CamCat
Books

Content Warning: This novel touches upon suicide and may be disturbing to some readers.

CamCat Publishing, LLC
Brentwood, Tennessee 37027
camcatpublishing.com

This is a work of fiction. Names, characters, places, and incidents are either products of the author's imagination or are used fictitiously.

© 2022 by Colleen M. Story

All rights reserved. Printed in the United States of America. No part of this book may be used or reproduced in any manner whatsoever without written permission except in the case of brief quotations embodied in critical articles and reviews. For information, address CamCat Publishing, 101 Creekside Crossing, Suite 280, Brentwood, TN 37027.

Hardcover ISBN 9780744305340
Paperback ISBN 9780744305388
Large-Print Paperback ISBN 9780744305470
eBook ISBN 9780744305456
Audiobook ISBN 9780744305555

Library of Congress Cataloguing-in-Publication Data available upon request

Book and cover design by Maryann Appel

5   3   1   2   4

Also by Colleen M. Story

Fiction
Loreena's Gift
Rise of the Sidenah

Nonfiction
Your Writing Matters
Writer Get Noticed!
Overwhelmed Writer Rescue

For my brothers, and for Mom.

"There is no despair so absolute as that which comes with the first moments of our first great sorrow, when we have not yet known what it is to have suffered and be healed, to have despaired and have recovered hope."

—George Eliot, from *Adam Bede*

D aniel A. Shepard would have been lost forever had not the lighthouse beam brought him back to life. In sweeping strokes it painted the blackness in ribbons of white, awakening his spirit with each pass over his body, gently drawing him out of the blackness into which he had fallen. He dropped his arm over his face, suspecting a crack in the hotel drapes, but the light shone through nevertheless, as if the sleeve of his fleece jacket were no more than a thin cotton sheet. He rolled over on his side. A sharp pain sliced through his thighs, forcing him fully awake. His legs were on fire. He slapped at the flames, but when he looked down, he was fully clothed, his limbs unharmed.

The ceiling twinkled, some sort of spray glitter he'd failed to notice before. But no, the sparkles were too far away. And the air smelled fresh, not the typical hotel air, heavy with the scent of old socks. He'd expected the usual lumpy beds and noisy cooling fans.

It wasn't long before he realized this was no hotel.

He was outside.

His gaze went first to the flashing light, emanating from an airport tower, he thought, until he heard the roar of the ocean below. Having grown up in Montana, he'd never been to either coast, but now long waves gleamed like threads of lace, appearing and then fading into the deep. He stared, half unsure of what he was seeing, and still they danced in and out under a moonlit sky, the lighthouse showing them off about every twenty seconds. A breeze caressed his face, bringing with it the scent of salt and seaweed, and then he noticed the sand cool between his fingers. He lifted one hand and let the soft grains trickle over his palm. The guys had spoken about heading for the beach after the Los Angeles show, but last he remembered, they hadn't made it out of the bar.

The pain returned, biting at his ankles, flames erupting about the hem of his jeans. He recoiled, crab legging through the sand, one hand slapping at the fire until he fell onto his back. The vision faded to reveal his jeans intact, white cotton socks covering his ankles, the fleece jacket unzipped, his favorite high-tops on his feet.

"I didn't drink that much," he said out loud, though his tone was less than convincing. He removed his Kawasaki cap and ran his fingers through his thick, brown hair, resting his hand on the back of his neck. Jay had asked him to join the others. They'd left the crowd on their feet, an audience of over a thousand shouting for more. They'd deserved a celebration.

"Jay?" Daniel called, "you there?"

The last show was a blur. All he could remember was his hometown of Butte, Montana, the old grandstand at the fairgrounds lit up with stadium lights as he and the six other motorcycle riders flew over the tops of hundreds of heads. But that couldn't be right.

They were in L.A. Their last show had to have been in L.A. Behind him, city lights danced in the distance, casting a hazy orange glow into the night sky. His last run up the ramp, he'd done the dead body and the cliffhanger. Or had it been the double grab and the superman?

The night answered only in waves, the sand whispering *hush*.

He had to pick up Tony in San Francisco. The thought came out of the blue. His little brother was attending the marine camp he'd drooled over for years. He'd be finished on August twenty-ninth. If Daniel weren't there, the kid would be left stranded. He glanced at his wrist, but his watch was gone. They were supposed to spend a couple of weeks together before Tony went back to school, though Daniel wasn't sure he was going to let his little brother return to their mother's house. Tony had been in that hellhole long enough. Daniel had an apartment now. They could both stay there.

He patted his pockets. No keys, no wallet. But something in the front right. He dug in and pulled out the Matchbox F-14 Tomcat. He'd received it as a present when he was young, for Christmas maybe, though he couldn't remember for sure. He'd passed it on to Tony on his fifth birthday, and then Tony had given it back before Daniel had left the hellhole for good. Tony had meant it as a good-luck charm, something to keep Daniel safe while he was performing his stunts. Daniel turned it over in his hand, puzzled.

A piercing whistle grabbed his attention. He tucked the toy away and stood up. Over the din of the ocean the whistle came again, a high-pitched tone that spiked and then dropped. He held his breath. There, at the shoreline, down and to the right. The waves crested and crashed, and then a distressed, wailing sound of something or someone in pain.

It wasn't easy running in the sand, especially in high-top sneakers. Salty grains poked at his heels. As if wanting to help, the lighthouse intermittently showed the way. *Here. No, over here.*

At the crest of the hill, he looked down on a long stretch of beach, the sand smoothed by the tide. To the right, where the moon's glow frosted the shore, loaf-shaped mounds lay marooned among the ocean's refuse, grounded vessels cast aside as if by a storm.

Daniel approached with caution. The shadows loomed larger with every step; great sea monsters with invisible faces. Ten feet away, he hesitated. Multiple torpedo-shaped bodies, twelve to sixteen feet long, all with aft-facing dorsal fins, lay stranded on the sand. Pilot whales. Tony had taped pictures of them on the walls of his room during his sea-creature phase, which had followed his dinosaur obsession. He'd liked the pilot whales best because they looked so much like dolphins, bulbous heads blunted in front, mouths angled up in permanent smiles. Daniel trudged past five, ten, twelve of them. Some exhaled out their blowholes, spraying weak fountains over their heads. One lifted its tail and then let it fall back with a thud. After fifteen, he stopped.

A new sound drew his ear, something shuffling nearby. He stumbled forward in the darkness and found a baby whale struggling to be near its mother. It was about a third her size, maybe five feet long, the smiling mouth deceptively cheerful. Half crouched, Daniel approached. At its side, he paused, extended his hand, and tentatively touched the skin. Slick and rubbery, it was like raw egg over a soccer ball. Tony would be devastated to see his favorite animals dying. The mother Daniel could do nothing for, but looking again at the baby, he shed his fleece jacket and squatted down. The young ones were only about 150 pounds. Tucking one hand underneath the tail, he raised his chin and slid the other under what he thought was the neck, wriggling his fingers through the sand to get a grip. Once he'd secured a good hold, he took a breath and heaved. The whale felt heavier than he'd expected. He pushed hard, forcing his heels into the sand, his thighs straining. Slowly, he rose, wobbled a bit, and finally stood upright. The weight settled hard and heavy against his chest. The whale squirmed and Daniel thought he might lose him, but then the animal went still. Daniel walked unsteadily toward the water, the whale's skin slick against his own. He went about ten feet until his shoes sank into the wet sand, and then a little farther until the ocean came up to his waist. With the current buffeting his body, he let go.

The baby swam out, turned, and went back to the shore. Flopping like a hooked fish, it called for its mother. The big whale whistled in answer. Daniel trudged back onto the beach, his chest heaving. Water sloshed in his shoes, his jeans heavy, the breeze cold on his arms. He scooped up the whale, balanced himself, and again carried it to the water. He walked farther out the second time, but still, the baby returned.

The dim glow of dawn cast a grey light on the mass suicide before him. He spotted movement in some of the shapes, but only occasionally did a blast of mist escape a blowhole or a low groan overwhelm the ocean's roar. The baby called to its mother in pitiful squeaks and whistles, but she no longer answered back. Daniel knew he should get help, but for most of them, it would be too late.

Orion stood tall in the eastern sky, the Big Dipper angling northwest, both dispassionately observing the scene playing out below. A gust of wind cooled Daniel's skin. He shivered under his wet clothes, retrieved his fleece jacket, and pulled it back on. Arms crossed, he walked up the hill. He would find help or the rest of the guys or something. They couldn't be that far off. The whales were nearly out of sight when the baby cried out again, a wild sound like a child's scream of terror. Daniel's flesh lifted off his bones.

He ran all the way back. In the water a third time, he waded forward until he could no longer feel the sand under his feet, and then did his best to swim even farther, clinging tightly to the rubbery skin. Kicking hard he managed a few more feet before the whale slipped away and disappeared into the ocean. Spent, Daniel waited, treading water, the wet jacket heavy on his shoulders as he scanned the shoreline.

Moments passed, but he didn't detect any new shapes moving. The waves tossed him up and down, playing with him. He blinked saltwater out of his eyes.

Come on. *Come on.*

There! Like a geyser, the spout burst from the water. It sparkled momentarily and then dropped and disappeared into the vastness of the ocean. Three times the whale's back arced into the night, the moon shaping its blow into a cream-colored cone until at last, everything was quiet and Daniel swam alone.

He leaned back and let the water take him where it would. He would rest for a moment and then swim back, find a phone, call Jay, and regroup. He'd have a hell of a story to tell Tony when he picked him up. A smile creased his lips, and then the pain returned and he doubled over with it, his gaze seeking but not finding the flames. With desperate motions, he swam back to the shore. Hands and knees in the sand, he panted hard until the burning cooled and he could lie down, the great sea monsters surrounding him in a silent embrace.

CHAPTER TWO

His recovery on the shore was short-lived. Just as he started to get up on his hands and knees, the sand collapsed underneath him, tilting him over onto his side. Feeling his hip and shoulder start to sink, he rolled onto his back to see stars dragging streaks of light behind them, the night sky spinning like a Ferris wheel. He was dizzy from fatigue, he thought, but the sensation intensified, the beach wide and then narrow, the night twisting as if wringing itself out. He remembered suffering a fever as a child, when everything appeared distorted and smaller than it should have been, rooms shrinking in size even while he seemed to grow, except this time it was the coastline and the lighthouse and the city lights expanding and elongating until they were nothing but colored ribbons. Around and around it all went, the vertigo so overpowering he closed his eyes. Gradually, the sensation eased and the world stopped moving, leaving him feeling as if he'd come to the end of an amusement park ride.

His childhood home materialized around him, a ragged trailer house on the outskirts of Butte. He sat crouched low by the living room window. Raindrops spattered the glass, the sky covered in dense gray clouds. Outside, donning a homemade headdress fashioned from a leather belt and taped-on crow feathers, Tony stood in the steady downpour, having taken up a post in the middle of the muddy front yard, if you could call the square of dirt between their trailer and the gravel road beyond a yard. Daniel peered through the part of the window that wasn't covered with brown spray paint. His little brother raised skinny white arms to the sky and started to run in circles. His feet pummeled the ground, shooting out muddy splashes of slop that fell back to stain his jeans. After five times around, he changed to a football shuffle, side to side with his arms pumping in front of him. Rain bombed his feathers and soaked through his black hair. Ten minutes later, he stood like a soldier, sent God a drenched salute, and ran back inside. Dropping the headdress on the TV tray by the door, he stepped out of his mud-covered sneakers and ran across the room to join Daniel. "Did it work? Did the rain stop?"

The memory faded, giving way to the sensation of hard stone poking into his cheek. He was outdoors again, one side of his body warmed by the sun, the other pressed against a mound of dirt that quivered underneath him. A train whistle moaned. Wheels clacked in a steady rhythm, coming, coming, and then a ding-ringing of bells. Under his fingers, a steel track vibrated. The whistle sounded again, louder this time, bombarding his ears and forcing his eyelids back. The steel monster was no more than fifty feet away. Scrambling to his hands and knees, he glanced with horror at the tracks where his fingers had lain. A gust of wind blasted his face as the engine barreled by, the whistle dropping in pitch with a mournful farewell. Daniel grabbed his cap and stumbled backward, down the incline and away from the tracks. In his rush he lost his balance and fell, rolling twice before coming to rest on level ground.

It was midday, the sun shining brightly above him, green fields covering the area on the other side of the tracks. He got to his feet, dusted off his jeans, placed his cap on his head and looked around. In front of him rested a tank trailer of some sort, several others parked nearby awaiting transport. Magpies croaked their disapproval from a clump of cottonwood trees on the other side of the lot. All around him stretched a country landscape rich with farm fields, a red barn and silver grain silo visible in the distance. He kept turning, surveilling it all, at one point rubbing the back of his head and then dropping his hand to his waist. How had he gone from the ocean to the plains? He checked his jeans, shirt, and jacket. All dry. Completely dry. Even his hair was dry.

On his fourth turn around he paused to study what looked like an eatery across the road, a single-story building painted barn red with white trim, a matching sign hanging from a tall iron post: The Old Biddy. Daniel narrowed his eyes. He didn't know this place. He wished he'd reconsidered Jay's advice about buying a cell phone. "It's 2014 Danny," his friend had teased numerous times. "You're acting like an old man." Still, considering that his wallet and keys were gone, a phone probably would have been stolen too. The café was his best shot at getting in touch with somebody.

He headed toward the place, gravel crunching under his shoes. An antique farm plow sat on the grass in front; two cars, a rusted truck, and a Suzuki motorcycle parked at the curb. On the other street corner rested a mechanic's shop and, down the way, three single-level houses worn and aged from too many winters without fresh paint.

He was about to open the door when a young couple emerged, both with tattooed arms and pierced noses. They passed him by without comment, an overhead bell announcing their exit. Daniel slipped in behind them, barely clearing the entrance before stiff springs slammed the door closed. An elderly couple sat in a booth by the wall, newspapers partitions between them. At a center table, a man with a buzz cut sliced into his steak, thick biceps framing his ribs. Sizzling sounds emanated from the back, the smell of beef in the air. Daniel looked to his right and jumped, startled. An oversized rooster stood just inside the door, its sharp yellow beak poised over his head.

The waitress, a portly woman with three hens on her apron, walked out in rubber-soled shoes, the kind hospital nurses wore to ease the wear and tear on their feet. Years of skin drooped from her arms, her wide face framed with curly black hair. Daniel waited, but she breezed by him, depositing the smell of cheap hairspray in her wake. She opened the door, looked left and right, then mumbled something inaudible and retraced her steps.

"Ma'am?" he called, but she didn't respond. "Ma'am, do you have a phone?"

The woman disappeared into the back. Daniel scanned the place. They had to have an office or break room or something. As he started after her, he sensed he was being watched.

The young woman stood at the side of her booth, intense green eyes focused on him. Thick auburn hair fell in choppy layers about her head, the bangs jagged over graceful eyebrows. Her fair skin was flushed at the cheeks and neck, her body thin and half hidden underneath the brown leather jacket she wore. "Daniel?"

There was something familiar about the eyes, something that made him hold his breath. She was too far away, but he could smell the musky perfume she wore, the spicy zing of it. He knew her silver earrings were shaped like an artist's palette, the circles of paint small indentations in the metal. He felt a moment's pleasure that she was wearing them but couldn't remember why. He took a step toward her.

Her grip tightened on the booth. "Daniel? Is that you?"

He could feel her hair in his hands, the kind of hair you could grab hold of without worrying about breaking it. Her lips tasted like the caramel candies she carried in her pocket. "Jolene."

She blinked rapidly, looked around the café, and then stared at him again. "But you . . . you're . . ."

"Jolene!" They'd walked together through a park where the ducks fanned their feathers in the sun. They'd gazed at paintings on a museum wall while arguing about their worth. She'd waited for him at the edge of the fairgrounds near the exit gate. "Where are we?"

"You don't know where you are?"

"We had a show last night, but . . ." He shook his head. "I can't remember." He could feel her small ear pressed against his chest. They had been standing outside a hotel on a late night. He'd asked if she had friends waiting, but she'd only stared at him with those startling green eyes, and then she'd stood on her tiptoes and kissed him.

"Daniel?"

"We were touring in L.A., I thought, but since last night . . ." He looked around. The place was covered in chickens, black and white pictures of hen houses on the walls, shelves laden with knick-knacks and ceramic figurines, chicks in bunches peering over the tops of woven baskets. Daniel's vision blurred. Swaying, he sought to steady himself. "I need a phone."

"Here, no . . ." Jolene flew to his side, and then hesitated a moment before touching him. When she did, a look of surprise crossed her face, but he was so unsteady she recovered quickly and with one arm around his waist, walked him to the booth and set him on the bench seat opposite hers. A glass of ice water sat untouched on the table. He drained half of it, the cool liquid dousing the fire that wasn't really there but still made him sweat. Uncomfortable under her intense gaze, he tried to look nonchalant.

"What do you have to do to get service in here? Crow?"

The waitress wouldn't acknowledge his existence, not even after he asked her twice for a cheeseburger with fries and a Dr. Pepper. He might have given her a piece of his mind if Jolene hadn't intervened, slipping in the burger with her request for a strawberry waffle. The waitress scratched the order down and then patted the young woman on her skinny arm as if she pitied her, saying she was glad to see her appetite had improved.

Country music played over speakers in the ceiling corners, the tables covered in red-and-white checkered tablecloths. "I've never been here before," Daniel said half to himself before he realized Jolene had heard him. "I don't even know how I got here." He glanced at her face. She was looking at him as if he was the last thing she had ever expected to see. In one hand she clenched a pendant that hung around her neck, a rich purple stone cut in a diamond shape. "Did we plan to meet here?" he asked.

"A long time ago."

"Not today?"

She reached out and touched his hand. His impulse was to touch her back, but she was studying the limb as if in science class, pressing down on the fleshy part between his thumb and forefinger and then against his wrist to check his pulse. He opened his hand to take hers but she withdrew and tucked both arms under the table. When he looked at her face she turned away as if embarrassed and rubbed her arms against a chill. The earrings were the ones he'd remembered, the artist's palette. He'd given them to her. Over a pizza dinner.

"Iowa?" he said.

"Harlan." She glanced at him. "About an hour and a half from Des Moines. You remember Des Moines, don't you?"

Des Moines.

Yes.

That's where they had met.

The memories returned like tentative kittens. The team did a show there. She'd come backstage afterwards to have merchandise signed. He'd asked her to stay another day. Then another and another until a week had gone by and the team had to leave for their next tour date.

The waitress brought the second glass of water Jolene had requested, then looked at Daniel's and paused. "Did I get that right?" she asked. "You wanted another one?"

"I'd like some more," Daniel said, pushing his empty glass over.

"It's fine," Jolene said with a forced smile.

"But I'd like—" Daniel started but the waitress was already walking away. Jolene pushed the new glass to his side of the table. "Don't you want it?" he asked.

"I got it for you."

He took it gratefully and drained half of it. When he set it down she was staring at him again. "What?" he asked.

"What *do* you remember?"

The ocean. It would make him sound nuttier than he already did. He took another sip and shifted his weight. "The last show we did," he said. "I think something happened. An accident or something."

"An accident."

"There was a fire. I can't remember . . ." He looked around the café again. How had he ever traveled from L.A. to Iowa with no memory of the time between? "You sure we didn't plan to meet here today?"

She sat stiffly in her seat twisting the edges of her napkin. "You don't know how you got here?"

More water. He felt so hot. Already his second glass was almost empty. "I woke up over there. By the tracks."

"Woke up?"

The waitress brought their meal and set it down in front of Jolene. When she'd gone Jolene pushed the cheeseburger over. It seemed rude to eat now with so many questions between them, but the aroma was too tempting. He took a bite. The meat was juicy and flavorful, the best he could remember tasting in a long while. It was only when he was nearly done that he paused to see Jolene still watching him, her lips shiny with syrup, most of her waffle intact on her plate.

"I need to pick up my little brother," he blurted.

She stopped chewing.

"August twenty-ninth," he continued. "He's at summer camp. What's today?"

She swallowed hard and set the fork down on the plate.

"If this is Iowa, I need to get going. I've got to get to San Francisco—"

She covered her mouth, a shadow passing over her features.

"What?" Daniel said.

"Is that what this is about?"

He stared at her.

"It's been over a year and now you want to say something? Is that what this is? You want to say something now?" She dropped her hand to the table. "You're supposed to be . . . I mean, they said you were . . ." Her mouth hovered open, her breath escaping in uneven gasps. "You know, don't you? You know. That's why you're here."

"Know what?" He opened his hands in surrender. "What?"

The front door opened and slammed closed. Tendons stood out in Jolene's neck. Her gaze jumped back and forth between his face and the new customers at the entrance. When the waitress thundered by, Jolene slid out of the booth.

"Hey, where are you going?"

She headed toward the back of the café. He took a few steps after her, but she hurried, soon disappearing under the wooden sign that read "restrooms." Daniel hovered in the breezeway. Over a year. It had been that long since what? Since they'd seen each other? It didn't seem that long, but then everything was turned upside down.

The restroom doors read "roosters" and "hens." On his right spread the kitchen, the cook busy at the grill. A few more steps and he came to a narrow opening and another door with a sign that read "office." He slipped inside. The room was about fifteen square feet, a worn leather couch resting against one wall, an L-shaped computer desk against the other. He spotted a cordless telephone behind the monitor. Finally. He dialed Jay's number. Pressing the cool handset to his ear, he waited. After three rings, Jay's voice came on with the same message he'd recorded when they'd first made it onto the motocross team. *Hey, I'm either ridin' or thinking about ridin', so leave it at the beep.*

"Jay, what the hell? Did I hit my head or something? I'm in fucking Iowa. You need to let me know what's going on. I'll try again. Do me a favor and pick up."

He pressed *end* and replaced the headset. Chewing on a knuckle, he paced back and forth and then eyed the computer. It was on, the screensaver showing chickens pecking at the ground. He sat down and opened a browser. It responded, the machine already connected to the Internet. On the Diamond Xtreme motocross website he found the main number and dialed. Erin's voice came on and he almost spoke before realizing it was the out-of-office recording. The group's manager rattled on about office hours. Daniel replaced the handset and checked the upper right corner of the screen. August twenty-fourth. He pulled up the calendar. A Sunday. The motocross office was closed. He glanced ahead to the twenty-ninth. Five days to get to San Francisco.

Checking the website again, he went to the performance schedule. There it was. Their last show. He blinked. That couldn't be right. It said August second, *Butte Silverbow County Fair*. Three weeks ago? He remembered a show just the night before. Besides, he hadn't been in his hometown that recently. He squinted, heat rising up the back of his neck. Underneath the event listing sat an isolated paragraph:

As a result of the tragic accident at our last event culminating in the loss of team member Daniel A. Shepard, we have canceled our next show in Salt Lake City, Utah, out of respect for our riders and the fans. It has been an emotional time for everyone, and our hearts go out to Daniel's family and friends. If you'd like to express your condolences, we've set up a fan page for Daniel, which you can find by clicking here. We plan to resume the tour in Denver, Colorado, on September 6th.

CHAPTER THREE

D aniel didn't know how long he'd been sitting in front of the computer when the office door opened. Jolene entered. She looked as if she'd been crying. It must have been the expression on his face because she hurried to his side and checked the screen. A moment passed, her hair tickling his ear.

"Come on." She pressed a key. The screen went black. "We need to go."

"But I—"

"We need to go *now*." She took hold of his arm.

"Did you see—"

"If she catches us in here there'll be hell to pay. Come on!"

She led him out the back door. Iowa's sprawling farms and vast sky remained unchanged, the sun beaming warmth on his skin. *Butte Silverbow County Fair.* That couldn't have been their last show. He'd have remembered that, a show in his hometown. Had his mother come? He knew the answer before he thought of the question.

But she could have come.

Jolene walked ahead of him, a sketchpad tucked under her arm. "Come on!" He obeyed, taking a couple more steps. If he'd been in Butte that recently, Tony must have told him then about the marine camp, unless he'd already left. Or had he come to the show?

"Daniel!"

Jolene waited for him at the front of the building. He trotted to catch up, scanning the trailer lot across the street, looking for his bike or a car or some other mode of transportation that would answer the question of how the hell he'd gotten here, especially if he'd been in Montana three weeks ago. Around the corner, he spotted the same Suzuki motorcycle he'd seen on the way in, blue and white with shiny chrome accents. It was hers. Right. They'd had motorcycles in common. He'd teased her about buying the wrong brand. She slipped the sketchpad into the saddlebag and put the helmet over her head. "It's kind of a small back seat."

. . . the tragic loss of Daniel A. Shepard . . . It must have been an accident. He looked at his arms. No wounds. No scars.

Jolene started the engine. He sensed the vibrations warm against his thighs, the smell of dirt and popcorn in his sinuses, earplugs muffling all but the announcer's voice. An event in his hometown. He couldn't see Tony's face in the crowd.

"Let's go." Jolene patted the seat behind her.

The ball of his foot tingled, his spine rigid. *It has been an emotional time for everyone*... There had been an accident, had to have been an accident, but he wasn't "lost," though even as he thought about it the ground dissolved underneath him, his footing no longer secure on the sidewalk.

Jolene appeared at his ribs, grasped his elbow, and pushed him forward. She was surprisingly strong. He forced his feet to move. On the cushioned leather his knees framed Jolene's hips as he placed his toes on the foot pegs.

A smooth change of gears and they were flying down the two-lane Iowa road, the sun warm behind them, the breeze cooling their skin.

———————

A single stoplight signaled their entrance into Harlan, that and a broad white sign that read, "Harlan: A Growing Tradition." Jolene eased through the intersection and took them onto what looked like the main road, past a department store and a Subway and a church and a car wash. At the Twelfth Street intersection she turned left and buzzed past a few businesses and shopping areas, then coasted alongside a tree-filled park and a humble neighborhood with an elementary school. About eight blocks later, she slowed by a cemetery. Daniel wondered if she planned to go in, but she went to the next crossway instead, turned left, rolled across the street to the first house on the right, and parked the bike at the curb. The place was a one-story brick-and-siding combo with a wide picture window and one-car garage. At the corner of the yard stood a small wooden sign that read, "Isabella Field, Psychic Medium."

Jolene dismounted and walked up the driveway. "You should probably come in," she called to him, and then slipped through the front door without a key. Daniel followed, wondering what they were doing at some psychic's house. Inside, the smell of incense assaulted his sinuses. Sandalwood, he thought, though there was cinnamon, too, strong cinnamon, as if someone had opened the wrong lid when pouring. Two candle flames flickered on a mahogany stand set against the living room wall. Behind him, the picture window facing the road was covered in heavy, dark drapes.

"Close it," Jolene whispered. She stood inside and just to the right of the door, her hands in her pockets, her gaze trained on the opposite end of the room where a slim woman—Isabella, Daniel assumed—sat at a desk, a computer screen to her left. The length of her hair was the first thing Daniel noticed, a long and tousled mane of cashew brown that hung over the back of the chair all the way down to the seat. He closed the door behind him and the room went dark, the computer screen suddenly the brightest thing.

"Remember, Bethany," the woman was saying, "you must never go forward in fear. You have so many other choices you could make in this situation." Her voice was soothing, a gentle mother's voice breathed along the radio waves linking it to Bethany's speakers. The young woman on screen listened intently, brown eyes alert over plump cheeks, dyed black hair short and spiky.

Jolene grabbed Daniel's hand and pulled him away. They found the kitchen, which was surprisingly sparse compared to the other rooms, the walls a fog gray, the countertops clean granite. Jolene powered through to the back door and stepped onto a porch.

She took the wicker chair on the left, propping her boots up on a matching footstool. Daniel closed the door behind him and stood to the right, hands in his pockets. This wasn't Jolene's house, that much was clear, so he didn't know why she'd brought him here, but she didn't seem in the mood for questions.

The back yard was about double the size of the front, the grass lush and still glistening from a recent sprinkle. Flowers bloomed in overcrowded beds at either side of the porch, in hanging baskets at its edge, and in two more circular beds out in the yard, one with a birdbath in the center. Two robins ducked and splashed while holding out their wings. When the back door opened and Isabella stepped out, they flitted off into the trees.

"This is a surprise," she said to Jolene. "I thought you'd be packing."

Jolene gave her a short hug, then stepped back to where she could look at them both. "That was the plan."

"Is everything all right?"

"I needed to see you."

"I have a break between calls." Her shoulders were bare except for the red bra straps that cut across her fair skin, velvet sleeves clinging to her upper arms. She caressed the leather fringe on Jolene's jacket. "I remember this. She wore it all the time. It's a little big for you, though."

Jolene pulled the zipper up about an inch. "I wanted something of hers. To take with me." She glanced at Daniel.

Isabella caught the glance and turned. Her gaze passed over him as if he weren't there. "What is it?"

Jolene stared at one and then the other. Isabella looked behind her again but it was clear she saw nothing. "What?" she said. Jolene retreated, one hand out to steady herself on the porch railing. A dog barked from somewhere down the road, a noisy truck grinding its gears.

"Should I introduce myself?" Daniel said. "Ma'am, my name is Daniel."

Jolene watched as the woman failed to respond. "You don't see him?" she asked.

"See who?"

"I think she's talking about me."

"Him!" Jolene pointed. "You don't see him?"

"What? Who am I supposed to see?"

Jolene thrust one hand into her hair and buried it on top of her head. Daniel looked from her to Isabella and back again, his frown deepening. Was the woman teasing Jolene on purpose?

"I thought they must have gotten it wrong," Jolene said. "It had to be wrong because he was just standing there and I could touch him and he felt real and . . ." She pivoted and hit Daniel in the chest. "He's there! Right there!" She thunked him again with the heel of her hand, then grabbed his face and turned it to Isabella. "You can't see him?"

Isabella cast her gaze around, her expression growing increasingly alarmed. "See who?"

Jolene released Daniel and backed away, shaking her head. "Oh my god. I wish Mom were here."

Daniel watched helplessly as Isabella took Jolene's hand and drew her back inside the house. The gray walls surrounded them again as she led the way through the kitchen and into the dining room, a separate room unto itself across from the living room.

There, she sat Jolene in the chair opposite a smaller window with gold-colored drapes. Taking her own seat on the other side of a grand mahogany table, she gestured between them. "Out with it."

The space looked like a meeting room for a secret society, the wood floor covered by a red oval rug laced with gold ornate designs reminiscent of royalty, the thick table an overbearing presence in the middle of it. Jolene clung to the purple stone around her neck. "The dream I told you about," she began, but then glanced at Daniel and gestured toward the woman. "This is Isabella." Another gesture. "That's Daniel."

Isabella's gaze darted about. "You don't mean . . ."

Jolene nodded.

"Des Moines Daniel? He's here, now?"

Des Moines Daniel? So Jolene had told Isabella about him. Though Isabella didn't seem pleased that he was there.

"What does he want?" she asked.

"To go to California." Jolene said it as if it were obvious.

Isabella lowered her voice. "San Francisco?"

Jolene met her gaze.

"You can't do that." She grasped Jolene's hand in both of hers. "We talked about this."

"Talked about what?" Daniel came to the edge of the table but Jolene held up her hand before he could say any more.

"Why can't you see him?" she asked. "You do this stuff every day."

Isabella looked around again and then sat back in her chair. Sunlight came through the gold drapes behind her, brightening the henna tattoo that snaked along the back of her hand. "Something must be different."

"That's what I'm worried about."

"I haven't seen any of the others either, though."

"But they were never here. They never came here. *He's* here."

Others? Daniel thought.

"They're your ghosts, honey."

"Ghosts?" Daniel said. "What are you talking about?"

Jolene cast him an exasperated look. "He's not really . . ." She stopped. "He's . . . solid."

"Of course I'm solid." Daniel waved his hands in front of Isabella, then looked back at Jolene. "What's the matter with her?"

Isabella rubbed her bottom lip. "Solid to *you.*" She arched a graceful eyebrow.

"So you think—" Jolene began.

"You're saying I'm a ghost?" Daniel blurted. "Is she saying I'm a ghost?"

"That is has something to do with you." Isabella said. "Your connection to him. Maybe?" When Jolene looked disappointed, Isabella got up and left the room, the scent of vanilla trailing after her. Jolene slumped, the tall back of the chair dwarfing her small figure in dark wood.

Daniel sat down next to her. "What are we doing here?"

"She was my mother's best friend."

"Was?"

"You don't remember that either?" Jolene grasped the lapel on her jacket and pulled it close, the way a child might pull a blanket near.

Daniel dropped his gaze, scanning his memory. "I'm sorry. It's just . . ." They had sent emails. He squeezed his eyes shut. "She was sick . . ."

"Cancer."

"Right. Stomach cancer."

"She passed in February. After that Christmas when I had to cancel my trip to see you."

Daniel stared at her blankly.

She sighed. "Just forget it."

He rubbed his forehead. He needed to talk to Dr. Reiman. Clearly he'd suffered a head injury. Or had Dr. Reiman already treated it and released him to travel?

"She might be able to help," Jolene said.

"Help what?" Daniel said. "Is this about that thing on the website?"

"It's not just on the website."

"You saw it somewhere else?" When she didn't answer, he sat forward. "I'm not some ghost." He tapped her shoulder. "You feel that, right? What ghost can do that?"

"None I've ever known."

"And how many have you . . . known?"

"A lot."

A lot? He stared at the artist's palette earrings. He'd found them in a quaint gift shop. The clerk had been an older man with thick gray hair who had teased them about being in love when they'd only been together two days. They'd existed in a world apart that week in Des Moines, a world of art museums and long walks and intimate meals and dark hotel nights. He didn't remember her ever talking about ghosts. "You trust this woman?" he asked.

"With my life."

"So why is she pretending not to see me?"

"She's not pretending."

"You can see me."

"That's no big surprise."

"Because you see ghosts."

"Since I was five."

Daniel wrestled with that one. He didn't believe in such things, but then he didn't think she was crazy, either. "You can't touch a ghost."

"Not usually."

"I'm *not* dead. Christ. I'm sitting here. You felt my pulse!"

"Fine." Jolene held up her hands in surrender, then crossed her arms over her chest.

Isabella returned, cutting their conversation short. She held a deck of oversized cards in her hand.

Jolene shook her head. "I don't want that," she said.

"But they could tell us—"

"I want to know what *you* think."

"But we need to consult with spirit. In case . . ."

"What?"

The woman hesitated, strands of hair dangling over the edges of her eyes. "We need help on this." Positioning herself opposite Jolene, she set the cards on the table and started to separate them.

Jolene stood up and slapped her hand on top of Isabella's, stopping her. "I want to know what *you* think. From your experience. What does it tell you?"

The two women faced each other across the table, the tip of Isabella's fingers trapped under Jolene's palm. Isabella dropped her gaze. "I don't know," she said, and then looked back up into Jolene's face. "I've never heard of anything like this."

"Not ever?"

"A ghost that feels solid? Even to just one person?" Isabella shook her head. "And showing up today of all days?"

"What's so special about today?" Daniel asked.

"I had planned to go to Washington," Jolene told him.

"I don't want to mess up your plans."

Jolene released Isabella's hand and walked around the table. "So what do you think I should do?"

Isabella crossed her arms over her chest. "I think . . ." She paused, gazing into Jolene's eyes, and her expression softened. "I think what you're thinking of doing is a bad idea. You should stick to your original plan. Go to Washington and work your way into that art school. But that's what I thought before. That hasn't changed." She scooped the cards off the table and disappeared into the back of the house.

Daniel watched Jolene. He didn't remember her ever looking so frightened. She was always confident, her steps quick and light, never this heaviness that seemed to weigh on her now. It occurred to him that he should leave. He was the one upsetting her, intruding upon her plans. But it had been so long since he'd seen her, since he had stood this close to her.

Isabella returned, a necklace dangling from her graceful fingers. "It's a sigil," she said as she clasped it around Jolene's neck. "A protective symbol. The 'J' shape has always made me think of you."

Daniel stepped closer to see, inhaling Jolene's scent, a trace of her musky perfume about her collar. The pendant was made of wiry silver with a shape that did resemble a "J," though the top line extended only halfway. It reminded Daniel of calligraphy or of Japanese writing.

Jolene let it rest beside the purple stone and raised her eyebrows.

"It will help protect you." Isabella pursed her lips. "On your way to California."

Jolene's expression turned apologetic. "You know what happened. And now he's here. There can be only one reason."

"You don't know that."

"But Brent says—"

Brent?

"You know what I think of him." Isabella rested her hands on her hips.

"But he's the reason I haven't . . ." Jolene glanced at Daniel, her expression suddenly guilty.

"*You* say that," Isabella said. "I don't give him credit for it."

"But he's helped me. You know? I'm in a better place now."

Isabella frowned. "I'm not so sure of that."

"Who's Brent?" Daniel asked.

"Does he know?" Isabella pointed surprisingly close to where Daniel was standing. "About him? Have you told him?"

Jolene shook her head.

Isabella threw up her hands. "I've told you what I think. Maybe you need to talk to someone more knowledgeable."

An uncomfortable silence hovered between them. A clock ticked noisily in the kitchen. Finally, Isabella reached out and gave Jolene a hug. When they broke their embrace, she pressed her lips into a half-hearted smile. "Take care of yourself. Please. Text me."

"I don't—"

"I know. No cell phone. But he has one. Text me. Let me know where you are." Isabella reached out and touched Jolene's cheek.

Jolene gave her a sad smile and grasped the pendant again. "Thank you." She turned and drifted out the front door, then paused a moment before moving on down the steps. Daniel followed, sucking his stomach in to slide past Isabella.

"Be careful," Isabella called from the landing. "She would want you to be safe."

Halfway down the driveway, Jolene cast a glance across the road to the cemetery. "I never hear from her. Strangers talk to me all the time, but never her."

"I know what she would have told you," Isabella called. "Go to Washington. And Brent. She would say he's no good for you."

Jolene released the kickstand on the bike. "Yes, she probably would have said that. But what would she have said about Daniel?"

"She wouldn't care about him. She'd care about you."

Jolene waved and put on her helmet. Daniel started after her, but then Isabella spoke again in a subdued voice.

"Daniel, if you care about her, if you loved her once, as she told me, you can't take her there."

He paused. The woman was talking to him now?

"Find another way to get to San Francisco. Don't take her with you. She can't go out there. Not now."

He walked back up the steps. Leaning close to her face, he spoke: "I don't know what game you're playing here lady, but just leave her alone, all right?" He paused, waiting, but she didn't appear to have heard him. When he turned away, she reached out suddenly. He expected to feel her fingers on his arm, but then her hand was on the other side of him and he hadn't felt anything at all. She stared blankly his direction. "Daniel?" she said.

He looked down at his arm. He could have sworn her hand just went right through it.

CHAPTER FOUR

Classical music played on the tinny desk radio, violins swimming gently over a floating melody while the basses supported them from underneath. His friend Jay, a die-hard rock fan, would make fun of him if he knew, but Daniel needed it to study. It was the only way he could concentrate. Knee-deep in his math homework, he was staring at the numbers and symbols, struggling to comprehend the formula, when Tony interrupted. "Betcha don't know what this is."

Half irritated and half relieved, he looked up to see his brother's arm extended through the doorway of their shared bedroom, a toy dinosaur clutched in his fingers.

The rest of him remained hidden behind the wall. "A dinosaur," Daniel said.

"Duh." Tony took the answer as permission and entered, making the dinosaur move through the air as if it were walking. Reaching the bunk bed against the wall he hopped backward, landing on Daniel's bottom bunk. "Betcha don't know what *kind* it is."

Guessing the dinosaur was a regular game between them. Daniel bought bags of the plastic toys whenever he could scrape the money together, ordering them from the man at the downtown toy store to be sure he never got the same bag twice. He set his pencil down to study the latest creature dancing in his brother's hands. It was Army green and had a short, stout head with two rows of spines along its back. "Stegosaurus."

"No." Tony drew out the word. "They have *big* spikes. He has little ones. And his head is smaller, see?" He lifted the dinosaur again for Daniel's inspection.

Daniel leaned his elbows on his knees. "Hmm. Is that the brachiosaurus, or whatever it's called?"

"No! The brachiosaurus has a *long* neck. This one has almost no neck at all." Tony tucked his chin down into his throat, trying to make his neck disappear and succeeding only at resembling a toad. "See his tail?"

Daniel covered his mouth to hide his smile. "Looks like a club."

"That's the clue!"

"Clubasaurus?"

Tony laughed, one of his belly laughs that scattered invisible sparks all around the room. "Clubasaurus! Ha ha!"

"So what is he?"

"Ankylosaurus!"

"Ankylosaurus? I don't see anything on him that looks like an ankle."

"No no no. It's because of the species he was."

"And what was that? The ankle species?"

Tony laughed again. "Nevermind!"

"So what is it? Meat eater or plant eater?"

"Plants."

"With all that armor? He has horns!"

"So the T-rex will leave him alone." Tony got off the bed and made the toy walk on Daniel's desk. "What are you doing?"

"Math."

"Can I help?"

"You haven't learned this yet. It's algebra."

Tony brought the dinosaur up to his brother's face, as if it were the one speaking. "When will you be done?"

"Another hour?"

"Then can we play apocalypse?"

The end of the world.

Tony's favorite game.

The day the meteors (baseballs and tennis balls) fell from the sky and the snow (shredded paper) blew from the north and the dinosaurs were wiped off the face of the Earth. Daniel promised to play as soon as his math was done if Tony would agree to something different this time, like death from volcanic explosions or Earth-wide fire. His brother wrinkled his nose, but then agreed to find a new idea, just not one of those.

A little over an hour later they were destroying the ancient world, though it wasn't snow and meteors this time but a disease spread by tiny bugs in the form of pebbles. Rashes (ketchup) and blisters (whipped cream) erupted on the dinosaurs' leathery skin until, writing in agony, they all fell to their doom, only to be brought back (wiped clean) by the god that was Tony Donati. When it was over, Daniel made macaroni and cheese out of a box and they ate while watching television. It was a good night because their mother had to work late and didn't come back until long after they'd gone to sleep.

A knock sounded at the door. Daniel sat up in bed. It took him a minute to realize he'd been dreaming about Tony and the apocalypse. The sight of the large television, heavy drapes, and cheesy flower prints on the wall brought him back to the hotel room Jolene had gotten for him. He checked the clock. A little past nine. He'd meant to lie down for a while but that was two hours ago. *Tap tap tap.* A gentle knock. He checked himself. He'd showered immediately after entering the room, but he had no clean clothes. The sweat-stained shirt he couldn't stand, so he'd left it off, going bare-chested and barefoot with only his jeans on. It would have to do.

"Daniel? It's me. Open up."

"Coming." He opened the door. Jolene stood half hidden behind a stack of folded clothes.

"Some clean ones," she said, handing them over. They settled solidly on his palms and smelled of fresh laundry detergent. "They may be a little small. He's not as tall as you are."

Daniel nearly dropped them. They were *his*. He stepped aside to allow Jolene in, then followed her, letting the door shut behind them. He ditched the clothes on the edge of the first bed.

"Some toothpaste and stuff." She set a white sack on the table by the window and then turned to look at him. Her gaze lingered on his bare chest. "You should try one on, be sure they're going to fit."

Daniel turned his gaze back to the stack of clothes. A price tag slid out of the pile. The accompanying shirt had a rich, dark green color, with long sleeves, buttons, and a stiff collar, a nicer shirt than he usually wore. It appeared brand new. He slipped his arms into it. "Well?" he said.

She smiled a little. "Looks good on you."

He finished buttoning and thrust his hands into his pockets, the F-14 Tomcat cool against his fingers. She had showered too, her hair damp and slicked back, her small frame hidden in gray sweats. She cast her gaze around the room and crossed her arms. It was too hot, the first time he'd noticed it.

"Oh, the food." She passed him by in a blink, headed for the door. "I didn't have enough hands."

"Let me help." He went after her, pausing only when he stood at the hallway in his bare feet.

"It's okay. I'll get it."

He found his shoes, pulled them on, swiped the key off the television stand and charged out after her.

There was no motorcycle in the parking lot. He spotted her hoodie over by a white Ford F-150. She was standing at the driver's side door. When he came up behind her, she handed him a warm paper sack that smelled like chicken, then reached in again and grabbed a second bag. "Pizza or chicken. Your choice." It smelled delicious. He followed her back inside, thinking only after the door had closed behind them that she'd had to buy it for him again.

She set her bag on the table by the window and then flopped down on the far bed where he'd been lying and tucked two pillows behind her. She looked tired for only nine-thirty. Daniel put his bag next to hers and glanced her way. His first instinct was to lie down next to her, but he took a seat at the table instead, dumped the bag on its side and pulled the Styrofoam cartons out. The first held the chicken. He grabbed the leg and took a bite. "Want some?"

"I already ate."

With Brent, most likely. He chewed for a while, then, "So who's this Brent anyway?" When she didn't answer, he tried again. "Your boyfriend?"

She shrugged. "He's . . ." she fiddled with the pillowcase next to her. "He's helped me a lot." "So he's your boyfriend?"

She rolled her eyes, signaling he'd get no more out of her.

He dropped the clean leg bone onto a napkin and took the thigh. "Thanks for this, by the way."

She pushed herself up, re-stacking the pillows behind her. "We have to talk about tomorrow."

"I'm calling Jay. My friend from the team."

"I know. I met Jay." Her gaze was curious. Did he remember? "After that."

"You know something else you're not telling me?"

"You saw what it said on the website."

He didn't need reminding.

The words kept bubbling up in his head. *As a result of a tragic accident . . .*

"And you saw how Isabella reacted."

"I think she was playing with you."

"She doesn't play that way."

He poked his nose into the first bag again and then the second one. Finding nothing to drink, he set the half-eaten thigh on a napkin and got up. "Water?"

"Thanks."

He returned with two full plastic cups, gave one to her, and sat down again. "I don't know what's going on with Diamond Xtreme. But clearly, I'm not dead." She didn't respond to that, so he wiped his lips and went back to eating, quickly polishing off the thigh. The next Styrofoam bowl contained mashed potatoes. He started in on that.

"I thought you'd probably like the chicken," she said.

"You want the pizza?"

She hesitated, then nodded. He took the food to her, along with a napkin. When she reached for it, their fingers touched.

"Thanks." She let the box settle on her lap.

"I'll call Jay tomorrow. Get it all straightened out." He swallowed another bite of potatoes. "You can go on your trip with what's-his-name like you planned. Forget you ever saw me." He regretted it the instant he said it. It came out cold, like he didn't care about seeing her.

Stupid.

She chewed, the smell of pepperoni filling the room. The air was still stifling. Daniel turned the dial on the cooler. The fan started to hum. He sat back down, drained the cup of water, and stood up to refill it. He glanced at Jolene's, but hers was still three-quarters full.

When he returned, she'd stopped eating, only one bite missing from her slice of pizza.

He gestured toward it. "Not as good?"

"It's fine."

He went back to his potatoes. He'd messed things up now. "Thanks again, by the way. For all this." He gestured to the food and the clothes.

She forced a tight-lipped smile that quickly faded. When he said nothing more, she replaced her slice of pizza in the box, closed the lid, and sat up. Poised on the edge of the bed, she glanced around the room.

"You didn't finish," was all he could think to say.

She walked past him to the desk against the wall. Finding the hotel notepad, she wrote something down, then tore the sheet off and handed it to him. "You can get me here. If by some chance you don't get Jay or whatever."

Daniel took the paper. Brent's cell phone, probably.

"We'll be leaving by ten, so . . ." She hesitated, then started for the door. Daniel stuffed the paper into his pocket and hurried after her. When she turned back, she scanned his torso.

"That's a good color on you." She gave him a parting glance and walked away.

A voice screamed at him to say something, do something to stop her, but he only stood in the hallway and watched until she was gone.

CHAPTER FIVE

T he artichoke-green linoleum was cracked in multiple locations, creating the perfect obstacle course for any rolling toy.
The worst had curled upwards, forming a dangerous ridge
hungry for passing toes. For that reason, it usually lay hidden
under the dining room table, but Daniel had pulled the table
into the living room and now sat under the kitchen sink, his back
against the cabinets. Tony had taken up a position opposite him
by the front door, his legs spread like bumpers. Today was dem-
olition derby day, a competition they held at least once a month.
Miniature vehicles of all types tested their metal over the great
ridge, some flying over it and others stalling in the middle of it.

Tony and Daniel rooted for the ones that would power through and stay upright all the way to the other side.

The F-14 Tomcat had been Daniel's favorite from his earliest memory. He'd kept it through all their moves, always in his pocket so it wouldn't get lost in the boxes like so many of his other things did. When he was nine years old and the new baby came, he'd used it to get acquainted, rolling it along the top of the crib and flying it through the space overhead. How fun it had been to see Tony's big blue eyes glued to the wings, his little arms and legs squirming with pleasure when Daniel dropped the jet closer to him.

The best part was the way he'd squealed with delight when the plane landed on his chest and then rolled across it, back and forth over the cotton shirt with the blue teddy bears. Later, Daniel would push it across the breakfast table with a *whoosh*, take off into the air, and bank around to drop a Fruit Loop bomb on the highchair tray, after which Tony would stuff it into his mouth and then thrust his hand out for the next one.

The plane soon became the source of several requests. "Play, Danny. Airplane!" Tony would wait to eat until the plane dropped whatever it was from the sky above. Their mother, Valerie, warned Daniel that he was setting himself up for a lifetime of plane feedings, but Daniel ignored her, dropping pieces of sandwich and potato chips and cut-up apples and macaroni noodles one after another onto the tray. Tony would wait to sleep, too, until the plane had made its tour of the crib. Later, he made up his own games, building new worlds for the plane to live in, from cardboard box multi-tiered hangars to undiscovered country behind the couch to burrowed shelters in the back yard dirt. But always he was happy to return the toy to his older brother.

Daniel knew he was growing too mature for such things, but he couldn't let the plane go until he turned fourteen and Tony was five. As the Christmas season approached, there was no money for gifts, Daniel having used all his earnings from his work at the mechanic's shop for everyday essentials like food and clothing. On Christmas Eve he looked around his room at all his toys and even thought about making one with a few nails and scraps of wood, but in the end, he wrapped the metal jet in some gently used holiday paper he'd found in the school trash can and left the present under the three-foot-high turquoise tree Valerie had confiscated from the bar's storage room. He feared it would be a disappointment, something old rather than new, but when Tony unwrapped it the next morning, his mouth curled up in a smile.

"It's just like yours, Danny!" He rushed across the room in bare feet, oversized cream-colored pajama pants threatening to fall off his waist.

Daniel smiled, determined to keep his mouth shut, but Tony caught the shift in his gaze. He examined the plane more closely. His smile faded. "This is *your* plane."

"I'm giving it to you for Christmas."

"But it's your plane."

"I want you to have it. I know how much you like it."

Tony extended his arm, the toy firmly in his grasp. "You keep it."

Daniel shook his head. "It's yours, now."

"But I don't want you to be sad."

Daniel studied his brother's face then and wondered where he had come from. There were no other presents under the tree. Valerie had already told them the pancakes they were soon to have for breakfast were all Santa could afford. She was stirring the mix in a bowl, the smell of cooking oil wafting up from the stove.

Tony set the plane in his palm.

Daniel pushed it back. "I'll be sad if you don't take it."

"That's what Christmas is about," Valerie said in her some-times-sweet voice as she set the bowl aside and reached for a carton of eggs, her sandy hair combed and soft against her face, cigarette a miniature chimney in her hand. "Giving."

Tony turned the plane around in his hands, and for a moment Daniel wasn't sure he was going to go along with it, but finally he grinned and wrapped his arms around Daniel's neck. Daniel wrestled with him after that, tickling him until he squealed and begged him to stop.

Back and forth on the kitchen floor, the Chevy Camaro and the Dodge truck and the CAT backhoe and the long red fire truck competed with one another to see which could overcome the great ridge.

From the point of view of the toys, it formed a rugged peak, sharp and intimidating like the mother of all frost heaves, the crevice at the apex a dark hole in which a set of tires could disappear and never return.

Taking a burst of power from Daniel's thrust hand, the Camaro flew over the top and landed upright on the other side. The truck made it over too, but then lost control and dropped onto its fender, slamming into the displaced table leg. The backhoe hit the first rise and stopped completely, its extended shovel draped uselessly in the air. The fire truck managed to get its front tires over but then got held up by its long midsection, the ridge poking its jagged edges into the truck's metal underbelly.

The boys commented on each vehicle's fate with a series of exclamations, groans, and shouts of surprise, but then there was only one vehicle left. A respectful silence fell over the kitchen.

"Okay." Tony rubbed his hands together. "Time for the plane."

To Tony it was always just "the plane." Daniel had explained what an F-14 Tomcat was, a fighter, a twin-engine war destroyer, but to Tony it would always be the plane. Ducking his head to get the best view, he waited, the tip of his tongue hovering at the corner of his mouth. Daniel revved the plane back and forth in front of him, eyeing the ridge. He would have to hit it just right, angled a little off center and propelled with sufficient velocity, or the toy wouldn't make it over. Instead it would likely hit, go airborne, and crash under the table, or plunge its pointed noise into the ridges and promptly land on its back.

He'd gotten it right only a few times out of the many he'd tried, but Tony was always ready to catch it, just in case. One, two . . .

Three!

The silver jet rolled, hit the ridge, and became airborne, the nose pointed toward the smoke-stained ceiling, tail fins aligned for a perfect flight out the small square window in the front door. Daniel watched, hopeful, but he had pushed it just a little too far to the right. The wing dipped, the rise not as steep as he had hoped. As it reached the peak of its ascent and was about to succumb to gravity, two small hands clasped around it.

"Altitude successfully reached, sir!" Tony opened his hands. The jet lay safe in his palms. "Let's try again. Straighter this time."

At nine o'clock the following morning, Daniel emerged from the hotel office having read eight online articles about his own death. Most were posted on motocross blogs and websites. One had appeared in the Butte paper, the *Montana Standard*. It gave the best overview of the supposed facts.

The Diamond Xtreme motocross team had performed at the Butte Silver Bow County Fair on August second, three weeks before Daniel arrived in Iowa. The last series of jumps were all crowd-pleasers. Then Shepard rode into place, paused at the starting line, and flicking a lighter, lit the top of a pointed object he held in his left hand. A sparkling flame ignited and danced, bright colors alive in the night. Something to give the audience an extra thrill, the announcer mused. They cheered as Daniel pocketed the lighter and still holding the flame, pulled the throttle and rode up the ramp. Once airborne, he thrust the flame skyward. The audience roared its approval. Then at the apex of his arc, he brought it back down. Time seemed to stand still as he hovered mid-air. Then there was a startling explosion, engulfing Shepard and the bike in flames and ejecting Shepard off his bike. The Kawasaki landed on the ramp and crashed into the dirt below. Shepard's body dropped at the edge of the arena, still encased in flames. Emergency crews put the fire out, but Shepard was pronounced dead on the scene. His mother, who lived in Butte, could not be reached for comment. The cause of the accident was under investigation.

Every post had a picture, but most were of the jump before the fire. In those, the rider wore Daniel's colors and rode a Kawasaki the same model as his. Other shots showed something burning in the air, but no details beyond that. Only one had captured the explosion itself, a ball of fire suspended between the ramps.

Daniel grabbed a bowl of cereal from the breakfast nook, ate it quickly, then retired to his room. He still hadn't been able to reach Jay, and when he'd called the office again there was no answer. His email inbox was filled with junk. Unable to remember his account number, he hadn't been able to gain access to his money. He'd written a note to Coach Greg, telling him that despite what it said on the website, he was alive and well and would be back in Reno soon. But after an hour at the computer, he was no closer to solving his problem than he had been before.

He glanced at the clock. In another thirty minutes, Jolene would be gone.

He sat on the bed and called the motocross office again. When he still couldn't reach anyone, he realized he had only one choice left. He winced at the thought of it. She would put him through the third-degree. For ten minutes he argued with himself before finally picking up the phone once more. Sucking air into his lungs, he listened, his heartbeat accelerating with each ring in his ear. Nine-forty-one. If she'd worked the night shift, she would still be asleep. Third ring. Fourth. Finally, a click.

"Yeah." A smoker's voice, gravelly and phlegm-filled. She coughed three times, the sound exploding in his eardrum. He imagined her head on the pillow, eyes still closed, sandy hair free of the ponytail she often wore but still holding the conical shape at the back of her head.

"Valerie. It's me."

"Daniel?" A quick intake of breath. Then, "Who is this?"

"It's Daniel. Sorry to wake you. I just need to talk for a second."

No response.

"I'm in Iowa, and I lost my wallet. Look, if you can lend me some cash, I'll pay you back double. Within a week. I wouldn't ask, but I'm kind of in trouble. Something weird has happened. Do you know if we did a show there three weeks ago?" The phone remained deadly silent. "Valerie?" *Click.*

Daniel stared at the earpiece, then slammed it down on the phone. "Damn it!" Typical. The one time he really needed her. He felt like throwing the whole thing across the room but after a few rapid exhales, grabbed the earpiece and redialed. No answer. He tried one more time but she was ignoring it now. He let fly a string of curses and clenched his fists. Nothing she did should surprise him, but for some reason this did. She'd never missed out on an opportunity to lecture him about one thing or another. He'd counted on that. He'd never expected silence.

He plunged his hand into his pocket and gripped the toy plane, feeling its solid metal shape against his palm. It was getting late, and he was out of options. With a long inhale, he moved his gaze once more to the phone.

He had to call Jolene.

Nine-fifty. He paced the room. She had a new boyfriend. She'd moved on. Nine fifty-two. He pulled the piece of crumpled notepad paper from his other pocket. Smoothing it with his fingers, he stared at the numbers she had written, allowing three more precious minutes to go by before approaching the phone once again. Tentatively, he reached out for the earpiece but then stopped. Nine fifty-six. They were going to Washington. He'd be messing up their plans. Swallowing hard, he picked up the phone. It rested solidly in his palm. Taking a breath, he dialed. She answered after the first ring. "Hello?"

"It's me." He gripped the earpiece hard to still his trembling. "I need your help."

She took so long to respond he feared she would refuse. "We'll be there in about twenty minutes."

He hung up and sat down. She was coming. It would be all right. He waited for the nervousness to fade, then got up, gathered the clothes she'd brought him, and leaving the key on the TV stand, headed out.

He was sitting on the green bench in front of the hotel when the Ford F-150 pulled into the parking lot. It looked intimidating, the shiny grill an open mouth baring fangs. Daniel moved to the edge of the blacktop, eager to get this part over with. The thought of meeting Jolene's boyfriend was enough to make him puke. He cast his gaze upward. The sun was already high overhead, the temperature at least eighty. It would be a blessing to ride in air conditioning at least. Hands in his pockets, he fingered the plane and tried to look nonchalant. Jolene's Suzuki was tied in the truck bed. It seemed an odd metaphor, her vehicle tied to his, strapped down with rope so it couldn't escape. He admonished himself. He didn't know the guy.

The passenger door opened, and Jolene slipped out. She wore jeans and a forest green long-sleeved blouse, the necklace Isabella had given her fighting with the purple stone for space at the hollow of her throat. Her hair was freshly washed and bouncy, and as she got closer she smiled, her green eyes sparkling like the surface of a lake.

"We match." She stopped in front of him and pointed to the green shirt he'd tried on for her the night before.

He refrained from telling her it was the only one he could stomach wearing. The rest of the clothes lay in a pile on the bench. "Wasn't that the plan?" he asked.

She blushed, then sobered. "Now listen." She moved in closer, suddenly serious, her voice low. "He doesn't know you're coming, but it's okay. He's not going to be able to see you. Just like Isabella. I need you to follow me into the back of the truck and keep quiet, and he won't even know you're there. All right?"

Daniel frowned. "Of course he'll see me." *He's just a guy, not a strange psychic lady,* he wanted to say, but didn't.

"I'm trying to help you. Will you just listen for once?"

The driver's side door opened. Daniel looked up to see a lanky man exiting the truck. Lean and relaxed, he paused to take a long inhale, his gaze pointed north, rich walnut hair cascading in waves past the neck of his black woven shirt. Dark eyes looked out from under a firm brow, a neatly trimmed Van Dyke framing a straight, thoughtful mouth.

"Keep quiet," Jolene whispered. "Let me handle this."

Daniel watched as the guy came toward them, his hands easy in the pockets of his brown khaki slacks, his shoulders so loose it was as if he were flopped in a couch rather than walking. He emanated the air of someone concentrating on something else, a busy brain noodling over a math problem or pondering the meaning of life, but what struck Daniel most as he approached was how *old* he was. The guy had to be in his thirties, late thirties, even, and this was who Jolene was living with? Daniel glanced at her, but she wasn't paying attention. She shifted her weight from foot to foot, obviously nervous about how all this was going to go.

"*This* is the guy?" he said.

"Shhh!" she hissed.

When he was nearly upon them, Brent glanced once at Jolene and then cast his gaze upward in a daydreaming sort of way, perhaps to check out the roof of the building or the air conditioning vents or maybe the brown gutters leading from the roof to the sidewalk. Daniel couldn't tell which, and wasn't really interested until the guy lowered his gaze and leveled it on his. The look was intense but removed at the same time, as if Brent was just as unhappy about meeting Daniel as Daniel was about meeting him, but in front of Jolene, wanted to act like he was unconcerned. "So you're Daniel."

Daniel glanced at Jolene. She looked from one man to the other, speechless. "And you're Brent," he said, going for the same long-suffering tone.

"How did you—" Jolene started, then stopped, her gaze on Brent. "I mean—"

Brent smiled, one of those sensuous, not quite all the way smiles that girls swooned over. "I saw your picture. The one of you and him at the museum. And you've been all secretive. Did you think I couldn't put two and two together?"

The picture at the museum. Daniel thought back. They'd visited an art museum in Des Moines. She'd worn a green blouse. They'd had their picture taken. He'd kept his copy in his desk drawer. She was wearing the same blouse now. The very same one with the ribbon tie at the shoulder.

Jolene's face flushed. "I'll get these." She picked up the pile of clothes from the bench and walked to the truck, leaving the two men to size each other up in her absence.

Daniel waited a beat, then, "I appreciate this," he said.

"What?" Brent said.

"She offered me a ride," Daniel said. When the guy looked surprised, he went on. "Mentioned you guys could maybe drop me off somewhere on your way . . ." He stopped. California wasn't on the way to Washington. "I was in an accident and lost my wallet—"

"He needs a ride," Jolene interrupted, coming back to stand in between them. "I told him he could go with us." She was smiling too much, her hand gestures jerky. "You know, for a ways. I didn't think it would be a problem."

Brent's gaze shifted from one to the other. Daniel could almost read his thoughts. This was his trip with Jolene, a new start for them somewhere else. *It's okay,* he wanted to say, *I'll find another way.* But there was no other way.

The three stood in awkward silence. Finally, Brent placed his hand on the back of Jolene's neck and gestured toward the truck. "Welcome aboard. You can have the whole back seat to yourself."

CHAPTER SIX

The trailer-home bathroom was too small for three people.
Cramped and dingy, it offered only a pale yellow light from a
single bare bulb in the center of the ceiling, the fixture having been shattered long ago. Tony, scratched and bloody, balanced
precariously on the edge of the pink bathtub, Valerie standing in
front of him armed with a wet washcloth.

Dressed in a threadbare white tank top that drooped low
enough to show her cleavage, she dragged the cloth over Tony's
arm, cleaning off the dried blood to reveal mostly pale skin with
a few mean-looking scrapes thrown in. Her strokes didn't change
whether she was on healthy skin or torn, and Tony grimaced

under her rough administrations. Daniel hovered in the doorway, feeling helpless.

"He was *your* responsibility," she said to him. "You're the adult here." She paused to take a drag on her cigarette and then placed it back in the ashtray centered on the toilet seat lid. "You have to watch out for him."

"I was." Daniel's gaze centered on Tony's tortured face. "Why don't you let me do that?"

"So you can mess this up too?" Valerie glared at him, dark circles under her hazel eyes. "That's all we'd need. Him getting tetanus or some infection because you didn't bother to clean him up right." She shoved the wounded arm low under the tub faucet, Tony nearly falling in after it. He stopped himself by grabbing the sink with his other hand. Valerie turned the water on and soaked the arm, the back of her thighs jiggling below green nylon shorts. That done, she directed Tony to stand up, turning his arm as if he were a marionette, and started in with the washcloth again, this time on the side of his bloody face. Tony squeezed his eyes shut. "My day off, and this is how I get to spend it."

"We were riding bikes. A crash was bound to happen."

"Bound to happen? He's six years old! You don't take a six-year-old on a gravel road! He doesn't belong out there with you and your buddies."

"I wanted to go," Tony mumbled.

"Sure you did, honey." She turned his face one direction and then the other, then started in on the back of his neck, working like she worked cleaning tables at the bar, what muscle she had in her thin arms bulging, her cheeks red. "You want to do what big brother does, but you're nine years younger. You need time to grow. Daniel should know that."

"It was just a short gravel road. He lost his balance is all."

"Yeah, and what happens next time, hm? He falls off a cliff somewhere. Then what are you going to tell me? It was bound to happen? For hell's sake, Daniel. I need some help around here. I can't do it all. I'm working sixty goddamn hours a week as it is."

"But last week you said they cut—"

"Trying to keep you kids fed is all I do." She rinsed the blood and grime from the washcloth and turned Tony around, pushing one arm and then the other as if he were a rotating display rack, ending with one final inspection of his face. Two scrapes marred his cheek, one on top of the other like lines on paper. "Look at this. We'll be lucky if it doesn't scar."

"Cool," Tony said.

"It is *not* cool. My baby's face, all torn up." She finished cleaning and kissed him twice, once on his good cheek and once on his nose, and then let him go. Looking down at his legs, she shook her head. "Those jeans. Holes in them now. I'll have to fix those, too."

"Give them to me," Daniel said.

"You don't know how to sew."

"Let me have them." Daniel waited until Tony took them off, then grabbed them and disappeared.

"You need to bathe now," Valerie said to Tony. "Come on." Daniel heard the water start and the stopper click. "Soap up everything," she commanded. "All those little stones need to come out."

"You already washed it!" Tony said.

"You heard me!" She shut the bathroom door and walked into the boys' room.

Daniel found the sewing kit and was sitting on the couch threading a needle when she emerged again, her sandy hair a bird's nest. She stopped behind him and watched, her breath stale and smoky. "You really think you can fix those?"

"I've got a patch." Daniel patted the patch he'd placed on the couch next to him.

"You're going to make a mess of it."

"Just go rest, or whatever you were going to do."

She hung back, exhaling smoke. "Use small stitches or it will bunch up."

Daniel obeyed, the material held near his nose now, the needle going in and out. "You said they cut your hours. It's why I had to take on more at Mike's."

"Yeah, well, doesn't stop them from keeping me beyond what they're paying me. You ask Mike for a raise?"

Daniel closed his mouth and stitched.

"You little pansy." She slapped the back of his head and padded to the kitchen. "You ain't got the balls for it."

"I haven't worked there a year yet."

"Where's the rule you gotta wait for a year?"

"When did *you* last ask?"

"They ain't gonna give me a raise at that place. The walls are barely standing as it is. Customers petering out every month, all of 'em headed over to that new place across town. Club something." She lit another cigarette and took a long drag.

"Why don't you apply there?" The water stopped running. Daniel heard a gentle *plurp* as Tony stepped into the tub. "You're always saying you want something better." No response. Daniel was about to turn around when he heard car keys jangling. Hopping on one leg in the kitchen, Valerie pulled sneakers over her bare feet, her cigarette dangling from her lips, the car keys tucked into one palm. An old familiar panic rose inside Daniel's chest, his fingers gripping the needle and fabric. Asking would be useless. He waited, holding his breath. When both shoes were on, she grabbed the windbreaker off the back of the dining room chair and opened the door. Before stepping through she looked back at him, her hazel eyes shiny, and pulled her cigarette out. "Sick of you saying what I do ain't good enough. You're spoiled, Danny, a spoiled brat. I should kick you out and let you see what it's like when it's all on your shoulders. Then you can tell me where to go apply."

She slammed the door behind her. Pictures rattled on the wall. A few seconds later, Daniel heard the engine roar on the old Pontiac, dirt kicking up against the side of the trailer as she spun out.

"That mom?" Tony called.

"She'll be back." He focused on the half-sewn patch.

"Where'd she go?"

Daniel paused. "Work."

"But it's her day off!"

"They called her in."

The water splashed. Daniel imagined his little brother punching it in frustration. But his own shoulders had come back down, his breathing returning to normal. The trailer was quiet, the smoke and tobacco smell dissipating. He pushed the needle through the denim and the patch. Small stitches.

Brent pulled off the highway and parked the truck in front of the rest area bathrooms. Daniel reached for the door handle, eager for some fresh air. He was hungry, too, but without cash or a credit card he couldn't raid the vending machines, and he wasn't asking Jolene for more money. High-tops quiet on the warm cement sidewalk, he headed to the restroom, where he splashed water on his face and tried to figure out how he was going to get hold of some cash. Coach Greg would float him some if he could reach him. The next time he had access to a computer, he'd ask.

Outside again, the sun beamed heat on his face. Cars whizzed by on the highway. Dreading the return to the truck and seeing no sign of Jolene, Daniel went the opposite direction, toward the back of the rest area grounds, behind the bathrooms and picnic tables, until he was looking out onto the countryside beyond. About a quarter mile away rested a single house, two more about the same distance behind it, a red barn just past the tips of the nearby trees. It was quiet and peaceful, a sharp contrast to the busy highway behind him. He longed to go toward it, find a place among the tall grasses, and lie down and stare up at the sky. Somewhere in his memory he recalled living in a place like this, before Valerie changed, a place where he ran around on a green lawn wearing navy blue swim trunks while she stood on the front steps trying to spray him with the water hose. He could hear her laughter as clear as it had once been and, for a moment, let the memory play, allowing himself to feel the water splashing his skin, Valerie's face scrunched up in delight as she tried to catch him without getting too wet herself. Then the yard and the hose and his mother's happy face faded from view, and he walked back toward the highway, the traffic noise growing louder in his ears.

Between the men's and women's restrooms he found a map hung on the brick wall. A red "you are here" star oriented him to his location. They were only about an hour out of Kearney, Nebraska. He'd slept longer than he thought. Behind him, the Ford was still parked up against the curb, the Suzuki secure in the bed. But there was no one inside.

"She wanted to draw a little."

Daniel jumped. Brent had managed to sneak up on him and now stood beside him looking out on the lot. He wore wire-rimmed sunglasses, his eyes in shadow.

"Her sketchbook," he said by way of explanation. Daniel remembered seeing her with it when they'd walked out of the chicken café. "She has talent," Brent said, "just lacks focus. Mind always . . ." He made a flitting motion with his fingers off to the side of his head.

"What?"

"Distracted." Brent took off the sunglasses and leveled a calm gaze at Daniel. "How did you guys meet, anyway?"

A Honda SUV pulled into the lot, drawing their attention. "She came to a show," Daniel said.

"A show?"

"Freestyle motocross." Brent looked at him blankly, so Daniel explained. "Motorcycles doing extreme jumps."

"Oh. They have shows with that?"

How old is this guy?

"Where?"

"Des Moines is the one she came to, but we tour all over."

Brent watched as a potbellied man exited the Honda and made his way to the restroom. When they were alone again, he glided to the nearest picnic table on the right, his loafers brushing easily through the grass. Daniel enjoyed the space of his absence, but then figured it would be rude not to follow. The table was shaded by a good-sized cottonwood and cool to the touch. He sat down opposite Brent but stayed alert, hoping to spot Jolene.

"Why would she go to something like that?" Brent said, continuing their conversation.

"Why not?"

He pushed a thumbnail between his teeth. "Can't imagine it."

"It's exciting. We go right over the audience's heads." Daniel was defending himself. He didn't know why he cared one way or the other.

"You're pretty high, then."

Daniel traced an arc over the tabletop. "You run the bike up the ramp and then you jump. While you're in the air, you do stunts. Flips, whips, turns, tail grabs."

"Tail grab?"

"You grab the back of the bike."

"While you're in the air?" Brent's eyebrows shot up. "So you could fall? I mean, before you hit the other ramp?"

The bike rolled down the ramp alone. Daniel shook his head, ridding himself of the haunting image. "If you don't know what you're doing," he said.

They both sat silent for a moment, then, "She came to your show, and . . . ?"

Daniel shifted his weight on the hard wooden bench. The guy was getting too personal. It wasn't his business. Still, he could remember it like it was yesterday, Jolene waiting in line after the show, joining the others who wanted to meet the riders backstage. She'd stood out, that shocking head of red hair.

When she'd shifted over to his line, he'd gotten nervous and signed faster, moving the other fans through until she stood in front of him.

"Your autograph," she'd said, pulling her sleeve down to bare her shoulder.

Daniel remembered the alabaster skin, the little red freckles in it, and though he'd tried he couldn't mar it with the Sharpie, so he'd kissed the shoulder instead and given her a free signed T-shirt. The guys had ribbed him about that one, but Jolene had given him a different smile then, one that was a little sad and a little smoldering, so that when an hour later he found her standing at the gate he couldn't say he was entirely surprised.

Brent was staring at him, a hard stare.

"It was a long time ago," Daniel said. "What about you? How did you two meet?"

"Art class," Brent said, "in Omaha. She was one of my students. She has a good eye. Was a fan of my work."

Was that all one needed to qualify as *having a good eye?* "How long—"

"About a year ago."

Daniel did the math in his head. Jolene had said it had been over a year since they'd been together. So this guy had come along . . . when? After they'd broken up? Daniel couldn't remember that part. They'd had an amazing week in Des Moines, then exchanged emails and texts for months. They'd planned to meet for Christmas but then her mother had gotten sick. After that? He must have done something wrong. "What kind of art do you teach?" he asked.

"Drawing and painting mostly."

"So Jolene . . . ?"

"Pencil. Charcoal."

Daniel nodded. "I appreciate you giving me a ride," he said.

"It's fine." Brent rubbed his nose and leaned forward, bringing one knee up to his chest. "It was kind of funny, watching her freak out." He smiled. "She was surprised I could see you."

Daniel's gaze jerked to his face.

"She didn't think that would happen."

"Why not?" Daniel uttered a half-hearted chuckle. "I mean, that would be weird."

Brent was still smiling in a secretive way. "Who knows. I can't figure her out sometimes." He glanced at Daniel. "All her talk about ghosts and all."

Daniel looked across the rest area grounds, turning that one around in his head. Either Brent was trying to act like he knew more than he did, or he *did* know more than he was letting on. He could have seen the articles about Daniel's death. But he acted like he didn't even know what motocross was. "So you—" Daniel began, but Brent was focused intensely on the table. Daniel followed his gaze and saw a black beetle making it's way across the wood.

Brent lowered one finger to follow along behind it. "You ever feel like it's right behind you?" he said in a subdued voice. "Sense it there, a hand just waiting to edge you over the cliff?"

"Not sure what you mean," Daniel said.

"You're up in the air. Your bike falls away underneath you. For a moment, you *must* feel it."

Daniel's stomach dropped, the image returning in his mind, the bike rolling down the ramp alone. *No. He didn't want to feel that again.*

"Even a creature as simple as this," Brent went on. "It knows. Something big is coming." He brought his finger down just enough to hold the beetle suspended, it's little legs struggling to propel it forward, its antennae waving wildly.

"I think it's just scared," Daniel said.

Brent waited another few seconds, then lifted his finger. The beetle scurried away underneath the table. "No way to tell,

I guess," he said. "It's just a bug, right?" He gazed at Daniel, put his sunglasses back on, then stood up, leaned back to stretch his spine, and started toward the sidewalk.

Daniel watched his back, wondering what the hell all that was about. Whatever it was, he felt shaky again, like he had after the train engine had nearly severed his fingers. He moved his gaze. On the other side of the rest area, Jolene approached through the grass. *Damn.* Despite his best intentions, he'd failed to spot her first. She and Brent met in the middle near the green metal trash cans and the Honda SUV.

There they hesitated, observing one another, and then Brent cupped his hand on the back of her neck. Holding her that way, he steered her toward Daniel. Jolene's gaze fell on him. Her smile came quickly, suddenly. An unplanned flash of teeth. It lifted Daniel out of his shoes. It was all he could do not to run to meet her.

Daniel and Tony crashed through the front door, stumbling on tired feet into Pastor Gus Handley's house. Daniel turned on the light, illuminating the interior of the modest home in the old part of Butte, the air smelling of cat food and faded coffee. Gus's nearly six-foot tall mountain man watched them from the corner of the living room. A wooden sculpture, it held a rifle against its ribs, beaver pelts slung over its shoulder, a long knife sheathed at its belt. The face was smoothed oak wood, eyes deep set under a heavy brow, lips curled as if it was looking into the sun.

"Don't shoot, Max, it's us!" Tony said to the sculpture as he passed, dragging his backpack behind him.

"He's still wearing the hat." Daniel eyed the purple stocking cap Tony had placed on top of the sculpture's head on a previous visit, the multi-colored pom-pom flopped over by its ear. It was the most recent wardrobe addition. Older items included one of their mother's pink beaded necklaces and Tony's old Superman belt.

"He's not a damn drag queen." Gus walked in behind them, balancing a large red cooler against his hip. A wiry man in his late sixties, he was still muscular, his arms tanned a golden brown. A black cowboy hat hid his bald head, making him appear younger than his years, cowboy boots clumping over the linoleum floor.

Tony laughed, dropped the pack by the couch and dashed into the bathroom. Daniel helped Gus set the cooler on the kitchen counter. "Why didn't you take them off?" he asked.

"Kid would just find something worse to put on him." Gus glanced at the sculpture. "Before you know it, the poor sonofabitch will be wearing a bra and panties."

Daniel grinned, then took the cover off the cooler. The three of them had hiked at least twenty miles around the Twin Lakes in a weekend. They were dead on their feet, the mountains having deposited the delicious heaviness of nature's fatigue in their muscles. Daniel was grateful for it, though, so he took over the job of storing away the leftover food and shooed Gus out of the kitchen. It was because of the pastor they were able to camp at all, say nothing of the other things he'd done for them. A pastor was supposed to serve his community, but Gus had gone overboard when it came to Daniel and his brother. Daniel didn't know of any other boys the pastor took camping or hunting, or whom he let crash at his house whenever they wanted to.

Cooler empty, food stowed in the refrigerator, Daniel parked himself in the forest green recliner. Gus had already settled into his favorite leather lounger and closed his eyes, his thick fingers folded over his belly. On the mantle, the antique mahogany clock rang out the late hour, eleven chimes hailing their return. Daniel's breathing had just started to slow when a cat meowed.

"Bones." Gus sighed. "One of these days I gotta teach you how to feed yourself." The calico purred and brushed white and orange hairs on Gus's jeans. It had been well fed, that much was plain. The bones so prominent when it first started coming around—the reason for its name—were no longer part of its physique. "Come on, you old cuss." Gus pushed himself up and out of his chair. "Let's see if you're really out of food or if you're just lying to me."

Tony emerged from the bathroom and dropped onto the striped couch Gus had picked up at the goodwill shop. On the wall over his head rested an oversized photograph of a bull moose. Daniel studied it, still impressed with the quality of the shot. The animal stared right into the camera lens, broad antlers for miles on either side of his head. Water dripped from his wide muzzle into the lake, a few strands of marshy greens held tightly between his lips.

"I ever tell you about that old moose up there?" Gus reappeared behind him, his hand on the back of the chair, fingers ripe with the smell of the trout he'd just given the cat.

Daniel winked at Tony, who smiled back with sleepy eyes. "It's been a while," he said.

"Let me paint a picture for you." Gus eased himself back down into his chair and held his hands up in the shape of a frame, his voice taking on the deep resonance he used for sermons. "You're up in those grand Rocky Mountains, a little time in God's good country. You make yourself a pretty nice camp in a clearing, you catch some fresh fish, fry 'em up, and sleep overnight in your tent. You wake up the next morning with your brain all fuzzy and head to the lake to snap some pictures and pump some fresh water through your little anti-bacterial filter."

Both boys had heard the story several times before, but some of the weariness fled Tony's gaze as he concentrated on Gus's face.

"You walk along, not thinking about anything in particular, half of you still zonked out in that sleeping bag. The air feels alive and you're looking forward to that first taste of fresh, cool lake water. You come around the corner and lift your head." Gus leaned forward and aimed his gaze at the photograph. "And right there in front of you, not more than fifteen feet away, is the biggest, most fierce dark-haired sonofabitch you've ever seen in your life."

Tony chuckled. It was always funny to hear a preacher swear.

"He's got eyes black as lava and mighty antlers big enough to carry a man to his grave, with a chest three times the breadth of yours and shoulders like a damn grizzly bear's."

"What did you do?" Tony asked, though he already knew the answer.

"I just stand there. I mean, this thing is massive. He lifts his head and looks at me like I'm intruding on him, you know? It's his home, and what the hell am I doing there?"

Tony chuckled some more.

"If he'd wanted to, he could have devoured that ground between me and him in two strides, no problem. I would have been no more for this world, fertilizer for the next batch of greens to grow up the following spring."

"But he didn't?" Tony said.

Bones returned from the kitchen, licking his chops. Gus reached down and ran his fingers along the animal's spine, the vertebrae curving in response. "He might have, if I'd done what I wanted to do."

"Run like hell," Daniel said.

"But I knew which one of us would win that race."

"So you stayed?" Tony was up on his elbows now.

"I stood there, shaking in my boots." Gus brought his hand back from petting the cat and stroked his chin. "I said to myself, 'I may not be as big. I may not be as strong, and I may not be as mean as this monster in front of me, but on this brilliant morning at the edge of this beautiful lake in the heart of these fine mountains, I have just as much right to be here, and there's plenty of room for the both of us.'"

The boys watched him, waiting.

Gus sighed and sat back in his chair.

"How long did you stand there?" Tony asked.

"We had a good long staring contest, that old bull and me, before I finally got up the nerve to look through my camera." He shook his head. "I'd planned to take a picture of the lake."

Tony turned to look at the photo above him. "That's a lot better picture."

Gus smiled, showing the one cracked canine tooth he'd never gotten fixed.

Daniel studied the photograph again, the bull just as Gus had described him, dark-eyed and oozing power from every brown and black hair on its body. "So you got your water, then?" he asked, wanting to hear the final punch line.

Gus pulled his shoulders up in a slow shrug. "I wasn't really that thirsty."

Both boys laughed, the sound of their voices filling the small living room, the old man watching them with a wry smile on his face.

CHAPTER SEVEN

"So, why San Francisco?"

Daniel glanced over his plate at Brent.

They were eating in a family restaurant in Kearney, something he thought would diminish the conversation, but Brent didn't seem to mind doing both. "Picking up my little brother," Daniel said. "You?"

Brent chewed like he did everything else, nonchalantly, the food enjoyed but not deemed important. "Brother?" Cooking oil glistened on his lips.

"He's at summer camp," Daniel said, and then quickly, "What about you? Why Washington?"

Brent hooked a thumb toward Jolene. "She wants to go to college there." He shrugged. "I don't see the need."

"We're going to San Francisco first," Jolene said, eyeing Daniel.

"You don't have to—" Daniel started.

"We want to," Jolene said. "I've never seen it."

"Ever been there?" Brent asked him.

Daniel shook his head and caught Jolene's eye. "This will be my first time too." Tony would be waiting at the Bay Area Discovery Museum, just north of the bridge where the boats would be. How he knew that he couldn't remember. It would be a good idea to call the place, confirm the kids would be there at . . . three o'clock.

Yes, it was three.

"So this stunt thing," Brent said. "It's like your full-time job?"

"For now."

"A regular Evel Knievel, then."

"He was raised in Montana too."

"No kidding?"

"You couldn't do it," Jolene said.

"Wouldn't want to."

"Be too scared to."

"I'm not a fool."

Jolene stopped at that, a bite of waffle dripping syrup off her fork. "It's only foolish if you don't know what you're doing. He does."

Brent opened one hand. "We all do foolish things when we're young."

As you're clearly not anymore, Daniel wanted to say.

Jolene stabbed another piece of waffle and stirred it around.

"Not everyone gets it," Daniel said.

"He's just doing this thing he does," Jolene said. "Ignore him."

"What thing?" Brent said.

"Your superiority thing."

"Am not."

"Are too." She glanced at Daniel. "He won't let me show anyone my work."

"You know why," Brent said.

"It's bad luck to show it when you're still a novice," she said in a mocking voice.

"I'd like to see it," Daniel said.

Brent shook his head. "Whether you praise or criticize, your opinion pollutes it." He spoke with authority, his teacher voice, Daniel thought. "She must find her way without any outside influence."

"I'm no art critic."

"Everyone has an opinion. Most can't help but share it."

The restaurant had calmed, the wave of lunch customers having receded. Daniel pushed his empty plates to the edge of the table and sat back in the booth.

"You want something else?" Jolene asked.

Daniel shook his head. "I'm good."

"Me too," Brent said in a snarky tone of voice.

Jolene shot him a scornful look.

Daniel shifted uncomfortably, then crushed the napkin in his hand and set it on the table. "Be right back."

He stopped in the restroom, then checked around the hostess' desk for a phone, but there wasn't one. No office he could sneak into either. He considered going back to the table, but at the last minute turned on his toe and slipped out the front door.

A siren whined from somewhere across the town of Butte, its alarm long and mournful. It was late February and everything was still covered in snow, about four inches of it whitewashing all the buildings and streets so that even the old part of town looked a little cleaner than usual. At night the white of it reflected the moon glow, making it nearly as easy to get around as it was in the daytime—a blessing as Daniel and Tony trudged up the sloppy hill, over the ridge, and down the sidewalk toward Gus's house.

They had left dirty dishes on the counter and socks on the floor, and there were cookies missing from the one coveted package of peanut butter chocolate chip, the ones Valerie liked to believe were hers and hers alone. She'd come home from work to the "mess" and had gone into one of her rages, waking them from their beds after midnight wielding a broom that landed a few good bruises on Daniel. He threw on his jeans and sneakers, plopped a coat on Tony's shoulders, and escaped with him out the back door. Valerie threw dirty shirts and underwear after them, shouting into the night: "I work my ass off and you boys don't appreciate nothing!"

Gus's house key waited for them in its usual place on the back porch, stowed under the upside-down ceramic planting pot. Groping through the snow, Daniel wished he'd remembered to stash gloves in his coat pockets. Tony had his and was waiting by the door, his shoulders hunched against the cold. It was far below freezing, judging by the way their nostrils stuck together on every inhale, and both were eager to be inside. As Daniel's fingers fell on the cool metal, he had a passing grateful thought. Gus was gone to guest preach at another church in Missoula, which meant they didn't have to worry about waking him up. It was always worse when they had to do that.

Once the door was open, he stowed the key back in its rightful spot and joined his brother on the linoleum landing. They both removed their snowy shoes before going in. Then Tony said hi to Max and set to warming up some hot water for tea. They'd both learned to like it under Gus's influence, and it would feel good on a cold night like this. Besides, it would help them get back to sleep more quickly, which was necessary on a school night.

Daniel dropped into the striped couch that would be his bed. Tony always took the twin in the spare bedroom, the one Gus had originally set up as an office. The bed had been added in case any church guests needed a place to stay, he'd explained, though it was obvious the bed was for Tony. No one else ever stayed at Gus's house. Daniel had laid on the bed once or twice and found it far better than the bunk bed he and his brother shared at the trailer home, which made it all the easier to retreat here when Valerie went into one of her rants.

Bones emerged from Gus's bedroom to stare at them with sleepy green eyes. Daniel wiggled his finger, enticing the cat to come over, but the animal only watched him with a bored expression and then meandered into the kitchen in search of something to eat. Tony passed him by as he brought over the tea, black with a splash of milk. "Should I give him something?"

"Is his dish empty?"

Tony set his tea down on the lamp stand and went to look. "It's full, but he's not eating it."

"Not like he needs it." Daniel took a sip of the tea and let it warm the back of his throat. He was dead tired after having worked on a busted U-joint all evening at Mike's, and the last thing he wanted was tea. Instead he longed to just lay his head down on the leather pillow and go back to sleep, but Tony, as frequently was the case, was wide awake after the excitement.

Sitting cross-legged on the floor, he turned on the television. Daniel knew what was coming next. If the kid would just watch and shut up, he might be able to sleep through the glow and the noise, but that wasn't what Tony would do.

Daniel waited, sipping the tea as quickly as he could without burning his tongue. Sure enough, after flipping through the channels, Tony landed on an old sci-fi show and started in.

"Would a spaceship really be that big? None of the ones we've ever built are that big. I can't see that it would be practical to build one that size." When Daniel didn't answer, Tony turned to him. "Huh? Would it?"

"I don't know," Daniel took another obligatory gulp of tea. "Just watch or turn it off."

Tony swiveled back to the screen. Daniel forced himself to drink the hot liquid quickly. His throat throbbed with the heat, but he finished and stretched across the cushions, gratefully closing his eyes.

"How come we don't get this channel? It always has good shows, but we don't get it."

Please, just shut up.

"How come, Danny?"

"I've told you a million times. Cable is expensive. I'm going to sleep now. Be quiet, or I'll turn it off."

"I'm not done with my tea yet."

"Drink quietly."

His breath was just starting to slow into a gentle, comfortable rhythm when his brother started in again.

He used a quieter voice this time, but that was almost more irritating.

"You should watch this part. It's gross. The lizard-headed monster licks up the guy's blood." Eerie music played over the television's worn speakers, the strings sounding as if they might break any second. "Here it comes, Danny. You should watch. Ewww, that's so disgusting! Look!"

"Will you shut up?"

"But you have to see this part!"

"I'm trying to sleep."

"He's got this forked tongue and he licks it up and it's so—"

"Tony!" Daniel rose on his elbow and glared at his brother. "It's bad enough you gotta go eating her cookies but now you gotta keep me up too?"

Tony clutched the teacup in both hands. "They were your socks on the floor," he mumbled.

Daniel pushed himself up and out of the couch. The pattern was too predictable. Every time this happened, they ended up in a fight. This time, he was changing it. He grabbed the remote from Tony's hand and turned off the television. "Bed. We have school tomorrow."

"I'm not done with my tea."

Daniel grabbed the cup. "You are now." He stormed into the kitchen and dumped the contents into the sink. When he turned back around Tony was watching him. "Bed."

"I don't have to do what you say."

Daniel glared at the small freckled face with the chapped red lips and felt his forehead getting hot. "Fine." He shut off the light and retreated into the office, slamming the door behind him. Collapsing onto the twin bed, he heaved a great sigh and closed his eyes. He had almost calmed his breathing again when the television came back on. Gradually, the sound level increased until it was booming through the thin wall, pushing against his cell membranes like expanding helium. His whole body about to burst, he leapt out of bed and stormed back into the living room.

It took him a moment to find it, but when he traced the cord from the television to the electrical outlet, he pulled it. The screen went dark. Without a word, he went back into the spare room and flopped down on the bed. His heart slammed in his chest. He waited, half expecting the noise to start up again any moment, but everything was quiet. A while longer and he dared close his eyes, his nerves still on edge. Gus had placed a battery-run clock on his office desk. The hands glowed in the dark. Daniel could just pick out the time: a little after one. He had to get up in less than four hours for his early shift at Mike's. The old mechanic was the only one in town who would allow such a haphazard schedule, and for a high school kid no less. He couldn't afford to be late. He tried to relax, but after watching another twenty minutes go by, he got up and tiptoed to the door.

It took some time for his eyes to adjust to the darkness, but soon he could make out Tony's form. His brother had curled into a ball in Gus's recliner, his hands pulled into his chest like a baby bird's, his knees up to his chin and his head on the armrest. Daniel stood in the doorway watching him, uncertain if he was asleep, but then he heard Tony's steady breathing in and out. He felt his own shoulders relax and returned to the office.

Lying in the twin bed, he couldn't help but feel guilty. After a few more minutes of tossing and turning, he crept back into the living room, scooped his hands under Tony's knees and shoulders and carried him into the office. When he laid him down

Tony turned onto his side, his back to him. Daniel covered him up and tiptoed out.

Finally he lay on the couch, the house blissfully quiet. When he had managed to get comfortable, he heaved a long heavy sigh. They couldn't keep doing this. He would have to be more careful about picking up their clothes. And the cookies. He would go to the store and get an extra package. If they had their own stash, he wouldn't have to worry about Tony sneaking any.

He felt a sudden weight on his belly and grunted. Bones had jumped up and landed in the center of him. Daniel moved the cat to the side but Bones didn't want to leave. He stood at the edge of the cushion kneading his paws back and forth. Once Daniel got comfortable again, Bones curled up at his ribs and nestled his chin on his arm, purring loudly. Daniel closed his eyes. Gus would be back tomorrow.

This had to be the last time.

The sun blazed as Daniel rounded the north corner and followed the sidewalk to the back of the restaurant. The day was already warmer than it had been when they'd walked in, but there was a welcome breeze. He longed for a bit of grass, but it was all concrete and asphalt, the bulk of the parking lot resting between the restaurant and a wooden fence beyond, tall cottonwoods casting shade on the few cars lucky enough to land the back spaces. There was a pickup truck in one of them, a newer Dodge model, navy blue and clean as if it had just rolled out of the showroom. The bed was empty and had one of those nice black liners in it. He checked around once more and then stepped up on the bumper and threw his leg over. Once inside, he laid down, found a comfortable angle, and heaved a sigh of relief.

Sun glinted off the edges of the leaves above him, their tips like blinking lights when the breeze moved them to and fro. He felt a dull ache behind his forehead and rubbed it with his fingers and thumb. For a long while he tried without success to attach some logical pattern to the last couple of days, to find a way to explain everything that had happened. He inhaled and exhaled, willing his mind to *focus*, to figure this out. He was still going over it all when he heard a *slap slap slap* approaching. Fearing discovery, he opened his eyes and lifted his head.

The sound came from the right, the opposite side of the building from where he had approached, the side where the yellow dumpster was. They came like the footsteps of his high school counselor, the one who wore flower print skirts and flip-flops with glued-on accessories like shiny fake gemstones and plastic miniature animals. She'd slapped-slapped down the hallway when she came to call him from class, to ask him how it was going at home, why he'd missed a day of school the week before, why he hadn't turned in his English assignment. As the steps approached, he ducked low in the truck bed, shrinking like he had at his desk, longing for a magical sort of invisibility that would cover him like his own personal cloud.

The steps stopped. Daniel peeked over the top of the bed frame. A figure had appeared on the corner, a girl no more than about sixteen. She wore a black tank top and red sweat bottoms, a cigarette dangling from her ample lips. A roll of fat separated her breasts from her waist, limp brown hair skimming pale white shoulders. She rested her back against the yellow dumpster, her gaze aimed at the edge of the lot, where the fence blocked the view.

Daniel dared not move. There was something in the girl's posture, her curved shoulders and somber expression, her slow movements, that said this was a private moment, one not to be disturbed. He felt suddenly out of place, as if he had been the one to intrude. She stood, arms crossed, one hand under the other elbow to raise the cigarette level with her mouth. She inhaled and then tapped it against her thumb. The ashes drifted like dust to the ground, her eyes unblinking as she pulled the nicotine again into her lungs. When it was spent, she squashed it out, toes curled as she rotated her foot over the butt. Both hands went into her pockets and she slid down until she'd rested her bottom on the asphalt, her back still pressed against the dumpster. Her knees fell to the side and she kicked off her shoes, bare heels the color of peach pits. Daniel heard a rattling like dice in a cup. The sound aligned with the movements of her hand in her right pocket.

He felt a whisper on the back of his neck and shivered. The girl pulled her hand out. The pill container flashed white and orange between her fingers and thumb. A prescription bottle. She reached into her other pocket and pulled out a plastic water bottle. Yellow-gold liquid sloshed around inside. Daniel crawled to the tailgate, moving like a cat. She set the pills down beside her, opened the water bottle, and upended the lid. It landed in the dumpster behind her. She took a small sip, squinted as if it were sour, and then set the bottle down. Crossing her legs, she picked up the pills again and brought them close to her face. With the other hand she reached inside her bra and emerged with a cell phone. Thumb poised over the screen, she scrolled. Three strokes, four.

Daniel looked around. The parking lot was still empty. Strange that no one had come out to claim a vehicle and drive away. He wiped perspiration off his forehead. He had to get back inside, but the truck had become a hiding place. He waited, hesitant to show himself, to break into what seemed the girl's private world.

A quiet voice spoke in the back of his head. The voice said he knew what this was, knew it as well as he knew his own hands, knew exactly what the pills and the bottle and the amber liquid and the phone were all about, but he couldn't listen, couldn't fall over that cliff into the darkness of his own thoughts. He'd been in that place before. He didn't want to go there again. His hand trembled on the warm metal, his stomach hollow. He was only a stranger here, he told himself. It wasn't his place to interfere. Someone else could handle it.

She stopped scrolling and looked up. Daniel held to the tailgate, knees bent as he squatted low. She looked behind her and then up at the sky and then back at the phone. She seemed to think about something, a pouch of skin thick under her chin. Finally, she set the phone down beside her. Again she took up the water bottle. Took another swig. Scrunched up her face. Obviously, she wasn't used to powerful liquor. She had no tattoos, her skin clean and smooth, a chubby baby on the floor playing with something she shouldn't be playing with, her eyes narrow slits in the sun.

Daniel's knees hurt. He had to move. If she spotted him, it was no problem of his. He looked down to check where he was placing his feet. Stretched one leg out. He was about to stretch the other when he looked back.

The girl was staring straight at him.

Balanced between the bed and the ground, he had to keep going. He placed the ball of one foot onto the bumper and then the other on the asphalt. Stable again, he dared look up. Her gaze followed his movements. He was caught, now. No sense in hiding. In that moment, it occurred to him that besides Brent and Jolene, this girl was the only one who had acknowledged him, who seemed to even see him. One hand still clinging to the tailgate, he paused, and then glanced down the sidewalk the way he'd come. He should just go, but he was stuck, unable to move. She remained focused on him, her expression calm but interested, as if he were an unusual-looking stray cat crossing her path. Hot air pressed against his skin. He would go around the other way, return to the restaurant, leave her be. Still watching him, the girl pushed the water bottle down between her thighs and used both hands to open the childproof cap.

"Don't." The word escaped his lips unbidden. He shouldn't interfere. But he could feel the bottle in his own hands, hear the thoughts in his head. *Just swallow them down. It will be easy.* Her life. Her choice. He didn't know her. Bile rose in the back of his throat. The white lid fell to the asphalt, tip-tapping back and forth before it settled. Daniel shook his head, but his voice felt trapped, his throat closed.

The girl smiled a little then, a calm smile as if his presence were a comfort, and then she tipped her head back and slid the pills into her mouth. So many pills. She took them all. When she brought her head forward again the bottle was empty. She chewed, her gaze on him, her expression like someone standing in line at the grocery store wishing the line would move a little faster. Daniel could taste the chalky powder on his tongue, the bitterness sticking to his upper palate. The sensation was so familiar, a dark night around him, a hotel room, the smell of old pizza and soda and the taste of chalky white pills in his mouth.

His stomach twisted at the thought of what had happened afterward, the cramping and the lurching and his face reflected in toilet water. He felt like he was going to throw up.

"Stop." He took a step toward her.

She took a long swig from the bottle, combining the two substances into a deadly cocktail, rinsing the paste from the insides of her cheeks. That was the part he'd been missing, the hard liquor. She was more prepared than he had been. Focused on her task, she no longer looked at him but concentrated on chewing and swallowing and washing it down. It was a job she had to finish, an unsavory task, but one she was determined to complete. Daniel knew it was already growing too late, the drugs sliding down her digestive tubes to make a beeline for her bloodstream. The doctors would try to pump her stomach. If the doctors got there in time.

She chewed faster, shook her head as if to clear it, and then downed the rest of the alcohol in three swallows. Panting now, she threw both bottles away. The water bottle rolled across the lot, coming to a stop under the back tire of a red Toyota. The pill bottle took a much shorter journey, out and back around to drop into the dip by the curb.

Daniel looked from the refuse back to the girl. She was a rag doll, slumped against the dumpster, her spine curled forward, feet splayed out. She let her eyes close and rested her head. The phone lay still and black by her leg, the flip-flops discarded and already looking like sandals someone else had left behind. Her chest rose and fell with breath. Her matted hair covered all but a rectangular strip of her face.

Daniel's heart thumped between his ears, sweat dripping down the back of his neck. Too much time had passed. Jolene would be looking for him. He shifted his weight from one foot to the other, then pulled his hand away from the truck and walked. He intended to go around, back the way he had come. None of this was about him. It was her life, her decision. But his feet betrayed him. He approached the girl, his own breath coming in sharp bursts. Her cheeks were flushed, sweat glimmering on her fleshy neck. His body moved with only half his consent, the other half arguing he shouldn't go near, that he risked falling back into the black hole that before had consumed him, it's mouth opening wider with every step he took.

He knelt by her side and touched her face. She opened her eyes and smiled at him, then lifted her head a little. "What's your name?" Daniel asked.

"Trisha."

He nodded, his gaze scanning her. Nothing else was moving, as if her head were the only part that remained alive. "What were those?"

"Happy pills."

The bottle lay against the curb on the other side of her. He retrieved it and read the label. Generic oxycodone. And she'd chewed them. He got the water bottle next. Sniffed. Whiskey. She was looking up at the sky, the smile stretched like plastic over her lips.

"I wasn't sure you were real," she mumbled.

"Are you here with someone?"

She raised one hand a few inches off the ground and waved it back and forth. "No one's asking you."

The steps ticked off in his mind. Call 9-1-1. Go back inside. Find out if there's a doctor in the restaurant. Get someone here to take her to the hospital, pump her stomach, put her through hell with physicians and counselors and maybe even a mental health institution. "Why?" he asked.

She laughed a little before her eyelids dropped. Her breathing slowed, then her body tipped over until she was lying on her side, her head just under the corner of the dumpster, legs still splayed, one arm trapped underneath her ribs.

"Trisha." Daniel took hold of her shoulder, then jerked back. Her body was already heavy. "Trisha!" He looked around. How could he be in this busy parking lot this long without someone walking by?

Cripe, son, move your damn feet.

Gus's voice in his head. Gritting his teeth, he scooped up the prescription bottle. There was a name: Philip Howell. He looked down at the girl. Back at the bottle. Read the instructions and then the doctor's name and address. These pills had been prescribed for pain, but not for Trisha.

He picked up her cell phone and had started to dial 9-1-1 when he heard footsteps behind him, steady strides with a cushioned heel. He whirled around.

Brent stood about ten feet away. He looked at Daniel and then at the still body behind him.

Daniel felt his spine stiffen, his throat close. The phone clattered to the pavement.

Recovering, Daniel picked up the phone and held it out. "We need to call 9-1-1."

Brent walked past him and dropped to his knees by the girl. Positioned just behind her shoulders, he bent at the waist to look more closely, his walnut hair falling over his face. Daniel went to dial the phone himself but the fall had smashed it, the screen broken and black. He pressed the buttons at the side and thunked his finger on the front.

Nothing happened.

"It's not working." He looked up to see Brent's hand on Trisha's breast, fingers curled in a predatory squeeze. The tank top strap came away from the little mole and inched out until it drooped over her arm, exposing the red bra. Brent lifted his other hand then, the one that had been on her neck, and brushed her hair back with a gentle touch, exposing her face. Trisha's body had rolled toward him as if in response until her back lay braced against his thighs, her right arm having fallen limp into his lap, her face pointed to the sky.

"What the hell are you doing?"

Brent didn't look up. "Beautiful, isn't she? Almost gone, but not quite . . ." He caressed her cheek. "The expression. It's . . ." He positioned his hands around her face, framing it.

"Get off her!" Daniel stormed toward him.

"Hold on, there, Montana." Brent raised one palm. "Not like you were rushing to her rescue."

Daniel looked down at the phone. Pressed buttons. The screen stayed black. "Get your hands off her."

Brent locked gazes with him. He searched Daniel's face as if gauging how serious he was about this, then relented and sat back, lacing his fingers in front of him. Trisha's body moved too, rolling, and Brent stood up, allowing her to come to a stop on her back, both shoulders now lying on the asphalt.

Daniel dropped by her side and replaced the tank top, positioning it as it was, covering the mole. Setting the dead phone beside her, he pressed his fingers to her neck. Nothing. Pressed again deeper. One minute it seemed there was no pulse, but then he sensed a faint thump.

"Do you have a phone?"

Brent stood over him, watching.

"Can you at least get Jolene?"

"She wouldn't get it, wouldn't understand . . ."

Daniel moved, intending to go inside himself, but leaving Trisha alone now was even more problematic than it had been before. "I'm going to get her. Leave her alone!" His shirt wet with sweat, he ran down the length of the parking lot. Sneakers slapping against the asphalt, he rounded the corner, poised to charge up the side of the building, only to run into Jolene. He stopped, high-tops skidding. "Do you have a phone?"

She took in his stricken face. "What happened?"

"She took these." He held the pill bottle out.

"Who?"

"Trisha. We need to call 9-1-1."

She pushed past him and jogged around the corner.

"Wait!" He followed her back into the parking lot. Beyond, Brent had a different cell phone in his hand. "What's going on?" she asked.

Brent pressed the phone to his ear and leaned over Trisha, his fingers on her neck as if for the first time. After a moment, he set the phone down, straddled the girl's belly, and started performing chest compressions.

Jolene bolted forward. Daniel followed, but more slowly, watching the drama unfold in front of him.

"The phone," Brent said between breaths as he worked. "Can you talk to them?"

Jolene rounded Trisha's head and slid to a stop at Brent's side. She pressed the phone—Brent's phone, apparently—to her ear. "Hello?" Her cheeks paled as she watched the girl jerk back and forth under Brent's weight. Yes, they were at the Perkins restaurant. The girl was unconscious. She had apparently taken some pills. Jolene looked up at Daniel.

It was like watching a movie. This wasn't the Brent he'd observed only a few minutes before, this hero trying to save Trisha's life, working together with Jolene to perform a last-minute rescue. As Jolene stared at Daniel, he realized who he was in her eyes, the guy on the sidelines, the guy without the courage to act.

She motioned for him to approach. Walking across the parking lot he spotted the water bottle still resting against the curb where he'd left it. He stooped to retrieve it, then handed both bottles to Jolene. She read the prescription label into the phone, then described the water bottle. She looked at Daniel, eyebrows raised. He went through the motions of smelling it. She took a whiff and wrinkled her face.

"Alcohol," she said. "Whiskey, I think." She set the bottle down. A few more seconds of silence, and then, "Okay."

The operator kept her on the line. Brent continued with the compressions, pumping up and down like an oil drill, Trisha's heavy body yielding and resisting in rhythm underneath. Every now and then he stopped and checked her pulse again, then resumed.

"I'm still here," Jolene said. "No. I don't know." She glanced at Daniel, and then held up the pills.

Daniel shrugged. How much time had passed? He had no idea.

"Fifteen minutes," Brent said.

Jolene repeated the figure. Brent looked practiced, like he'd done this before, his laced fingers above the breastbone, his rhythm steady, just enough pressure. A siren sounded in the distance. Daniel stepped closer. It wasn't going to work, what Brent was doing. Daniel figured he knew that.

Brent waited until the siren sounded again to stop his CPR. "We have to go."

Jolene looked up.

"We can't be here when they come." He spoke in a soft voice, not wanting to be heard on the other side of the call. Sitting back on his heels, he panted, catching his breath. "They'll have questions." He looked up at Daniel. Jolene followed his gaze.

Keep going, he wanted to tell them, but Trisha was already gone. They wouldn't be able to save her. No stomach pumping. No mental institution.

Jolene looked at the bottles in her hands.

"Here." Brent made a "gimme" motion. She handed them over. He wiped both bottles on his shirt, ridding them of fingerprints, and then set them down by Trisha's side. He cleaned the girl's smashed phone and lay that nearby too, then motioned for Jolene to hang up. "Let's go." He grabbed his phone back and offered her his hand. She hesitated, and then took it. They started across the parking lot together. Trisha's tank top was mussed from Brent's pumping and Daniel longed to straighten it, to prepare her for when they would come with their gurney and their machines, make her as presentable as possible for the strangers who would try to save her life. He imagined his own body in the dirt, flames licking at his leathers, security personnel dousing the fire, and then the fire medics arriving in their red vehicle with flashing lights. He saw them surround him, observe his unresponsive body, remove his helmet to reveal weeping red cheeks, then start cutting off his blackened jacket and pants with scissors. The paramedics were right behind them and then he was on a gurney being rushed into the ambulance, the double doors slamming shut.

"Daniel!"

Jolene's voice, but he couldn't see her, only the red-and-white lights, the dust, the smoke.

"Come on!"

He looked her direction, trying to clear his vision. His body swayed, the heat rising on his skin. The accident. There had been an accident. A fire.

"Daniel." He felt her take his hand, her small fingers in his. "Come on. Hurry!"

His feet moved. Behind him, Trisha lay still on the asphalt, her skin slowly sinking deeper into her bones.

CHAPTER EIGHT

Morning sunlight glowed through the window, casting a yellow-gold hue on the brown carpet and brightening the aluminum foil that formed the tallest hill in Tony's world of Dinotan. Lying on his bottom bunk, Daniel heard his brother whispering and then humming, a happy tune like one might hum while walking. After a few moments of that, the melody changed to a more ominous one, background music to a suspense scene. Daniel sat up on one elbow, his eyes still heavy with sleep. The air felt cold, his arms sprouting goose bumps. At least the sun meant a nicer day than they'd had the day before, when the snow had fallen for so long it covered Tony's knees when they'd walked home from school. Casting his gaze to the bed above him, he was surprised his little brother was awake already. It had been tiring work, shoveling a path down their driveway. Fortunately a neighbor had plowed out the gravel road going up the hill, so they had only to clear the way between the trailer house and the edge of the road. The end had been the hardest part, where the tractor blade had built up a ridge blocking the driveway. Daniel had done most of it, but Tony had pitched in as best he could and crashed on his bed that night with his clothes still on.

Now, Daniel could hear him whispering an argument between two characters, then more humming. He soon caught on that the danger music was for the shark and the happy music for the pilot whale. He had ordered the bag of sea creatures after Tony had started talking about them. His brother had checked out a thick hardcover book on marine life from the library and absorbed it like a sponge. Once Daniel had gotten him the toys, they were always with him, especially the shark and the pilot whale, often squaring off against one another.

"Boys, breakfast!"

The humming stopped. A small face framed with a mop of black hair peeked over the top bunk. "Breakfast?"

Daniel looked at the closed bedroom door as if he might see through it. He smelled eggs cooking, and . . .

"Is that bacon?"

They dove out of their beds, Daniel scrambling for his jeans while Tony, still fully dressed, opened the door. Stepping into the living room, they were met with a rare sight: Their mother in the kitchen. Cooking.

"What are you standing there for? Come eat." She had even brushed her hair. It hung loose and soft around her cheeks, dark roots showing at the side part, blonde ends frayed and split but clinging neatly to one another.

"Mom, you made breakfast?" Tony said.

"Let's see. We got eggs, bacon, toast, some grapes, oh, and three Danishes with berry filling. Sound like breakfast to you?" She held up the plate for them to see, flipping the eggs with the other hand, her movements smooth with the expertise she'd gained over the years working in kitchens, serving up breakfast to thousands of customers but rarely to her own boys.

Daniel felt his stomach stir. Tony must have felt the same as they both bolted forward at the same moment, racing each other and sliding into their chairs at the dining room table. Tony's legs swung back and forth as if powered by an engine, his hungry gaze taking in all the bounty before him. Daniel felt the same. It had been so long since he'd had anything but cold cereal in the morning, often without milk. He watched his mother, looking for signs. Was this about a new boyfriend? He cringed at the thought, and then leaned out a little, trying to see past the kitchen and down the hallway to where her bedroom was.

"No one's there," she said, reading his mind. "Can't I just make breakfast for my boys?"

He straightened but didn't answer. It couldn't be that easy. It was never that easy. Still, when she piled his plate high and set it in front of him, he couldn't help but close his eyes for a moment, his senses bathing in the smell and heat of the food. Tony wiggled in excitement next to him, their mother clattering dishes in the sink and then sitting down to join them.

They ate in silence, all of them like refugees presented with their first real meal in months. Once the initial cravings were satisfied, Tony started talking. It was always what he did when he was happy or nervous or, more often, some combination of the two.

"When did you get all this, Mom?"

"This morning, while you boys were asleep."

"But it's only eight-thirty. Were you up that early?"

"I'd have to be, wouldn't I? Besides, you boys worked so hard clearing the driveway, I had to use it." She took a swallow of coffee. "And no snow this morning either, so you've got a break."

Tony watched her, elbows on the table, the empty fork at his lips. "I didn't know you could make all this."

"I'm your mother, for chrissake."

"Well yeah, but . . ." He didn't finish the thought. "It's really good!"

"It is good," Daniel said. "Thank you."

Valerie cocked an eyebrow at him.

"Is it someone's birthday?" Tony asked.

"No one's birthday."

"No . . . new boyfriends?" Daniel asked, her good mood giving him the courage to venture in.

"Had enough of them for a while." She glanced at Tony. "Haven't we?"

Tony kicked his feet with more vigor.

Daniel wondered if he could believe her. The last one had been so filthy. He had found a cereal bowl full of the guy's nail clippings while cleaning the back bathroom. "A new job?" he asked, but she shook her head.

"Not yet."

It had been three weeks since she'd been laid off. If it weren't for his job at Mike's, they wouldn't have been eating much at all lately.

"Aunt Carrie sent us some money. For Valentine's Day."

Aunt Carrie, then. Daniel wondered if Valerie had made one of her usual calls asking for help or if his aunt had just sensed that it was time.

"Is she coming to see us?" Tony asked, grape jelly stuck on the corner of his lip.

"It's too cold right now. Maybe later in the spring."

Tony swallowed his last bite of toast and sank back into his chair. His belly poofed out under his soiled shirt and he patted it three times as if assuring it that digesting all that food was well within its capability. All that was left on his plate was the frosted Danish, which he'd pushed into the center and now sat ogling. "I never had one of these before."

"I saw you looking at them."

"When?"

"When we were in the store last month."

Tony's eyes sparkled. He looked at his mother like he hadn't seen her for a very long time, and then got down from his chair and went over to her side. When she turned to him, still holding her fork in one hand, he held out his arms. For a moment she didn't move, an almost frightened expression on her face, and then she set the fork down and leaned over to hug her son.

"Thank you." Tony pressed his cheek into her shoulder. "This was a great surprise."

Daniel couldn't see his mother's face, but he was frozen in time, watching the two of them as if he were looking in on another family in another town, where breakfasts like this were commonplace and such touching moments always within reach. When Tony pulled away and returned to his chair, his mother wiped her eyes on her sleeve and looked back toward the stove so they couldn't see her face. Tony didn't notice, poking the tip of his finger into the Danish filling and then placing just the tiniest bit on his tongue.

Daniel returned to his own food. If she caught him staring, she would be embarrassed, so he kept eating like it was normal, knowing the gap between the two of them was too large for him to offer a similar gesture. Even getting off the chair and starting toward her would be like stepping onto a two-inch-wide beam stretched across the Grand Canyon. Mostly, the gap felt comfortable, the familiar place they had settled into over the last several years, but this morning, with the fluffy scrambled eggs, warm toast, and tender bacon melting together like sugar on his tongue, he wished it wasn't so.

When she turned back around, her face was dry, the faraway gaze restored to her eyes.

Jolene checked them into a Fairfield Inn in Cheyenne, Wyoming. It was a clean and fresh-smelling hotel, not very old, the cobalt blue color in the carpets still richly pigmented and contrasting neatly with the gray. As Daniel followed the other two into the elevator, he wondered why Jolene was always the one paying. The guy had to be a leech as well as a jerk. Not that Daniel had room to talk.

She'd gotten two rooms, one down the hall from the other. Daniel ducked into his and shut the door behind him. He had a half hour before they were supposed to meet for dinner. He tried his series of calls again: Erin, Jay, and Valerie. Erin answered but couldn't hear him, Jay's number clicked on with the same voicemail, and Valerie didn't answer. He changed into some of the new clothes Jolene had bought for him at the Walmart before the hotel, then ran down to the guest office to check his email. Nothing but junk. Not even Coach Greg had answered the email he'd sent from Harlan.

Frustrated, he grabbed his key and took the stairs back up to his floor. It was almost time for them to meet. As he approached Jolene and Brent's room, he heard voices and slowed down. They were arguing about something. He paused, listening. He should go back to his room. But he remained, suspended, in the middle of the hallway.

"She was like that when I got there," Brent said.

"Why didn't you do something?"

"I did." Pause. "Why aren't you asking him? He was there before I was."

The image of Trisha's face flashed in Daniel's mind. He crossed to the wall and, checking to make sure he was alone, slid up next to the door. One of them had left it open a crack, the swing bar lock propped against it to allow a convenient no-key entry.

"It was just . . . scary," Jolene said. "Her face was so white. And you were pushing on her chest, and it was like you were pushing on a, on a . . ." Her voice was rising, her words coming fast between breaths. "On the bottom of a pot or something, the way it was popping back and forth. I was afraid you were breaking her ribs."

"I didn't break her ribs."

Daniel held his body at the ready, his gaze alternately on the door and on the hallway behind him.

"She was dead," Jolene said. "Gone, just like my mother was. She wasn't sleeping the way you make it look."

"I do not make it look like that."

"You do. Your paintings are all peaceful and serene like it's all so perfect. It's not how it really is."

"It's how it *can* be."

"And you say I'm the amateur."

Score one for Jolene! Daniel thought.

"Come on, you're making too much of this."

"Why aren't you? It happened at the very restaurant where we were eating, at the same time—"

"Why aren't you asking him about this? He was there first."

"He didn't know what was going on."

She was protecting him. Daniel pulled his hand over his mouth.

"So he's excused then," Brent said.

"At least he's upset. I don't see how you can be so calm."

"Upset? He slept the rest of the way here!"

"He passed out in the parking lot! You saw him. He collapsed."

"So what did you want me to do? Fall apart? I think that's your specialty."

Daniel clenched his fist. *Such a jerk!* He was tempted to barge in and give him a piece of his mind.

"Did you see her ghost?" Jolene asked.

Brent chuckled. "I don't believe in that nonsense. You know that."

"Yeah, that's what you say."

"What's that supposed to mean?"

"Nothing."

Silence. Then, "Did *you*?" he asked.

"No."

"Well that's good at least."

"According to you."

Brent heaved a heavy sigh. "Can we drop this? It's time to go."

Daniel stepped away from the door, then stood in the middle of the hall unsure what to do with himself. In the end he hurried back to his room, slipped inside, and holding the door open a crack, waited. When he heard their door close, he opened his and stepped through.

"You're ready." Jolene greeted him with a friendly smile. "I'm hungry. Where do you want to go?"

⁕⁕⁕

He thought they'd return to the hotel when they finished dinner, but Brent drove them across town instead, over the railroad tracks and under the highway, down to a long, gray building with a red-and-yellow sign on top. *Outlaw Saloon*, it read. He parked in between two other Ford trucks, turned off the engine and glanced at Jolene. "Ready?"

"I'm tired," she said. "Do we have to do this tonight?"

"Do what?" Daniel asked.

Brent raised an eyebrow at Jolene.

"It's stupid," she said.

"She had a . . . bad experience," Brent said, "so she's afraid to go into bars now."

"So why are we going in?" Daniel asked.

"We must face what we're afraid of," Brent said in a singsong voice.

"Let's just get it over with." Jolene got out of the truck.

Outside, they all stood looking at the building, which appeared more like an auto service shop than a bar, the siding a nondescript gray, a long awning covering the sidewalk to the front doors. "Besides, these are great places to observe human nature," Brent told them. "Vices, sins, deception, they're all here for the taking at a place like this. Perfect for informing one's art." He cocked an eyebrow at Jolene and then started walking.

"I thought we were on vacation," Jolene said, following him.

"Best time," Brent said over his shoulder. "Creativity thrives on vacation." He walked faster, clearly eager for the observing to start.

Daniel slid in beside Jolene. She had put on some makeup, her eyelashes darker and longer, bringing out the green in her eyes. "We don't have to do this."

"It's okay."

"I'm tired too."

"We probably won't stay long. Just enough to make him think I'm getting over my fear." She emphasized the last four words, then gave him a weak smile.

Daniel pursed his lips, wondering what the "bad experience" was, and why she always went along with Brent, even when she didn't want to. He could sort of see it before. She was alone then. But she wasn't now. He decided he had to do a better job of showing her that.

Ahead, people stood in small groups at the side of the building, most of them smoking. He wrinkled his nose at the smell. It always reminded him of Valerie. They walked through the door and onto a black-and-white-checkered linoleum floor. The open room was crowded, dotted with tall round tables and black cushioned stools with a warehouse-like smell of open air and dust. Brent led them to the bar, where they found a couple of empty seats between two groups of women. A country band played on the stage beyond, a familiar rocking rhythm powering the dancers already on the floor. Jolene looked back at Daniel, but he gestured for her to take the last remaining seat. Brent asked for everyone's fancy.

"Just a Dr. Pepper, or Coke, or whatever they have," Daniel said. "Someone's gotta drive us back."

"I'll drive," Brent said. "I can always drive, unlike some people." He raised an eyebrow at Jolene.

Jolene averted her gaze. Daniel noticed the reaction. "It's the cocky ones who get in trouble," he said to Brent.

Brent laughed. "You would know," he said.

Daniel glared at him, heat crawling up his spine. "I'm gonna look around," he said. He waited to see if Jolene might go with him, but she didn't get off her stool, so he went alone, heading back the way they had come. Three was definitely a crowd, and he could stand it only for short periods of time.

Outside again, he ran into another smoking group to the left of the front doors, so he turned the other direction and walked away from the building, toward the trees and open ground in the distance. The last of the sun's glow laid a long bruise on the edge of the horizon. He felt the dusk like a blanket on his shoulders, his tense muscles releasing. A few outdoor tables lay scattered nearby. He left them behind and skirted the parking lot, headed for a clump of shadowed cottonwoods in the broad patch of grass at the edge of the lot. It was dark out, but the moon was up, and his eyes soon adjusted well enough to make his way. He'd thought to sit down somewhere among the trees but spotted a couple kissing nearby, so he kept walking, moving farther back on the property until he found a space where he could be alone. Settling down and bracing his back against a mature trunk, he looked out on the saloon and the lights of Cheyenne beyond. Many times, he had watched over the lights of Butte from a similar vantage point, though it was usually from the seat of his Kawasaki rather than from behind a saloon. The country band played on, energizing the night with their beat, turning the planet in the fantastical way it turned at night, with colored lights and moving feet and heady drinks and the feeling that this was a place everyone wanted to be. Daniel listened from afar while his thoughts tumbled over one another. He had believed his memory would improve with time, but it seemed instead to be doing the opposite, the scenes from his life on the road with the Diamond Xtreme fading like ink on aged paper while his memories of living in Butte came to the fore, vivid and raw as if he'd lived them only a few days ago.

He tried to force himself to remember what had happened before Iowa, before his dream of the beach and the whales, but when he did, all he could see was the ground falling away like it did when his bike left the ramp, his bodyweight dropping into his heels. Soon after came the fire and then the pain. He pressed his palms against the grass, allowing the cool blades to calm the heat. Sweat prickled under his arms and over the back of his neck. He didn't want to soil the new shirt. Jolene had picked it out, navy blue with a sharp collar that made him look higher class than he was. He released two buttons and dropped his head back against the bark, willing the pain to subside.

Tony was waiting for him. He dug the Tomcat out of his pocket and brought it close to his face. He had to get to San Francisco, that was all. Looking at the dark head of the pilot inside the cracked window, he knew this like he knew the beat of his own heart.

CHAPTER NINE

A thud sounded against the wall outside Daniel and Tony's room. They both looked up, startled.

"On the left!" Valerie shouted.

"Shit, woman!" A man's voice. Another thud and then the bathroom door squeaked opened and closed. The boys knew what would come next. They directed their attention out the window but couldn't help but hear the tinkling sound of a belt buckle and then the beer-fueled urine stream gushing into the toilet.

"He wanted to slide on the ice, you see." Keeping his voice low, Daniel started the story he'd promised about Harry the Horse and the missing ice skate. He'd backed himself into a corner when Tony had asked him for the umpteenth time why they'd named the Big Dipper the Big Dipper. It didn't look like a dipper at all. What would you have named it, Danny? When Daniel blurted out "ice skate," Tony had demanded he explain himself, and Daniel had launched into a story to keep his little brother's mind off the chaos in the next room. "He tried gliding on his hooves, but he couldn't control himself. They would get all packed with snow until they were round as baseballs."

"An ice-skating horse." Tony shook his head. "Lame."

"You haven't heard the rest of the story."

The man exited the bathroom without flushing. Heavy footsteps receded and then more footsteps, lighter ones, approached. The door closed again. Someone flushed, and then a quieter stream of urine. Sally, Daniel guessed, one of the new waitresses Valerie had invited. Strange to imagine her doing her business only a few feet away.

"So he'd try to glide on them," he continued, "but he'd end up sprawled out on the ice with his legs like the points of a star." Daniel's back ached. Too many hours underneath a Chevy truck to get at the transmission. He lay on his side, one hand holding his head near the edge of the cut-up cardboard box that began the world of Dinotan. The woman in the bathroom started talking on her cell phone.

"I'll be home soon," she said in a subdued voice, though the walls were thin enough that the boys could hear. "Are the kids asleep?" Pause. "You're just getting dinner? It's eleven thirty." The toilet flushed. "It's one night, John." Tony's gaze moved from Daniel's face to the floor. "McDonald's is fine. It's just late." Water ran in the sink. "I know but—" The water continued and then shut off. "No, you don't have to. I have a ride. I gotta go." The door squeaked open and the woman returned to the living room. "I swear, he's such a baby!" she shouted.

"Come on, Sally." Valerie's voice. "It's your turn!"

"Does the TV have to be so loud?" someone else said. It sounded like Joe, the bouncer from the bar where they all worked.

"Come on, sweetheart!" another man shouted.

Daniel pushed Dinotan to the side and maneuvered his body to create a border between Tony and the door. "So the town blacksmith made Harry some ice skates," he went on. "They slid easily over his hooves, and they had long leather straps that wrapped around his forelegs." More laughter from the other room, but at least the bathroom was mercifully empty for the moment.

"Knock it off, Bruce!"

Tony jumped.

"Christ, woman, lighten up."

"Keep your hands to yourself."

"Not like you didn't want it."

"In your dreams."

Men laughed and jeered. Glasses clinked. The front door of the trailer opened and slammed shut.

"Harry especially liked the way the blacksmith decorated the straps with red ribbons that flew behind him like flags when he soared over the ice."

Tony rubbed one eye and pulled his knees close. "So how did he lose one of them into the sky?"

"I'm getting to that." Daniel shifted again, trying but failing to get comfortable on the hard floor. "It happened one winter day. Harry liked to skate in the afternoon, when it was bright and warm. At first, no one bothered him, but soon word spread around about this horse ice-skating. It wasn't long before Harry had a good-sized audience that would gather around the perimeter at two o'clock every afternoon to watch. Once in a while, Harry would even show off a little."

"Like you do on your motorcycle?"

"Hey, who's a show-off? I saw you hanging upside down on the monkey bars for that girl."

"What girl?"

"The blonde one. What's her name?"

"Oh." Tony looked down at his hands. "Maizey."

Daniel pointed at him. "You were showing off."

"Was not."

"Uh-huh."

"Wouldn't matter. She thinks I'm a loser."

"Sure. That's why she was watching you."

"Just to make fun."

"Girls always watch you just for a chance to make fun."

"They do."

"Whatever. So Harry's doing turns and jumps and the people are clapping and smiling, and everything is great. But then one day Harry's owner, Martha—." He stopped.

"What?"

"Shh." Daniel looked toward the closed door. The trailer home had suddenly fallen silent save for the television, which was emanating the distant sound of car engines racing. He sat up and listened, then checked the clock. It wasn't even midnight yet. Too early for the party to be over.

"So what happened?" Tony whispered.

Daniel hesitated. It was too quiet. But when he heard nothing more, he continued. "Martha used Harry for work, to deliver the mail up in the mountains. She liked her job because people were always glad to see her coming. Especially when the weather was bad, they would go on about how dedicated she was."

Someone rapped heavily on the front door, the sound a muffled thump in the boys' room. "Sally! Open this door." A booming male voice. More thumping, six hits. "Sally! I know you're in there." Footsteps approached. Daniel drew his feet underneath him.

Tony turned toward the door. It opened.

"Stay there." Valerie pushed a woman inside and quickly shut the door again.

"Bitch, get out here now!"

"John, give it a rest!" Valerie called, her footsteps receding.

The television volume went down to near nothing. The woman—Sally—stood in shadow, the only light coming from a small desk lamp in the middle of Dinotan. The boys watched, unmoving, as she remained at the door, one hand on the surface of it, the other on the wall next to it, her body poised for escape. "You should have left him," she mumbled in a subdued voice. "I keep telling you to leave him and you're a damned chicken-shit about it. Now look what he's doing. Look what he's doing now. Shit." She took a step back from the door, her fists clenched at her sides.

Daniel stood up slowly, eyeing his baseball bat by the bed. The woman smelled of beer and cigarettes and a heavy pour of rose perfume. Standing about five feet six, she was a stick, maybe one-hundred-ten pounds. In the light of Dinotan's moon, he could see his brother's gaze pointed at the woman's back.

"Open this door," John bellowed from outside. "I need to talk to my wife."

"She already left," Valerie answered. "Said you were having trouble with the kids."

"The kids are fine and I'm not having any goddamn trouble. Open this door."

"Not when you're talking like that. You're drunk."

"It doesn't matter what the hell I am. Where's my wife?"

"I told you. Give it a rest."

"Open the door, or I'll fuckin' open it for you!"

Silence filled the rest of the trailer, but in the small room Daniel heard Sally's quick inhales of breath, the sniffs and choked sobs. "Dammit!" she whispered. "One night. I can't even have one fucking night." She turned to the side so she was leaning her shoulder against the doorframe.

Everything fell still.

And then a mighty crash rocked the trailer home.

Daniel grabbed the baseball bat, flew to the door, and gripped Sally's shoulder. She jumped, startled to see him, but he only pushed her aside and slipped through. "Lock it!" he hissed.

Walking down the hallway he could see the lights had been turned off, probably because they'd been watching a movie, the light over the range the only one shining. In its shadow loomed the figure who'd collided with the door, a man over six feet tall and thick like a bodybuilder. He stood in the middle of the dining room an angry bull, nostrils flared over a thick mustache, his small eyes darting back and forth, searching the room.

"Valerie?" Daniel called.

She didn't answer. He took a couple more steps, his gaze wary on the intruder. To his right two other waitresses, Kendra and Joan, cowered on the couch, Joe and Bruce on the floor in front of them. Bruce held a bowl of popcorn in his lap. The air smelled of stale beer and salsa. Everyone was watching the big man. The door stood open, still upright but skewed, the top part hanging farther away from the frame than usual, the hinges undone. Daniel still couldn't see Valerie.

"Where is she?" John looked right at him.

For the first time, Daniel realized he was the only one standing between John and his wife. The big man glowered at him, his chest as wide as China. "What you gonna do with that bat, son?"

Daniel took another step forward. "My mother. Valerie. What'd you do?"

"Guess she was going to open the door after all. Got there a little late." Daniel looked down. On the floor behind the crooked door, Valerie lay still. "Your turn," John said. "Where's my wife?"

Daniel lifted the bat and moved until he stood at the edge of the living room. "Get out of my house."

"Your house? Who the hell are you?"

"I live here. Get out."

John took a step toward him, a mountain moving in the dark. "I'm not going anywhere until you tell me where she is."

"Come on, John." Joe's voice from behind. "Let it be."

John registered Joe-the-bouncer's face. "You gonna let her hide like this?"

"She needed a break. She'll be home later."

"A break?" John set meaty hands on his hips. "Since when are you her calendar boy?"

"I'm off duty." The bouncer made his way forward, his voice close behind Daniel's ear.

"Sally?" John called, scanning the rest of the room. "You got five seconds to get out here or I'm tearing this place apart."

"What the hell?" Joe said. "Calm down. I'll get you a beer."

Daniel turned the bat in his hand, getting past the wood slicked with his own sweat until he found a good grip again. The others stayed where they were, frozen in front of the TV. A click. A long *squeak*, the familiar sound of the bedroom door opening.

Daniel whirled around. *Get back!* he wanted to say, but the air shot out of his lungs, John's fist a boulder between his shoulder blades. The bat dropped onto the carpeted floor as he fell forward, just catching himself on the back of the couch before Joe stepped up to stop the big man. John grabbed the bouncer's shoulder and shoved him aside too.

Another squeak and the bedroom door closed again.

"That door ain't gonna stop me." John stormed into the hallway.

"This was my night!" Sally yelled, her voice muffled from inside the boys' room.

"Just like every other night is your night." John grabbed the doorknob and shook it. "I work all day while you sit around on your lazy ass, and then I come home to a messy house and hungry kids and it's your night?" He jerked the door back and forth inside the frame.

Daniel righted himself, retrieved the bat, and hurried down the hall, fully aware of how flimsy the door lock was and how close the big man was to blowing in and scaring the shit out of Tony. He came up behind Joe, who'd recovered first and now waited just behind John.

"Go on outside," Joe said. "We'll bring her out."

"Sally!" John banged on the door. "Get your ass out here or I'm breaking this door down."

"You're tearing up the lady's house," Joe said.

Daniel's blood pumped hot through his veins. Tony was in there, probably frozen on the carpet where he'd left him. "Hey, shithead."

John paused.

"That's my room. Get the hell away from it."

The big man paused, then turned around slowly. "That's your room?" He hooked a thumb over his shoulder.

Daniel looked from the door to the shadow of the man's face. *Shit.* Why did he phrase it that way?

John slid past Joe with a twist of his shoulder. "Your room? You got my wife in *your* room?"

"Aw hell, John," Joe said. "He's a kid. Will you give it a rest?"

But John was walking back to the living room, which is what they both wanted, though Daniel didn't particularly like where this was going. He backed up in the wake of the man's advance, Joe following, until the three of them stood by the couch. Daniel cast a glance to the left and found the others gone, the bowl of popcorn abandoned on the coffee table, night air entering the broken front door to cool the back of his shirt.

"How old are you?" John said.

"Not your business."

"When you're sleeping with my wife it is."

"I'm not sleeping with her!"

"She's been with us all night, John. The kid wasn't even around."

But John hadn't taken his gaze off Daniel. He took a step closer, forcing Daniel back onto the linoleum. "Sally's been sneaking out for weeks now."

"Will you listen to yourself? The kid's a mechanic. He works all hours. Sally ain't been hanging out with him."

Daniel looked behind him. Valerie no longer lay on the floor. He checked the kitchen, but she wasn't there either. Casting his gaze to her room, he saw the door was closed.

"Sally, come out and defend your lover boy!" John started toward Daniel, faster now.

The trailer was closing in on him. There was only the kitchen, his mother's closed door, and the cold air outside. As John descended, he chose the cold air and bolted.

"You little shit!" John tore after him.

"I'll call the police!" Joe said.

Yes, for chrissake. Call the police. Daniel ran until he stood clear of his home and turned around. When the big man caught up, he thought about running again, but his brother was still in the back room, his mother in the front one, and there was nowhere to go but the snow-covered hills. The ground was hard under his feet, slick with a thin layer of ice. Valerie's outside light was on, and as he stood in the glow with the big man coming on like thunder, he gripped the bat and said a prayer that he'd make it out of this alive.

Hoping for a jumpstart he swung first, but it was like hitting a wall. John grabbed the bat, jerked it out of his hands and threw it wide. It hit the back of Ms. O'Brien's Ford Focus. Then the big man took hold of his shirt with one hand, his other crunching Daniel's shoulder.

"You think it's fun to go fucking another man's wife?"

"I didn't fuck her!" he yelled. "You oversized piece of shit!"

His feet left the ground and then he was sailing through the air. He fell hard on his tailbone and then his hip, his head colliding with the mailbox post. Groaning, he turned to the side and blinked, trying to clear his vision. John was coming at him again. Where the hell was Joe?

As if in answer, the bouncer came up from behind and grabbed John's shoulder. The big man whirled around to meet a solid punch in the face and then another. He staggered back, his hand on his cheek. "Joe, this ain't your business," he spat.

"Quit picking on the kid and go on home."

John turned on Daniel. He hesitated a minute, and then strode forward and grabbed him by the shirt and the pants. Daniel felt himself lifted as if he were no more than a sack of trash.

"John, goddammit!" Joe came after him.

With his left hand, Daniel punched the man in the gut. It had no effect. John threw him again. Daniel turned in the air and landed hard on his knee. White light pulsed into his brain.

Joe went to work. Daniel heard the punches, the grunts and the groans. The guy knew where to land a hit. Rolling on the ground, Daniel tried to get up, but his knee buckled and he fell back down in the snow. Another punch and the big man cried out.

"All right, all right!"

The punching stopped. Daniel heard breath coming fast and couldn't be sure if it was his or theirs. He gripped his knee, arms shaking, unbidden tears flowing down his cheeks. Behind him, footsteps, fast ones, and then a face in front of him.

"Danny? Danny, you all right?"

Tony. "Get back into the house!"

But his brother was crying, his small hand on Daniel's shoulder. "Should I call the doctor?"

"Get back in the house. Go. Now."

The bouncer was talking the big man down. He should go home, get some rest. Sally would be there soon; he would make sure of it. This wasn't doing anyone any good. Tony's shoes crunched the snow as he walked away. Daniel laid his head back and tried to get control of the pain. In the shadows, it was hard to see, but then he heard it, his little brother's voice shouting through a strained throat.

"That's my brother! You leave my brother alone! You leave him alone!"

"Tony." Pain drove any other words from Daniel's mouth.

Back at the Fairfield hotel in Cheyenne, Daniel's room felt claustrophobic. He was tired, but too revved up to sleep. He'd discarded the new dress shirt on the back of the chair, wearing only his T-shirt and a pair of cheap sweats Jolene had gotten him. He had the cooler on high, but he was still too warm. He splashed cold water on his face, brushed his teeth, and tried to relax on the bed, but it was useless. Throwing on his shoes, he pocketed the slim plastic key card and went back out into the night.

The front door led to the parking lot. Then it was a short distance to the streetlight and the main road leading into or out of the city. Across the way stood the shopping mall that had been so crowded only a few hours earlier. It lay dark and quiet now, the yellow parking lights casting a dim glow on the empty asphalt. Daniel scanned both ways and decided to turn right. The traffic was still fairly steady for the late hour, exhaust and dust entering his lungs breath after breath. It felt good to walk, to move. After another block he spotted a convenience store up ahead. The lights were on, and since it was nearly midnight, that was fortunate. There was coffee to be had in there, and maybe a candy bar.

The bell rang when he walked in the door, but the clerk—a lanky man with salt-and-pepper hair—paid it no mind. Daniel checked the coffee maker and found it empty. A cold dread crept over his shoulders, but he walked back to the checkout counter anyway. The clerk was no longer there. He looked around and found the man in the snack aisle. "Sir?" He was stocking chips on the shelves a few feet away. Daniel set his jaw and walked up to him. "Sir?" When the man still didn't respond, Daniel reached out to touch his shoulder. His hand fell through it as if the clerk were nothing but a projection. Seemingly unaware that anything had happened, he stocked the rest of the chips and walked away.

Daniel stared at the space he had left behind, and then at his hand. His heartbeat raced, his mouth gone dry. He turned to find the clerk had retreated behind the counter. Steeling himself, he walked around and tapped him again on the shoulder. His finger fell through the guy's skin as if he were gesturing through empty air. He jerked it back, stumbling into the shelf behind him. The clerk paused and turned as if he'd heard, then went back to organizing his papers.

Out on the street, Daniel ran as fast as he could back toward the hotel, his skin breaking out into a sticky sweat. The plane. He'd forgotten the plane. It was still in his jeans pocket. He had to get the plane and then everything would be all right. The craziness of that idea was not lost on him, but at that moment it made perfect sense.

He raced through the parking lot, found the side entrance, and used his key to get in. All he could think about was his small room and the plane waiting for him in his jeans. He spotted the sign that read "stairs," powered through the door, and started up, taking two at a time.

On the second flight, he found Jolene.

He saw only the top of her head at first, that thick crown of red. Then he saw the bloody pocketknife. Next to it, the pale skin of her arm, marked with two mean cuts that dripped red blood down onto the carpet.

Daniel froze, one foot on the landing, the other on the second stair. The knife, the blood, the cuts. His gaze moved from one to the other and back again. Jolene's arm was so scarred with old cuts it looked like a bar chart. They were all evenly spaced, forming a pattern of ticks like one might make in a cave to mark the passing days.

She looked up at him, cheeks red, then brought the knife in, her fingers closing the blade with a practiced tuck and pull. Slipping it into the pocket of her fleece hoodie, she stared at him like a nervous dog that had just been caught in the chicken house. Daniel stared back, aware he'd intruded on a private moment. He should excuse himself and move on, but the sight of her was just the focal point he'd needed, the element keeping him from spinning off into that black hole. He reached out and with a trembling hand, took hold of her shoulder.

His grip held, her flesh firm underneath his palm. He squeezed and released, feeling the cotton under his fingers, the smallness of her muscles and bones. He squeezed three times before dropping his head to breathe, his breath the loudest thing in the stairway. Finally, he lowered himself to sit on the stair below hers. Pressing his back into the wall he let his legs relax, his chest heaving, and almost without realizing it, reached out and took hold of her ankle, his fingers wrapped around the soft cotton sock. When his breath finally calmed, his gaze registered only Jolene's legs.

She was wearing navy blue sweat pants and pure white socks, no shoes. He folded inward until his head rested on her thigh, and then remained there, the one hand still around her ankle. For a long while they only breathed together, and then he felt her fingers in his hair.

He closed his eyes.

The lights in the examination room were too bright. Daniel dropped his arm across his eyes to ease the glare. He didn't remember the ride across Butte to the hospital, didn't know it was Joe who had taken him until Tony told him later that night. He did remember John's muscled fists and, as soon as he regained consciousness, was quickly reminded of all the places they'd landed. Shortly after that the drugs took hold, and then everything was a blur except the bright lights and the raising and bending of his leg. In the end the doctor diagnosed him with a fractured kneecap, adding that he was incredibly fortunate because it was a clean fracture, the bone intact. A couple months' rest and it would heal just fine.

They prescribed a contraption called a knee immobilizer. It was more convenient than a cast as long as Daniel followed directions, the doctor said with a stern look over the top of his glasses. While Daniel waited for them to bring him one, Tony filled him in. Joe had driven them to the hospital in his pickup truck, then left to take Sally to a hotel. Daniel felt grateful for the bouncer's actions, but both boys knew what that meant. They had no ride home.

"Is there a light on the desk?" Daniel asked.

"Yeah," Tony said.

"Turn it on, would you? Then turn this one off." He pointed at the fluorescent light on the ceiling. Tony complied and the bright light vanished, to Daniel's great relief. Resting on the table, he inhaled the antiseptic air, his leg naked and straight, his jeans discarded somewhere he couldn't remember. "Did you see Valerie?" he asked. He didn't want to care how she was, but now that it was all over, he couldn't help but wonder why she hadn't come.

"She saw us leave," Tony said.

"So she's okay?"

"I think so."

A plastic clock on the wall ticked off the seconds. "She say anything?"

Tony shook his head.

She couldn't have been hurt that badly if she'd made it into her room and then out again when they'd left. She could have gotten into her car and come to the hospital. He rubbed his hands together. "Frickin' refrigerator in here."

Tony got up and walked out.

"Where you going?"

The brown door swung closed and latched. Daniel stared at it. Looked at his knee. Stared at the door. He had almost made up his mind to get up and go after his brother when it opened again and Tony returned carrying Daniel's jeans and a thin hospital blanket. He set the jeans on the chair by the examining table, pulled the blanket from the pile and brought it over.

Daniel wrapped it around his shoulders. "Now I look like an old lady in a shawl." He raised his eyebrows, but Tony only plopped on the doctor's stool and started rolling it back and forth, his body slumped, his hands limp in his lap. He spun around twice, then pressed his toes against the wall and pushed himself backward. The chair sailed across the room and collided with the cupboards under the sink. Daniel winced, afraid someone would come to see what was making the noise. Tony turned, pushed off again, and sailed across the other direction.

"You got anything going on tomorrow?"

Slam against the wall.

"There's a dinosaur thing."

"What dinosaur thing?"

"It's called Jurassic Quest. The whole fourth grade is going."

Daniel lifted himself up on his elbows. "What's Jurassic Quest?"

Tony twisted left and right. "They've built these life-sized dinosaurs that move and make sounds. They're going to have them at the civic center. They've got food and stuff, too."

A field trip. He would have needed a signed permission slip for that. And *money*. "Sounds awesome. We'll get out of here and get you ready to go. Think you can stay awake all day after being up all night?"

"I don't want to go."

So he hadn't asked Valerie to sign the slip. Either that, or she'd forgotten. Daniel laid his head back against the pillow. He wasn't up to this. Not now.

"It will be dumb anyway. Miss Turner said those of us who stay behind will get to have lunch at our desks."

"Sure. Who wants to see life-sized dinosaurs? Walk among them like they were still alive. Stupid. Much better to sit at your desk and draw pretty pictures and then eat your baloney sandwich while Miss Turner reads her book."

"Miss Turner's going on the field trip."

"Even better. Who, then?"

"Some substitute."

"Outstanding. Whoever it is, I'll bet she'll be hot. Maybe only sixty years old this time."

Tony sailed across the room and thudded up against the cabinets. "How long are they going to make us wait?"

"You're just chicken. Chicken to go because you know that girl is going to be there. What's her name?"

"Am not."

"Are too. It's the perfect chance to hang out, but you don't have the guts. Chicken chicken chicken. Bauuulk, baulk bauulllllk." Daniel flapped his elbows, his arms rubbing against the examination table.

"Cut it out."

"Bauuulk, baulk bauulllllk, be-gaaaaullllk!" After years of listening to Mrs. O'Brien's birds, he could do chicken all day long.

"That's not it!"

"Exactly, and I know what *is* it. You wanted Mom to do it. 'Mommy, sign my permission slip. Mommy I need twenty dollars.'" An unexpected wave of anger swelled over Daniel's chest. "You know I would have signed it for you, would have given you the money weeks ago. Why didn't you ask me?"

Tony twisted back and forth in the chair.

"How many times you going to do this? You know how it goes. You knew it before you even asked her. Yet off you go again, down the same old path like some little baby who doesn't know any better. Do you like sitting there all red-faced because Mommy didn't come through for you? 'Wah, wah, Mommy didn't do what mommies are supposed to do.' You ever get tired of that?"

Tony's cheeks flamed, his eyes swelling.

"I'd think you'd get tired of it. *I* get tired of it. Instead you'd rather miss out on the best field trip ever and sit on your hands in class while some substitute teaches you how to make smiley faces. Maybe someday you'll figure out I'm the one who's here for you. I'm the one trying to make it better for you."

Voices out in the hall, but no one came in. Daniel gritted his teeth. He wanted out of this place. Out of his mother's house. Out of fucking Butte, Montana. Restless, he raised himself up on his elbows again.

He'd meant to glare at the doorway in the hopes his anger would produce someone who would finish the job and let him go. Instead his gaze connected with his brother's. Tony glared back, eyes looking up from under dark eyebrows. Daniel recognized that glare and morphed his face to be just as stern. "What?"

Tony said nothing.

At first Daniel was glad to see some backbone there, a little fight in his brother's eyes. But as he looked again, he saw something else, too, something that wasn't so good to see.

"I shouldn't have to rely on you for everything."

Daniel shifted his elbows to better support his half-upright position.

"I can never do anything. I have to ask Mom, or you. I can't even ask Gus, because you're always telling me not to bother him. I don't like having to ask everyone all the time."

"You know I'll do it for you. And you know that odds are, she won't."

"So you think you're better than she is."

Daniel's mouth opened but nothing came out.

"You said she couldn't help drinking and smoking, that there was something in it that made it hard to stop. You said she was lonely and sad."

Daniel listened, dumbfounded.

Was Tony really protecting Valerie? After having watched John beat him up while she'd hid in the back room?

Tony stood and zipped up his coat. "I guess she needs someone besides us. It doesn't mean you have to blame her all the time."

"She hid in her room while that guy beat me up. He could have killed me! If Joe hadn't been there, who knows what would have happened."

Tony met his gaze. "You were brave, Danny." He stood there a minute more, looking at him with round blue eyes that glistened with tears. Then he turned around and opened the door.

"Where are you going?"

"Home."

"You can't go by yourself."

"I can."

The door clicked closed behind him.

Daniel and Jolene sat together on the Fairfield hotel stairway for a long time, a bubble of warm air surrounding them as they breathed into the narrow space between the walls, their temporary sanctuary undisturbed until the door opened on the first floor below.

Metal clamped against metal, the security latch depressed and extended. A space of silence, and then the latch clicked closed. Daniel heard footsteps. He stood up and then, unsure where to go, simply remained standing. The steps paused for a moment, the newcomer perhaps uncertain how to proceed, and then resumed, this time descending instead of ascending, the course reversed. The door opened and closed again, returning them to their private space, but the energy had changed. Jolene stood up and without a word, started climbing.

"Wait." Daniel reached for her uninjured arm and felt it firmly in his grasp. "Where are you going?"

"The bench." She looked at him calmly, then took his hand and led him along behind her, dropping it only to open the door. They went through, turned right, and started down the hallway. Daniel's room was the other direction, but the room Jolene and Brent shared was coming up. Jolene passed it by, padding soundlessly on the thin carpet in her stocking feet, and when she reached the wooden bench at the end of the hall, sat down.

"No." Daniel took her hand and pulled her up.

"What?"

"You need water. Bandages." He guided her gently back down the hall.

"You don't have any bandages."

"Someone can bring us some." He gripped her hand more tightly, ready for increased resistance, but she didn't give any. Instead, she walked beside him easily until they reached his room, and then waited patiently for him to unlock it. As they went in, he remembered he hadn't picked up before leaving. The shirt lay on the back of the chair, the dirty underwear and socks glaring on the floor, the jeans on the corner of the bed.

He had an impulse to grab the plane out of his jeans' pocket, but he was okay now. He picked up the socks and underwear instead, stuffed them into the backpack Jolene had gotten him, and then guided her into the bathroom where he drew some warm water in the sink. This he had practiced numerous times with Tony. He knew how to clean a wound. But she hesitated when he gestured for her arm, so he set the washcloth near, handed her a clean hand towel, and exited, closing the door behind him. "I'll call for bandages."

The receptionist couldn't hear him over the phone. As he hung up, the vertigo returned, the hotel room spinning before his eyes. He grabbed his jeans, retrieved the plane, stuffed it into his right sweats pocket, and sat down on the bed. *It's okay,* he told himself. *Suck it up.*

Jolene came out with the white towel wrapped around her arm, her face shiny with perspiration. She cast a glance at his face, and then went to the phone herself. After a short conversation, she replaced the handset and sat on the bed opposite him.

"We're quite the pair, aren't we?" She smiled a little.

Daniel glanced at the clock. One-thirty in the morning. He wondered how she could be gone now without Brent worrying about her, but he didn't want to mention the guy. He gestured toward her injured arm. "Anything I can do to stop you from doing that again?"

Someone knocked. Daniel jumped up but Jolene laid her hand gently on his arm. With one look he knew what she meant—he wouldn't be seen. He followed her anyway. A woman in a housekeeping uniform stood in the hallway. She was older, with thick brown hair and brown eyes that widened in concern when she saw Jolene.

"Okay?" She looked at the towel-wrapped arm while handing over a box of bandages and a tube of antiseptic cream.

Jolene nodded and thanked her. The woman half waved and walked away. A few minutes later, Jolene emerged again from the bathroom with two bandages on her injured arm. She'd stopped the bleeding, but Daniel could still see all the other scars marching their way up to her inner elbow, small, half-inch marks placed one next to the other like rows of dominoes.

"Months since my mother passed," she said by way of explanation. "Plus an extra one here and there."

"I could get you a notebook. A whiteboard. Piece of wood?"

She retrieved cups of water for them both, then settled again onto the other bed. "For the longest time, I couldn't feel anything. I didn't even cry at her funeral."

Daniel sipped the water, watching her.

"I felt like a zombie. Then one night, on the one-month anniversary of her passing, I was just sitting there playing with it." She pulled out the Swiss Army knife and held it lightly in her fingers. "She gave it to me when I was ten." She started to show him how to open it, but he held up his hand, casting her a warning glare. She tucked it back into her pocket. "I just wanted to feel something. And it was no big deal. Just a little cut."

He gazed at her smooth arm, the fair skin now riddled with scars that would never completely disappear.

"After that, it was like I had to return, I had to mark the anniversaries. If I let one go it was like letting her down." She tucked her chin low into her neck. "Plus I thought if I was hurting, you know, physically, maybe she could hear that."

"You mean, from wherever she was."

"But it's not working."

"You've never . . . heard from her?"

Jolene shook her head. "Many others. At least thirty. Never her."

Daniel removed his shoes and lay back on the bed. He couldn't remember her talking to him about this before, but maybe she had. And maybe he hadn't been sensitive. Maybe that was why she'd broken up with him.

"When was the first time?"

Taking his cue, she laid back against the headboard and wriggled her feet under the blankets. "When I was four. It was an old lady. Her name was Mrs. Daley. She babysat me sometimes. One day when she wasn't babysitting me, she walked by our house. She was just standing there in the yard, so I went out to talk to her. Her cat Midnight was lost, she said, and there was no one to take care of him. I told her I would look for him. That made her happy, and she walked away. I looked all afternoon, and around about dinnertime found Midnight under the stairs that led up to Mrs. Daley's front door. I took him in my arms and knocked, but no one answered. I called out to Mrs. Daley, but she didn't come, so I took Midnight home. I was petting him in the dining room and telling Mom what had happened. When I finished my story, I looked up and she was just staring at me. I thought I was in trouble for taking the cat." She paused and ran her hand over the comforter. "Mrs. Daley had died three days before. I found out later Mom wasn't sure how to tell me, first big death in a child's life and all. She thought I'd made the whole story up, that maybe I'd heard about Mrs. Daley's death and was in denial or something. But I hadn't heard anything."

"Did she ever believe you?"

"Not 'til years later."

Daniel stared at the opposite wall, soaking in the quiet space with just the two of them. "What happened to the cat?"

"We kept him. He lived until he was fifteen years old. He was the first pet I ever had."

Daniel pictured the cat and the little girl playing with it. "What did you think about it? After your mom said Mrs. Daley had died?"

"I didn't believe her. I told her I had seen her and that she would be coming back for Midnight. I waited for days, checking her door, knocking, looking around her yard. It wasn't until Mom took me to the funeral and showed me Mrs. Daley in her casket that I finally started to wonder what had happened. But then I thought they must have gotten the days wrong, that I had seen her before she died. I thought that for a long time."

"What changed your mind?"

"A girl in my first-grade class named Jenny." Jolene shifted so she was on her side facing him and tucked the pillow under her head. "She died of appendicitis because her parents wouldn't take her to the doctor. It was forbidden by their religion."

"How old was she?"

"Seven. She used to sit two rows behind me in Mrs. Gilliam's class. She was quiet, kind of skinny, with stringy blonde hair and a long face, but I liked her. We paired up sometimes to study flashcards for addition. She was smart, and she was always patient with me because I took twice as long as she did figuring them out."

The cooler clicked on and hummed, sending cold air into the room. Jolene pulled the blanket up higher on her shoulders, so Daniel got up and turned it off.

"The teachers tried to make it sound like she'd just died, but the story spread around. Her parents had let her suffer. I could see her in my mind, clutching her side and crying. But when I got home from school and found her in my room, I thought maybe it had all been a mistake. I was so happy to see her I went to hug her, but my hands went right through her. That was freaky."

Daniel's breath caught in his throat. *My hands went right through her.* "What did you do?"

"I was scared, but she was my friend, you know? So I asked her what happened. She said she got sick and her parents tried to help but they couldn't. I told her they should have taken her to the doctor. She said they prayed and prayed, but God didn't hear them."

It was too far, the distance between them. Daniel hesitated by the cooler, waiting for her to continue. When she didn't, he walked around to the far side of her bed and laid down next to her. His heart pounded in his chest as he waited for her to pull away or say something in protest, but she turned and gave him a pillow instead.

He stuffed it under his head. When she settled again, she finished explaining how the two girls had talked for hours, Jenny saying she was scared and wanting to go back to her parents, Jolene asking her if she had tried to talk to them. Daniel gradually relaxed in the space next to her, his attention on her story even as he inhaled the scent of the soap on her skin. Jenny tried to talk to her parents, but they couldn't hear her. She was all alone, so Jolene had told her she could stay as long as she wanted to. They'd played card games all afternoon. Jenny couldn't hold the cards, so Jolene had to move them for her. At one point Jolene's mother came in, looked right at Jenny, and asked Jolene who she was talking to.

That's the moment Jolene knew for sure something was different.

"She was gone the next day," she said in a soft voice. "I never saw her again. I wondered for a long time if she was okay, but when the other kids would talk about her in school, I didn't say anything. Everyone thought of her as this girl rolling in pain while her parents stood over her praying. But we'd played cards for hours that day and I'd seen her smile and laugh, and that was my last memory of her. I knew something they didn't, and I felt sort of peaceful about it."

Daniel inched his hand over to take hers. She didn't pull away. "You said her parents couldn't hear her," he said. "Do you think there's something about parents and children, something that prevents your mother from hearing you, or maybe, you from hearing her?"

Jolene shook her head. "That doesn't make any sense. Mom and I were close. She should be the easiest to hear."

"Maybe that's not how it works."

"What do you mean?"

"Maybe the connection is not based on love."

She looked at him in the dim light. "I loved Mrs. Daley, and I was fond of Jenny. They were the first two I saw."

"But you've seen others?"

She turned her gaze back to the ceiling. "Yeah. A lot."

"What about them?"

"One was a teacher who'd been unable to save her student from a school shooting. Another was an old lady who couldn't find her husband. Three were teenagers who'd committed suicide." She shook her head. "They said they did it because they heard the voice of a Walking Sam."

"A what?"

"A Walking Sam. It's a Native American legend. A demon that lures people over to the other side, people who are depressed, you know, or struggling. It stalks them, whispers to them until they're convinced they should commit suicide. They don't know he's a demon until it's too late."

"Creepy."

"All three of the girls said they'd heard him talking to them, encouraging them." She turned to him. "They made a pact and committed suicide together. I felt bad for them. They were so lost."

Daniel could feel her body heat on his side, hear her breath flowing gently in and out. "They needed your help." When she didn't respond, he went on. "Mrs. Daly wanted to make sure Midnight was okay. Jenny needed a friend because she was scared. The teacher felt guilty, and the girls. Sounds like they regretted what they did. I can't imagine how that would feel, alone and unable to talk to anybody." Daniel lifted her hand. "But they could talk to you."

Jolene's body tightened. It was a slight movement, but Daniel felt the change through her fingers. "Yeah, I've thought that too."

They laid together in silence. Daniel tried to think of something else to say, but nothing came to mind. Her breathing grew erratic, her inhales irregular, and he felt a strange space open up between them. Rolling onto her side, she withdrew her hand and slipped out of the bed.

"Wait," Daniel said. "Where are you going?"

"It's late. We're supposed to meet early in the morning."

"I'm sorry," he said, getting up too. *What had he said wrong this time?*

"Don't be sorry." She wrapped her arms around herself and started walking toward the door.

Daniel came around to meet her. "I'm glad you told me, you know, about everything."

"You think I'm crazy now too?"

"Of course not." As the words came out, Daniel realized the truth of them. Strange as the stories were, he'd believed every word. Why wouldn't he, after what had happened to him that night? He could tell her about it, prove it to her that way, but she was already leaving.

"In Salt Lake," she said. "There's a guy giving a talk. His name is Richard Wells. He knows more about all this stuff than I do. I've read his blog and some of his books. I'm hoping we can hear him."

"You think he can help you, with your mother?"

She shook her head. "With you."

Daniel's eyebrows shot up. "Me?"

"You know."

"I don't need any help."

She rolled her eyes and opened the door.

"Jolene, wait." He grabbed her arm, realizing too late it was the injured one. She winced but held her position, so he took her shoulder instead and turned her toward him. The door closed. She looked up at him, her green eyes gazing into his with that same trusting look she'd given him back in Des Moines outside of the hotel, and he bent low to kiss her.

When she kissed him back, his body burned. He scooped one arm underneath her and pulled her close. His fingers pressing into her spine, he kissed her again and again, his other arm around her shoulders. She was so small but so warm against him, her lips like another world—a world he never wanted to leave.

When she stopped him, she was breathing heavily, one hand on his chest. She didn't say anything, only rested there. Daniel's blood pumped wildly through his body. He waited, holding it all back and at the same time reveling in the feeling of having to hold it back. How much more real could one be than this? How much more alive?

She gave him a tender smile. "Goodnight," she said.

"You don't have to go."

She put her hands in her pockets, drawing her arms into her ribs. When she looked at him again, she was smiling. "I'll see you in the morning."

He held the door open for her and watched until she'd reached her room with Brent, then walked back inside and sat down on the bed. A slow grin crept across his face. Everything was going to be all right. Better than all right. He looked at the hand that had held hers, then shed his clothes and went in to take a cold shower.

CHAPTER TEN

B rent pulled the Ford up to the side of a humble café and turned off the engine. They'd been too late to make the free breakfast at the hotel, so they'd decided to stop at this home-spun charmer before hitting the Interstate. Hand-painted blue with yellow trim, the place had a flat roof, wood paneling, and three motorcycles parked at the side of it. Daniel hungered for some fried eggs and pancakes, but dreaded repeating the scene they'd already played several times on this trip. Jolene would have to order for him again, and she would pay while he'd be the guy going along for free. Inside they took the last booth in the corner by the window, Brent sitting next to Jolene, leaving Daniel eyeing the painted cow skull that hung on the back wall. On one horn rested a cowboy hat, and he had the urge to drop it on his head. That would get a smile out of Jolene, but Brent was there, so he left the hat and took his seat across from them.

Their waitress arrived at their table in a bustle of activity, setting two water glasses down and then withdrawing her order pad and pen with one hand while handing out straws with the other. She had a square build with straight brown hair extending past her shoulders, her face weathered and tan. When she didn't even look at him, Daniel told Jolene what he wanted. Soon they had their coffee and everything settled into a normal routine until Daniel's gaze shifted to Jolene's lips. She had tilted the mug and was sipping, just a little to avoid burning her tongue. She glanced up at him and paused. His blood warmed and he looked away. But why should he feel guilty? She and Brent weren't married, and hadn't she kissed him back? Still, it was uncomfortable with Brent there so he turned his focus to the spruce tree beyond the parking lot. Brent blathered on about the decor of the place and what style it was, quizzing Jolene on the few paintings that hung on the walls. Daniel remembered another café much like this, only it was dark outside and he had been short enough at the time that he could still rest his head on the back of the booth. Tony had sat on the other side, maybe three years old, his little body towering above Daniel's, elevated by a booster seat.

"Neat!" he'd said, looking around the place with wide eyes. They hadn't gone out to eat often, so it was a big deal to his brother. Daniel had to have been about twelve years old. He'd been wearing his new sneakers, one of the last pairs Valerie ever bought him. They were black and silver with bright blue accents, and he hadn't been wearing them long because they still felt tight on his feet. "Almost done." Tony held up his glass of chocolate milk, proud that he'd nearly finished it.

"Drink it too fast and it will be all gone," Daniel said. "No more."

Tony's smile faded. He looked from Daniel to his glass, then set the glass on the table. Daniel remembered the serious downturn of his wet lips. It had made him instantly sorry for saying anything. "You can have the rest of mine," he told him.

Tony grinned at that, then drained his glass in two gulps, his head tipped back to suck out the last few drops. Daniel pretended to try to beat him, his neck cranked around to the side, but by the time Tony set his empty glass down with a solid *whap*, Daniel had taken barely a mouthful.

"I didn't know you could drink so fast!" Daniel pushed his glass across the table. "Here you go."

Tony took the prize in both hands as if it were a treasured birthday present. "What about you?" he said, pointing at Daniel.

"You have it."

Tony thought about that for a moment, then grabbed his own empty glass and started to pour the chocolate milk from one to the other, slopping some on the table.

"Hey," Valerie said, "you're making a mess." She dabbed at the liquid with a napkin while Tony pushed Daniel's now quarter-filled glass back to him.

"Both of us!" he said, and raised his glass high as if in a toast. Daniel lifted his in return. They clanked them together, dropped their heads back, and gulped. The cool, smooth liquid filled Daniel's mouth and he held it over his tongue for a moment, then remembered himself and checked Tony's progress. His brother had already finished and was watching him.

Daniel stopped drinking.

"You want more?" he said.

"You finish." Lips covered in chocolate, Tony watched him with fierce blue eyes.

Daniel drained the last of it, put the glass down, and wiped his mouth with the back of his arm. "Delicious."

Tony copied him, smearing milk all over his gray cotton shirt-sleeve. "Delicious!"

"Boys," their mother said, "I just bought those shirts."

They both ducked their heads, but when she looked away again, they grinned at each other, the game belonging only to the two of them.

Daniel studied the wooden wagon menu holder at the edge of the booth. His throat felt tight, the memory too close. Here he was again, living in the past. When he looked up, Jolene was watching him. She held her coffee mug in one hand, her head angled toward the window, but her eyes focused on his. He felt a warm flush as something passed between them, and then she turned to face Brent.

"So, we're going to Salt Lake today, right?" she said. "I want to see someone there. His name is Richard Wells."

Brent had taken a small notebook out of his pocket and was sketching with a dark-lead pencil. He held it lightly between his fingers, first making fast, vibrating movements and then slower, sweeping strokes. It wasn't long before he'd created a copy of the cow skull hanging behind Daniel's head, minus the quirky cowboy hat. He darkened the edges of the paper so the skull stood out a stark white. "Who's that?" he asked.

"Richard Wells," Jolene said. "He's doing a talk tomorrow night."

Daniel resisted the urge to add something that would make it plain she had already told him about it.

Brent held the drawing out to study it. "A talk about what?"

The waitress brought the food before Jolene could respond. She set the breakfast burrito in front of Brent, the banana waffle in front of Jolene, and the breakfast sampler in the middle of the table.

"Anything else I can get you?" she asked.

Daniel grabbed a menu and pointed.

"One chocolate milk please," Jolene said. "No, make that two."

The waitress bustled away. Brent frowned, his gaze appraising the drawing. "Are we ten years old now?"

"It's good for you," Daniel said. "Calcium and all that." He caught Jolene's eye and put the menu back. It pleased him that she'd ordered one too. He looked forward to finding out how she might approach it, something to think about instead of the fact that the waitress, like everybody else, was ignoring him.

Brent tucked his notebook away and cut off a large piece of the burrito. "You didn't answer the question."

"Let's let it be a surprise." Jolene added butter and syrup to her waffle. "I couldn't really explain it anyway."

"More of your mumbo jumbo?" He wobbled his head, making fun.

"You're one to talk."

"What's that supposed to mean?"

"You're just as interested as I am." She pointed at the drawing.

"What? It's a skull."

"Right." Jolene cut her waffle carefully along the lines. Daniel winced watching her, remembering the lines on her arm, swollen and red. He turned his attention to his breakfast, pleased that it tasted as good as he thought it might. Their waitress returned with the chocolate milks. Jolene inspected hers through the clear glass, then noisily started stirring, her spoon flashing silver as it went around and around. Some of the chocolate syrup clung to the edges of Daniel's glass as well, so he joined in.

"What is this," Brent said, "synchronized stirring?"

Jolene's mouth turned up a little, and they both moved their spoons faster, hitting regularly against the sides of the glasses. *Clink-a-chink-a-clink-a-link.* They started to sync up. Daniel stared at Jolene's spoon, striving to match her moves. Jolene did the same and then laughed.

Brent pointed at her. "*This* is what I'm talking about. This childishness."

She flicked a half spoonful of milk his way.

"Hey!" He found the spill on his shirt and wiped it off with his napkin. "You really want to go there?" He scooped up a forkful of refried beans and held it poised at the edge of his plate.

Jolene raised one hand in defense. "No, no, I'll stop." Brent waited until she pushed the glass away and then put the forkful of beans in his mouth.

Daniel grinned at Jolene. She smiled in return, her eyes dancing, and took a long drink of the milk. Daniel made a note of it. He'd have to order more in the future. At least it was something she would actually consume.

"So," Brent said, "this Richard, what does he do?"

Jolene dabbed at a banana with her fork. "Like I said. It will be a surprise."

"Just wondering what kind of a crackpot has suckered you in this time."

"You don't have to go," Jolene said.

"It's all fake. I keep telling you. These idiots prey on people who are mourning. He's going to do the same to you. Find out about your mother and then play with your emotions like a yo-yo. I don't know why you'd set yourself up for something like that."

"Better to pretend like you do I guess."

"What's that supposed to mean?"

She shrugged.

Brent's chewing was noisy. He kept his lips closed but created such suction in the back of his mouth that it was like listening to a dog wolfing down a can of wet food. "If you'd just accept that your mother is gone, you'd feel a lot better."

Jolene held her fork suspended over the plate. "And how would that make me feel better?"

"You wouldn't keep chasing after these idiots looking for some way to talk to her," Brent said. "Just accept that she's gone. It's what everyone has to do."

"Sure. Accept that I can speak to God knows how many other dead people, but not her. That's supposed to make me feel better?"

"You don't speak to other dead people. You just *think* you do."

Jolene's eyes blazed, her cheeks red. She set the fork down, snatched up her water glass—which was still a quarter of the way full—and with a quick, jerking motion, tossed the water into Brent's face.

"What the hell?" He opened his hands and looked at himself, water dripping over one cheek and down onto his shirt, some of it pooling on the table in front of him. "Christ." He dabbed at his face with his napkin, then got up, threw the napkin on the table, and walked away.

Daniel watched him go into the back where the restrooms were. Jolene sat stewing, breathing audibly now. He let her be, his gaze drifting to the two burly men who sat eating pie at one of the nearby tables. Eventually she grabbed her napkin to sop up the water, so he added his napkin to the effort, then retrieved a few more from the next table until it was mostly dried. When they finished, Jolene sat back against the booth, arms crossed.

"You're going to ask him, aren't you?" he said. "Richard Wells. You're going to ask him." When she didn't answer, he got up, intending to sit next to her. He started sidestepping out of the booth when the front door whined and a lanky young man walked in, a black backpack slung over one shoulder.

A jolt of adrenaline shot through Daniel's gut. The kid wore a dark hoodie, skinny jeans, and combat boots, his hair long and stringy, skin pale. He made his way to the last booth on the other side of the room. Half sitting, half standing, Daniel watched as the young man threw his backpack in and then dropped onto the cushioned bench. Black hair the texture of a girl's fell limp over his ears, one stray strand hanging down the center of his face.

"What?" Jolene said.

The word startled Daniel. He shifted his gaze.

She had moved to the edge of the bench, one foot in the aisle. "You know him?"

He could hear his heartbeat thumping in his ears. Retreating, he eased himself down into the booth. His face felt flushed, his breath hot against the back of his throat. "Get back," he whispered to Jolene, waving his hand. *"Get back."*

She obeyed, bringing her legs in under the table, but continued to lean over so she could see around the corner. As if on cue, the young man dropped his gaze to hers and smiled, bright red lips pulling into his cheeks. It wasn't a friendly smile. Daniel thought of the way some teenage boys leered at girls, the type of teens who went around in packs carrying knives in their back pockets. "We need to go."

"What about Brent?"

"He'll come out when he gets done. Come on." He pushed his plate toward the center of the table. He didn't know why he felt the urgency. Not like this was the first rude teenager he'd run into.

Jolene drained her chocolate milk. "Where's our waitress? We need to pay." She dug into her pocket.

Daniel scanned the room but couldn't find her. Jolene started counting out bills. Shame crept over his shoulders. She was paying for all three of them. And she'd paid for his clothes and the hotel rooms and all the meals he'd been eating. It was humiliating.

He had to find a way to pay her back.

"We should ask that one." She pointed to another waitress in a pink shirt who was cleaning off the bar counter. Daniel glanced toward her, then felt his gaze pulled back to the booth across the room.

The young man was gone.

"Where'd he go?" Jolene asked.

They were both still looking when a harrowing scream ripped through the café. Everything stopped. Forks held suspended. Conversations halted. Cleaning rag paused on a dirty counter.

"Get out!" Daniel whispered to Jolene. "Go. Now!" He waited until she was on the move, then hurried across the café, making his way around the other customers, most frozen in their seats wearing confused expressions, one of the burly men getting up as Daniel passed.

Through the swinging doors behind the bar, he paused and looked left.

There was their waitress, doubled over, one hand clutching her belly, the other clinging to the edge of a long, white table covered in condiments, napkins, and salt and pepper shakers. She uttered a raspy groan, knees bent over her rubber-soled shoes, the black apron ties straining at her lower back. Another moan and her knuckles turned red on the table, her body lurching to the right. "Oh God. Oh." A deep red stain widened on her gray T-shirt.

Behind her the young man stood holding a hunter's blade covered with blood.

"Ronny?" she said. "Help me!"

She knew him?

One hand still on the table, she tried to steady herself, but her knee dropped onto the cement floor, the rest of her body teetering after it. Daniel got there in time to slow her descent. Cradling her head, he looked down at her face. The fluorescent lights reflected a harsh white glare in her hazel eyes. Her cheeks were covered in sweat and tears, lipstick smeared. "Ronny?"

The young man held the knife in front of him as if he weren't quite finished yet, his own face calm, skin dry.

"Daniel?"

Daniel glanced behind him. *Jolene.* "Get out of here!" He pointed. "Call nine-one-one!"

"You won't be calling anyone."

Daniel's gaze jerked to the young man's face. He had *heard* him. But there wasn't time to wonder how or why. The bastard was advancing on Jolene, knife raised. Jolene bolted, and Ronny went after her. Daniel leapt to his feet and slipped on the bloody floor. He caught himself on the table, but not before cracking one knee on the cement. He winced and forced his body up.

"Oh my God!" The waitress in the pink shirt appeared in front of him and then just as suddenly stood behind him.

Daniel whirled, chills racing up his spine. She had walked straight through him.

The woman stared at her colleague bleeding on the floor. She covered her mouth with her hand, then rushed to the cupboards against the wall and retrieved a stack of clean towels.

"Daniel!"

Jolene. He charged back into the dining room, then stopped. Bright sunlight streamed through the large windows. *Where was she?* Another beat and then he saw Ronny standing at the second booth inside the doorway. Clutched to his chest, her head in the crook of his arm, stood Jolene, her neck taught, the bloody knife to her ribs, inches away from her heart.

"Anybody moves, she dies." Ronny spoke like the shy kid in class, but the place was so still, everyone heard him.

Daniel raised his hands over his head. "The woman. She'll bleed to death."

Dark eyes met his own. "That was the plan."

"What was the plan?" The burly man who had been the first to stand now faced the teen, hands ready at his sides. He wore a black beard, bright orange T-shirt, and matching baseball cap. "What did you do to Patty?"

"Sit down, Hank." Ronny glared at him, his grip firm on the knife, until the big man obeyed. "Anyone else moves, or tries to use their cell phone, she dies." He glared around the room. Two college-aged kids sat in a window booth on the far side of the front door, a nicely dressed older woman alone by the wall, and at a central table, a small family with a boy about six years old. Everyone was quiet.

No one moved. Then a squeaky hinge whined in the back. They all turned to see the waitress in pink standing behind the bar, her chubby face wet from crying, her pink shirt stained with blood.

"She's dead." Her voice cracked as she looked around, as if someone might tell her she was wrong, that Patty was fine. When no one said anything, she started crying again and turned to go back through the double doors.

"No one leaves or she dies!" Ronny barked, tightening his grip on Jolene. The waitress stopped, then backed into the café and grabbed the bar counter to steady herself. Ronny took one last look around, then, seemingly satisfied, bent Jolene's body, forcing her to her knees so he could sit at the edge of the booth. She squirmed but couldn't break free, her breath coming in audible gasps.

"Who was she?" Daniel asked, hooking his thumb behind him.

"Fake mother number four."

"All she ever tried to do is help you," Hank said.

"You don't know everything," Ronny said.

"Look, you can let her go." Daniel said. "Take me. I'll go willingly."

"Who said I wanted to go anywhere?"

"Who the hell you muttering at?" Hank said.

Ronny shot him a dark look. "Him!" He nodded his head toward Daniel.

Hank's eyes shifted left to right. "Who?"

Ronny leaned forward, the knife cutting into Jolene's skin. Red blood swelled on her neck.

"Hey, watch it!" Daniel started toward them, his arm extended.

Ronny's gaze jerked back to Daniel. He pulled Jolene in, pointing the tip of the knife in warning.

Daniel halted, his hands above his head.

"Patty should have taken you to the darn nut house," Hank said. "I told her as much."

"You think juvie was bad." Hank's partner, a bald guy in a white T-shirt, tapped his coffee mug on the table. "Wait 'til you try jail."

Ronny brought the blade around so the tip hung near Jolene's earlobe. Looking up from underneath slim eyebrows, he focused on the two men. "Ever seen a girl's ear cut off?"

Daniel felt his mouth go dry. The other customers stared helplessly, the little boy mute between his parents, the waitress still clinging to the bar. Jolene's eyes were squeezed shut, air hissing out her nostrils. Daniel glanced to the right. Where was Brent? He might have called for help, but considering what he'd done at the Perkins, Daniel couldn't put faith in that option. The cook must have gotten away. He or she would have called the cops. It wouldn't be long before the place erupted in blue and red lights, and then there would be nothing stopping Ronny from doing what he planned to do, a final blaze of glory pulled red across Jolene's neck.

He stepped brazenly into Ronny's line of sight. "So this is it, then?" He threw his hands up. "Your last stand?" Looking around, he shrugged. "It's all right, I guess. I mean, the best someone like you can do."

"You need to shut up and sit down."

"I am sitting down!" Hank huffed in exasperation.

"I wasn't talking to you!" Ronny shot him a hateful look and flexed his arm—

"Fine fine!" Hank raised both hands, palms open.

"He doesn't know what he's doing," Hank's partner grumbled.

Daniel forced a laugh. "He's right, you know. You're sitting there in an ugly old booth in some breakfast café in Wyoming, holding what, maybe ten people hostage?" He looked around. "Any minute now Hank's going to get his big, meaty paws around your scrawny neck, and then what?"

Ronny glanced at Hank, his dark eyes shifting. "She'll be dead," he said.

"No one else is dying," Hank said.

Daniel leaned forward, his hands on his knees. "Cops come and throw you in the slammer for the rest of your life, that's what. Big reward there! Your plan sucks, man."

"It doesn't."

"You kidding? Look around! You'll be on the news maybe two days, and then it will be done. All these witnesses. No way you're getting out."

"I know."

"Know what?" Hank said.

Daniel blinked as if surprised. "*That's* the plan? How are you going to do that, anyway? Some Japanese hari-kari in the belly with that dull knife of yours? That'll be pleasant."

Ronny glanced at the blade. Jolene hadn't moved. Her eyes were closed and Daniel could no longer hear her breathing. "Shut up or she goes right now," Ronny said.

"You hearing voices?" Hank said.

Daniel laughed out loud. "Pathetic!"

"Shut up! Both of you! I'll do it!" "For crying out loud!" Hank said. "No one's said nothing here but me and you!"

Still laughing, Daniel dared another step closer.

"He can't see me, Ronny, or hear me. You're the only one who can." He turned toward Hank. "Hey Hank! Yoo-hoo! Over here." He waved his arms and when Hank ignored him, gazed back at Ronny. "Only you, Ronny." He walked over to the waitress. "Hey, can I get some coffee?" Waved his hands in front of her face. "Hellooo?" She didn't respond. Daniel skipped over to the small family, then the single woman and the college kids. Again and again he spoke to them, only to be ignored. Pushing laughter from his gut, he jogged back over to Ronny, getting closer than he had been before when the kid remembered himself and braced against Jolene like a dog guarding his bone.

Daniel stopped, bent at the waist, and stared into Ronny's eyes. "I'm your worst nightmare, kid, the demon you summoned back there by your dark deeds." He pointed to the double doors. "Now I'm here to tell you that there's no halo, no streets of gold, no big reunion with your long-lost puppy. You do this, you're going to wind up right back here just as you are, a lonely, pathetic kid with a grudge. And no one will give a shit." Daniel pointed a finger in Ronny's face. "No one . . . will give . . . a *shit*."

Ronny's gaze shifted to Hank. In that moment, Daniel sprang forward and grabbed the kid around the neck. The knife clattered to the floor. Jolene slid away. Gritting his teeth, Daniel pressed his thumbs on the fleshy indentations of Ronny's throat. Somewhere in the distance a siren wailed. Ronny fought back, punching Daniel's chest and then his shoulders, but he couldn't break his hold. Elbows out, Daniel held tightly to the throat, the skin thin and moist, and when the hitting stopped and Ronny's eyes started rolling back into his head, Daniel pushed him down hard. The kid dropped into the booth, hitting his shoulder on the table and coming to rest on the bench seat.

Daniel stood back, out of breath. Jolene lay still on the floor. A strong wind passed through him. Hank on the move. The big man stood in front of him now, observing Ronny's still form. Daniel dropped down by Jolene.

Her eyes were still closed, her face red. Hank's partner grabbed her under the arms and pulled her clear. She lay among the chair legs, red marks on her neck from where Ronny had held her, the thin cut having left a trail of moist blood. "This girl needs help!"

The older woman approached with a cell phone in her hand, a butterfly brooch on her jacket. "I've got 9-1-1," she said. As if in answer, the sirens sounded again, closer this time. Hank lifted Ronny from the seat, dragged him away from Jolene and dropped him on the linoleum by the front door. The young man collapsed on his right shoulder. "Damn lunatic," Hank said.

The butterfly woman walked to the window, still talking to the 9-1-1 dispatcher. "A young woman," she said, checking the parking lot and the road beyond. "I think she passed out."

Hank turned to his partner. "She all right?"

"I don't know." The partner crouched on Jolene's other side. "She's breathing."

The college kids stood helplessly nearby. The waitress sat on a bar stool staring into space, the bloody towel still in her hand. The mom had the little boy in her arms, the father watching Hank and his partner. Under the "restrooms" signs, Brent had appeared, the water stain still dark on his shirt. Daniel caught his gaze. The guy's expression was stone cold, his eyes emotionless. He started walking toward them as if nothing had happened. Instinctively, Daniel reached his arms over Jolene. She breathed steadily, her chest rising and falling.

"They say to stay with her," the butterfly woman said. "That everyone needs to stay." The student typed something on his cell phone. The mother spoke in soft tones to her son, rocking him, the father now on his cell phone too.

"What about Patty?" the waitress said.

The woman glanced at her, then told the dispatcher, "We have another injured . . ." She paused. "Dead woman, I believe." She glanced at the double doors. "Okay." She walked across the café, hesitated, then pushed through. "Yes. She's on the floor." A long pause, then the woman moved forward, disappearing from view.

Hank paced between Ronny and Jolene, looking at one and then the other and then toward the double doors. Finally he stopped by his partner and leaned close. "Did you see what happened?" he said in a low voice.

The partner shrugged his shoulders. "A seizure or something? He kind of shook and then fell back."

Daniel frowned at them, irritated. He wanted to argue, but they wouldn't hear him anyway. He checked again for Jolene's breath, touched her face and found it warm but clammy. Brent hovered at the edge of the group, his expression strangely calm. Rotating red-and-blue lights reflected against the windows, the sirens loud and then suddenly quiet. Soon the café would be filled with medical technicians and law enforcement personnel. A new weariness took hold of Daniel's limbs, sweeping over him as if he'd been drugged. He laid down on the floor next to Jolene. He longed to close his eyes too, if only for a few moments.

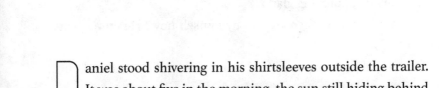

CHAPTER ELEVEN

Daniel stood shivering in his shirtsleeves outside the trailer. It was about five in the morning, the sun still hiding behind the Montana mountains, the porchlight off. He'd found his spare key where he always left it tucked under the step. He fumbled around until he got it into the keyhole, then hopped inside, doing his best to maneuver with the crutch the hospital had given him. Both Valerie and Tony were probably asleep, assuming Tony had gotten home all right.

The lamp came on in the living room. He looked up to see Valerie staring at him from over the back of the couch, her hair sticking up at the crown. She still wore the tight orange tank top she'd worn for the party, a gold chain twisted haphazardly about her throat. "Where you been?"

Daniel gave her a quizzical look. "The hospital."

"All this time?"

"Not like I went out partying." He leaned on the one crutch and waved as Jay drove away, then shut the door. He'd hated having to bother his friend to come get him, but Jay in his usual way had made it seem like he'd intended to get up at five anyway.

"Who brought you home?"

"Jay."

She scanned for a cigarette; found a pack on the coffee table. "Tony got here a couple hours ago."

Daniel glanced at the closed bedroom door and felt a wave of relief. "Tony didn't have a fractured kneecap." He set the crutch against the dining room table and hopped his way to the kitchen. Valerie stayed where she was, holding him in the sternness of a mother's disapproving glare.

"You letting him go around by himself now? He's nine years old."

"Not like I could stop him." Daniel found the cereal and milk and hopped back to the table.

"And who's fault is that? No one asked you to go pretending to be some hero. Swinging a fuckin' baseball bat at that giant of a brute. That'll be a whale of a hospital bill. How am I supposed to manage that?"

Daniel dumped cereal in the bowl. It overflowed onto the table.

"If you would have left well enough alone, it would have been fine."

The milk slopped out of the carton over the brown O-shaped pieces. With one hand on the back of the chair, Daniel managed to lower himself into it. A word search on the back of the cereal box served as a welcome distraction. *Oats*. Straight across.

"I don't know what was going through that stupid head of yours. We don't have insurance. And look at you now." She pointed at him. "How you gonna work like that? And don't think I'm putting my wages toward your bill. You'll be paying that on your own."

"No surprise there," Daniel mumbled.

Valerie exhaled a cloud of smoke and stood up. She'd replaced the skinny jeans she was wearing earlier with gray sweats. They hung precariously from her hipbones, too big for her like most sweats were, even the small sizes. "You'd think you'd be worried about it. We're barely surviving as it is, and I can't do any more hours. If you'd get your head out of that blasted two-wheeled killing machine, you'd see that."

Daniel pulled the cereal box closer, ducking his head behind it. It always came back to the motorcycle. The only thing that gave Daniel any hope of one day breaking free of this hellhole was the point of contention between them, and the older he got, the more sense it made. He used to think it was all about how Tony's dad had died, flying off into oblivion and an early death on his "two-wheeled killing machine." But lately he didn't think that was it. She wasn't worried about his safety. She was worried about her own.

She rummaged through the kitchen cupboard by the fridge, found a bag of chips, and slammed the door shut. She'd wake Tony up. Daniel checked the clock—just a few hours before the dinosaur field trip. He rubbed his temples. *Spoon*. Straight down on the right. He shouldn't have to worry about it. She was the one who was supposed to be worried about getting her son to field trips. She was the one who was supposed to take care of the bills, who was supposed to make it possible for him to launch his own life in just a few months' time.

He rubbed his knee through the brace. The pain was starting to return. The prescription for painkillers rested in his back pocket, folded up into a square, but he'd go without it. Who knew how much the hospital bill would be? She was right about that. It would take him months or more to pay it back. He shut his eyes and pictured himself on the Kawasaki. He'd been practicing stunts with Jay, flying between the hills north of town, but he'd have to stop now until his knee could heal. *Bowl.* Vertical on the left.

Valerie grabbed a beer from the refrigerator, popped the top and leaned back against the counter, chomping potato chips, the cigarette butt discarded in the sink. "How long before that heals?"

"Six weeks."

She dumped a quarter of the can's contents down her slim throat. "What are we going to do during that time?"

"You could stop buying so much beer."

Her eyes flared. She descended on him and shoved the can in his face. "This. The only thing I've got to help me deal with you and this house and those bills." She gestured wildly toward the corner of the counter where the bills lay piled up like used tissues. "You think it's easy taking care of you two?"

He'd never talked back to her, never argued with her, but the stiff brace on his knee coupled with the throbbing pain everywhere compelled him to meet her gaze with a stern one of his own. "We didn't ask to be born, *Mother*. That was your choice, not ours."

Her face hardened, the lines prominent around her eyes. She set the beer on the table and raising a trembling finger, pointed at his face. "You . . . you were not . . ." She shook her head, her cheeks flaring red, then tucked the finger into a fist. "I did not . . . that man, that sick, disgusting excuse for a human being that was your . . . your . . ." Her face shook with fury, the tendons popping at her neck. She picked up the beer can again, raised it to her lips, but then without taking a drink set it back down. "You ungrateful bastard. You have no idea. No idea what it took for me to *allow* you to be born." Trembling all over now, she nearly spat her words. "For me not to . . . I came so close . . ."

Daniel stared at her, sweat pricking under his soiled shirt. The unknown father for all these years. It was clear what she was telling him now, clear in the way her whole body expressed revulsion as she stared at him, the way her eyes took on the rage, her biceps showing under her tense, skinny arms. In that moment, the shades were opened between them, the light illuminating what had been hidden in the shadows, and he understood who he was and why things were as they were, and why no matter how hard he tried, they would never be any better.

She downed the rest of the beer, threw the can away, and retreated into her room, slamming that door too. Daniel stared at his bowl of cereal. Cheerios floated on the milk like little brown life rafts. They suddenly looked unappetizing, his stomach turning at the sight of them. Wincing in pain, he got up, dumped the contents in the sink, rinsed the bowl and left it drying on a towel. With damp hands he grabbed his crutch and hopped down the hallway to his room.

He couldn't be sure if Tony was still asleep. Doing his best to maneuver quietly, he pulled his backpack from underneath the bed and stashed a few things inside. Underwear, socks, T-shirts. He would put anything else he needed in the front pocket when it was time. Once his knee healed, it would be an easy getaway. With the backpack prepared, he pushed it under the bed and looked at his lumpy mattress. He'd never be able to sleep there now. He tore off his blankets and put one the floor. The other, he used to cover himself as he stretched out next to Dinotan, the lamp that served as the moon hovering close to his ear. Settled, he waited for sleep to overtake him. His sore muscles complained about the hard floor, but at least his leg was straight rather than falling off the edge of the bed.

"Danny?"

Daniel grunted.

"Does it hurt?"

"A little." *Please go back to sleep.*

"I heard you and Mom arguing."

"It's okay. Go to sleep."

"I'm sorry I left you at the hospital."

"Just as well. You've got school tomorrow. And the field trip. Only a couple of hours away."

His brother's breath was unsteady, his nose plugged again. "I'm hungry."

"You didn't get dinner?" When Tony didn't answer, Daniel sighed. "Give her a few minutes. Then, if you're quiet . . ." He waited, expecting his brother to come down the small ladder, but Tony didn't move.

"Why are you on the floor?"

"It feels better."

"You want mine?"

"No thanks."

The top bunk squeaked as Tony shifted positions. "What were you arguing about?"

"Either go eat or go to sleep. You're keeping me up."

Tony sighed. Daniel had almost drifted off again when another question floated down from the bed above. "Danny? Are you going to leave?"

Daniel didn't answer. Didn't want to answer. Didn't want to think about that part of it, about the part of his escape that required leaving his little brother behind. It was different for Tony. He was the one she wanted. He could see that now. See why she cleaned Tony's wounds while berating Daniel for taking him biking on the wrong road, why she smiled whenever Tony came around and blamed Daniel for not making sure his brother's hair was combed, why she hugged Tony often but kept her distance from him. She'd never hurt Tony, he knew that, though the drinking and the smoking and the parties wouldn't stop. And the boyfriends. The boyfriends were the worst part.

"You are, aren't you?"

"Go to sleep."

The hospital appeared like a beacon up ahead, a white light emanating from the lookout over the emergency entrance. The words Cheyenne Regional Medical Center glowed prominently under the glass windows. Daniel longed to slow down, his body a heavy weight he dragged along with every step, but he was already late. He'd passed out again, as he had after Trisha's suicide, and when he'd finally regained consciousness on the floor of the café, the day had gone, the sun already set behind the long open horizon.

Running back toward town, he'd planned to steal a cell phone off someone for directions, but then he'd spotted the road sign pointing the way to the hospital. A swell of relief eased the tension in his shoulders. Lucky for him, it was only a little over a mile away.

Now within sight of the building, he pushed on, trying to ignore the fact that the streetlights were already illuminated, darkness shrouding Cheyenne in shadow. Jolene hadn't been hurt that bad. They wouldn't have kept her overnight. He ran down the street, slowing only when he stepped inside the emergency room doors. The smell of disinfectant filled his nostrils, the air sterile and cold against his face.

He hurried to the desk to speak with the nurse. When she didn't even glance up from her computer, he checked the hospital map and set to searching the building. He tried speaking to a few other nurses and patients when they passed by, with no success. Emboldened, he began checking every room, opening doors and stepping in without regard for patient privacy. In some, he found families visiting. In others, the patients were alone, frail bodies lying wilted under bleached sheets. No one objected or spoke to him. He picked up his pace, his gaze searching for only one face and not finding it, up elevators and down elevators, scouring each hallway, rechecking the map and looking again. About a half-hour later, he stepped through the emergency sliding doors onto the sidewalk, his limbs trembling with weariness.

"Looking for something?"

Brent leaned against his truck on the other side of the street, his arms crossed. Jolene's motorcycle no longer rested in the bed. Relieved but confused, Daniel walked forward, seeking Jolene's face. "Is she all right?" he asked. "Did they release her?"

Brent watched as Daniel moved to the passenger side of the truck and looked inside. "What do you want, Montana?"

"Where is she?"

"Not sure you ought to know."

"What's that supposed to mean?"

"I don't think you should be around her."

Daniel circled back until he was standing by the tailgate. "Me? Where were you? She could have died in there."

"Because of *you*."

"What? It's not my fault some crazy kid came into the café."

"In *our* café, where *we* were having breakfast, in out-of-the-way Cheyenne, Wyoming, of all places." Brent spoke as if lecturing in a classroom. "Then there's the girl at Perkins, who just happened to commit suicide while you were out there watching. And oh, she's dead too."

"Like you helped with that."

"Not my point." Brent slid his hands in his pockets. "All these things happening. I might be happy about it. Since you've dropped into our lives, I've been drawing more than usual. I was almost looking forward to the rest of the trip." He cast his gaze toward the hospital. "But then Jolene got caught in the middle. And that's not something I can allow."

"*I'm* the one who got her out," Daniel said. "You hid in the back."

"You would have preferred I surprise the guy, so he could have pulled his knife across her throat?"

"You could have called for help."

"Who says I didn't?"

Daniel cast him a sideways glance, disbelieving. "If you did, you waited long enough."

Brent gazed at him in that superior way Jolene had talked about. "You're lucky it went the way it did. You took a big risk in there. Which brings us back to my original question: What do you want? Because you shouldn't even be here, Daniel *Shepard*."

Daniel blinked. He'd never told the guy his last name.

"Yeah, interesting message on your motorcycle website. Diamond Xtreme, is it? It seems Daniel Shepard's been dead for weeks."

Daniel gazed up at the sky. This was proving to be a waste of time. "A mistake. Obviously."

Brent cocked his head as if the comment were amusing, then plunged his left hand deep in his pants pocket. Daniel watched as he emerged with something in his palm, then stepped forward and stuck out his right hand. "Show me."

Daniel hesitated, then grasped the guy's hand. To his relief, there was no passing through the flesh. Instead Brent returned the grip with a firm hold, then quickly opened his other hand, exposing a pocketknife. Jolene's, unless Brent had its twin.

Daniel started to pull his hand back, but Brent held on. "Show me." He turned Daniel's palm up and cut a thin slice in the middle of the fleshy skin. Daniel winced, but didn't pull away. Brent lifted the knife and watched as the blood began to pool along the cut.

Daniel watched it too, almost grateful to see the blood himself. "Believe me now?" he said, but Brent didn't move. More blood seeped across Daniel's palm. Brent watched until it started to drip down onto the asphalt.

Finally, he replaced the knife in his pocket and then in an unexpected move, touched the wound with his forefinger and brought the new blood to his tongue.

Daniel grimaced. "What the hell?" He reclaimed his hand with a tug.

Brent moved his tongue around as if trying to detect the flavors. His brow lifted, then he cocked his head. "Oh right. Of course." He focused on Daniel. "You don't remember?"

"Remember what?"

Brent scratched his cheek and rested his hands on his hips. An evening breeze blew his bangs up and he swallowed, his throat shifting with the motion.

Finally, he gave Daniel a departing look and reached for the door.

"Hey!" Daniel came up behind him. "Where is she? Where is Jolene?"

Brent paused, reached into his back pocket, and pulled out something long and white. "Your ticket to San Francisco." He held it out while Daniel stared at him, then reached into his other back pocket and pulled out a stack of hundreds. He counted out five and slid them underneath the ticket. "Your best offer. Take it or leave it."

Daniel looked from the money to the guy's face. At one point he considered knocking him out and taking the keys, but he still wouldn't know where to go. He opened his bloody hand. "You saw for yourself. There's been a mistake."

"Yes." Brent nodded. "Definitely some sort of mistake . . ." He moved his jaw as if still tasting the blood.

"At least let me say goodbye to her."

"You need to stay away." He pushed the money and the ticket forward one last time. "Take it or leave it."

Daniel looked from Brent's face to the papers. At least he would have a way to get to Tony. "Is Jolene okay with this?" Brent's gaze held firm, a signal that Jolene probably knew nothing about it. He withdrew the papers. In a desperate move Daniel grabbed

them. Brent nodded as if they'd just concluded a business trans-
action, then slid into the driver's seat and shut the door.

Daniel immediately tried to open it, but Brent was too fast
with the lock button. "You can't just leave me here," he said.

Brent started the engine and opened the window a crack.
"The bus stop is a few miles down the business loop. Keep going
along there," he pointed, "until you get past the park. You'll see it."

"She won't be happy about this!"

Brent closed the window and started backing the pickup. The
guy was going to leave him alone on the street, and Daniel would
never find Jolene again. He grabbed the door handle. "Brent!"
The truck paused as Brent shifted into drive. "Hey!" He slapped
the window. When Brent pulled forward again, Daniel vaulted
into the pickup bed. The truck stopped, pitching him into the
window. Daniel righted himself and peered inside to see Brent
ducked down, looking for something? Then he opened the door.

"Get out," he said.

Daniel was about to argue when he saw the nine-millimeter
pointed at him. The world stopped, his feet frozen.

"Get out," Brent said again.

The weapon hovered in the space between them, its simple
presence changing everything. Daniel glanced at the hospital, his
thoughts turning to Jolene. To what Brent might do if she pushed
him far enough. When his gaze shifted back to Brent's face he saw
a calm, cool man holding a gun on another man like he'd done it
several times before. "What are you doing?"

"You're dangerous, Montana. You shouldn't be around her,
and I'm going to make sure you're not. Now get out."

Daniel climbed out of the bed. "She doesn't belong to you,"
he said, backing away with his hands in the air.

"Actually, she does."

Daniel stopped. "I will find her."

Brent kept the gun on him. "Try again and I'll use it. At least now, I know it will work." He gave a little smirk, then got back into the truck, locked the door, and drove away.

✦ ✦ ✦

It wasn't an overly large class graduating from Butte high school that year—under three-hundred students—but still, the recitation of names dragged on. One by one, the students climbed the stairs in their purple caps and gowns while friends and family clapped and hollered. Daniel sat nervously tapping his foot, dreading the silence that would accompany his name, but when his turn came, Jay and a few of his friends sent up a chorus of whoops and whistles, saving him the embarrassment.

He was relieved when it was all over, though happy for the diploma. It was his ticket to freedom, and he was eager to use it. He threw his hat in the air and then found himself flowing with the crowd out to the front of the community center. Once there he paused to look for Jay, his gaze passing over clumps of families offering congratulations, mothers and fathers posing grown children for pictures. He stopped cold when he saw Valerie standing at the edge of the crowd.

She wore a pretty burnt-orange flower-print dress with a high collar and keyhole neck, a wide yellow belt at the waist, and a pair of flip-flops, her hair pulled back in a clip. Under her right hand stood Tony dressed in the only button-up shirt and tie he owned, his dress pants already too short for him. Tony waved and smiled. Valerie's expression remained hidden behind her oversized plastic-rimmed sunglasses. Daniel started toward them, making his way through the crowd of graduating seniors, his deep purple gown flowing behind him.

"Hey, man!"

A strong arm pulled him to a stop. Daniel turned to find Jay grinning, his hat and diploma in one hand, his latest girlfriend in the other. Daniel embraced his friend.

"Can't believe they let the likes of us through." Jay's black hair stood straight up on his crown. The girl was a stick with brown hair. "Something wrong in the record-keeping department."

"Shh!" Daniel hovered close. "Will you shut up? We're almost out the door!"

"Ah, they won't stop us now. They've already got their eye on the next batch of idiots to come through. Speaking of, where's that brother of yours?"

Tony had come up behind them while they were talking and now smiled at Jay. "Smarter than you," he said.

Jay grabbed Tony and pulled him in, his arm thick around the boy's neck. "Yeah, well, who's stronger, little runt, huh? And always will be!"

Tony squirmed and then ducked, turned, and escaped. Jay looked up in surprise. "Hey, when did you teach him that?"

"Marine moves," Tony boasted.

"The old man." Jay shook his head. "Where is Gus, anyway?"

Daniel hadn't seen him, but Gus was there, he was sure of it. He continued scanning, but then saw Valerie standing awkwardly a few feet away. He slapped Jay on the back and started toward her.

"Party at my place," Jay called. "Come when you're ready."

Daniel waved as his friend disappeared with the broom-like girlfriend in tow. He hadn't even gotten her name. When he turned around again, Valerie had secured Tony back by her side. People milled around them, some gradually leaving the lobby area, others lining up for more photos, families big and small dressed in their best clothes.

"Guess it's real now." Daniel handed his mother his diploma.

She surveyed it in a glance and gave it back. "I didn't think you were going to do it." She still hadn't smiled, her face maddeningly camouflaged behind the dark frames. "You'll have to make your own way, now."

I've been doing that for years, he wanted to say, but didn't argue. Not here. Not today. Part of him wanted to tell her the news, that now that his knee had healed, he and Jay were going to Reno to audition for the Diamond Xtreme freestyle motocross. He was so excited he could hardly stand keeping it secret. He was determined to make it. He wasn't spending his life on a concrete floor covered in oil and engine grease. He'd get to travel, see things he'd never seen, all while doing what he loved. It was nearly bursting inside him, but he didn't tell her. Couldn't tell her. Instead, he said, "How about I take us all to lunch? Your choice."

Her expression remained unmoved.

"Pizza!" Tony said.

"Her choice," Daniel repeated. "I'm buying. Something nice."

She turned her dark gaze his way. "Uptown, then."

The Uptown Café. One of the best in Butte. Daniel nodded. "Then we're off. Where did you park?"

They ran into Gus on the way out. He stood near the door in his black jacket and western tie, a dark cowboy hat on his head.

Daniel brightened at the sight of him and shook his hand, but Gus pulled him close and Daniel hugged him back. He wanted to stay and talk, but Valerie was already headed for the door. He cast a look her way. "We're going to lunch," he said.

Gus's gaze followed Valerie. "You paying?"

Daniel nodded.

"Good boy." Gus gripped his shoulder. "Proud of you, son." He handed over a white envelope and smiled, his small eyes sparkling. "Be sure you come by later. I need help getting the violets out."

Daniel took the envelope, his cheeks hot. He couldn't remember the last time someone had told him they were proud of him. The envelope contained money, he was sure, and his first instinct was to refuse it, but he knew that would be useless, so he folded it up and put it in his pocket. "Thanks."

Gus tousled Tony's hair. "So you're the big man now?"

Tony looked down at his feet. "Not very big yet."

"Look up, boy! What are you worried about? You've always been the smarter one anyway." He hooked a thumb at Daniel. "You'll soon be showing him a thing or two."

Tony smiled. Daniel could no longer see Valerie, so he said goodbye and guided his brother away, shouting another thanks over his shoulder and promising to stop by later.

They found Valerie already out of the building and headed around the corner. She walked faster now, as if she'd been released from bondage and couldn't wait to escape. They jogged to catch up, and then slowed about twenty feet behind her, content to let her lead them to the car. Daniel waved to some more departing students who called to him. Everyone was everyone's friend on graduation day.

"Can I go to the party with you?" Tony said.

"Jay's party?" Daniel paused. "There'll be drinking."

"So?"

"Valerie wouldn't approve."

"She doesn't have to know."

"It's a graduation party. She's going to know."

"Tell her you're taking me to Chad's house."

"She'll see right through that." They crossed the block and stepped up onto the next sidewalk. Daniel spotted Valerie's green Pontiac another block down, parked parallel to the side street. "Did you convince her to come?"

"Mom?" Tony looked up at him. "No. She was the one hurrying me."

Daniel digested that answer and watched his mother's dress swaying behind her in the breeze. "She looks nice."

"Yeah."

They made it to the end of the next block and turned right. Valerie took her keys out of her purse. "I'll ask her, after lunch," Daniel said. "See if you can come."

"Cool." Tony skirted around a fire hydrant as Valerie neared the car. "I hope she says yes. Will Gary be there?"

Jay's friend who played the guitar. Tony thought he walked on water, especially after he'd heard him play "Hotel California." Daniel pulled the gown off over his head and folded it into a haphazard pile. "Probably. But I don't know if he'll be up to teaching today."

A few more steps and they would be at the Pontiac. Valerie was already opening the driver's side door. "Danny." Tony grabbed Daniel's arm. "How long, you know, before you go?"

Daniel stuffed the robe under his arm. He could feel his hair sticking up, the gown having left a charge of static electricity.

Valerie was getting in. She wouldn't have much patience for waiting. He had planned to talk to Tony about Reno, tell him everything, but not today. "Don't worry about it right now. Let's go have lunch, and then we'll go to the party. Deal?" He tapped Tony's shoulder, but his brother didn't smile.

"But you have to promise."

"What?" Daniel tucked the diploma in on top of the gown.

"That you'll tell me when. That you won't sneak out." He walked in front of the car, headed for shotgun seat. "Promise."

"I wouldn't sneak out."

"But you already packed."

Of course. His brother would know about the bag under his bed.

Tony paused before opening his door and gave his older brother a long look. "Promise." The breeze blew his hair back from his face, revealing the few freckles he still had on his forehead. He squinted in the sunlight, lips set together. Seeing him standing there like that, so grown up in his shirt and tie, Daniel didn't know how he was going to do it, how he was going to leave him here in this, this old Pontiac and this trailer in the mud hole in this town with this mother. The impossibility of it pinched his gut in a vice-grip even as the thought of getting out, of finally getting out, offered him the first chance he'd had to truly breathe. He couldn't do it. Couldn't leave him behind. Not here. At the same time he couldn't see how he could stay. The very thought of returning to that trailer for even one more night made his skin crawl.

"Come on, we ain't got all day!" Valerie honked the horn, her voice muffled through the windows. Tony jumped and opened the door, then looked back at Daniel.

"Promise," Daniel said. Tony nodded, but he had a look on his face. Daniel knew that look. Valerie's favorite or not, Tony feared being left alone.

<hr />

Standing alone on the street in front of the hospital, Daniel stared down the road. He'd watched Brent's truck until it was out of sight, all the while picturing the gun pointed at him. It wasn't so much the fact that Brent had a gun. In Montana, it seemed everyone had a gun. It was the way Brent had used it, calmly threatening, making it clear that if pressed, he would pull the trigger and not think twice about it. Daniel already knew he was a control freak, but this? Brent apparently thought it was perfectly fine that he should decide who Jolene associated with and who she didn't.

He started walking, gaze down as he worked out the details. They had to be at the same hotel where they'd stayed the night before. After everything that had happened at the café, Jolene wouldn't have wanted to go somewhere else. She would crave familiarity. Safety. *And maybe to be away from you.* The thought came on him unbidden. He wanted to push it away, but there it was, a possibility he didn't want to consider but a possibility nonetheless. She might feel the same way Brent did. She might blame him for what had been going on, and for what had happened that morning.

I can't talk to you anymore. Don't call or write. I won't answer. I'm sorry.

He stopped abruptly by a red-leafed tree, the memory hitting him like a boomerang to the forehead. An email from Jolene. He could see it on his laptop screen. After their week in Des Moines, they'd communicated for months. Even planned to meet over the summer. Then she'd emailed him. Broken up with him. His vision blurred over the gnarled tree trunk. It had been in May, when everything turned green in Butte. He'd tried responding, tried to get her to explain, but she was true to her word. She didn't answer him. He'd never heard from her again. Eight months down the drain.

A siren sounded from across town. He looked back toward the emergency center, then hurried on. Brent wouldn't have wanted Daniel to find them. He would have suggested changing their location. But he'd also want to make Jolene happy. Daniel concentrated, trying to put himself in Jolene's shoes. He felt the sting of the knife wound on his neck, the sore throat. *I can't talk to you anymore.* She had surprised him before by pulling away. She could be doing that again.

Hands in his pockets, his shoulders hunched inside the hoodie, he steeled himself against the night breeze blowing over his sweaty skin. The hotel was back the way he'd come, closer to the Interstate. The farther he walked, the more he could see Brent's plan taking shape. Comfort Jolene after the incident. Stay by her side at the hospital. Take her back to the hotel. Promise her he would check on Daniel. Find Daniel and buy him off with a bus ticket and some cash. Tell Jolene Daniel wanted to head out on his own.

Or, do what Jolene asked and tell Daniel to leave them both the hell alone.

He picked up his pace, car exhaust pervasive in his nostrils. Soon he came to another intersection. Old town buildings flanked the road going right, but on the left stood a Grease Monkey and beyond that, a Kum & Go gas station. Daniel jogged over. As usual, the clerk couldn't see him, so he got water, a sandwich, chips, disinfectant, bandages, and a city map for free. One advantage to being invisible. In the restroom, he cleaned and bandaged his palm, then consulted the map. Tracing the route with his finger, he memorized it, then returned the map to the rack. Back outside, he paused again at the intersection. When the light changed, he crossed the street, unwrapped his sandwich, and settled in for a long walk, praying that he was right. She had to be at the hotel. She had to be wondering where he was.

CHAPTER TWELVE

Daniel and Tony managed to make it to Gus' old white house while there was still daylight to be had. From the street, the shape of the porch resembled a giant mouth, stout columns on either side, the "teeth" the twin railings that framed the three steps covered in green outdoor carpet. The front door was the focal point, split-paned windows on either side of it, the roof an inverted "V" with green shingles.

The boys rang the doorbell and, hearing no answer, walked inside and through the place calling Gus' name.

"Out here, you noisemakers," they heard from the direction of the back yard. "Why don't you holler less and help more?"

Tony ran through the laundry room and out, letting the screen door slam behind him. He got a glare from Gus for that and apologized, then bounced over and took up one of the dirty pots Gus was cleaning.

Edging up to the old man's side, he held it out for some water. Gus obliged with the hose. After he'd let enough into the pot, he flicked a few drops into Tony's face. "That's for slamming the door."

Tony shook the water out of his hair and smiled, then swished the pot around, cleaning the edges with his hands. "You gonna try roses this year?"

"I ain't trying roses and you know it. Damn things grow like weeds and then they don't flower like they're supposed to and pretty soon all you have is a bed of thorns."

Tony grinned at Daniel.

"Why don't you grow your own roses if you're so keen on them?"

"I don't know where I'd put them." Tony set down one clean pot and picked up the next dirty one, his back to the white shed in the corner of Gus's yard.

"A confusing thing for sure. There's no room at your place."

"I don't mean that. It's just, a rose should be special, in a special place."

"So make a special place and grow your thorns."

"Like where?"

"Wherever you want! It's your place, isn't it?"

Daniel went back inside and emerged a few minutes later with three Dixie cups full of cold water. Gus drank gratefully and looked up at the fading light in the sky. "You boys took long enough getting here. Where you been all day?"

"Jay's party." Tony had already set aside his cup and was cleaning out the next pot, having taken the hose from Gus. "Gary was there. He played his guitar."

"Learn anything?"

"The G chord. I know two now. C and G."

"Well, ain't that something. All you need is an instrument to practice on."

"Think I could get one?"

"Well gee, I don't know. This is America. In America you get a job and earn money and then you can buy whatever the hell you want."

"I've already cleaned out Mrs. O'Brien's hen house."

"*That* was a fun job." Daniel stood nearby, watching, unsure what else needed to be done.

"You made her happy with that one," Gus said. "Now she can have those birds waking you up in the morning for many years to come."

Both boys groaned. Mrs. O'Brien's chickens were lively ones, and she always had at least one enthusiastic rooster that didn't seem to know when sunrise was over. Tony finished washing out the last pot and went to turn the water off. "You know of anyone else who needs help?"

"It's almost June, son. Get yourself out there and mow some lawns."

"I don't have a lawnmower."

"*I don't have a lawnmower*," Gus mocked. "So what you're saying is you don't want to work." Pulling out his pocketknife, he opened a bag of fresh soil and another of small white stones, then started filling one of the pots.

Tony returned to help. "I can't mow their lawns without a lawnmower."

"Smart boy, this one," Gus said to Daniel. "You been teaching him?"

"It's true!" Tony said.

"The families you'd work for would have them." Daniel had found the new plants on the porch and brought them over two-by-two to set within reach. "You just use theirs."

"Oh," Tony said.

"Yeah, *oh*," Gus said. "Always an excuse not to work, boy. Find a way to make it happen and get you that guitar."

Tony finished half-filling the next pot and stood up. He was smiling.

"What's got your gizzard now?"

"By the end of the summer, I'm going to have a guitar."

"That's more like it." Gus finished his pot, set it in the row they'd started and backed away, reviewing the line. He pointed at the new plants Daniel had set nearby. "All right, now, you put a few stones in the bottom of each pot, then a little soil, then you put the plant in and fill in the rest with soil. When you're done, they go up on the front porch."

Gus dusted off his hands and went inside. The boys fell in to do as they were told. For Tony, it was always fun, whatever Gus had them do. For Daniel, it was a small way to try to repay the old man for everything he'd done for them over the past many years. Hands in the dirt, he ruminated over the days to come. He'd soon be leaving Tony behind and setting out on his own. He wanted to talk to Gus about it, but it would be difficult with his brother around, so he wriggled the little green violet out of its temporary pot and placed it carefully in the new larger one. Satisfied it was straight, he filled the rest with dirt, added a little water, and set it aside. It looked lonely and small, drooping a little after the move, but Daniel had seen Gus's violets before. By the end of the summer it would be bursting with blooms and smiling happily at the sun. He'd just finished setting up the third one when Gus hollered from inside.

"You boys come on with those plants now."

Tony finished filling his third pot and stood up with all three collected in his hands and arms. Together he and Daniel carried them carefully around the side of the house and up onto the porch, lining them on top of the wooden railing.

They didn't notice Gus at first, but when they turned around to go back, he stood by the front door with a long black case in his hand.

"You have a guitar?" Tony said.

"Go wash your hands," Gus said.

Tony flew inside the house. Gus took a seat in one of the wooden porch chairs, easing into it with a grateful sigh. He rested the case beside him on the floor. A second chair sat next to him, but Daniel figured Tony would want that one, so he pulled a third from the other side to position himself at an angle to them both.

Tony returned, hands shiny damp, and almost let the door slam again before he remembered and caught it. He clicked it closed and spun around to glance first at the guitar case, then at Gus, than at Daniel.

"Come sit down," Gus said.

Tony sat on the edge of the other chair like an eager puppy.

"A friend of mine gave me this years ago. He was on his way to the good lord at the time. He wanted to be sure it got a proper home, and it has. Now, I ain't giving it to you. You need to work and buy your own, but until then, if you want to play something, you come over here and play it as long as you're careful with it."

Tony's eyes were wide as oranges as Gus opened the case. A brilliant purple fur lined the interior, the instrument a stunning contrast of liquid yellow in the middle and sunset red-orange around the edges. "That's an old Gibson Hummingbird," Gus said. "Sunburst, they called that design." He leaned forward and pointed. "That's a tortoiseshell pick guard under the sound hole."

Daniel rested his elbows on his knees. The instrument was gorgeous. Tony dropped down by its side but didn't touch it.

"Well, go on," Gus said. "It's not going to play itself."

Tony waited another beat, then slid one hand under the neck and the other under the body. Gently lifting it out of its case, he didn't take it into his own lap, but handed it to Gus instead. "Can you show me?"

The old man sat back a little, surprised. "Nah, you go ahead."

"Please?"

Another pause, and finally Gus took hold of the instrument. For a moment, Daniel thought maybe he didn't know how to play it, but then he pulled the guitar into his belly and his right arm came over the top like an arm might come over a loved one, gentle, easy, remembered as if he'd done it many times before, the left settling loosely over the fret board, the eyes gazing down at the strings.

The fingers of the right hand hovered over the sound hole, then seemed to remember themselves and found their strings, the left fingers following suit on the neck. When he finally started playing, the sound rang with a welcome sonority, one single string plucked and then the next to create a walking bass line, the other fingers alternately strumming, and then a voice out of nowhere—a little tenuous at first, but then stronger from deep in Gus's throat.

Daniel recognized the song: *Blue Eyes Cryin' in the Rain*, an old Willy Nelson tune he'd heard on the radio, but in that moment it sounded new, Gus's curled fingers striking the bass notes in descending rhythm, the accompanying chords strummed with less force, his voice deeper than Willy's, without the nasally edge. As he listened to Gus sing about parting and never meeting again, he glanced at Tony. His younger brother caught his eye and grinned, then quickly shifted his gaze back to Gus's fingers, as if he might memorize their movements.

Gradually, the boys let the music wash over them as the old man they'd known for years seemed to change into someone they had just met, someone who had talents they were completely unaware of. As Gus' confidence grew and his voice strengthened, Daniel thought he saw a younger version of their friend, a slimmer, stronger version in a military uniform sitting on the edge of a bunk and strumming the chords while the other men listened, some of them reading books, some writing letters, some staring into space wondering what they were doing in a place so far away from home while the ground shook with the vibration of distant explosions. He imagined Gus might be thinking something similar, that maybe those memories were why he'd hidden the guitar away, just like he hid the scar on his neck with high turtlenecks and bandanas so that only the tip could be seen just behind his ear.

That he'd agreed to Tony's request and was playing now was testament to how difficult he found it to deny Tony what he asked for. That he was willing to surrender what was obviously a treasured possession to the boy, even temporarily, was also a sign of how he cared for him, and as he went into a guitar solo in the middle of the song, wiggling the strings to create a vibrato on the held notes, his other hand snapping from one chord to another like the carriage return on a typewriter, Daniel realized that any conversation he'd planned was unnecessary. There was no doubt Gus would look after his brother once he was gone. If anything, the old man was throwing the door open even wider. Tony stared at him with stern concentration, his gaze drinking in the patterns Gus's fingers made on the strings. Daniel watched the two of them as if he were watching a film that gradually panned out at a greater and greater distance, his viewpoint rising into the sky as his part of the story came to an end and the guitar strings vibrated against his own heart at the realization that he was, indeed, leaving, and that from now on nothing would ever be the same.

Wheels rattled across a tile floor, stacks of dishes clanking against one another nearby. A child asked if he could go outside while other children's running feet pounded the floor. Somewhere, a television blared. These and other sounds penetrated Daniel's consciousness slowly, accompanied by the low hum of quiet voices, morning voices of people not quite awake. Over it all wafted the smell of bacon and eggs and toast. Daniel opened his eyes.

The hotel breakfast nook was too bright, the sunlight blazing through wide windows and setting the southwest colors on fire. Red, orange, sky blue, and yellow came at him from the chairs, tables, and wall coverings. People milled about, gathering food from the counters along the perimeter, some sitting in the brightly colored chairs and couches, eating, talking, reading their cell phones and tablets, one old man with a print newspaper in his hands. Suspended from a wall brace, the television gazed down on them all, the reporter blathering the day's news. Behind the front desk, the hotel receptionist milled about, now and then checking the computer, her blonde hair slicked back into a neat ponytail. She wasn't the same one Daniel had tried and failed to talk to the night before, but he doubted he'd have any better luck getting this one to hear him.

Slowly, he eased himself into a sitting position and rubbed his sore shoulder. Seeking to avoid anymore unpleasant pass-throughs like he'd experienced with the waitress and Hank at the café, he'd hidden himself away on the floor in the corner. No one had bothered him, but it wasn't the most comfortable place to sleep. Using his other hand to rub the muscle, he was reminded of the knife wound, a sharp sting abruptly stopping his movements. He lifted the bandages and saw a new scab forming where Brent had cut him, the night's events returning to him in a rush. He'd been relieved to find Brent's truck in the hotel parking lot shortly after he'd arrived, Jolene's bike parked just two spaces down. He'd wondered then if she'd gone looking for him, but his attempt to get any information from the receptionist had been useless. It was too late to go knocking on doors, and anyway he didn't want to face Brent again, so he'd hidden himself away in the breakfast nook, robbing the couch of a pillow for his head.

Now, he feared he'd overslept. The round white clock on the wall read eight-forty. The three of them hadn't left until after nine the morning before. Surely, he hadn't missed them, but still he walked through the area, scanning, and when he didn't see them, headed for the front door.

The morning air felt warm against his skin, the parking lot emanating heat in airy waves. An old woman sat on a bench to his right. She held a cane at her side, a black purse at her hip. A bright orange scarf covered her gray hair, a few curls escaping over her forehead. Moving his gaze from her to the parking lot, Daniel spotted Jolene's motorcycle. Brent's truck, however, wasn't where it had been the night before. Moving into a jog, he covered the length of the hotel and then continued around to the back. There he found another exit door and had a flashing thought that they could have sneaked away, but Jolene wouldn't have left her bike. Brent had to have gone out to get something. He'd be back. It was the logical explanation.

But as Daniel returned to the front doors, his heart was racing. He passed the old woman and walked inside. The receptionist, as expected, neglected to answer his questions, as did the other guests. After quickly searching the halls, he walked back out the glass doors.

Green Wyoming grasses shimmied in the empty lot beyond. Cars passed by on the busy road, crows complaining atop the telephone wires. Daniel stood on the asphalt, the pavement warming the bottom of his high-tops. Not knowing what else to do, he walked over to Jolene's bike. There was nothing unusual about it. It sat as any bike might sit when parked, the key out of the ignition, the front tire turned, the kickstand down. He touched the leather seat, feeling the sun's heat, then went back inside.

Three couples stood in line waiting to check out, one with two children bouncing up and down on restless toes. The hotel staff had started to shut down the free breakfast, a short woman with curly black hair tackling the hot dishes first, carrying steel bins of eggs and bacon into the kitchen in back. Daniel took a couple steps toward her, unsure what else to do. He was about to turn around again when someone spoke.

"If it's the girl you're all up in arms about, she's already gone."

Daniel's gaze jerked left. There by the window, nearly hidden in one of the booths, sat the old woman who'd been on the outside bench just moments before.

Somehow, she had slipped in without him noticing. A powdered-sugar donut rested on the table in front of her, a smear of red jelly marring her upper lip.

"That's who you're looking for, ain't it?"

"You saw her?" Daniel slid into the bench opposite her. "The girl with the short red hair?"

The woman cut off a piece of donut with a plastic knife and put it into her mouth. Closing her eyes, she savored the taste, her tongue poking into her cheeks and then under her lips.

"Ma'am, please," Daniel said. "I need to find her. If you saw her—"

"A polite young man would allow me to finish my breakfast, so I wouldn't have to talk with my mouth full." She glared at him like a stern principal.

Daniel brightened. "You can see me then?"

The woman's glare deepened, one hand clutching her napkin.

"I have to find her. She's about this tall . . ." He held his hand suspended over the space beside the table. "She wears a brown leather jacket with fringe and black riding boots, like motorcycle boots."

The woman took a sip of her tea and set to cutting another piece of donut.

"She might have been with a taller guy, wavy brown hair, artist type. They would have left in a white truck with an extra cab."

"I'm no damned security camera. I like to sit outside is all." She pointed at him with the plastic knife. "You young people always got your faces in your gadgets, don't even know where you are half the time. Fall off the cliff staring at those damn things."

Daniel didn't know what to say to that.

"We never had anything like that. Looked around. Saw what was happening. If you'd tried that, you probably wouldn't have lost your girl." She put the piece of donut in her mouth and sat back, one hand gently gripping the handle on her teacup.

"You said you saw her?"

The woman wiped her mouth, missing the jelly stain on her upper lip. "I don't know you from Adam."

"I'm a friend. We got separated last night."

She eyed his sweaty shirt, day's worth of stubble, Kawasaki cap. "The other man have something to do with that?"

"So you did see them? The two of them?"

"Got in a fight, did you? I guess he came out on top."

"You saw them leave. In the white truck? What time?"

The old woman toyed with the last piece of her donut. "What kind of trouble you in? I sure as hell don't want none of it."

"Please." He leaned over the table, his hands inches away from hers. She smelled like cheap perfume. "I need to know. Did you see what direction they went?"

She hesitated, studying him. "She's got her boy. So who are you?"

"Did she look happy?"

"How the hell do I know if she was happy? She's a girl. She walked out with a boy. What do I care?" She turned her teacup back and forth. "I waited until they were all gone, hoping to eat in peace, and you gotta come over here and ruin it."

Daniel sat back, confused. She had called out to him, but now she seemed to want nothing more than for him to leave. He looked around. Much of the breakfast was already gone, but there were some Danishes left, plus the cereal and milk. He wasn't sure he could eat, but it seemed the wise thing to do, so he got some cereal and a cherry Danish, grabbed a few napkins, and sat back down. When he noticed her donut was gone, he tried to find another, but there were no more of the same flavor. He picked a chocolate one instead and returned with it, setting it in front of her.

She pushed it away. "I don't want that."

"I promise. I'll leave you alone. Just tell me what you saw." The receptionist tapped her fingers on the computer keyboard, the sound tick-tacking against Daniel's temple. The staff member with the curly black hair cleaned off the breakfast tables with a red rag. The old woman held her hand over her teacup as if to protect it from being whisked away.

"Are you here with family?" Daniel asked, trying another approach.

"Family's family. They don't give a damn about an old woman."

"Then who are you here with?"

"Myself!" Her eyes sharpened. "I have to be here with someone?"

"But . . ." Daniel drew his hands back to his sides. The clock was ticking. He stuffed cereal into his mouth.

"Fort Collins," she said eventually. "My granddaughter lives there. She's getting married. Some engineer. Boring piece of shit." She shrugged. "I thought I might go to the wedding."

"Have you met him?"

"Seen him. From a distance." She licked the tip of her forefinger and then touched it to the empty plate, picking up crumbs of powdered donut that she put in her mouth. "Pudgy looking.

Doesn't exercise. Thick glasses. Don't know what she sees in him. All he seems to care about is himself."

"The other guy with Jolene," Daniel said, "the red-haired girl. He's like that too. Selfish. She thinks she owes him because he helped her through a hard time. Doesn't see the other side of him."

"And you do?" Another judgmental glare.

"I have. A couple of times." He paused. "The girl's mother. She died of cancer a while back. She was all alone because . . . well, because we broke up. And this guy was there for her, I guess. So now she thinks she has to pay him back."

The woman met his gaze. "Her mother died? But she's just a young thing."

Daniel nodded, restraining himself. The woman *had* seen her.

"Why would she go with him, then, if he's such a bad guy? Why didn't she wait for you? I'm not sure you're so lily white."

She went with him? So he was too late. They were gone. "I wouldn't hurt her. This guy. He's charming. You know how they can be. But he's dangerous."

The old woman looked away, tilting her head a little to the left. In that motion, Daniel could see an echo of the girl she must have been, a pretty girl with long hair and slender fingers.

"They came through about seven-thirty this morning," she said. "I was on the bench. I like to watch the sunrise, smell the fresh air."

Seven-thirty! Nearly two hours ago.

"They were arguing between the two sets of doors there." She pointed halfheartedly. "I couldn't hear most of it, but I did hear one thing." She looked at him. "She said it couldn't be the same between them."

The kiss. It had to have been their kiss. But no. Daniel checked his ego. It was because Brent had hidden himself away while Ronny threatened Jolene's life. That would be enough to change any girl's mind.

"He didn't like that, the charmer," the old woman said.

"What did he do?"

"He came out and she went after him. Said she was sorry. Said she owed him a lot and she didn't want to hurt him."

"What did he say then?"

She pulled her cuffs down to the ends of her wrists and lifted her chin, then took another look at the chocolate donut. "People were going in and out, you know. Cars parking, engines running, children shouting."

Daniel clenched his fists underneath the table.

"He kept walking away, your charmer. She kept following. From what I could gather, he suggested they go have breakfast and talk it over." She stirred the tea. "She had that jacket you mentioned, the one with the fringe. The breeze was blowing it around like little flags behind her. She was thinking about it, I could tell, and then she turned and looked right at me." The woman pointed at her eyes. "I mean, right at me. People don't usually do that. They don't pay attention. They don't see."

Daniel stopped chewing.

They don't see.

The woman glanced out the window. "That's why I remembered her. She was unique."

Daniel studied her with new eyes. She looked just like any old lady would look. But she could see him. And she thought it unusual that Jolene could see her. He stirred his cereal around, wondering. How was one to tell a ghost if he saw one?

"Then she looked back at the hotel like she had left something behind," the woman went on. "Maybe that was you?" She raised both eyebrows, directing the question at him, but didn't wait for an answer. "Either way, she looked back at me, and I got the feeling she wanted to ask me something, but instead she confirmed with Mr. Charming that it was only breakfast and they would return to get her bike. He assured her that was the case. She thought a little more, then told him to give her a moment. That's when she went over to that bike there." She pointed out the window. Jolene's bike. "She fiddled with those bags on the back but what she was doing I couldn't tell. When she finished, she looked at me again, directly at me. I could swear she was trying to say something, but then she went with him. She got in the white truck you mentioned, and they left."

"Did you see which direction?"

"Barreled out of here like he was going to a fire, your Mr. Charming. Around the corner and didn't even stop at the light. Turned and headed that way." She pointed out the window.

Toward the Interstate.

Daniel slipped out of the booth. He had already taken a couple steps toward the door when he stopped. Returning, he leaned over and wrapped his arm around the old woman's thin shoulders. "Thank you," he said. "And have fun at your granddaughter's wedding."

He had almost exited the breakfast nook when she spoke. "She won't see me," she said. "She doesn't see me anymore." Daniel looked back. She had turned halfway so he could see her profile, the light shining through the thin material of her scarf to highlight one side of her white hair in a pale orange glow. "She's wearing my pearls." Her hand went to her neck, one bony forefinger resting there in the hollow. "My daughter gave them to her three days ago." With effort, she pushed herself around a little more so she could see him. "Don't stay here, young man. Go on. Rescue your girl if you must, but then you need to go." She paused and looked down at the table. "After a while, even the free donuts aren't worth it."

The staff member with the curly hair came by with her rag. The old woman reached for her tea. "I'm not done with that!" she snapped. The employee wiped down the table anyway, the hand with the rag passing through Daniel's dishes as if they weren't there. Finished, she started to walk away. The old woman pursed her lips, picked up the salt shaker, and threw it hard. It passed through the employee's head and disappeared into the wall without a sound. Daniel could hear the old woman grumbling as he dashed out the front door.

Jolene's left saddlebag held napkins, a bottle of water, some lip balm, a clean pair of socks, a pick comb and a few other odds and ends. In the right one, Daniel found the sketchpad. When he lifted the cover, he felt like he was opening her diary, but it was the only possibility left.

He'd planned on flipping through the pages, but the pictures slowed him down, demanding his attention. There were several figures with wings, angels he guessed, though they all seemed more troubled than peaceful, one page filled with a glorious pair of wings, the face looking upward, a blindfold over the eyes. Another figure had sparse wings outstretched as if a storm had blown off some of the feathers, the hair covering the face, the arms reaching for something below. There were ghostly images, a female in a white dress, her face in shadow, a mist of a child sitting on her shoulders, both of them floating in a dark ether. Many of the portraits were of the same woman, Jolene's mother he guessed, though he'd never met her. She was another slight woman like Isabella, with fine bones and lifted brows, as if she were always just a little bit in awe at whatever she was seeing. Studying one image after the other, Daniel realized that Jolene was good, exceptionally good, surely not the amateur Brent tried to make her out to be.

He'd nearly reached the end of the pad when he came across two drawings that stopped him cold. One was of a small figure on the beach with a very large ocean coming toward him, the moonlight glow emanating from behind. It looked like Tony to Daniel, though the view was from the back, so there were no defining features. He stared at that figure for some time before he turned the page and again felt his heartbeat quicken. Here was another beach and another ocean, but this time there was a whale on the shore. He couldn't see its face, only the tail and the long rise and fall of the creature's mighty back, the sand untouched around it. He stared at that picture for a long time before turning the page. At the bottom right-hand corner he found a note scrawled in pen: *Salt Lake City Library, 7:00. Hurry. Key in other bag inside sock.*

A flush of heat spread through his body, followed by a welcome relief. She hadn't wanted to leave him behind. He checked the rest of the pad, but that was all there was, so he tucked it away and buckled the saddlebag closed. It didn't take him long to find the key tucked inside a sock in the other bag. The gas tank was full. She had thought of everything. All he had to do was catch up. He started the engine, let it warm, then backed around.

Gently releasing the clutch, he coasted out of the parking lot. It was like nothing had changed, like he was back where he belonged, the handlebars familiar under his palms, his knees close to the frame. He rode to the light and turned right, and by the time he hit the Interstate he was flying, his body low and forward, gaze intent on the road.

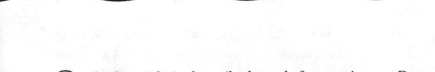

CHAPTER THIRTEEN

On his last night in the trailer home before moving out, Daniel received the toy plane back from his brother. He'd nearly finished packing when Tony surprised him with the gift, handing it over as if suggesting he needed to add it to his backpack before he zipped it closed.

Daniel eased off the wrapping as Tony sat somberly beside him, both of them on his bunk bed in their old room. The jet was a little worse for wear, a few more black and white nicks in the silver paint, the numbers faded on the nose, but it was as familiar as his own fingers.

"This is your plane," Daniel said.

Tony's eyelids were heavy. He looked older than his nine years, the cheeks having lost their chubbiness, freckles faded on his fair skin. "You should have it back now."

"Why?"

"It was your plane. It won't feel right having it here once you're gone."

"But I gave it to you."

"I'm nine years old now."

"I was fourteen when I gave it to you."

"Big baby."

Daniel held the plane in his palm. "You don't want it?"

"I want you to have it." He met Daniel's gaze. "It might bring you good luck."

Daniel thought again of offering to take him along. It was still summer. School wouldn't start for another many weeks. But he didn't know what a nine-year-old boy would do among a gang of bikers.

His friends weren't the best examples. He couldn't even be sure it would be a better place for Tony than he had here with Valerie, though even as that thought crossed his mind he couldn't help but counter himself. At least with him, Tony would have a full belly.

"You think I'll get out someday too?" Tony said.

"You'll go on to some fancy college and become that whale biology dude or whatever you call it."

"Marine biologist."

"That. You gotta finish school though."

"When are you coming back?"

Daniel leaned forward, resting his elbows on his knees. "If I get on the team, I'm not sure. They tour around the country.

It would depend on the schedule." A sticky silence hovered between them. Daniel looked at his brother's back, at the shoulder blades poking through the thin T-shirt, the hair that was too long on his neck. "I'll come as soon as I can."

"You'll get on. They won't have anyone better than you."

"Jay's better than me."

"Not as gutsy."

"You mean not as stupid."

"You said it."

Daniel smiled a little and turned the plane in his palm. He thought of when he'd first run the toy around his brother's crib. Had that really been nine years ago? He slipped it into his jeans pocket. "I have a present for you too." Without waiting for Tony's response, he walked out past the kitchen, stuck his head in the coat closet, and emerged with a large box.

Tony followed him out. "It's not my birthday, and I'm not leaving."

"This isn't for any of that."

"What's it for?"

"Like the plane."

"'Cuz you're leaving."

Daniel pushed the box across the table. "I'll be back soon. Then we can use it."

Tony looked at him, waiting for more.

"Are you going to open it or not?"

They were alone in the trailer, their mother at work. She wouldn't be around to say goodbye. Daniel thought that was just as well. He didn't need more lectures about his "killing machine." Tony took his time lifting the flaps. When there was nothing left to do he reached inside. His eyes shot open. He poked his nose over the edge of the box. Daniel took hold, stabilizing it while Tony pulled out the helmet.

"Whoa," he said, holding it in front of him. "I can ride with you?"

"Not yet. Valerie would kill me. But when I come back."

Tony turned the helmet in his hands, examining all sides, and then put it on his head. Daniel reached out to help, but Tony pushed his hands away. "I can do it." His brother struggled with the clasp, threading the nylon strap in and out of the buckle and then pulling it tight.

Daniel took hold of it and wiggled. "It's a little loose."

"I don't have a big head like some people."

"I thought for sure it would be the right fit. Here, take it off."

"No!" Tony grabbed the helmet with both hands.

"It doesn't fit right."

"I'm keeping it."

"You have to have one that fits right."

"It's mine!" Tony stepped back. "I can tighten it more." He adjusted the strap again, pulling it down so hard on his head he had to squint. "See? No wiggle room now."

"It's not supposed to hurt."

"It doesn't." He hit it with his knuckles, making a hollow rapping sound. "I can show Mom now and she'll know we're being safe."

"Don't do that." Daniel set the empty box next to the front door where he'd remember to take it out to the dumpster. "You don't want her confiscating it."

"Can we take a ride now? Just a little one?"

Daniel wanted to say "yes." It would improve Tony's mood, make the whole leaving thing a little easier. "We have to wait until you can reach the foot pegs."

"I can reach them now."

"You don't know that."

Tony averted his gaze.

"Do you?"

A sheepish shrug.

"You've been sitting on it?"

"I measured."

"How?"

"The space from here to here." Tony pointed to his belt and then his sneaker.

"With what?"

No answer.

"We need to wait until you turn ten."

"You said as long as I could reach the pegs—"

"I thought that would be when you were ten. You're growing too fast."

"So you're going back on your word now?"

Daniel opened the refrigerator. No milk. If he didn't get some, it was hard telling when Tony would have it again. He reached for the house key on the wall. "Come on. We need milk."

"So we *are* going to ride?"

"We're going to walk. You need to stash that, now." He pointed to the helmet. "Somewhere Mom won't see it."

Tony hesitated, then slowly unlatched the clasp. Holding the helmet in front of him, he looked it over again. "It even has cushioning. No way it can hurt, no matter how tight I pull it."

"We need to get going. They close soon."

Tony took the helmet back into their room. He was gone for several minutes, enough time for Daniel to deposit the empty box in the dumpster. He was tempted to shout out that he'd changed his mind, that they could ride to the store and back. It wasn't far. But Valerie would never forgive him if she found out, and besides, the fit of the helmet bugged him.

Give it another six months. Maybe his brother's head would grow into it. Meanwhile it would give him something to look forward to.

Tony emerged with his old nylon jacket on, the one that was too short in the arms. He'd pulled the cuffs up to his elbows. Even in summer, the evenings were cool in Montana. "Are we going to see Gus on the way?"

"Good idea. We'll see if he needs anything."

They walked together out to the gravel road and turned left. It was a pleasant evening, the sky clear and already filling with stars, the air cool and fresh. As they settled into a comfortable stride, Tony slid his hands into his jacket pockets.

"Think we'll ever have a snowball fight again?" he asked.

Daniel looked out at the road they'd walked together so many times. It angled gradually up the hill in front of them, out of the hellhole and to the crest where they could see most of the city below before crossing a short span of level ground and descending back down into old town. "Sure," he said. "But remember, if you have any trouble—"

"I go to Gus's place. I know."

They walked in silence until they reached the top of the hill. Then Daniel paused. Tony kept going until he realized his brother was no longer beside him. "What?"

"It's kind of a pretty town, isn't it?"

Tony followed his brother's gaze. "If you like mining holes."

"Beyond that. Look over there." Daniel pointed to the mountains up north. "How many people have that in their back yards?"

"I'd prefer the ocean. A few dolphins playing. A whale spout. Some fishing boats."

"You haven't even been to the ocean. You don't know what it's like."

"I will someday."

Daniel looked at his brother. Standing there in the shadows of dusk with his hood hanging behind his head, Tony had grown. His crown would reach near Daniel's throat now.

He remembered the day the little boy had performed his anti-rain dance in the mud, his sneakers sending out splashes of brown water that covered his jeans. A lot of time had passed since then. He stepped up beside him. "We could take a ride out there, just the two of us."

"To the ocean?"

He imagined what it would be like, his first glimpse of the Pacific. "I'll be in Reno. That's not far from the ocean. I'll scout out the place. Find the best spots."

"Where the whales are."

Car headlights moved up and down the small streets. The stadium lights were on too, a baseball game in full swing.

"San Francisco would be good," Tony said. "Killer whales there sometimes."

"Really?" How far was San Francisco from Reno? "Valerie would never let you."

Tony started walking again. "She doesn't have to know everything."

Daniel raised his eyebrows. That was new. "Not like we can escape on a bike without her knowing."

"Gus would help us."

"He would *not* help us lie."

"We wouldn't have to. We could tell her it was a school trip, a summer field trip out west. Gus could drop me off at the bus stop. You could pick me up in San Francisco."

"And if Valerie calls the teacher?"

"She wouldn't. It would be summertime."

"Next summer, you're thinking?"

"Or this one."

"When you're ten. Next summer."

They started down the hill toward Gus's house. Tony was right. Valerie would never check on it. The plan could work. Next summer, when Tony's school was out, if he could convince Valerie the class was taking a field trip, it just might work. Daniel would send money for the bus ticket to Gus. They'd go see the whales. His step a little lighter, he broke into a run and passed his brother by. "Beat ya there, slow poke!"

Tony dug in behind him, his sneakers slapping the sidewalk. This time, Daniel didn't wait, but flew down the hill, his strides gulping up pieces of Butte and spitting them out behind him.

<hr />

Growing up, Daniel remembered public libraries as stodgy old brick buildings with plain rectangular rooms full of equally stodgy bookshelves bursting with rows of musty books. The Salt Lake City library was about as far as one could get from that. Had he not known what it was, he never would have guessed as he approached. He'd have thought it was a new technology company maybe, or an art gallery, a place he might have taken Jolene to look at paintings. As he moved across the wide swath of brick walkway in front of it, the unique wedge shape of the glass wall caught his eye, and he couldn't help but look up to admire the sun's light reflected on the surface. From the long row of glass front doors, he picked one and stepped inside.

This was where Richard Wells was speaking, where Jolene had promised she would be. Daniel had found the event listing online during a quick stop in Park City, and now here he was, only a few minutes late. The space opened around him like an oversized greenhouse, a high glass ceiling criss-crossed by metal beams, the wall on the right a waffle design separated by open space and glass railings, the left a series of levels with columns exposed. Trees in planters lined the walkway ahead of him, a row of airport-style shops attracting customers to their wares. People milled about in quiet groups or sat at round tables working on their laptops. Everywhere he looked he saw glass, the floor bathed in the color of the setting sun, and the air—such glorious air for an indoor environment. He took in a deep breath. The scent that came to him was a mixture of coffee and freshly baked cinnamon rolls.

He looked for someone who could direct him to the event. About halfway into the building on the left, glass elevators took patrons to the various open floors. Beyond that, a spiral staircase wound its way up, white and elegant like a ribbon with a glass railing, landings offering panoramic views at each floor. Daniel found a young woman at a reception desk. He hesitated, quite sure he knew how it would go, but finally asked her for help anyway. Of course, she couldn't hear him, so he hunted around and found a sign announcing the Richard Wells event in Conference Room B. Following the directions, he backtracked and then turned right to go down the hall. At the end of it he opened a door and walked into a meeting room filled with about thirty people.

They sat theater style facing the speaker, who stood to the side of a screen showing a picture of a sunrise with the words "Spiritual Living on a Daily Basis." Daniel recognized Richard Wells as the same man he'd seen on the website, though he was a little shorter than he'd imagined he'd be, maybe five-foot-nine. The bleached-blond hair, dual strips of dark hair framing his chin, and the large navy-blue stone hanging from his neck all fit the guru image.

The guy glanced at him as he stepped through the door—had he really seen him?—but otherwise made no move to acknowledge his presence.

Pressed up against the back wall, it took Daniel a moment to find Jolene, but then he spotted her in the second row on the left side of the room. Her red hair made her an easy mark. He caught his breath, nerves lighting up along his spine. She was here. It would be all right. He started to relax but then scanned left and found Brent glaring at him from the aisle seat. The look was so scathing it sent a jolt of adrenaline through Daniel's body. At least the control freak wouldn't have his weapon here. Brent returned his attention to the speaker and draped his arm possessively around Jolene's shoulders. Daniel watched her, hoping she'd shrug him off, but minutes passed and she didn't move, her attention fully on Richard Wells.

Daniel thought of going to her, but that would interrupt everything, so he decided to wait. Eventually the presentation would be over. When he looked forward again, he found Wells watching him warily as if he presented some sort of danger. The look surprised Daniel, mostly because he'd grown used to being ignored, but also because he seemed to have ignited a true fear in the guy. He looked down at himself and couldn't see anything unusual, but still Wells kept glancing nervously at him, so he found a seat in the back row and took it.

"So the question is," Wells said in a gentle tenor voice, his fingers touching together in front of his waist, "what do you believe? In your heart of hearts, in your private moments, what do you think will happen after you leave this Earth?"

Daniel glanced at Jolene. She was listening intently. Brent had tilted his head back a little, his chin forward as if he, too, were fascinated with the guru's talk. *Get away from him*, Daniel thought, wishing he could grab her and run out the door. The guy had fondled a dying girl, left Jolene to die at the hands of a murderous teen, threatened Daniel with a gun, and tricked Jolene to get her away from the hotel. What might he do next? Deep in thought, Daniel's gaze burrowed into the back of the guy's head until he realized that Wells had stopped speaking. Glancing up, he saw the guru staring right at him.

"I sense that someone is visiting us here today," Wells said. The audience murmured in surprise. Wells opened his hands in a welcoming gesture. "Someone who wishes to say something." He glided over until he stood at the end of Jolene's row. "Miss, what is your name?" Jolene gestured to herself. When Wells nodded affirmation, she answered him. "And Jolene, where are you from?"

"Iowa."

The room fell silent, all eyes trained on the interaction. "I think there's someone here to see you, Jolene. Do you sense his presence?"

Jolene looked around the room, her gaze passing over Daniel. "Did you say *he*?"

"He's pretty tall with dark hair. Slim build. Do you know him?"

Jolene checked again and frowned. "I'm not sure."

Daniel stood up. "It's me." He waited, but Jolene didn't respond. "Jolene, he sees me. It's okay." But her gaze remained on Wells.

"He's trying to speak to you," Wells said. "Do you know what it is he wishes to tell you?"

Daniel's gaze was a laser on the back of Jolene's head. She looked a third time and still appeared not to see him. Panic shot through his limbs.

Wells cocked his head in Daniel's direction. "Your name, sir?"

Daniel couldn't stand it anymore. He stormed around the room to Wells' side. "Jolene, it's me. He's talking about me!"

Jolene looked confused. "Did he say what his name was?"

Wells turned to Daniel, waiting. Sweat broke out across Daniel's back. No, not her. Not her too. "Jolene!" he said, but she looked right through him as if he weren't there.

＊◦＊ ◦ ＊◦＊

The door to the meeting room opened, and a young woman entered. Slim, mousy-haired, wearing gray slacks and a pastel pink blouse, she addressed the group. "I'm sorry." She smiled, but her worried gray eyes didn't match her expression. "I have to interrupt. They need us to evacuate the building."

The group stared at her.

"I need you all to get up and walk out with me. Right now. I need you to come with me. Now, please."

The group murmured in confusion.

"We'll have to reschedule the event. I'm very sorry. Please, I need you all to leave with me now."

Finally convinced, the people began to get out of their chairs and start moving toward the door. Everyone seemed to have forgotten what had been taking place only a moment before. Wells glanced at Daniel and then moved to the front of the room. "I'm sure we can reschedule." He lifted his voice above the hum of the crowd. "And don't forget, the name of the book is *A Beautiful Life After Life*. Find it in your bookstores, and of course the library here has copies."

Some of the attendees smiled at him, but most concentrated on getting out, the group now pressed against the one open door.

"Mr. Wells, you too," the woman said. "We need everyone to evacuate."

Wells scooped up his books, laptop, and water bottle, and started following the group out. Daniel let him go, his gaze fixed on Jolene, but she had gotten up too and joined the crowd at the door. He moved up beside her and whispered her name, but she didn't respond. Brent had his hand on the back of her neck, fingers pressed into her skin. Daniel spoke her name again, but she walked past him unmoved. Brent smirked—apparently *he* could still see him—but kept his gaze forward, and then they were through the door, following along with the rest of the group, the young woman checking to be sure they were all coming.

"Jolene!"

Daniel shouted it this time, but she still didn't respond, and neither did any of the others. Wells came up behind him, his hands and arms full. Out in the hallway, he turned back and settled a nervous gaze on Daniel's face. The guru could see him, there was no doubt. Daniel ignored him and tried to get through to Jolene, but the people were crowding the hallway now, more exiting from other rooms as they went along, the pace increasing.

The general mood had become more fearful, the crowd stepping lively to keep up with the young woman. A few checked to be sure Wells was following. One woman asked if he had received any messages from beyond.

"The angels speak only when they need me," he answered.

"Sure they do," Daniel said.

The guy glanced at him, then walked a little faster.

They soon emerged into the main room, the vast space greeting them like freedom. Daniel made his way to Jolene's side, but even when he leaned down next to her and spoke her name, she didn't respond. He took her arm and tried to turn her toward him, but she pulled it back as if bitten by a bug. She glanced at the place where his hand had been, looked about as if trying to determine what had disturbed her, and then stumbled forward as the other people came along behind her. The young woman was still guiding them, having turned toward the entrance doors now, encouraging them to follow. Daniel stared at Jolene's retreating form. Brent had taken hold of her arm and was ushering her out, the two like fish swimming along with the current. Wells lagged behind, at one point pausing to get a better hold of his stuff. Settled again, he lifted his gaze, then stopped, a look of dread crossing his face. Daniel followed his line of sight.

"Jolene!" he shouted in alarm.

She froze, then whirled around, but when she searched the area her gaze moved right past him.

She couldn't see him.

Brent pulled on her arm, but she resisted, her gaze moving upward. There. She saw it. She took a step back inside, Brent still clinging to her. The young woman called for them all to come through the doors, you too, Mr. Wells. The psychic looked from the woman to Daniel, and then together all their gazes tilted up-ward.

At the top of the spiral staircase, a young man with short brown hair, a black T-shirt, and faded jeans sat on the beautiful glass railing, his feet dangling over the side. One hand encircled the handrail, an angry-looking switchblade in the other. Below him a few people had stopped to gawk, their necks craned to see above them, but much like the young woman, the other library staff members were ushering them out, paid personnel in dress clothes talking in firm voices. The young man turned around, waving the blade to be sure the security guard behind him didn't try anything, then pushed forward onto the railing so that even more of his long legs were dangling, orange and blue sneakers hovering over the vast empty space.

"Everyone outside now!" the young woman called. "Mr. Wells!"

Daniel turned to see Brent had dropped Jolene's arm to stare at the young man on the railing. His jaw slack, he glided back inside the library as if drawn by some sort of magnet, a renewed fascination playing on his features.

Jolene searched the area in front of her. She was looking for him, Daniel was sure of it. He called her name again and her head jerked toward him, but her eyes didn't see.

"Mr. Wells!" The young woman stormed back inside, head-ed straight for Wells' position. "Miss?" She called to Jolene. "We need to go now." The psychic nodded his assent but kept his gaze on Daniel. The young woman tugged on Wells' arm. "Please, Mr. Wells."

Wells started to go with her and then turned back to Daniel. "Help him."

"The authorities are on their way, Mr. Wells," the young woman said. "Now please, come with me."

Daniel watched the woman try to pull Wells away, but he was gently resisting her. "You have to help him."

"How?" Daniel asked.

"They've called 9-1-1, Mr. Wells," the young woman said, assuming his statements were directed to her. "They'll be here any minute. We must get out so they can do their jobs." Dragging Wells by the arm, she called over her shoulder at Brent and Jolene. "Sir, we need to evacuate now. Miss? You must come immediately!"

Brent stared transfixed at the young man, hands in his pockets, a nonchalant observer happily entertained. "Come on, William," he murmured in a low voice. "It's now or never."

Daniel looked hard at Brent's face.

William?

He knew the kid's name? Behind them, Jolene remained where she was, still searching the space in front of her, her gaze alternating between it and the young man on the high railing. The library employee was farther away now, focused on getting Wells to the door, Wells going along for the moment. Daniel glanced up and saw the teen—William?—balanced precariously on the railing, his gaze fixated on the hard floor below. He meant to jump, it was plain, and the fall, more than thirty feet onto the hard tiles, could be deadly.

"Daniel?" Jolene called.

"Here!" Daniel said, but then a murmur went up from the crowd. The young man moved from a sitting position to a crouched one, his heels on the railing as if he meant to frog-jump into the space before him. The security guard stepped up to help, but the teen opened the blade again to stop him, waving it back and forth in a threatening way. Back on the ground floor, the library employee had taken Jolene's arm and was dragging her toward the entrance. It seemed she was going to succeed in getting Jolene to the other side of the glass doors. A panic rose inside Daniel's chest. Once Jolene was on that other side, he feared he would lose her forever. An irrational fear, perhaps, but it possessed him with a powerful fist.

He ran after her.

"Go help him!" Wells shouted. "You're the only one who can!"

Daniel's gaze jerked to the guru's face, the cheeks like soft bread, the eyes narrow but firmly fixed on him from just this side of the library doors.

"Emergency personnel are on their way, Mr. Wells." The young woman with Jolene in tow addressed him. "We must clear the area." Again, she tried to get the stragglers out the door. As they got closer, Jolene wrenched away from her and took a few steps back inside. Daniel ran toward her, calling her name, telling her to wait, that he was there, only a few feet in front of her. She seemed to hear his voice and turned her head. Suddenly Brent appeared beside her, looped one arm into hers and jerked her back. The young woman took up the other side and the two of them carried her away like a feed sack.

"Wait!" Daniel called.

Jolene struggled against the clamps around her arms. She had just managed to break free of the young woman's hold when her gaze jerked from searching for Daniel to the staircase above.

"No!" Wells shouted.

A wide grin spread across Brent's face.

Daniel turned just in time to see the young man fall.

The body crumpled onto the tile, a pool of blood oozing from underneath the ear. The face, pointed Daniel's direction, was near invisible behind the mop of black hair.

Someone screamed. The employees renewed their efforts to get everyone out. Most of the patrons hurried through the doors, needing no more encouragement. Others moved back, gawking and pointing, covering their mouths in horror.

Jolene's face was ashen, her gaze fixed on the floor.

"Come on," Brent said, turning his attention to her. "We gotta go." He urged Jolene to move. The young library employee tried to help. "I got her," Brent said, and with a backward glance at the body, wrapped his arm around Jolene's waist and pointed her toward the door.

Daniel ran after them, but Brent moved quickly, determined now. Jolene struggled to get her feet underneath her. "Wait!" she said.

The young woman had one hand on the long silver door handle and was beckoning with the other for Brent to follow. Jolene pulled away from him, bracing herself with one arm against the doorframe so he couldn't take her through. She called Daniel's name. Daniel called back and reached for her outstretched hand but swiped only air. The door receded in his vision. He tried to take hold of the frame, but it was as if he couldn't reach it. He heard Jolene's voice and sought out her face, but it too was receding, falling below him, getting smaller, as if the whole world were sinking into a giant hole. Both arms out, he tried to find something to hold on to, some way to stop this sensation of flying up and up. He could see the top of Jolene's head now, and then Brent's as he came toward her and again took her arm. A group of four emergency technicians rushed inside, passing by Jolene. Daniel reached for her hand again, but his fingertips seemed miles away from hers, his feet no longer touching the ground.

"Jolene!" A new desperation took hold of him, a feeling as if he were slipping away and couldn't stop it. He cried out but his voice was small, muffled. He searched for something, anything to hold onto. His gaze caught the young man crumpled on the floor behind him, the emergency technicians racing toward him, the spiral staircase winding away from the body like a flag raised in tribute. The round tables stood empty, some still holding unfinished cups of coffee and plates half filled with sandwiches and pastries. The technicians dropped to their knees around the young man and Daniel realized he was seeing them, too, from above, looking down on the tops of their heads as they checked for vital signs. He was leaving it all, rising like smoke into the glass ceiling.

"No!" Something gripped his wrist. He looked down and saw a distorted version of Wells' face somewhere beneath him. His arm stretched to twice its length, it seemed, his fingers encircling Daniel's skin just below his palm. The gentle smile was gone, his mouth firmly set.

"Hang on," Wells said.

CHAPTER FOURTEEN

((W here are we going?" Daniel asked.

"My place," Wells said.

Daniel followed the guru across the length of the parking garage, one hand on his shoulder as if he were blind and Wells his guide. "I've got a motorcycle," he said. "Her motorcycle." He turned back. "Jolene—"

Brent and Jolene followed them, Brent's arm around Jolene's shoulders, but Jolene didn't respond.

"I don't think she can hear you," Wells said.

"But before—"

"It's all right. Just hang on."

Wells gripped Daniel's hand on his shoulder, making sure he didn't let go.

Daniel looked behind him again. Jolene had her head down and was walking like she did when she was angry, except her skin looked pale and she was clutching her necklaces together at the hollow of her throat. She hadn't looked at him since they'd left the library. Daniel turned back around, his legs a little unsteady. At least the world was the right size again.

Wells stopped at a crossover SUV, midnight blue, and unlocked the doors. Brent whispered to Jolene and gestured off somewhere else, but she shook her head vehemently and moved closer to Wells' vehicle. Brent spoke more urgently, but Jolene ignored him and got into the back seat. "I'll be right behind you, then," he said, and glared at Wells. "You sure—"

"She'll be fine," Wells said.

Brent pointed at Daniel. "*You* were supposed to be gone."

The image of the gun flashed in Daniel's mind, but he was too angry to care. He felt himself drop down into his shoes, his blood warming as he took a step toward the guy. "*You* tricked her into going without me."

Brent came toward him, his fists clenched at his sides.

"Gentlemen." Wells stepped up to interfere. "All this negative energy." He opened his hands, beseeching them, and then grabbed Daniel's arm above the elbow. "Let's go." He led Daniel around to the passenger side, after which Brent left to go find his truck. When they were all belted in and the engine humming, Jolene spoke.

"Is he here?"

"Right next to me." Wells backed out of the parking space.

Daniel looked at Jolene, but she stared blankly past him.

He reached out to grip her knee but touched only air, his hand dropping against the console before he pulled it back.

"You're out of phase," Wells said as he shifted into drive.

"What?" Jolene asked.

Daniel clenched his fist, trying to still its trembling. He couldn't touch her. Even she was beyond his reach now.

"Not in sync with one another." Wells pulled out of the garage, checking the rear-view to see if Brent was following. Seeing no one, he hesitated, then grumbled and moved out onto the street. It wasn't until they'd turned onto one of the main roads that he seemed to notice Daniel staring at him. "You're dead, right?" Wells said. "You died?" When Daniel didn't answer, Wells sighed and turned on his blinker. "Come on, you have to know that much."

"He can't remember." Jolene stared out the window.

"They say I died," Daniel said. "But I'm here. I have a heartbeat. I'm solid . . . well most of the time." He grasped his wrist as if to prove it.

Wells pulled up to a stoplight. "It's probably not going to last."

Daniel turned to him in alarm. "You mean that—" he pointed back toward the library—"could happen again?"

"*Will* happen again, and worse."

"What will be worse?" Jolene asked.

"He started to fade, back at the library."

"Fade?" Daniel and Jolene both said it at the same time.

The light turned green. "You know how ghosts are—" he glanced at Daniel— "well, usually are, transparent? He's moving into that phase. That he can be solid at all is amazing." Wells looked at him again in awe. "I've never seen it."

"Me, either," Jolene said.

Wells glanced again in the rear-view mirror. "You . . . ?"

"Since I was five."

"Me since I was eight." Wells smiled. "Freaky, right?"

Jolene didn't answer.

"But you can't see him?"

"I could. Until now I guess."

"Right. Like I thought." He smiled to himself. "Out of phase."

"Yeah, can we get back to the fading?" Daniel asked. "Why is it happening now?"

Wells shrugged. "It's a spirit's natural state. This solid state is the one that's strange."

The sky had turned nearly dark, the clouds heavy overhead, but the city was alive with lights. Daniel wished he'd gotten in the back so he could sit next to Jolene. "Why can't she see me anymore? I was just talking to her yesterday."

"We were just talking yesterday," Jolene said. "And now I can't see him."

"I'm guessing you two are tethered?"

"What's that mean?" Daniel asked.

"How do you know?" Jolene said at the same time.

Wells looked from Daniel to the rear-view mirror. "This is so wild."

Both of them frowned at him.

"I'm sorry. It's just been so long since . . ." He gestured in Daniel's direction. "I mean, the last time was when I was a kid. I figured I'd lost my touch. That after puberty it . . ." He splayed both hands in front of him. "Gone, you know? Poof!"

"So what," Daniel said, "you've just been duping people?"

"Of course not. I'm the real thing!" He glanced at Daniel, dark eyebrows high on his forehead. "Lucky for you, right?"

Daniel had to give him that. "So what do you mean, tethered?"

"Spirits. Sometimes, to survive here, they tether themselves to a living person. As to who you're tethered to . . ." He tilted his gaze at Jolene. "I'd guess that part of the mystery's been solved. Part two . . . why her?"

Daniel thought of the kiss. Surely that had to be why, but he didn't share the thought. Jolene didn't say anything either.

"Oh, so it's *that* kind of relationship," Wells said with a smile. "That would do it."

The other two didn't comment as he got onto the highway and sped up, driving them north toward Ogden. Once he'd accelerated to seventy-five miles an hour, he sat back and exhaled as if leaving the city had been taxing. Daniel watched him out of the corner of his eye.

The guy couldn't be more than twenty-eight, twenty-nine years old. A gold ring adorned each ring finger, a gold chain around his right wrist, the blue jewel around his neck. The vehicle was new, no more than a year or two, the bleached-blond hair color fresh. Everything about the guy spoke phony con artist, yet somehow he'd brought Daniel back from a place he couldn't even define. "How did you do that?" he asked finally. "Pull me back like that."

"Surprised me too." Wells grinned like a kid, but when he caught Daniel's serious expression, he sobered. "I was the obvious conduit."

"What?"

"Like an electric current. I gave you the power you needed to regain your physical form." He left a clump of traffic behind, merged into the right lane and rested his left elbow on the door.

"So you've done that type of thing before."

"Not exactly. But I've read about it. I'm kind of a nerd about this stuff." Wells reached over and squeezed his arm. Daniel glared at him. "Just checking." Wells said.

"How does it happen?" Jolene said. "I mean, someone being here, like he is."

"Hell if I know. I mean, nobody really knows. I've read theories though. Some say if he has a strong enough tether, a spirit can exist in a more physical way. Others say if someone has a really powerful reason for being here, nothing can stop them." Wells lifted one open hand off the steering wheel. "Another theory goes that if a spirit has help from the world beyond in the form of some sort of physical object, that can give the ghost form for a time."

The plane. Daniel touched the lump in his pocket. But the plane wasn't "from the world beyond." He glanced at Jolene. It had to be her. His tether, if he were to believe any of this. But now he couldn't touch her. "It's okay," he said, but she couldn't hear him.

"Your boyfriend," Wells said to her, "is he like you?"

"He's not my boyfriend," she snapped. Then, "I don't know. He thinks it's all crazy, he says, but he's been able to see Daniel all along."

Wells cocked an eyebrow at Daniel. "Interesting."

"Fascinating," Daniel said in a mocking tone.

"So what does that mean, about Brent?" she asked.

Wells shrugged. "Some people don't want to admit they can see ghosts."

"That's not it," Jolene said.

"He just likes putting you down," Daniel said, but of course she didn't hear him.

The traffic was lighter now, with the city receding behind them. Daniel thought of the young man at the library—*William,* if Brent was right—and wondered if the emergency personnel had been able to save him. "Why did you want me to help him?" he asked suddenly.

Wells glanced at him, quickly interpreting his meaning. "He was in your dimension at that point, shifting from life to death, you might say."

"The young man?" Jolene said. "That was awful."

Daniel thought of Trisha and Ronny. They had been near death when they saw him. A taut string pulled up his spine. It was all making too much sense. The old woman in the hotel, though. A spirit? No one else had registered his presence except Jolene and . . . he checked his side mirror, wondering if the headlights behind them belonged to Brent's white truck.

"So what happened, anyway?" Wells asked, breaking into his thoughts. "To you, I mean?"

Memories flashed through Daniel's mind, flames rising over his body, the bike falling away toward the ramp without him. "There was an accident. A head injury, I figure."

"But you died."

Daniel squirmed. *I'm sitting right next to you*, he wanted to say.

"No one can hear him," Jolene said, "not even on the phone."

"My mother did."

Wells tapped his finger on the steering wheel. "It's not uncommon for a ghost to take a while to realize what's happened. I mean, it could happen to any of us. You're going along living your life and then bam!" He slapped his palm on the steering wheel. "A car slams into you and plunges you into a telephone pole." He twisted his finger in the air to illustrate. "Next thing you know you're back in your house with your family and you seem perfectly fine, except they can't hear or see you. They're sitting around crying and wondering what the hell happened, and you're standing there trying to convince them that hey, here I am!" He waved his hand, clearly enjoying the scenario. When Daniel stared at him, his lively expression disappeared. "It would be confusing for anyone."

"She can hear me." Daniel tilted his head toward Jolene, grasping at the few arguments he had left. "At least she could until today. And my mother heard me. Brent can hear me." He nearly choked over the name. "You can hear me."

"What's he saying?" Jolene asked.

"He says he's not dead."

"Even she will tell you," Daniel went on, unable to help himself. "Ask her. She sees ghosts all the time. And she's never seen one like me."

Wells returned his gaze to Jolene's. "How long since you first saw him?"

"He showed up on Sunday," Jolene said.

"This last Sunday?" Wells returned his gaze to the road. "And he's already fading." He opened his hand as if releasing a puff of smoke. "That is kind of fast."

"How long does he have?" Jolene asked.

Daniel frowned. He wasn't some terminal cancer patient.

"If it hasn't been quite a week, I'd say not long. A couple of days, maybe."

"I'm going to pick up my brother." As if that settled the matter. "On Friday. Three o'clock."

Wells glanced at him but didn't comment.

The yellow lines on the road ran steadily past their tires, the city lights smaller behind them. The mountain peaks formed jagged shadows on the right, but Daniel could peer up and find the occasional light at the top, a signal to a plane, perhaps, or the location of a tower of some sort.

"So you have a brother," Wells said. "And he's still alive?"

Daniel's eyes popped. "Why the hell would you ask that?"

Wells held up his hands in surrender. "Don't have to bite my head off."

They drove north for a good while before Wells exited the highway and took them east. Daniel watched as new neighborhoods sprung up around them, subdivisions with names like Canyon Vista and Northwood Hills, the homes all of modern design and most with two levels. The road rose and then fell into what looked like mini canyons the closer they got to the mountains, the landscape more varied and interesting than it seemed in the city. Wells checked the rear-view mirror. "Think he'll find it?" "He has GPS," Jolene said from the back.

Daniel groaned inwardly, wishing Brent's GPS would malfunction.

They kept going east for a few more minutes and then Wells circled a roundabout, turned north one last time, drove about a half mile, and pulled up to a house on the corner. "Home sweet home." He parked the vehicle and they all got out, Daniel and Jolene following up the stairs to the door. That they were just about to walk into a stranger's house didn't seem strange at all. The guy had saved Daniel from whatever oblivion he'd been fading off into.

That was enough to earn anyone's trust.

Wells jiggled the keys and stood back. "Welcome."

The entryway floor was sandstone-colored tile, a coat closet on the right and a magazine stand on the left. Daniel saw Wells' face beaming from the top cover. In the living room beyond rose a high ceiling, a fan twirling at the top, light emanating from a handful of floor lamps scattered about. In the corner, a quilted pillow rested opposite a simple wooden cabinet about three feet high, on top of which stood a bronze rendering of the sun. An L-shaped couch and love seat marked the edge of the living room, a potted tree behind it, the coffee table oval-shaped with a glass surface. Beyond lay the dining room and kitchen, a built-in bar offering a row of tall wooden stools.

Within minutes, Wells had set out a tray with four clean glasses, a pitcher of water, fresh lemon slices and ice. He invited them to sit and soon delivered a second tray filled with sliced strawberries and apples, tiny squares of cheese, crackers, and cut-up carrots near a small bowl of ranch dressing. Daniel waited for Jolene to start, but she only sat with her arms crossed, so when Wells handed them each a paper plate, Daniel helped himself.

"Is he sitting next to me?"

Wells nodded, watching one and then the other as if they were new pets he'd just brought home.

"Why can't I see him?" Jolene said. "Is he eating?"

Daniel stuffed another strawberry in his mouth.

"You'd better hurry, or there won't be any left," Wells said, an amused look on his face. He put the containers away and then sat down on the stool opposite them. Jolene was staring at the food tray.

"It's different when you're out of phase," Wells said. "You can't see what he's doing."

Jolene frowned.

"The way I understand it, he's caught between this world and the next, in a space like a corridor or a tunnel. Another dimension of sorts." He moved his hands to demonstrate, cupping the heels of his palms together, his expression eager, like a performer who'd finally found a captive audience. "He travels through these corridors for a time, and it appears to him as if he's operating in the world, but we don't see any evidence of it." He dropped his hands into his lap. "By 'we,' I mean normal people, not folks like you and I. They don't see him, his food, his plates, or anything he manipulates, because he's in these corridors that block their vision. You and I, we can see into these corridors."

"So all that food I thought he was eating just went untouched," Jolene said.

Wells nodded.

"What?" Daniel stared at her. "I always ate it all."

Wells raised one finger. "It's harder with people. They have their own energy." He turned to Daniel. "Can you touch them? Regular people?"

Daniel stopped chewing. His first thought was of Isabella's hand going through his arm, then his own hand dropping through the clerk's shoulder at the gas station, and now, falling through Jolene's knee.

Wells nodded, reading his face. "So that fits the theory. He can't interact with people unless they're phased in with him somehow."

Daniel pushed his food away and rested his forearms on the table.

"The problem is, he can't survive very long in this dimension," Wells went on. "The energy that's keeping him there—after a while, it's starts to burn out. Sort of like a candle."

"And then what?" Jolene asked.

"He dissolves," Wells pulled his hands apart.

Daniel swallowed, a hollow feeling in his gut.

"The fading," Jolene said. Wells nodded. She shifted her weight and looked down, considering, then asked: "Why do some people return as ghosts and some don't?"

Good, Daniel thought. *She's asking him.* Maybe Wells could help her understand her mother's absence.

"Different things happen to different people." Wells leaned against the counter. "Some go on to the next world, their path a smooth highway. Others simply can't let go, so they hang around as the ghosts we typically tend to think about. Then there's a whole other group that doesn't follow the rules." He gazed at Daniel. "Some don't really intend to come here, not consciously. They're brought back by something else."

Jolene stiffened. "You mean, like, for revenge?"

Wells popped a piece of cheese into his mouth. "Could be for anything. If something is powerful enough to jerk you back here, there's not much you can do to resist it." He moved to the sink and refilled his glass of water, then hung the towel on the refrigerator door.

Daniel watched Jolene's gaze dart around the kitchen as if she were searching for something she couldn't find. "What's wrong?" he asked, but she didn't respond.

Wells turned around.

"Something you said spooked her," Daniel said.

"Try not to worry," Wells said. "It will take time to re-establish the connection, but I think you'll be able to. If you two were separated recently . . . ?" He looked from one to the other.

"Brent tried to get rid of me," Daniel said.

"Yeah." Jolene shifted nervously in her chair.

Wells poured Daniel another glass of water.

"Why are you giving him another one?" she asked.

"In his dimension, he's out."

Daniel drank from the second glass. "So if all this is true, I don't see how Brent can still see me. I'm not tethered to him, but he's been able to see me this whole time, even at the library."

Wells glanced toward the front door as if fearing the guy would walk in at any moment. "Could be he just sees ghosts?" "Brent?" Jolene asked.

Wells nodded.

"He's never acted like it." She paused. "I think he's just lying."

Wells glanced at Daniel.

"Not a good guy," he said. "But she's catching on."

Jolene glanced beside her, a lost look in her eyes. "Tell me more about this tethering thing. How long before I can see him again?"

⚜ • ⚜

They talked for a few minutes more, then Wells asked to be excused. When he was safely behind Jolene's back, he motioned for Daniel to follow. Daniel eyed Jolene, wishing she would look at him just once, but she sat with her chin in her hand, staring at the table, so he glided past her and followed Wells through another doorway to the right of the kitchen. He was surprised to find himself in an office—a thick, opulent room that might have belonged to a wealthy lawyer, the far wall lined with cherrywood bookshelves full to bursting with books. A heavy desk took up most of the rest of the space, on top of which sat an oversized flat-screened monitor, speakers and microphone equipment set up on one side, files stacked on the other, a tall maroon leather chair the focal point of it all.

"We have to talk." Wells sat down in the tall chair, its wheels rolling a gentle retreat under his weight.

Daniel was left with his choice of two other chairs with shorter backs and wider seats. He took the right-hand one and felt himself sinking into the cushion.

"First, you've got to get clear on what's going on here. You're dead. You're a ghost."

Daniel stared at him, unable to agree.

"Okay, let's try this." Wells swiveled in the chair. "You had an accident. Remember anything about it?"

Flames. Flying. The crowd in awe below him. The bike landing on the down ramp by itself.

"You don't have to share if you don't want to. But after the accident, when you . . . what did you do? Wake up?"

It was close enough. Daniel nodded.

"Since then, have you noticed anything strange?"

"Most people ignore me."

"Who doesn't, besides Jolene and Brent?"

Daniel shifted his weight. "Trisha and Ronny, and this old lady at the hotel."

"And what was happening when you saw them?"

"They were . . ." He paused. "Trisha. A girl behind the Perkins restaurant. She . . ." The image of Brent performing compressions flashed in his mind. He winced.

"Committed suicide," Wells finished for him.

Daniel arced an eyebrow in surprise. The guy was good. "Ronny, he killed his mother, and then, I think, he was planning

on killing himself too, but we stopped him. And the old woman."
He shrugged. "She seemed normal enough." Though of course
she hadn't seemed that way at all.

Wells stroked the strips of hair on his chin and then stood up.
"That's all?" He counted on his fingers. "Jolene, Brent, two others
on the brink of death, an old woman, and me."

Daniel opened his mouth to correct him, but there was no
one else, not since he'd landed in Iowa. The realization shouldn't
have surprised him, but it did, the stark reality of it in front of his
face.

"Tell me more about them."

Daniel hesitated. "Trisha swallowed a bunch of pills along
with some alcohol. Ronny stabbed his foster mother and then
held a knife to Jolene's throat before I got him off her."

"And the old woman?"

"It was because of her that I got here at all."

Wells waited.

"I don't know." Daniel looked out the tall windows that took
up most of the wall on the far side. "She could see me, but the
waitress couldn't see her. She wiped off her table as if she weren't
there." Something was ticking. He looked around and found the
source, a clock on the wall opposite the windows, high up and
only about a foot tall. It was in the shape of an angel, the wings
extended on either side of the clock's face, which was centered on
the round belly. As he looked at the figure, he knew he couldn't
escape the logic of what he'd just laid out. In a matter of days, he'd
crossed paths with three other people who'd committed suicide
or intended to do so (if one counted William), and one ghost who
had already passed away—who knew by what method?—likely
years before. He pressed his fingers into his temples.

Wells turned to the bookshelf behind him. Running his finger along the spines, he searched one shelf and then another above it, then cast his gaze higher. Finally, he pulled a step stool from behind a file cabinet. "Anything else?"

Daniel thought back to Isabella, the way her hand had seemed to pass through his arm. And Hank wondering what had happened to get Ronny away from Jolene. His veins felt like ice, his heel bouncing rapidly up and down.

"Something like intangibility." Wells reached for the book he'd targeted and pulled it out. "Passing through walls and that sort of thing?"

Daniel pressed his hands together. "No." *But people passing through him. Yes.* When Wells continued looking through the pages, Daniel got up and approached the wall. Slowly, he raised his hand until he felt the painted drywall against his palm. He waited a moment and then pushed, but nothing happened.

Wells sat down at his desk. "What about any other family, friends? Have you spoken to them?"

Daniel shoved his hands in his pockets. "I tried to call my best friend and the motocross office. No one seems to be able to hear me."

"Was your mother the only family you called?"

"My brother doesn't have a phone."

Wells turned a page, read a few lines, and then, "And she heard you?"

"Yeah, but she hung up." He shrugged. "No big surprise. She never listened to me when I was alive."

The words fell to the floor. Space expanded around him in a quiet breath. Then a powerful *boom* in his head. His breathing stopped, his words echoing in his ears.

When I was alive.

He stared at Wells' white face, now turned toward him. The space reversed direction, the walls pressing in. He put his hands on the back of the chair.

"It's okay." Wells hurried to his side. "Just breathe now. Easy. In and out. It's okay."

Daniel shook his head. *No.* The words kept echoing in his mind. It couldn't be.

"We don't need all the answers right now. Focus on your breath. Right here." Wells pinched his thumb and forefinger together in front of Daniel's face.

It made no sense. He wouldn't have gone flying off the bike. You always stayed with the bike. Even if you let go, it was only for a fraction of a second. He'd practiced endless hours. He knew what he was doing. But he could see the bike landing without him and then coasting down the ramp while he flew off to the side, the crowd diminishing in his view. "I have to pick up Tony," he said, breathless now. "He's waiting for me. I can't be . . ."

"Breathe," Wells commanded. "Stay calm. Is that your brother?"

Daniel nodded. "He's in California at summer camp. I'm picking him up on Friday afternoon. It's up to me because Valerie is unreliable. I have to get him, or he'll be there alone."

"Who's Valerie?"

"My mother. He can't count on her. He asked me. I'm the one who's supposed to get him. I can't be late or he'll be stranded there and I don't know what they'll do, if they have a place he can stay—"

"Okay, okay." Wells' voice was soothing, his touch firm on Daniel's shoulder. "Sit down." He gestured to the chair. "You don't have to figure all this out now. You have a couple days. Plenty of time. It's going to be okay."

"It's not okay!" Daniel stepped back and looked frantically at the doughy face in front of him. "If I can't get him because . . ." He glanced down at himself. "If I'm . . ." He raked his hand through his hair and rested it on the back of his neck. "Shit."

Wells tried again to guide him into the chair, but Daniel resisted, so he let him be. After watching him another moment, he walked back behind his desk. "You're you. That hasn't changed. So whether you're on this or that side of what we might call 'the Earth experience' doesn't really matter. You're still alive, just in a different form."

The Earth experience? Daniel rubbed his forehead with the heel of his hand. "Oh God. Tony. He's going to be all alone."

"Don't go there now." Wells raised one palm. "One step at a time. Concentrate on what you're here for."

"What I'm here for?"

Wells took another look at him and then dropped his gaze. "Never mind."

"No, wait. What do you mean?"

Wells raised one palm in a "stop" gesture. "It's enough for now. You need to sit with this. You can stay here tonight. I have extra rooms. You and Jolene and Brent, if he comes."

Daniel grumbled. "If you can sense half what you say you can, you know he shouldn't be allowed to stay here."

"I can't lock him out. Jolene wouldn't go for that."

Daniel leaned over the back of the chair.

Wells slid a piece of paper inside the book he'd been looking at to mark the page, then closed it, tucked it into his hand, and started toward the door. "Come on. I'll show you where the rooms are. You can shower and change. I must have some clothes some-where that will fit you."

Daniel stood where he was for a moment, then remembered Jolene and went back into the living room. She still sat at the counter, leaning her weight on her forearms. Daniel was about to grasp her shoulders when he heard the front door open. Turning, he saw Brent walking into the living room.

"Thought you might be hungry." His long denim shirt bil-lowed out at his sides as he breezed into the dining room, a pizza box held aloft in one hand. "Nice digs."

Wells gave Brent a cursory glance and a nod.

Daniel glared at the guy, resenting the fact that the pizza smelled so good.

Brent opened the box. "Got a pizza cutter?"

"Second drawer to the left of the sink." Wells started up the stairs. Brent found the slicer and divided the pizza into eight pieces.

"Paper plates in the cupboard below you," Wells called. "I'll be back." He glanced at Daniel but didn't encourage him to fol-low.

Brent found the plates and handed one to Jolene. "Want some?" He made a point not to offer any to Daniel.

The pizza was tempting. Daniel thought about snatching a slice just to irritate Brent, but he couldn't stand being in the room with the guy, so he headed toward the front door. On the threshold he paused, the memory of the fading sharp in his mind. Going off alone now might not be the best choice. He looked back and saw Brent serve Jolene a piece of pizza. *Shit.* He stepped out and closed the door behind him. He wouldn't go far.

At the end of Wells' driveway he turned left and walked down the road the way they'd come. The sidewalk pressed hard against his high-tops, a welcome sensation after the fading, the cement squares clean and bare. The night air was a little cooler here in Ogden, a refreshing change from the plains, and he sucked it in, filling his lungs. When he got to the stop sign, he paused, unsure of where to go next. Left would take him up the hill and farther into the darkness, the streetlights ending about a block away. Right would take him down the hill alongside the other housing developments, bright stadium lights gleaming in the distance. He decided on right and jogged for a time until he spotted a park on the left and crossed over.

Six stadium lights illuminated three tennis courts, one of them in use. A playground rested on the other side, also lit up, but it was empty, the slide and swings waiting for the next group of young children. A smattering of picnic tables populated the dimmer corners, the park a perfect square set amidst the neighborhood blocks, a small refuge. He made his way to the table closest to the courts and sat down to watch.

Two lanky teenage boys played, their sneakers squeaking on the asphalt as they dodged back and forth, knees knobby below the hems of their shorts. They were fairly accomplished, typically keeping the ball in play for at least six volleys before one hit it out of bounds or missed the return. The boy in the far court had a lean physique, dark hair, and wore a midnight-blue T-shirt that lit up his face. The other had lighter brown hair and wore a lime-green shirt with a gecko in it, his nose too large for his face, with wide ears to match. His ready smile belied his awkward features, and he constantly teased his companion, mocking his shots and swings, though the other was beating him by three points.

They finished the first game, the dark-haired boy handily defeating Lime Shirt, so the other challenged him to the best two out of three and set up to serve again. Daniel watched with envy. He'd never been good at tennis, but he'd played a few times, and now he wished he had a racket and a few balls and an opponent like that one, someone who would return his serve with a fierce forehand and a ready smile. Still restless, he got up and looked around. All he could see were more neighborhoods full of two-story houses.

The burst of energy he'd felt in Wells' office was quickly leaving him, replaced by a bone-deep exhaustion. When he tried to think of the problem before him—the idea that he could have really died—his mind only imagined the solace of the empty bed in one of Wells' upstairs rooms.

He walked. His legs took him closer to the courts and the two young men playing. At one point he got brave enough to test reality and shouted out, "Hey, why don't you guys let someone else use the court?" When they paid him no attention, he knew that they, too, couldn't see him. A heavy sigh escaped his lungs. Gaze lost in the grass, he didn't notice the younger boy until he'd nearly stumbled over the top of him.

"What are you shouting at?" The boy, no more than six or seven, looked up to meet Daniel's gaze.

Daniel stood, dumbfounded. The kid was sitting cross-legged in the grass at the edge of the courts, two racket covers, a net sack of balls, and a small cooler resting next to him. He held a tablet in his lap, some sort of game flashing on the screen, a black hoodie pulled up around the back of his neck.

"There are open courts over there." The kid pointed to the right. "You don't have to be rude."

"I'm not playing," Daniel said.

"Then what are you shouting for?" When Daniel didn't answer, the kid looked up at him again. "Quit standing there. You're bugging me."

Daniel lifted his foot, intending to move on, but he couldn't. This boy had *seen* him, and from what he could tell, he was nowhere near dying or contemplating death. Besides, his pale skin and startling blue eyes reminded Daniel of Tony. "You like planes?"

The kid acted like he hadn't heard, his fingers tapping on the screen.

"My brother does."

"I know your brother?"

"Don't think so."

A tennis ball hit the fence hard and bounced back into the court. "That your brother?" Daniel pointed to the winning player.

The kid glanced up. "So?"

"He plays well."

"Everyone says."

"You play?"

"Hate tennis."

Daniel wondered if the boy was older than he'd guessed. He dared take a step closer. "That more your speed, then?" he asked, pointing at the tablet.

The kid didn't answer.

"I've never seen that game."

"Obviously."

"You that guy, there?" He pointed to a burly, Viking-looking warrior.

The boy made a few more hits on the screen and then pressed a button.

Everything stopped. "Something you want?"

Daniel took the question as an invitation and sat down. "Actually, yeah. My name's Daniel, and I need some help. Right now, you're the only one I can ask."

At the word "help" the kid looked puzzled. "You want help, you should go to him."

He pointed to his older brother.

"I think I'll have better luck with you."

"He knows karate."

"Not surprised."

"You know him?"

"No, but he looks pretty athletic."

"Everyone says." The kid stared at his screen where the mighty Viking towered over the others, held suspended in attack. "So what help?"

Daniel braced himself on his hands and extended his legs straight out. The cool grass felt good under his palms. "What's your name?"

The boy considered a minute, then said, "Matt." He dropped his gaze to the tablet and, with a tap of his finger, the Viking leveled the last of his opponents.

"I'm Daniel." He glanced at the screen as Matt loaded up another game. "I have a little brother, too. I'm supposed to meet him in two days. If I'm not there on time, he'll probably freak out. He doesn't have any other way to get home."

Matt tapped away on his tablet.

"But I have another friend here and she's in trouble. She's with this guy who's no good for her."

"Punch him in the throat." Matt touched his throat in the center briefly, about where the Adam's apple would be, then returned his fingers to the tablet. "Scott says they can't breathe then."

"Right." Daniel eyed the older brother on the court. Scott. "Kind of hard to just do that out of the blue, though. I mean, she might feel sorry for him."

"So just watch him."

"I was going to do that, but I've got to get my brother."

"Where?"

"California."

"And your girlfriend is here."

"I didn't say she was my girlfriend."

Matt grinned, new front teeth large for his mouth. The two older boys finished the second game and moved into the third.

"You can see why I need your help."

Tap tap tap on the screen, then a lurch forward and a swipe right.

"If you were in California, waiting, and your brother was supposed to come get you, but he had a *friend*," Daniel emphasized the word, "who he thought was in trouble, what should he do?"

"Bring her with him." Matt angled the screen as if using it to steer.

"I thought of that." Daniel sat up. "There's one more thing I didn't tell you. I think I'm traveling a sort of dangerous path. Like your Viking there."

"Viking?" Matt frowned.

"That guy." Daniel pointed to the big one on the screen.

"He's not a Viking! He's a warlock."

Daniel cocked an eyebrow. "Think of me as that warlock then."

Matt cast him a doubtful glance.

"Just imagine, okay? Wherever I go, dangerous, desperate people show up. One tried to hurt her already."

"Punch 'em in the throat." Matt punched the air, demonstrating. "Second punch, to the gut. First you can't breathe, then you're doubled over. Advantage, warlock." He thrust his arm in the air, then dropped it quickly back to the game.

Scott lifted his racket and served. Lime Shirt was distracted by something behind him and missed the ball. It hit the fence and dropped. "Weak move," he called. "That the only way you can win?" He cast his gaze outside the court, and Daniel wondered if he was looking for Matt, but then he turned around and hit the ball back.

"Not my problem if you're daydreaming," Scott said, dancing on the balls of his feet.

Matt's screen lit up with another explosion, the sound effects distorted through the small speakers. "So what are you going to do? Take her with you?"

Daniel looked down into the brilliant blue eyes and felt a swell of gratitude for the boy's kindness. It helped, just to talk to someone. He tapped his pocket. He could give the kid the plane, but that would probably be a mistake. This wasn't a kid who would enjoy an old metal jet anyway. "I don't know," he said finally.

Matt turned and looked across the park. "That her?"

Daniel followed Matt's gaze and felt a smile crease his lips. "Yeah."

Jolene had her hands stuffed into her pockets, her shoulders forward, her neck low into the collar of her mother's jacket. As she got closer, she moved into a jog and didn't stop until she reached the courts. Panting, she watched the young men play for a moment, then looked down at Matt. "You see another guy around here, kind of like them, tall, skinny, a little older?"

Matt pointed at Daniel. "He's right there."

Jolene looked blankly at the space beside her. "Daniel?"

Matt frowned. "You can't see him?"

"She's blind," Daniel blurted out.

"She doesn't look it."

"Dark hair, kinda thick, longish back here?" She drew her fingers along the back of her neck.

"You his girlfriend?"

"Knock it off," Daniel said.

"He's all worried about you," Matt said.

Jolene stared blankly into the night. "He needs to come back."

Matt dropped his gaze to his game.

"You saw him then?" Jolene said.

"He's standing right next to you."

"Daniel, you need to come back with me now."

Lime Shirt shouted something about last point and I'm up this time, sucker. Matt made a few taps and swipes and then switched off the tablet. "I gotta go. You guys work it out."

Jolene watched him get up and walk to the fence. "Cute kid," she said. "But don't get your hopes up. He's a ghost too."

Daniel stared at her.

His shoulders slumped. He'd hoped someone normal had seen him. Just one normal person. He wanted to ask her how she could tell, but she wouldn't hear him.

"You can feel the energy." Jolene said. "Makes the hairs stand up on the back of your neck. Well mine, anyway." She turned to where she thought he was, on her left. "Wells said you could start fading again, you know, without the tether?"

Daniel watched as the boys played their last round, then came out and started gathering up their things. Matt waited by the light post, but they paid him no mind.

Jolene turned and started walking back across the park. "You coming?"

Daniel started to follow her, but then stopped and turned around again. The two older boys slid their rackets into the protective sleeves and collected the balls into the net bag. Matt drifted to stand next to his brother, but the older boy didn't acknowledge him. Lime Shirt, too, was oblivious to the boy's presence. Daniel pitied him. A boy that young. Stranded. He waited until Matt turned to look at him again, then put his hands into position as if he were holding a sword. He slashed the air a few times, taking grandiose steps forward, and then thrust the imaginary weapon into the air. "Vikings rule!"

When he looked down again, Matt was smiling at him. The older boys, their arms full of gear, walked off down the sidewalk. Matt waved at Daniel and then turned and followed them, his head down, the hood shielding his face.

CHAPTER FIFTEEN

J ay came out of the back of the apartment wearing gray sweatpants and a white towel around his neck.

"We got any pizza left?"

Daniel sat at the rickety table they'd found at a garage sale shortly after moving to Reno, his gaze on the back of the cereal box.

He could feel the morning sun warming his neck, the rays streaming through the kitchen window behind him.

Jay poked his wet head up above the refrigerator door. "Dude, you're seriously playing the game on the back of the Fruit Loops?"

"What else do you want me to look at?"

Jay closed the refrigerator door and popped open his laptop on the counter. After hitting a few keys, he brought it over to the table. "How about that?"

The screen showed a picture of a Diamond Xtreme rider doing a rock solid. The photographer had caught him suspended at the top of his arc, both hands out at his sides, his body flying over the top of his Kawasaki. The colors were blue, Jay's colors. "Yeah, well the photographer obviously doesn't know his form. If he had, it would have been my rock solid on there."

"Dream on." Jay tousled the towel over his damp hair, threw it onto the couch and returned to the refrigerator. "Eggs?"

"Sure." Daniel read the article as he finished his cereal.

Jay emerged with a carton of eggs and set them down by the stove. "Little brother calling today?"

"It's Sunday."

"He missed last week."

Daniel shrugged as if it were no big deal, but Jay knew as well as he did that it was. For Tony to miss a Sunday call was unusual. He'd only missed a couple since Daniel had moved out, and it had been almost a year.

Jay melted butter in the pan, the sizzle making Daniel's mouth water. "You never heard anything?"

"I'm sure he'll call today." Daniel finished the cereal and stood up to put everything away, tamping down the uneasy feeling in his gut. His Christmas visit had been awkward at best. He and Valerie had hardly exchanged two words over the four days. She had a new boyfriend, plain by the way she fixed up and went out three different times, but Tony wouldn't say much about him, and Daniel never met him. He paused at the calendar Jay had hung on the cupboard by the sink. It was the Diamond Xtreme calendar, each month featuring another rider doing a different stunt. He knew only four of them, the others having moved on since the pictures were taken, off to other teams or opportunities. Jay had marked the dates of their tour performances, and as Daniel lifted the pages he saw again that he had some time off the first week in April.

Jay slid four perfect over-easy eggs onto a plate. "Don't know how you do that every time," Daniel said.

"It's the heat." Jay separated the group of four in half, slid two off onto another plate and then took both to the table. "And the special touch, of course." He wiggled his hands, a smile playing over his narrow face, then returned and grabbed the hot sauce out of the cupboard. "You thinking about going home again?"

"Can't believe you ruin them with that stuff." Daniel joined him at the table. "You make these great eggs and then you ruin them."

"Just because you can't handle it." Jay tapped the bottom of the bottle and it spit dollops of burnt red over the eggs.

"I like to taste my eggs."

Jay scooped up a big bite, then looked back into the kitchen. "I forgot the toast."

"I'll get it." Daniel got up and pulled the bread out of the pantry.

"So you going?" Jay pulled the computer over and started browsing the Internet.

"You think Coach would be all right with it?"

"Your time off. Your choice."

Daniel dropped two slices in, depressed the button and put the rest of the bread back.

"Just tell him what it's for. He's a sucker for family."

"I would get rusty."

"It's only a few days. You'll be fine. Besides, you check on him, find out he's okay, your head will be in a better place."

Daniel couldn't argue with that. He crossed his arms and leaned against the counter. A small window behind the sink looked out on the rest of the apartments in the neighborhood and a brown hill beyond. It was nothing like the hills in Montana, only about a quarter of the size. He'd enjoyed working on his stunts at the arena, but missed being able to explore the wide-open spaces. During his Christmas visit there had been too much snow, but in the spring the Montana hills would be begging for a rider.

The toaster release jerked him back to the present. He pulled the slices, buttered them, and returned to the table.

Jay swallowed nearly half a slice in his first bite. "After he calls then," still chewing, "tonight. We hit the casinos. Try our luck."

"I don't have anything to gamble." Daniel cut into the egg, allowing the yolk to seep out rich and yellow onto the plate. "Especially if I'm going home, I'll need the cash."

"They have tables with a two-dollar limit. You'll be fine. You can't sit in Reno all this time and not hit the casinos. I keep telling you. That's like going to New York City and not seeing the Statue of Liberty." Daniel opened his mouth to protest but Jay pointed his fork at him, dark eyebrows low over his brown eyes. "No. We're going this time. No arguing. No excuses."

Daniel returned to his eggs. He couldn't deny being curious. The other guys had been telling him he was missing out, particularly because of the hot girls they said were always hanging around the craps tables.

He'd worried about feeling out of place, but after several months on the road, he was one of the team now.

He glanced at the clock on the wall. Almost ten. Tony usually called at noon. He took a bite of his toast and pointed at the computer. "Next time, it'll be me."

Jay typed something on the keyboard. "Want to put your money where your mouth is?"

"Fifty cents."

"That's confidence." Jay watched the screen while it changed. "'Course you'll lose unless you start pointing your toes a little."

"I'm not a fucking ballerina."

"Your legs are floppy. I keep telling you. Point your toes, and your legs will line up. Make a prettier picture." He glanced over and grinned, red lips playing out over smooth white teeth.

"Fine Baryshnikov. Should I wear a tutu?"

Jay's attention was already back on the screen. "Do that and you're *sure* to get your picture taken."

Daniel finished his eggs and stretched his legs to the side, a half of slice of toast still in his hand. His gaze fell on the front door, and he marveled again at the solidity of it, the thick width and heaviness so unlike the flimsy particleboard on Valerie's trailer home door. He couldn't help but feel guilty for how secure he felt behind this door, for how, together with the full-sized bed in the room he had to himself, it created a home where he slept better than he could ever remember sleeping since he was a child. It was when he felt most secure and at peace that he'd remember Tony alone behind that flimsy door, still in the top bunk in that back room with the air purifier whisking the cigarette and dope smoke away.

The uneasy feeling returned to his gut. Jay pecked away at his computer. The warm Reno sun rose higher in the sky and Daniel got up and put the plates in the dishwasher, growing more certain by the passing minute that he needed to go home, even if only for a couple of days.

———— ❖❖ ——— • • ——— ❖❖ ————

The smell of bacon woke him up. He wondered why Jay was cooking breakfast again but then opened his eyes and saw Wells behind the stove. While the guru whipped eggs, Daniel lay on the couch, a lightweight blue quilt over the top of him. He ran his hand over the soft surface. He didn't remember crashing after returning from the park, or finding a blanket to cover up with.

He sat up and wiped his eyes. Four plates had been set on the bar counter along with four cups of orange juice and four glasses of water. He hadn't slept through any sudden departures, thank goodness. He ran his tongue over his teeth. Gross. He needed a toothbrush. He started for the downstairs bathroom, then stopped. Wells looked up, catching his eye.

"Spare clothes there." He pointed to the corner of the coffee table. A pile of garments sat waiting. Daniel popped outside first to check Brent's truck, but the backpack he and Jolene had stocked in Cheyenne was gone. Brent must have dumped it somewhere along the way. Grumbling under his breath, he went back inside, grabbed the stack of clothes off the coffee table, and ducked into the bathroom. There, he took one of the longest showers he could remember. Refreshed, he pulled out a clean navy-blue T-shirt from Wells' pile. It was a large, so it fit okay. Grimacing, he checked the underwear and decided to change that too, along with his socks, retaining only his jeans. He was missing a razor, so he'd have to let the stubble be. Finding some toothpaste in the cupboard, he used his finger to clean as well as he could and combed his hair. By the time he opened the door again, he felt like a new person. He replaced the pants he hadn't used on the coffee table, then stood for a few moments, hands hanging uselessly at his sides. Jolene hadn't come down. She must still be resting. He wanted to see her, but he couldn't go barging into the rooms upstairs.

"I think Brent's showering next." Wells arched an eyebrow at him. "He just asked me for an extra towel."

Was he so transparent? Daniel glanced at the staircase and decided to go on up. He'd walk carefully. Be quiet. On the second level, he paused by the first closed door and heard water running. He listened for a moment and then crept down the hallway. The first room on the right had been Brent's. The guy's black bag lay at the foot of the bed. He walked on to the last room on the left and found the door cracked open. Inside, Jolene was humming. He knocked softly.

She poked her head out. When she saw him, a big smile spread across her face. "Hey." She wrapped her arms around him. Daniel was too surprised to respond at first. Last he remembered she still couldn't see him, but now here she was, her small body pressed against his. He could smell the berry scent of her shampoo, her wet hair tickling his chin. He returned the embrace and closed his eyes. They clung together for a few moments, then she let him go and stood back to look at him. "I was a little worried I'd never see you again."

"No big loss." When she hit him lightly in the chest, he smiled. "Me too."

"Come on." She checked the hallway, then gestured for him to come in and closed the door behind him. Daniel stood awkwardly on the sand-colored carpet. A four-poster bed took up most of the space, with one nightstand on the far side and a matching dresser on the opposite wall. He noticed these briefly before focusing on Jolene again. She was wearing another long-sleeved shirt, this one a purple print with a cityscape on the front, her blue jeans hugging her backside.

"You sleep all right down there?" she asked.

It was her. She had given him the blanket at some point during the night. "Fine." He stood in the middle of the room watching her. "I was glad you were still here, you know, when I woke up."

"Yeah." She stuffed a shirt and some socks into the backpack, deodorant and toothpaste lying on the bed. "What happened yesterday morning won't happen again. He pressured me into leaving." She shrugged. "I figured that's what he was doing. That's why, you know ..."

"The note."

She glanced at him. "The old woman told you?"

He nodded.

She continued packing. "I had to be sure. I guess I didn't believe he'd really do it."

He pulled a gun on me.

Daniel wanted to tell her, but it didn't feel right. He didn't want to whine about it. As he watched her, her movements quick about the room as she cleaned up and packed, his chest squeezed tight, the sensation of losing her flooding his body with adrenaline. "Why did we break up?" he asked.

She paused, one hand still inside the backpack. Her face stilled, her gaze unblinking. Then she resumed, tucking the deodorant into a front pocket. "You don't remember?"

"You sent me an email."

"That was it, pretty much." She glanced out the window.

Daniel followed her gaze. The housing development stretched to the mountain range beyond, its rocky base covered in evergreen trees. "Did I do something wrong?" He sounded pitiful, but he couldn't help it. He wanted to know.

She pulled the zipper closed. "It was just a bad time. My mom was gone."

"I should have been there. I should have come."

"You had stuff going on too."

"What stuff?"

She looked at him then with that haunted look he'd seen several times on this trip, the one where she receded into herself, leaving only a shell of a body behind. "It wasn't your fault. Trust me on that, okay?" She gave him a halfhearted smile. "Besides, it doesn't matter now." She retrieved a pick comb from the nightstand and ran it through her damp hair a few times. Tossed the comb into the bag. "We need to go. It's a little over seven hours."

"To where?"

"Reno." She zipped up the bag. "I figured you'd know that."

Home.

Daniel felt a spark of excitement at the idea of his apartment, his room, his friend. Then he remembered that Brent ruled their transportation. "We could take the bike," he said.

Jolene cast a last look around the room, checking for any remaining belongings. "The bike's still in Cheyenne," she said.

Daniel chuckled. "I parked it at the library."

She came up to him. "In your dimension maybe. In mine, it's still in Cheyenne. Remember what Wells said?"

He frowned, trying to make sense of it, but then let it go. She was standing near. He wanted to kiss her. Worse, he wanted her to go with him and leave Brent behind.

She slung the backpack over her shoulder. "It's weird, I know. But it means we gotta take the truck."

"We could get a bus ticket."

Concern flitted over her features. "You dislike him that much?"

Daniel glanced out the window again. Stuffed his hand in his pocket. "He doesn't treat you right. He's always bringing you down."

She studied him a moment, then sat down on the bed and patted the space next to her. Once he had joined her, she lifted her wrists and held them out for him to see. Daniel noticed the faded scars, one line at the end of each palm. "Several months after I lost Mom. I was in the bathroom with my knife. I was done." Her eyes glazed over. "He stopped me."

Daniel pictured it, that horrid knife poised over her arteries. The part about Brent stopping her he couldn't imagine, but there it was. He took her arm and placed his palm over her wrist.

"I wouldn't have seen you again," she said.

Daniel reached his other arm around her shoulders and pulled her close. "You don't owe him. It doesn't work like that. You're with someone because you *want* to be, not out of obligation."

"Sometimes," she said.

"All the time."

She let him hold her but didn't relax, her shoulders stiff. "I just . . . can't. Not yet." She took hold of the necklaces and gripped them tight. Daniel rubbed her arm, but she stood up, pulling away from him.

Daniel waited a beat, then, "How did he know the kid's name?"

Jolene turned back.

"The kid at the library. He knew his name. He spoke to him, right before it happened."

Her eyebrows knitted together. "How would he . . . ?"

"I thought you would know."

She scratched her neck above the collar. "He was on the news this morning. The kid." She glanced at the small clock radio resting on the nightstand. "Critical condition at the hospital. They don't know if he'll make it. He'd been planning it for weeks." Her gaze returned to Daniel. "It wasn't your fault."

He searched her face, her lips a little dry, the shirt collar gaping over her delicate neck. She was scratching where Ronny had cut her with the knife. "He was the third one," he said. "There could be more. Maybe it's not safe—"

"Smells like Wells has breakfast." She ducked her head, grabbed the backpack, and slung it over her shoulder. "You find yours?"

"Not in the truck."

"That shithead."

Daniel thought again that he should tell her about the gun, but she stormed out of the room. "It's all right—" he called after her.

"It's *not*." She turned back, eyes flashing anger.

"Then let's go. We don't need him."

For the first time, he thought she just might. She looked fierce standing there in the doorway, her grip firm on the straps, her body poised to move. Then she looked down the hall, and he knew he'd lost her. When she turned back again, the fierceness was gone.

"At least I can see you again." She held out her hand and smiled. Daniel took it and followed her into the hall. The shower had stopped running. Jolene dropped his hand and raced down the stairs. "I can see him again!" she called to Wells.

"You've reconnected," Wells answered happily.

"Just like you said."

Daniel picked up his pace. He'd managed to avoid Brent so far. He didn't relish a confrontation now. Just when he thought he'd escaped, Brent opened the door. He was dressed in a pale green V-neck, a sheen of moisture on his face and a towel in his hand. Seeing Daniel, he narrowed his gaze, thick walnut hair in damp waves about his ears. "Well, Shepard. Here we are again. You've wormed your way back in, it seems."

Daniel steeled his spine and looked into Brent's dark eyes. "Not too smart, leaving the bike behind."

Brent ran the towel through his hair, mussing it up. "So we'll survive a couple more days, then you'll be on your way. You have your brother to see, after all." He lowered the towel and closed the space between them. "And just so we're clear, you're *not* taking her with you."

Daniel gave a little shrug. "I think that's up to her."

"It's not happening." He stared deeply into Daniel's eyes, his own seeming to darken even more. "I didn't stop her just to have you drive her over the edge again."

Daniel frowned, unsure of the guy's meaning until suddenly, it dawned on him. Jolene's prior suicide attempt. His own limited time left. *Drive her over the edge . . .* The thought was like ice in his blood. She wouldn't. Would she? Trisha. Ronny. William. He took a sharp inhale. *Jolene?*

Brent wiped his face. "You said I didn't own her, but you're wrong. She's *mine*. If you doubt that, remember—I'm the one who sees you. Fading away like steam into the walls." He twiddled his fingers. "Pretty soon she'll be all alone again just like she was before, and I'll be the one to pick her up. Just like I did before." He dropped the towel on the rack, then started to slip past.

Daniel grabbed his arm, stopping him. "How come you can see me? I thought you didn't believe in ghosts."

Brent cocked his head to the side. "I said *she* shouldn't believe in all that nonsense. It only makes it worse for her, with her mother gone and all. And then of course, there's you. Gone from her life. And now back. Sort of. It's too much for a woman with a . . . fragile hold on life." He emphasized *fragile*, then turned and started down the hall. "She needs me, and she knows it. You? You're a fond memory. Nothing more."

⋅⋅⋅⋅⋅⋅⋅⋅⋅⋅ ⋅ ⋅ ⋅⋅⋅⋅⋅ ⋅

After breakfast, Jolene helped Wells clean up the dishes while Brent left to load up the truck. Daniel could hardly imagine sitting behind the guy now, but they were already talking about Reno and what they would do once they arrived. As he stirred his last bite of pancake around in the syrup, Jolene cleaned off the counter and then ran past him toward the stairs.

"Come on, Danny, it's your schedule we're trying to keep!"

He smiled at her use of the familiar name, then thought of Tony and touched his pocket where the plane still rested. *When I was alive.* How was he ever going to tell him? His stomach ached, and he set his fork down, unable to eat anymore.

"All done?" Wells asked. Daniel nodded and Wells whisked the plate away, rinsed it off, and placed it in the dishwasher. Drying his hands on a kitchen towel, he tipped his head toward the office. Daniel got the hint and followed him inside.

"Did you find anything about Brent?" he asked.

Wells shook his head. "Nothing concrete, but he's hiding something."

"Doesn't take a psychic to see that."

"You need to watch over Jolene. You know that, right? You can't leave her alone with him."

"She's been alone with him for a year."

"And you see how that's affecting her." When Daniel looked puzzled, Wells sighed and leaned back against his desk. "Haven't you noticed how thin she is? She didn't touch anything last night, not even the pizza, and barely a bite of her pancake this morning. Does she ever eat?"

Daniel recalled the many waffles left behind, mostly untouched.

"And she's cutting." He made a slicing motion across his inner arm, making it clear he'd seen the scars.

"Her mother died—" Daniel began, but Wells held up his hand.

"Doesn't matter. Her business. But there's a strange dynamic playing around the three of you, secrets each of you are keeping."

"I'm not keeping any secrets."

Wells arched an eyebrow. "It's not just you. It's her. And it's him. And I'm afraid one or all of you are going to get hurt."

"Am I putting her in danger?" Daniel took a step toward him. "You mentioned all the . . . *people* I've seen along the way—"

"I don't think so." He raised his hand to his chin. "Even if you are, it's far more dangerous for her if you leave. With you gone, there's nothing stopping him, nothing to keep him from . . ."

"What?"

"He's sucking her dry, Daniel. Watch. You'll see."

But Daniel already knew. He'd just never thought of it that clearly.

Wells glanced at the door and lowered his voice. "You're here for a reason."

"To pick up my brother."

Wells paused, a look of effort on his face like a father working to maintain patience with a child. "Answer me this: Why Jolene? Why are you tethered to her?"

She's my girlfriend. He didn't speak it, but searched for another explanation. "She was there," he said finally. "When I got to Iowa. She offered me a ride."

"And you just happened to appear where she was?"

Appear? The word startled him. Had he just appeared?

"You two are tethered," Wells went on. "We know that. You may want to examine for yourself why that is." He arched an eyebrow, then went on. "But then we have Brent in the picture, and he can see you. Always. Even when she can't."

"That's what I was asking you: why can he—"

"*You* have to figure out why that is." Wells spoke seriously now, his voice resonant like a true guru's might be. "This is about you and her, but it's also about you and him."

"I don't know him."

Wells cocked his head. "Maybe you do."

Daniel frowned. It didn't seem possible he could have forgotten a guy like that, but then his memory had been unreliable.

"You have to find out why he's in this triangle." Wells tented his fingers. "As long as you and Brent keep at each other's throats, you'll never discover his secrets, and if you don't bring them out into the open . . ." Wells threw up his hands. "I'm not saying be the guy's best friend. Just get him to let his guard down. I don't know what it is, but it's something . . . When I look at him, I see . . ." His gaze moved up to the ceiling. "A blurry edge, like you might see around an object on a really hot day."

Daniel heard the front door close. Jolene would come looking for him.

"You could stay a little longer," Wells opened his hands. "Give me some time to figure it out."

Another day delayed, and possibly a late arrival in San Francisco. The statement launched Daniel into action. "I have to get my brother." He put out his hand. "Thanks man, for everything. Really. I owe you."

Wells hesitated, then accepted the grip. "Be careful," he said. "And watch out for her."

"Daniel?" Jolene called.

Daniel opened the door.

"Oh! There you are." She looked at one and then the other, her gaze taking in everything, and Daniel got the feeling she knew exactly what they'd been talking about. "Are you ready?"

Daniel glanced back at Wells. "The fading. What if it happens again?"

Wells shrugged. "If she's your tether, she'll help. Stick with her. But either way, it won't last."

Daniel's gaze met Jolene's. Her expression was calm, her face relaxed. Almost *too* relaxed.

"Good luck," Wells said.

"Thank you." Jolene walked over to him and kissed him on the cheek, then grabbed Daniel's hand and pulled him down the hallway.

CHAPTER SIXTEEN

When Brent drove up the hill toward Daniel's apartment complex, it was after six o'clock in the evening. The sun cast a rich yellow glow over the Reno valley, the distant hills turning a reddish brown under its rays. Beyond, city lights winked at what was left of the daylight, preparing to take over the job of coloring the night sky as soon as the sun turned its back. The casinos itched for the nightlife to begin, traffic pulsing toward them filled with tourists and gamblers and families looking for fun. Seeing it all again, Daniel felt a warm rush of homecoming. He'd lived in Reno for only a little over two years so far, but though he missed the Montana mountains, this was home.

This was the city where he'd finally found his freedom, where the heavy burden on his shoulders had lifted and, for the first time, he'd felt like he was truly alive—never more so than when he was flying through the air, the crowd cheering below him. Reno had welcomed him with open arms, offered him belonging on the Diamond Xtreme team and a home that was a true sanctuary with Jay, his friend even more generous than he had been in high school. Daniel tried to dampen his expectations, but he couldn't help but hope that Jay would be home.

The truck downshifted. After climbing for about half a mile, at Daniel's direction, Brent turned into a neighborhood filled with three-story apartment buildings all painted gray with white trim. Flowering oleanders broke up the spaces between them, the short lawns green and well-kept.

Brent found a parking spot and Daniel jogged to the second stairway, racing up two steps at a time only to find his door locked. He checked his pockets, then remembered and flew back down the stairs, passing Brent and Jolene on the way. He found the spare under the evergreen bush in the flowerbed where he'd always kept it, ran back up, and opened the door.

"Jay?" The place was empty. Jay would have had his music on, the Eagles, America, or Bob Seger, or the television turned to NASCAR or the latest motocross event. Daniel checked the dining room, but the table rested clean and ready for the next meal, one of the two placemats having been removed. He stared at the empty space, then scanned the kitchen counters, but they were clean too. In the living room, the television was off and the old green yard-sale couch bare, so he slid open the balcony door and stepped out onto the four-foot wide cement flooring near the metal table and chairs. It had been his favorite place, this small balcony where he could sit outside and enjoy the fresh air. He could never get enough of the fresh air, untainted by cigarette or weed smoke, the brown hills clean and bare beyond.

"Hello?" He heard Jolene call behind him and went back inside. She and Brent stood in the living room, clearly unsure of what to do with themselves. Daniel passed them by and went down the hallway and straight into the master bedroom, which was Jay's. The door was open so he stepped in. The bed was made, the dresser missing the wallet and keys Jay usually stored there, the closet doors closed. Daniel checked the bathroom, but most of the items had been taken from the medicine cabinet, only an extra floss, some antibiotic ointment, bandages, and a few razor blades left behind.

That meant one thing—Jay was gone.

He went back up the hallway toward the other bedroom—his. This door was closed, so he opened it and stepped through, then stopped. Besides the bed and the one dresser, it was empty. The pictures he'd had on top of the dresser were gone, as well as the Kawasaki posters he'd hung on the wall. All his clothes were gone too, even those he'd had in the closet. He checked under the bed and in the corners, but the place had been completely cleaned out, even vacuumed.

Pausing in the middle of the room, he had a hard time believing what he was seeing. It had been only a few weeks. Finally, he plopped down on the corner of the bed. At least that was as he remembered it.

Sensing the familiarity, he scooted back against the wall and stretching his legs, sat there in a sort of stupor. Jolene and Brent talked in low voices in the living room. Somewhere outside a lawn mower started up. The sunlight beamed golden rays through the window, which shared the same view as the balcony, but he didn't turn to look, only stared straight ahead. Despite the absence of his things, the room was still his room, and sitting there, he felt safe and unsettled at the same time.

"You all right?" Jolene appeared in the doorway.

He tried to smile but didn't succeed. "This was my room."

She stepped in and looked around. "Real personality." He nodded, acknowledging the joke, but couldn't muster anything more. "Cleaned out already," she said. When he didn't respond, she added, "It has been a few weeks."

"I thought he might . . ." His throat tightened. *Wait*, he was going to say, but wait for what? Jay thought he was dead. And he was. Dead. He wrapped his hand around his wrist to feel the pulse beating against his finger.

The mattress moved. Jolene joined him on the bed and stretched her legs out. "This yours?" She tapped the quilted top. Daniel nodded. She rubbed her hand on the soft surface. "Kind of peaceful in here."

"Most of the time. Once in a while the neighbors argued, but . . ." Already he was talking about it in the past tense. "Yeah. It was nice."

"Your roommate?"

"Must be out on tour." But the next tour date wasn't until September. "Or visiting his family maybe."

She turned to face him, crossing both legs underneath her. Resting her elbows on her knees she played with the purple stone hanging from her neck. "You remember anything more about that night?"

Fire, lights, the bike rolling down the ramp alone. "This can't be real," he said. "It can't be that I'm really . . ."

"Because you're not." She took his hand and pressed his palm against hers. "Not really. You're here with me. I'm starting to think, you know, that maybe it's just a different way of being alive."

He caught her gaze. "You think I'm a ghost."

"You're different than any ghost I've ever seen. So maybe you're not a ghost." She brought his hand up under her chin. "You can't keep denying that something's changed, but I can't keep insisting you're just another ghost."

Daniel rubbed his face with his other hand, the stubble on his cheeks harsh against his fingers. "This was the first room I ever had to myself. Took me a while to get used to it, but then . . ."

"You liked it."

He fished the plane out of his pocket and held it between his fingers. "I guess this is all I have left."

Jolene's gaze fell on the toy.

"My brother and I passed it back and forth a few times. I gave it to him, he gave it back to me." He closed his fingers over the wings and rested his mouth on his knuckles as if he were blowing on them. "It's the only thing I had in my possession when I . . . got to Iowa." He looked at her, but she had turned away from him, her cheeks flushed. "Jolene?"

She let go and stood up. When she spoke, there was a crack in her voice. "You hungry?"

He'd said something wrong. Tucking the toy away, he sat up. "You guys can use the bathroom, the kitchen, whatever you need. I'm sure Jay wouldn't mind."

"He might wonder who got into his apartment while he was gone."

"I could leave him a note."

"That would freak him out."

Daniel felt himself smile. A final trick on his friend. It seemed like a great idea. He got off the bed and started for the door, then stopped and looked back. Jolene had drifted over to the window. "I'm glad you were there at the chicken café," he said. "Question your choice of dining facilities, but . . ." He paused but she didn't respond. "You have to tell me sometime about this thing you have. This ability to speak to, well, people like me."

She swayed back and forth, her hands clutching her arms as if she were hugging herself. "I'm glad too, that you came. It helped . . . clarify some things."

Daniel waited, expecting her to say more. She continued to sway back and forth, rubbing her arms. Standing by the door he could almost hear Jay calling him from the living room, shouting something about *you gotta see this guy he's insane with the way he holds the handle with one finger.* He remembered running down the hall to see the jump, flopping onto the squishy couch and grabbing a handful of Jay's popcorn. The voices faded, leaving him standing in the doorway of an empty room. Jolene snuffled, wiped her face, and shook her head. "So we're going out, right?" she said.

"You okay?"

"Fine." She glanced back with a forced smile and then turned to the window again. "I need to change clothes?"

His plan. Daniel had suggested it on the way into the city. "Hell yes. Get dolled up. We're hitting the town." He waited, thinking how it would be, how tonight he would get Jolene to smile again, but then she left the window and came toward him. Her face had lost the warmth that had been there when she came in, her eyes taking on that glassy, far-away look. She passed him by without acknowledging him and went back up the hallway. He heard her ask Brent for the keys, tell him they could use the bathroom to change. Daniel looked back at his room, but it was no longer his. It was as if he were gazing at the remnants of someone else's life. The emptiness that had consumed him at the library licked at the edges of his skin. He took hold of the doorknob and pulled it closed behind him.

· ────── ❖❖ ─ · ─ ❖❖ ────── ·

The Peppermill casino glimmered a gleeful welcome as they approached the dome-shaped entrance, its elegance reflected in the Greek-style columns. Old English streetlamps lined the sidewalks, fuchsia-colored flowers tucked under the lanterns. Beyond, the Peppermill sign replayed a firework light display. Down the way, a row of classical sculptures overlooked fountains trickling into shimmering pools.

Jolene walked toward it all awestruck, her face reflecting the pink light. When Daniel caught her eye, she grinned, a vibrant expression that reminded him of the week they'd spent together in Des Moines. She'd grinned at him a few times after that on their video calls, but he couldn't remember those as well. The question of why she'd broken up with him arose again in his mind, but he pushed it away, determined not to let that ruin their night.

Once they'd stepped through the front doors, he took the lead, striding confidently past the buffet with the lit-up dragon and the other restaurant with the seahorse hanging from the ceiling. They saw the pink fountain resting inside the wall and slowed to study the myriad Greek paintings, additional graceful sculptures beckoning from one corner and then another. Big-screen televisions advertised trips to New Zealand and Ireland and Switzerland and then, San Francisco. They paused when the picture of the Golden Gate Bridge came up, then moved on through the slot machines and into the blackjack room.

Butterscotch strip lights dressed up a series of half-moon tables, each with a set of charcoal-gray velvety chairs. The dealers were dressed in white collared shirts, red bowties, red vests and black slacks, the carpet a deep red with waves of yellow and blue and green snaking throughout, like little trails leading nowhere. More television screens clung to beams above, just under and to the side of the hanging lamps, the bar stretching a welcome space on one side of the room. The ultimate destination—the cashier's box—sat back and to the right. Daniel headed that way, reaching for his wallet and then remembering he didn't have it. He slowed to make sure Brent was behind him, now knowing that the guy had a stash in his wallet. Brent didn't resist, eyeing Daniel as if to make a point that nothing could proceed without him, until Jolene poked him. He promptly handed her a one-hundred-dollar bill. She exchanged it for a stack of fives.

"Now what?" she asked.

She was wearing the long-sleeved navy-blue blouse that lit up her fair skin, her eyes bright again like they were when she'd entered his old room at the apartment. Daniel stared at her, taken in by how beautiful she was. "Let's start at the ones that allow a five-dollar limit. We have to see if this is going to work."

"Chicken," Brent said.

Daniel raised his eyebrows. "Want to go higher?"

"We're not going to make anything on five dollars."

Daniel spotted a ten-dollar table with only one player. "This way then."

Brent circled around to take the seat next to a bald man, who wore a red polo shirt and leaned heavily against the bumper, one hand on a stack of chips. The dealer had dealt him two, a jack and a deuce, and he was now staring at the dealer's upright card—a six of hearts. Brent nodded at Jolene and directed her to place all the bills on the table.

The bald man scratched for another card. It was a three of spades. The man caressed his chips, then scratched again. The dealer— a messy blonde with hazel eyes and a petite figure— pulled a card from the shoe . . . a five of diamonds. She had hands like darts, here and there and back as if they had never moved. The bald man put a palm over his cards. The dealer turned her own remaining card up—a four of diamonds. She pulled a second card—a four of hearts. A third time she dealt—an eight of spades. The bald man smiled. The dealer acknowledged his victory with a nod, then handed him his winnings and turned to address the cash in front of Brent and Jolene. In a quick swipe she exchanged it for chips, leaving them to determine the amount of their first bet. Jolene decided—two red five-dollar chips in the betting circle. And the cards came on.

It was time for Daniel to move. He stepped up behind the dealer, hesitated a moment, and then looked at the shoe. Checking those cards would be difficult, replacing them in time nearly impossible. He turned to the dealer. She had both her cards on the table, the faceup one a ten of clubs. Daniel reached over, dangerously close to her arm, and lifted the corner of the facedown card, then quickly replaced it and pulled his arm back. His heart slammed in his chest, but the blonde didn't seem to notice. He showed Brent nine fingers.

Brent smiled to himself. That meant the dealer had 19, and she'd have to stand. He and Jolene had a ten and a five. He scratched for a card and received another five. Daniel clenched a fist in celebration. Brent put his palm over the cards, signaling his desire to stop, then leaned over and whispered to Jolene while the dealer turned to the bald man. He had seventeen and was thinking, then finally shook his head. The dealer turned her card over. Nineteen. She paid Brent his winnings and swept chips away from the bald man. He grumbled but then pushed over another bet. Brent and Jolene did the same. Daniel inhaled and waited, and when the cards were dealt again, he lifted the facedown one and told Brent the number. Jolene watched carefully, her gaze switching from Daniel to her cards and back again. The second hand they lost, but after that they won three more. Daniel grew more confident and gradually, Brent bet higher and higher amounts.

Soon Jolene got the hang of it and started making her own decisions, creating a separate stack of chips as Brent continued to build on the first. Both piles grew, taking up more room on the table. The old man commented a time or two on their luck, but after about an hour of play began to regard them with suspicion, as his own stack of chips remained woefully limited. Other players gravitated to the table, a middle-aged woman with bleached-blonde hair and another older gentleman wearing a fedora. The two tilted their heads together like an intimate couple, conversing over each play. At one point the bleached-blonde woman told Jolene she needed to borrow some of her luck, and even went so far as to get up and rub her hand on Jolene's shoulder.

The lights twinkled around them, the waitresses circulating with drinks. Jolene ordered for the three of them, and soon there was a Dr. Pepper sitting on the table beside her sparkling water, Brent the only one with alcohol, a bloody Mary. Daniel took a break during one hand and sucked his soda down gratefully. Brent still won his hand. Jolene lost. Daniel hurried back behind the dealer. The play went on, cards going out, cards coming back in, Daniel checking the facedown card, revealing the information. No one else noticed him standing there. No one even looked at him. It was unnerving at first, but then it started to be fun.

It was after the second hour the dealer started watching them more carefully. Daniel noticed her gaze settling on one and then the other a little longer than before. She started talking to them, congratulating them, saying things like, "It's your lucky night," or "Another good one for you, huh?" She'd make brief eye contact and then go on, but there was a change in her body language, more movement in her neck as her gaze took in the goings on around the table.

"It's time to take a break," Daniel announced. "Let's go cash out."

They played another hand, but Daniel didn't turn up the card. Jolene got the message, smiled at the dealer and gathered up her chips, saying something about how it was time for dinner. She'd tucked her winnings up against the edge of the table and it took her some time to gather them all. Eventually she opted for putting them into the small purse she'd brought with her, which was fortunately big enough to hold them. She glanced at Brent.

"Soon," he said, and put a small bet on the next hand. Daniel accompanied Jolene to the cash cage. She came away with two thousand forty dollars. She held the cash in her hand, staring at it as if she'd never seen cash before. Daniel steered her away, encouraging her to stuff the bills out of sight.

"Two thousand!" she said. "Can you believe it? Two-thousand dollars." She looked up at him. "And it was so fun!"

Daniel pulled her close, his hand on her shoulder. "The dealer was getting a little worried. We should go eat, then try another table."

"With a bigger limit."

Daniel laughed. "Okay."

Brent still sat at the table. "We need to get him out of there," she said. "He'll lose everything." But when he spotted them he gathered his chips, passed them by without a word, and went to cash out. They waited, gradually moving toward the edge of the room where they could make a quick exit.

"He won more than I did," Jolene said. "Oh, I almost forgot." She pulled out her wad of cash and started counting it.

"What are you doing?"

"Splitting it with you!"

He pushed her hand back toward her purse. "Whatever we earn in the next round, you can give me some of that."

She hesitated, but then did as he asked, looking back for Brent. "You've done this before?"

"Won like this? Never. But I did win about two hundred once." When she looked curious, he continued the story. "Jay brought me. We'd been touring for several months and everything had gone great. I mean, the audiences loved the stunts and neither one of us had screwed up. Surprising, since we were the new guys on the team. So when we got back, we came here to celebrate. We didn't have much, Jay more than me, so he let me borrow some of his. We went to the blackjack tables, as it's the only game we really knew, and we lost at first, but then we got the hang of it and walked out that night with about four hundred between us." Daniel scanned the room and found the table where they'd played, remembering Jay's happy voice in his ears.

"Four hundred dollars!" he'd exclaimed. "We just won four hundred dollars! And we're superstars on the Diamond Xtreme team!" He'd slapped Daniel on the back. "It doesn't get better than this, my friend."The memory dissipated when Brent walked up to them, his hands in his pockets.

"So?" Jolene asked.

"We going to get something to eat?"

"Come on, give. What did you get?"

Brent strolled out into the hallway, forcing them to follow him. "Not much. Was rather disappointing actually."

"You're begging for it." Jolene growled.

"So hostile." He smiled at her. "Fine. About three thousand."

Jolene squealed and jumped up, then looked around to be sure no one was watching. "Three thousand?" she whispered. "That means we have five thousand between us. Five thousand!"

Brent nodded as if it were an everyday occurrence. "I'm guessing we can get more before the night is through?" He glanced at Daniel.

"The best buffet is this way," Daniel said. "Then yeah, I figure we can come back, go to a different table." He started down the hall and soon felt Jolene's arm loop through his. He grinned but then saw she'd done the same with Brent, who now walked on her other side. Daniel led them on toward the restaurant, Brent loping his usual easy gait in his peripheral vision. He tamped down his irritation at Jolene being so nice to him.

"This one?" Brent paused, pointing.

Daniel looked inside and spotted the full-sized shark hanging from the ceiling. "This is the one," he said.

The Oceano. He and Jay had always passed it by on their way to the cheaper buffets. Now their pockets were fat with winnings, so

Daniel was eager to try it out. He'd always been curious, mainly because of the shark, but also because the scent of the seafood was always so tempting. The drinks came first, a red wine for Brent, sparkling water for Jolene, and Dr. Pepper for Daniel.

"Is that all you're going to get this whole trip?" Brent asked, pointing at Jolene's water.

Jolene dropped her gaze to the table, her hand glued to her glass.

"Just because she doesn't care to bomb herself out of her mind," Daniel said.

"Oh, she's been bombed," Brent said. "Maybe not while you were around."

"Cut it out," Jolene mumbled.

Brent shrugged and took a drink. "Truth."

She turned away from him, red crawling over her neck and into her cheeks.

Brent took a sip of his wine and turned his attention to Daniel. "Danny here is a teetotaler I guess."

"Just don't particularly like the stuff."

"That because of your mother?"

Daniel's gaze shot to Brent's face. "What about my mother?"

"Got the feeling she enjoyed the drink."

Daniel glared back at him. *Maybe you do,* Wells had said. He wracked his memory, but nowhere in his past could he find anyone resembling Brent.

"Overindulged quite a bit, didn't she?" Brent said.

"How would you know?"

Brent shrugged.

Daniel knew he should stick it out, find out more, but it was too uncomfortable, especially with Jolene looking like a rabbit ready to run. Besides, after the tall Dr. Pepper, nature was calling. Just as well. Another minute and he would pop the guy in the mouth. "I'll be back," he said and headed to the restroom.

The urinals were placed against an inside wall, hidden from view until after he entered and rounded the corner. In the mirror, his reflection looked the same as it always did, his hair wavy on his head, the collared blue shirt Jolene had given him dressing him up, his jeans a stonewashed blue. He wondered if he really looked that way or if it was some illusion, some trick of this other dimension Wells had talked about, his real form a skeletal shadow of who he'd been, or maybe a burned-up body draped onto walking bones. Longing to sit down, he went into one of the stalls, shut the door, and sat, his elbows on his knees. He had to be at the pier the next day, no later than three o'clock. His thoughts roiled about as if in a lively stew, Tony and Jolene and Brent and back to Tony again. He couldn't miss the appointment, but what would happen to Jolene? He couldn't just say his farewells and allow her to stay with Brent, particularly now that he had Wells' warning in his ears.

The door squeaked open. Footsteps clicked on the tile floor and then a belt buckle clanked followed by a steady urine stream. "You alive in there?"

Brent. Daniel winced, flushed the toilet, waited a moment, and walked out. Brent was just zipping up and headed to the sink, his gaze on Daniel in the mirror. Daniel took the next sink over and washed. Brent finished first, shook the water off his hands and went to the towel dispenser. Daniel took the one on the opposite wall.

"Guess I stepped in it out there," Brent said. "Didn't realize you hadn't told Jolene about Valerie."

Daniel squeezed the half-wet towel in his hands and dumped it in the trash.

"I thought for sure you had, what with you two being so close and all. Valerie was the problem all along, wasn't she?"

Daniel turned, massaging the back of his neck. "Do I know you? Because if so, I don't remember."

Brent stood over the trashcan drying his hands. "Don't be too hard on yourself. I didn't remember you at first, either." He shrugged one shoulder. "Understandable. I encounter a lot of people in my walk of life. And let's face it, most of them don't come back!" He chuckled, discarding the towel.

"Your walk of life?"

He turned back toward Daniel, a soft smile on his lips. "You could say we were friends for a while, you and I. When you really needed a friend."

Friends? Daniel crossed his arms over his chest. "When was that?"

"You were having a tough time of it." Brent copied the movement and leaned against the wall behind him. "I helped you out. It's what I do."

"You help out. Like you're helping Jolene?"

Brent's smile faded. "She's different."

"She says you helped her."

"After her mother died, yes. She was having a tough go of it too. A little like you."

"I don't remember having a tough go of it."

"That *is* interesting." Brent narrowed his eyes. "A blessing in the way of things, I suppose."

"The way of things?"

"When you step through to the other side."

Daniel extended his cut palm. "So what was this about?"

Brent stared at the rough red line carved into the flesh. "I was confused. I've never seen it before. This ..." He gestured down the outline of Daniel's body. "Form. I was curious. And, I needed to get a taste of your blood." He brought his finger to his lips. "That brought it all back for me."

Daniel recalled the action with a shudder. "Brought *what* back?"

"What happened. Before." Brent's expression sobered, his gaze more intense.

Daniel tried, but he couldn't place the face. He opened his hands at his sides. "I give up. Who are you?"

They stood staring at one another for a moment, then Brent came toward him. Daniel stepped back only to bump into the wall. There was nowhere to go. Brent grasped his hand, the same one he'd sliced two nights before. Fire seared Daniel's skin and he jerked his hand back, but Brent held firm. Flames erupted in Daniel's mind, the sensation of falling returning in a rush. He squinted his eyes shut and pulled harder, struggling to retrieve his hand. When the relief came, it was sudden and powerful and he fell back against the wall, mouth open in a desperate gasp for oxygen. New visions played in his memory, vivid and bright in their recovered recollection. He was back in the Butte arena getting ready to jump, his bike angled toward the ramp, the engine purring underneath him, the crowd alive and yelling. It was the last jump of the night. He'd planned to do the cliffhanger, but there was something different in his left hand. He focused and saw it was a sparkler bomb. Like the ones he and Tony had played with on the Fourth of July. Except bigger, with more sparklers tied together. In his other hand he held a cigarette lighter. He touched the flame to the single sparkler that extended from the top, the one that served as the wick. It glowed and spit multi-colored stars. He tucked the lighter back in his pocket, held the sparklers high, and pulled the throttle.

Shepard's lighting up the place tonight, ladies and gentlemen! Adding a little excitement, isn't he? And here he goes on his last jump, flames blazing just inches from his face and oh, he's airborne . . .

Daniel saw himself ride up the ramp and fly into the air. Poised where he would usually start moving his body, he held the sparklers high for the audience to see, glanced right to check their reaction, then looked down into the gaping hole that was the Kawasaki's lidless gas tank, about a quarter full. Beyond the lights of Butte gleamed a thoughtless farewell, the mountains dim shadows against the stars. He waited one more long second for the wick to burn, then pushed the sparkler bomb down into the hole. At first nothing happened. Gravity took hold and he started his descent. Then the tank exploded, a torch between his legs. The bike shook underneath him, then the handlebars jerked out of his hands. The seat fell away from his knees as the flames erupted around him, his leathers curling but resisting the consuming heat. He was flying alone with nothing to hang onto, hovering long enough to see the bike fall to the other ramp and roll down, coming to rest several feet beyond in the dirt, the wheels still turning as it dropped on its side.

He watched it lying there all ablaze, regret rising up in his throat as his own body began to fall, turning and twisting so that he saw the stadium lights and then the audience and then the dirt and then the stadium lights, but he couldn't hear anything but his own thoughts and the one voice in his head saying, *It's all over now. Be at peace.*

Daniel opened his eyes. Fluorescent lights blazed over the bathroom tile. *The voice.* It echoed in his ears. *It's time to be done. You don't need to do this anymore. You'll be okay. Come.* He heard his heart beating in his ears. The voice! He pushed himself up, his back pressed against the wall. Brent was gone. Another man washed his hands, the same bald man who'd been playing blackjack with them. He pulled a couple of towels down and dried off, then walked out without a word. Daniel stood on the cold tile floor, the last moment of his life playing over in his mind, the raw truth gradually sinking into his brain.

He'd done it. He'd caused the so-called accident. He'd done it on purpose. And he'd died that night in the arena with Brent's voice in his ears.

⁕⁕⁕ • ⁕⁕⁕

The hand Brent had grasped still burned. Daniel tried to shake the pain free. When the heat remained, he brought his palm to his face. The flesh looked normal except for the redness in the center. He stared at that, trying to remember more, like what had happened before he rode out for his last jump, what he'd been thinking, why he'd made the choice he'd made. With every passing moment the truth sank more deeply into his consciousness until he realized that Wells was right. He was caught in some in-between world, not alive but not exactly dead, in most ways completely lost and alone. Part of him still resisted the knowledge, for wasn't his body as real as he remembered it? Hadn't the pain shot through his nerves?

The questions came and went, peppered with new worries. Clearly, as Wells had said, he didn't have much time left. The thought that he might soon be parted from Jolene pained him, but even worse was the thought of Tony. The boy would be left alone to manage with Valerie as best he could. He would grow up hardened and scarred, forced to live with the knowledge that his brother had left him *willingly*, that his desire to leave had been stronger than any bond the brothers had shared.

It was another five minutes before he went to the sink, splashed new water over his face, then let it run over his reddened palm. He dried off while looking at himself in the mirror. It was strange, seeing his reflection, feeling himself standing there on the tile floor when he was supposed to be dead. Why hadn't he just died? Gone to heaven, or the other place, if there was such a thing? He threw the towel away and leaned on the sink, staring into his own brown eyes. Was this Gus's doing? His friend had died of a heart attack less than a year after Daniel had left town. Had Gus somehow worked it so that Daniel could be here long enough to say goodbye to his brother? Or was this something more sinister, some sort of punishment for the choice he'd made?

He looked down at the drain. He had to decide what he was going to do. Whatever Brent was, he wasn't normal, maybe not even human, and he was waiting out in the restaurant with Jolene. Fear sliced through his gut. *Trisha, Ronny, William, and . . . Jolene.* Was Brent whispering in her ear too? He turned, angry, ready to fight for her right then, but then remembered. Brent had stopped her, she'd said.

He'd encouraged the others, watched them as if entertained, but Jolene he had stopped.

He's draining her, Wells had said.

Daniel paused, his gaze on the tile floor. *She's mine.* Brent's words echoed in his ears. He was using her for something. Daniel had to help her see that, convince her to give up her obligation to him. Yes. That's what he needed to do. Decided, he walked to the door and lifted his hand to open it, but he couldn't. His palm burned, throbbed, and trembled. He threw it down in disgust, but other parts of him were trembling too. He could feel it about his shoulders and in the small of his back. He couldn't go out there like this.

He was *afraid*.

With the realization, the fear flooded over him as if finally allowed out of its cage. He broke out in a cool sweat, his stomach twisting. He went into a stall but nothing came up. The last time he'd felt like this, he'd been fourteen years old.

The memory unfolded over the tile floor. He, Gus, and Tony had gone to Quake Lake in Gallatin National Forest, and they'd all stayed in the same big tent. The old man had slept quietly on his left, Tony on his right with a little snore going on. Daniel was still awake when he heard a rustle in the wild grasses. Lifting his head, he listened, detecting a soft footfall. He held his breath, afraid to move until the rustling changed to a deep-throated grunt and a huff, and then a large shadow pressed against the side of the tent. Daniel shook Gus's shoulder.

"Gus, Gus!" he whispered. "Wake up. Something's out there."

The old man woke instantly, his military training strong in his bones.

"I think it's a bear!" Daniel whispered.

Gus reached for the rifle he kept by his sleeping bag.

"You're not going out there?"

The old man pulled on his cowboy boots and pushed forward onto his knees. "Can't run from fear, boy," he whispered. "The only way is to run toward it. Get your gun."

Daniel reached for the shotgun Gus had given him the year before. It was already loaded like he'd been taught, the safety on. He clicked it off.

"You come on out after me, and if I'm shootin', you shoot, you got it? Just be careful of your aim. I don't want any pellets in my ass."

Daniel slipped his shoes on and waited while Gus moved toward the opening and slowly unzipped the flap. The grunt and rustle sounded again just to their right, not a foot away from where they were sitting, only the thin nylon separating them from whatever man-eating beast was nosing around outside. Daniel had never been more scared in his life, and though he tried to force his body to move, all he could do was sit and cling to the gun. Gus finished unzipping the flap. It dropped open. Through the new space Daniel could see only darkness, not even the outline of the trees visible on the moonless night. Gus grabbed the flashlight hanging from the top of the tent, tucked his rifle against his ribs, and looked back. "Ready?"

Daniel nodded. What happened next, he never forgot. Gus tucked his toes underneath him, then burst out into the night in his underwear and boots and fired off a shot. "What the hell you think you're doing here? This ain't your campground! Get the hell out, you son of a bitch! Get the hell out of here!" Another shot. "Go now, git!" A third shot and finally Daniel moved, but by the time he made it outside the tent, Gus was no longer aiming his gun.

Daniel waited, but couldn't hear anything. "Is it gone?"

"Yeah, it's gone." Gus shone the light on him. "Where the hell were you? Leave an old man to die out here."

He switched the beam to the ground.

Daniel stood, shaking, ashamed but too afraid to step forward. "What was it?"

Gus shined the light on a set of tracks in the dirt. "Big cat. Hoping for a free dinner. Didn't expect to run into a rude ol' cuss like me. See here?" He focused the beam, but Daniel didn't move. "Come on, boy! Move your legs!"

Sure he heard the cat lingering nearby, Daniel took a few steps forward as Gus shined the light on the big paw tracks, bigger than he'd imagined they could be, bigger than his own hands. They were all along the side of the tent, only inches from where he and Gus had been sleeping.

"Hey, what happened?"

They both turned to see Tony poking his head out of tent. He rubbed one eye, his hair standing straight up.

"Just a big cat trying to get free food," Gus said. "Guess he didn't bother you none, huh?"

"A cat? What's a cat doing up here?"

"Probably looking for a juicy little boy, I imagine."

"To what? Take him home?"

Daniel and Gus looked at one another and then broke out laughing, Gus's voice echoing joyfully into the night. Gradually, Daniel's fear subsided. He took hold of his gun and made a promise to himself. He'd never sit inside the tent again.

Staring at the stall door at the Oceano seafood restaurant, Daniel felt his courage return. Whatever Brent was, he was dangerous, but he could see him, which probably meant he existed in the very dimension Daniel now seemed to be walking through. If that were the case, they were on equal ground. He walked out to the sink, drank some water out of his cupped hand, then grabbed a towel and sopped the sweat off his forehead and the back of his neck. Checking himself in the mirror once more, he combed through his hair and then walked toward the door. He reached for the door handle and then paused, noticing for the first time an image on the wall. It had been hand-painted, simple black words on white tile: "The smarter you play, the luckier you'll be." Over the words were painted the four suits from a deck of cards: spades, diamonds, hearts, and clubs.

It could have been a message from Gus himself. Daniel walked out.

———————

Jolene's gaze found him as he emerged from the back of the restaurant. Brent lounged beside her, his lower body angled toward hers as his upper body slouched back in his usual relaxed, nonchalant manner, his hand on what looked like a second glass of wine.

"There you are!" Brent sat up a little. "We were wondering if you'd been flushed away."

Daniel put on his friendliest expression. "Something I had for lunch I guess."

"It was gourmet fast food!" Jolene smiled but watched him carefully, her expression concerned. He sat down and took a drink of his Dr. Pepper.

"We got all that seafood coming," Brent said. "You can't let it go to waste."

"Don't plan to." Daniel looked around for the waitress, wondering how long it would take to bring the food. He was suddenly quite hungry. "So." He looked at Jolene and then Brent. "We're not far out now. What are you guys going to do once you get to San Francisco?"

"Don't think we'll be staying long." Brent eyed Jolene, but she didn't react.

"You have some money now," Daniel said. "You could look around, have fun."

"Fun is overrated. Not really what life is all about."

"Oh?" Daniel kept his voice even. "What's it about, then?"

"I think you know." Brent's gaze sharpened. "I think you know exactly."

"Not really. I mean, right now it's about good food and good luck." He winked at Jolene. She didn't smile, but she brightened a little.

Brent twirled his wine. "I would have thought for sure, as your memory returned—"

"You remembered something?" Jolene asked.

Daniel looked down at his napkin. *Damn.* The guy had pulled him the wrong way again. He hesitated, then decided to go along. "A few minutes ago. Another reason why I was so long in there." He shifted his fork and knife out of his way and leaned his elbows on the table. This would be the hard part, telling Jolene. He tried but couldn't look into her eyes. "I remember now. That day. The accident. I . . . died." *There. He said it.* "Just like it said on the website."

Dishes clanked in the back kitchen. A noisy family walked by, the youngest child complaining about being tired. "Are you okay?" Jolene asked.

Daniel waited until the family drifted off. "It was on my last jump. I fell. Well, sort of." He shifted in his seat. Swallowed. "I . . . did it. I made it happen." He paused. "The accident. On purpose." He forced himself to look into her eyes.

She didn't seem surprised.

Or disappointed.

She seemed *scared.* "Did you . . . remember anything else?" she asked.

Anything else? He searched her face, bewildered. "That was enough," he said.

"You don't remember . . . why?"

The question opened a dark hole inside him that he had no desire to explore. "That was all."

"How did you do it?" Brent asked. "I mean, if you don't mind telling us."

"Brent!" Jolene said.

"I'm just curious!" Brent threw up his arms.

Daniel sat up straight and focused on Brent's dark eyes. "I dropped a sparkler bomb in the gas tank," he said.

"Whoa." Brent sat back in mock surprise. "Did it . . . explode?"

Daniel cocked an eyebrow.

"Fire and flames, that sort of thing?" Brent's eyes glistened.

"You need me to draw you a picture?"

"Out with style as they say." He lifted his glass of wine as if in a toast. "Have to admire that." He took a long drink.

Jolene glared at him.

"You never answered the question." Daniel stirred the straw around in his glass. "What's life all about?"

Brent set the glass down and wiped his lips with the back of his hand. "Oh that? Nothing. It's about absolutely nothing. You figured that out." He tipped his glass Daniel's way. "Fairly early on, I might add, which means you were smarter than most."

"How's that?"

"You realized it all amounts to nothing. You get old. You lose everybody and everything. Nothing you do matters. It all goes to dust. So why bother with it? Why muddle through? Anyone with a brain can sense it, but only a few have the courage to do something about it."

"That's not what I thought," Daniel shook his head. "That wasn't it."

"No? What did you think, then?"

Daniel heard the tone, the toying, almost gleeful anticipation in it. Like a dog eyeing a bone, Brent wanted the story, wanted to roll around in it and soak it up much as he had the presence of Trisha's dying body and the scene where William hovered at the railing. He'd probably even sat peering around the corner at the café while Ronny held Jolene at knifepoint.

"Never mind him," Jolene said suddenly. Leaning forward, she lifted her glass. "Tonight is about fun, and I declare anything else completely off limits."

Daniel lifted his Dr. Pepper. "Agreed."

Brent seemed unwilling at first, but finally lifted what remained of his wine. "Fine," he said. "To fun, then."

They clinked glasses and drank. Over the rim, Daniel saw Brent's dark gaze edged in steel. The battle lines had been clearly drawn. And, for the first time, Daniel felt like he had the upper hand.

The food was surprisingly good.

Daniel savored it, if for nothing else than to honor Jay, who had always said they'd go there someday. When everyone had finished, he stood up, intending to take them back to the blackjack tables, but Brent suggested they call it a night. "Better not tempt fate," he said, his eyes bloodshot from his third glass of wine.

"Ah, come on." Daniel licked butter off his fingers, the lobster warm and satisfying in his belly. "You said you wanted to try the higher-limit tables. We know what we're doing now, so let's go." He glanced at Jolene, and she smiled back. Digging into her purse, she pulled out some cash, tucked it under her nearly full plate, and slid out of the booth. Together they returned to the blackjack tables, Brent dragging along behind.

Daniel chose one with a ten-dollar limit and set himself up behind the dealer, a dark-haired young man with thick eyebrows. Soon they were racking up the chips again, Jolene having caught the dealer's eye. He kept smiling at her, and she was smiling back, fully enjoying the attention. Daniel watched it play out with his own bemused expression, because through it all Brent was becoming less exuberant, his energy gradually waning until he finally excused himself and left the table. Daniel watched him head toward the restrooms, then turned his attention back to the cards.

In the nearly ten minutes that Brent was gone, not once did Jolene turn around to check on him. When he finally did reappear at the back of the room Daniel spotted him immediately, and for a few seconds took his eyes off the cards to watch. Jolene had amassed at least another thousand on only a two-hundred-dollar investment, and though the dealer was still smiling at her, it was obvious he was watching a little more closely. They'd have to leave before long. Daniel had already planned his next step, but now he watched Brent, observing the way he leaned on a nearby slot machine. It was the lean of someone fighting fatigue or too much alcohol or both, and it took him several moments before he started walking again. Daniel glanced at Jolene, her face radiant as she placed another bet. Then he shifted his gaze back to Brent. It seemed the happier Jolene was, the more fatigued the guy became.

"Just a few more," he told her quietly. Jolene cocked her head in acknowledgment, then slid a large stack of chips into the betting space.

"Feeling lucky?" the dealer asked, but Jolene didn't respond. Daniel eyed the cards and by the time Brent arrived at the table, Jolene had won the bet and was gathering the extra chips. She smiled wide, but as soon as Brent came near, the energy drained from her face, her eyes losing the sparkle they'd held under the blue and purple lights. When he touched her on the shoulder, she flinched and whirled around.

Recognizing him, she showed him her winnings, her face growing paler even as Daniel watched. Strange that he hadn't seen it this clearly before. The effect was so obvious. But then she'd rarely been more than a few feet away from the guy. She talked with him for a moment, and Daniel could tell by the look on Brent's face that he was trying a different tactic. He was tired, he said. Was she done playing? She looked at his downturned lips and sad eyes and nodded, then gathered her chips and took them to cash out. Brent hovered at her shoulder, close enough to whisper in her ear.

Daniel cast his gaze around the building. The next part of his plan would be tricky. He had to find a way to convince Jolene to go with him. Brent would tag along in the end. He'd have to, if what Daniel was beginning to believe was correct, but regardless, Daniel wanted to convince Jolene to go. With the guy working on her sympathies, he'd have to modify his plan.

The two returned from cashing out, Jolene tucking more bills into her purse. Daniel met them halfway. "Another fifteen hundred," Jolene told him. "Five hundred for each of us."

Daniel gave her a big hug. "You can keep mine. Get you started in California."

"No way. You're the reason we won so much. You probably should get more."

She started counting out bills.

Daniel placed his hand over hers. "I can't use it anyway."

She looked up. "Oh." Dropping her gaze, she stared at the money for a moment, then slipped the bills back into the pile and zipped her purse closed.

"Man, I'm beat," Brent said. "You guys ready to turn in?"

Daniel looked at him. "If you really want to, I guess we can." He dropped his tone of voice and shrugged his shoulders, then put on his most somber face.

"What?" Jolene said.

"It's just . . . I don't know how many days I've got left, you know? I'm picking up Tony tomorrow, and after that . . ." He cast his gaze over the casino. "I've already faded once. And well, I guess I haven't had this much fun in a really long time." He glanced at Jolene. "I don't want it to end."

She tilted her head in that sympathetic way she did, and even though her eyelids were drooping, she turned to Brent and said, "He's right. How often do we get to do something like this?"

Brent rubbed his Van Dyke as if he were thinking, then touched his fingers to his temple. "Just a bit of a headache—"

"I have aspirin." Jolene dug into her purse and pulled out a miniature bottle of the pain reliever.

Brent eyed Daniel from underneath his bangs, then took the bottle and dumped out two small white pills, popped them in his mouth, and swallowed. "Is there anything left to do?"

"Let's walk around." Daniel focused on Jolene. "I wanted to show you the pools, anyway. They're really cool. And this place is huge. You ought to at least check it out before we have to leave tomorrow."

Jolene stepped toward him, then looked over her shoulder at Brent. "You can go get us some rooms if you want. Get some rest."

Brent's gaze darted to Daniel. "No, I'm game. Lead on."

Daniel smiled, grabbed Jolene's hand, and pulled her toward the exit. "This way!"

They walked out of the gaming area and down the brightly lit hallway, Brent's gaze on the back of Daniel's neck, but he had Jolene's hand in his and for the first time in a long time, was determined to have things go his way.

He led them outside to check out the many fountains that lined the front of the building, stone sculptures of Greek figures inside and around them. Jolene ran up the stairs behind one and looked down on Brent and waved. He waved back weakly and then glanced out onto the street where the cars rolled by. The lights of the Peppermill lit up their faces in white and pink and blue, and at one point Daniel dipped his hand in the fountain and flicked water drops at Jolene until she grabbed a whole handful and splashed him back, dousing one side of his hair. He shook it out and then grabbed his own handful. She ran, laughing, down the sidewalk.

"Chicken!" he called after her, and she leaned over her knees, catching her breath, and then scooped out more from the last fountain in the row and came charging after him. Daniel ducked and managed to escape the spray. It landed on Brent's face instead, stopping him cold. He stood with his hands in his pockets as the water dripped down the sides of his cheeks. Jolene apologized and went to him, wiping the drops with her fingers and laughing at the same time. He formed his lips into a fake smile until she pressed her wet palm against his forehead.

"It might make your headache better," she said, and then took off running again.

Daniel ran after her, around the corner and down the side of the street until they reached the back of the building. Coming to another parking lot, Jolene slowed and rested her hands on her knees again, tiring quickly, it seemed. Daniel took advantage of the moment to grab her around the waist and spin her a few times before setting her down. She weighed no more than a feather. She squealed and laughed and when they finally stopped they stood staring at each other, breathless. Daniel wanted nothing more at that moment than to kiss her.

"You're wearing yourself out." Brent ambled up behind them, his hair pushed back and still damp from the spray. "Is this what you wanted to show us?" He gestured to the parking lot. "Have to say, I'm not impressed."

"Come on," Daniel said. "This way." He took Jolene's hand again and they jogged past the rows of cars and trucks. The air felt warm on their skin, the lights too bright to see any stars overhead. As the traffic noises dimmed behind them, they kept going, the building ebbing and flowing into the concrete with its curves and angles until they came to another corner and jogged left. A different parking lot stretched out to the right, this one a bit smaller than the last, and in front of them lay another group of buildings, a clear glass door ahead. "I think we have to go this way," Daniel said.

Jolene looked behind her. Brent was coming, but he was lagging. "He's getting a little irritated."

Daniel nearly spoke his first thought but bit his tongue. "Do you want to go back and check on him?"

Brent still had one hand in his pocket, the other easy at his side. Jolene seemed to fight an internal battle as she looked ahead and then behind, and finally up into Daniel's eyes. "Let's go!" she whispered, and dropping his hand, dashed toward the glass door.

"Hey!" Daniel ran after her, through the door and down the hallway, a mile-wide grin on his face. It was working. It was working! Little by little, he would break Brent's hold on her, and then the guy would have no choice but to melt away into whatever dimension he was from.

She stopped at a hallway intersection. "Which way?"

He pointed right and she smiled and then ran again. He ran after her, full out this time. Rounding the corner he saw her flying down the hallway, her boots light as she stayed on her toes, her blue sleeves rustling about her arms. He would catch her. He would kiss her before Brent showed up again. He would convince her that she didn't need him anymore.

CHAPTER SEVENTEEN

Daniel exited off the highway and rode into Butte, Montana, coasting easily down the hill on his Kawasaki. Most of what remained of the late winter snow had melted off, clean pavement showing through in a wide swath between the dark, wet shoulders. He shivered, his riding leathers lacking the insulation needed for the early spring weather. He should have known that Montana would be about 15 degrees colder than Reno this time of year.

He moved through the intersection and headed toward the old part of town, a familiar anxiety rising in his gut, his skin shrinking into his bones. Butte looked smaller to him now, more subdued and gray, lacking the bustle and bright lights of Reno. Only the thought of seeing Tony kept him on the road to the trailer house, as he'd arrived too late in the day to meet his brother at school. He would have preferred to have skipped the possibility of seeing Valerie altogether, but it was too late now. It was near dusk when he slowed to a stop and looked down at the hellhole. The trailer home looked humble, even poor. It still lacked any sort of lawn, surrounded in wet mud and traces of snow, the old junk cars permanent residents out back. Shame crept over his shoulders like a chill, and he nearly turned around to go find a hotel room when he spotted the Toyota pickup sitting in the narrow driveway.

The sun had already set, but there was enough light to see the truck was jacked up higher than usual, plenty of breathing room between the body and the wheels. Parked on the far side of the lot, the headlights pointed toward his and Tony's bedroom. Meanwhile, there was no sign of the old Pontiac. Daniel checked his watch. Six o'clock. Valerie's shift usually went until midnight. Even if she was home, it was unlikely she would have bought a new vehicle, and certainly not a little pickup. The Toyota had to belong to the boyfriend he'd heard about at Christmas.

He let gravity take him down the hill, going easy over the muddy road. When he leveled off again he downshifted and applied the brake, approaching the trailer home in stealth mode. Before he reached the driveway he stopped, parked the Kawasaki on a relatively dry spot of gravel, left his helmet on the seat, and walked the rest of the way. The Toyota gleamed as he passed it by, a black leather interior visible through the window.

Something made him tiptoe up the steps, careful to avoid making any noise. At the front door he paused, his ear bent near the hinges. Nothing. Surely everything was fine. He opened the screen door and checked the main doorknob. It was unlocked.

Inside, the same old smells assaulted his sinuses, cigarette smoke and the musty scent of dirty carpet, and something else . . . pizza. A half empty beer bottle rested on the kitchen counter, an open pizza box on the table with half a pizza still in it. Daniel looked around, slipping the door closed behind him. Tony's name hung on the edge of his tongue, but he didn't utter it. Instead, he crept into the living room, his gaze on the couch, sidestepping the old creaky board that lay just beside it. There was another beer bottle on the coffee table, this one drained. Next to it sat a can of root beer. Daniel stared at it. They rarely had soda in the house, yet the brown can sat there, brazen in its cool attractiveness, the top popped back, enticing. His gaze lifted to the bedroom door.

It was closed.

Sweat wetting his shirt, he sneaked down the hall, pausing every couple of steps to listen. As he got closer he heard something, a quiet voice. *No. Leave me alone.* Within a few more steps he was at the door, and in the next instant he pushed it open. What he saw he would spend the rest of his life trying to obliterate from his mind. When he did remember, it was a blur of light and color and skin and body parts, the man's hairy belly the most jarring, and after that, Tony's bare skin against it, both shirtless, Tony's worn leather belt in the man's hand. He remembered the monster's hair, what he had left of it, sticking straight up on the back of his head as he lifted it from the pillow, *Daniel's* pillow, for they were in the bottom bunk, the man's stocking feet hanging over the edge, holes in the heels showing darkened pads of skin. The forty-something-year-old wore a grin the likes Daniel had never seen before, something soft and tender about the thin lips and scruffy chin, brown eyes murky like low river water. He saw Daniel and it all changed, the brow dropping back, the smile fading. But it was Tony's face that lit the dynamite in Daniel's breast. The boy looked sick, the blood having fallen away from his skin, his arms limp at his sides as if he had lost all power to move them. A blob of tomato sauce stained his cheek, his lips chapped and separated, his blue eyes dull and sunken into his head. He turned when Daniel entered the room but that was all, the rest of his body unresponsive. The monster recovered quickly, pushing himself out of the bed to face Daniel, already babbling his excuses while Tony remained as if paralyzed, his feet bare on top of the blankets.

What Daniel did to the man remained a bloodstained memory, his vision shrouded in a red-rage fog for the entirety of the scene, which lasted maybe ten minutes, though it felt longer than that. The old baseball bat he'd always kept at the foot of the bed flew into his hands, and then he remembered only the blows, the first several to the head as he sought to smash the ugly face, break the sick grin off the lips and teeth, and once the blood began to spatter and the eye swelled shut, he moved to the bare torso, striking ribs and belly, the god awful sickening white skin of the belly with the black hairs marching down into the belt buckle, over and over again he hit that belly until the monster, clutching it in a wounded fist, scurried out the bedroom door on his hands and knees like a dog. Daniel pursued him, landing the blows on his bare back, his mind bent on breaking the vertebrae that poked through the skin, hammering each knobby bone down until it was no longer there.

Three times the man fell, his hands above his head pleading for it to stop, but Daniel didn't hear him, only saw that he was still moving, still talking, still living under all that repulsive skin, and he kicked and swung and hammered and struck until finally the man tumbled out the front door and down the stairs. He landed in the muddy dirt, bare skin a muted cream against the dark brown of the wet ground. In the glow of the sunset the blood stained rich, and the sight of it brought Daniel to a pause at the top of the steps. He watched with greedy eyes as the stains grew, spreading outward from the monster's body, until a heavy weariness overtook him, and he longed for the thing to be gone. He walked slowly down the steps, the bat aloft, but the monster saw him coming and found the strength to get up and crawl, what was likely a broken arm held close to his ribs as he managed on three limbs. Daniel pursued, his arms aching from the attack. He remembered opening the door of the Toyota and waiting, impatient for the man to get in and drive away. When the monster finally did pull himself up into the seat, his face a bloody, pulpy mess, Daniel leaned in and whispered to him. He wouldn't remember later exactly what he'd said, only that the thing refused to look at him in his hurry to start the engine. When the Toyota sprung to life with a nauseating roar, Daniel pushed the bat inside and rested it on the bruised cheek.

"You *ever*." The thing shook his head, babbling pleas, until Daniel shut the door.

Long after the headlights had disappeared over the top of the hill, he was still standing outside. Eventually the cold woke him. He shivered, pulled the leather jacket close, and walked back to the trailer house.

Tony stood in the doorway.

Daniel stopped and knelt in front of him. He looked into his eyes intending to say something, to make it clear no one was allowed, no matter who it was, even if it was a mother's boyfriend, that he should never allow anyone, that he should scream and run and do whatever he could to get away, to let someone know. The words ran on in his head as he looked into his brother's eyes, but the more he looked the angrier he got, the hollow space behind Tony's gaze something he'd never seen before, the paleness of the cheeks holding on like a bad infection. A new rage rose inside him, but this one was different. This one was directed at the one person he couldn't disassemble with a bat. "That wasn't your fault." He pointed down the road where the Toyota had gone. "You know that, right?"

Tony stared blankly.

The leftover pizza sat cold on the table. He picked up the box, the beer bottles, and the root beer can, and threw them all into the trash, then scoured the place for other traces of the stain their mother had brought. He found two cigarette butts he knew weren't Valerie's by their length, for she always smoked hers to the nub. Tony stood by the door watching him. When Daniel had finished his third round, his little brother pointed toward the television.

"The game," he said.

The monster had bought Tony a game, but they didn't have a system to play it on. It sat on the floor wrapped in plastic. He picked it up and stared at the Tyrannosaurus rex on the front. Into the trash. Then he scooped up the bag and hauled it out to the dumpster, heaving it over the edge and letting it fall into the abyss to be surrounded by rotting food and empty paint cans and old vomit. Once he'd rid the place of all traces of the white-skinned slime, he stood panting, his breath coming in clouds, and looked around.

Winter hadn't completely loosened its grip. In Reno it was long gone, but here, the season held on in the gray clouds and the sharp air and the white mantles on the mountains, the trailer homes still shrouded in hibernating silence, the sounds of living muted, as if the place had been evacuated and he was looking at the remains of a community long gone. As he allowed the chill to cool his fury, something shifted inside him. This could go on no longer. This *would* go on no longer.

He'd saved some money, and Tony had a helmet. He let his gaze drift back to Valerie's trailer, and saw his little brother standing there in the doorway. He had the screen door propped open, his body between it and the frame, bare feet hanging over the edge. Daniel stared at Tony's pale face. What a fool he was. Already, he was too late.

Daniel and Jolene wound their way through the hotel hallways until they came to another glass door. As luck would have it, it opened into the middle of the central pool area, just where Daniel had hoped to lead them, the sand-colored tiles a sharp contrast from the brightly colored carpets. Jolene stopped short and stared, the lights glowing a gentle yellow and white, the same streetlamps with the fuchsia-colored flowers they'd seen at the front of the casino lighting the pathway here as well, more of them on a second-level balcony that overlooked the pools. Arborvitae bushes and blooming flowers filled the knee-high stone beds that curved around the edges of the space, cardinal chaise lounges placed in groups of three and four near the water. The pools themselves were lit from within with a turquoise glow that gave the impression one had entered a tropical hideaway, from which Poseidon himself might emerge at any moment.

Daniel came up behind Jolene, quieting his steps to avoid disturbing the scene. It was having the effect he'd hoped it would, the same effect it had had on him the first time he saw it. Her gaze looked alive, cheeks flushed, as she took in the sight before her. Daniel had known she would like this area. It had always been his favorite, particularly at night. During the day, it was busy and noisy and bright, the sounds of children generating a playground sort of atmosphere, but at night it was magical, the butterscotch lights and turquoise glow lending it the aura of a faraway place, as if here one had entered a fantasy land or island resort somewhere deep in the Pacific.

He took Jolene's hand. She gave him a little smile and together they walked alongside the first pool. The water reflected the lights around it, the blue depths clear for the viewing of the curved flower-and-stem designs etched into the bottom surface. They kept close to the streetlamps and flowerbeds, finding a path between the pool's edge and the many lounge chairs set around it. Daniel looked ahead but could see no one else about.

Had they gotten lucky enough to have the place all to themselves?

He gripped Jolene's hand a little more tightly and tried to still the excitement rising up inside him, but it bubbled anyway, gathering in his throat, so he drew her hand up to his chest and held it there over his heart.

"You've come here before, haven't you?" she asked.

He nodded. "Usually after Jay and I spent some time at the tables, he'd find some girl he wanted to talk to, and I'd come here."

"Why didn't you find some girl?"

"They would always look at him first. He had . . . has a certain charm about him." The thought of his friend pained him, so he looked down at the top of Jolene's head. "Besides, I wasn't really looking for anyone."

"I can see why you liked it." She leaned close to him.

After a few more steps, he finally let her hand down again, giving her more movement. Ahead was the second, larger pool, the one with the sculpture he wanted her to see. He fought to keep his steps steady. His tendency was to pick up the pace to get there now and see what she thought of it, but he continued to stroll as if they had all the time in the world. As they passed the bushes on the left, he glanced back. Brent could catch up anytime.

"Come on, I have to show you something." Unable to hold back any longer, he stepped ahead, drawing her to the right. They were at the second pool's edge, but the sculpture was down at the other end. Already Daniel could see its outline, the angles cutting the night air above it, the lights casting the bronze in an even darker, richer shade. From here, it was hard to tell what it was if you didn't know, for all you could see were the sharp fins on the tail and the overall shape of something held high above the water.

They came near the second hot tub, and Daniel led Jolene to the inside of it, close to the perimeter of the rotunda where they'd be less easily spotted by Brent coming through the far door behind them. Daniel was going to do a grand flare to introduce the sculpture, but as they left the hot tub behind he realized Jolene had already spotted what he'd planned to point out.

"Whoa," she said.

His gaze roamed over the mermaid for the umpteenth time, admiring her beauty, the details of the fins so elaborate, not only on the tail but all along the lower body, the breasts small and pointed, the thick hair flying behind and above the head, making it clear she was swimming down into the ocean, her face smooth and young, the eyes deep-set and gazing at something in front of her as if she were going somewhere important. Her lips were soft and serious, arms slightly bent at the elbow. In each hand she held a small seahorse, heads pointed forward, her two friends on whatever journey she was on. Daniel got as close as he could and then stopped, watching the water splash on the large tree trunk underneath her, some of the drops rising high enough to wet her hands or the curled tail of one of the seahorses, a layer-cake fountain solid underneath the tree, the smaller layer spilling over into the larger one and then down into the pool, lit from within by the turquoise light.

Jolene stared into the mermaid's face, her arms also bent at the elbows, her hands open as if ready to receive something the sculpture might have to give her. Daniel moved to better see her expression, eager to find proof he'd just introduced her to something magical. He'd meant it as a reprieve from the heaviness she seemed to be carrying, but as her face came into view, he was surprised to find that it didn't reflect the happy wonder he'd expected. Instead, tears flowed down Jolene's cheeks, the skin on her neck flaring red. She bent forward, her belly drawn toward her spine, her shoulders moving into her chest. Daniel looked from her face to the sculpture and back again, puzzled.

The mermaid's gaze focused on something in the unseen depths, her arms forward to receive it. Jolene reached out her arms in return, her eyes filling and her mouth spreading open over her teeth. She wavered, her gaze so desperate on the sculpture she was losing her balance. Daniel grabbed her by the shoulders, but she shriveled like burned paper and fell at his feet. Hands pressed into her skull, she bent her head down until it nearly hit on the stone. Daniel got behind her and pulled her up. Her sobs became audible now, and she pounded her thighs with her fists, dropping forward again until Daniel repositioned his arms around her ribs and pulled her close.

"Jolene, Jolene stop!" His hands shook even as he held her, the stone biting into his knees and ankles. "It's okay. I'm here." He kept talking to her, but she seemed not to hear him, her body wracked with the efforts of her lungs. Daniel could feel her ribs under his fingers and realized with alarm just how skinny she really was, her body so light he could have carried her under one arm. He stood up then and pulled her away from the pool, her feet dragging behind her, her arms limp over his. He back-tracked to the flowerbed and sat down in front of it, bracing his spine against the stone behind him. She rocked forward again, her hands covering her face. "No no no," she said over and over again. Daniel looked around, wondering if he should take her somewhere.

He feared someone coming upon them now, someone who would find her this way and call security, which would only make things worse.

He was about to attempt carrying her away when she erupted in his arms.

"No!" She leapt to her feet and spun around to face him. "You will *not* comfort me! Not you."

He got up and moved toward her, but she shouted at him again.

"Stop it. Just stop it!"

"Stop what?" Daniel opened his hands. "What's wrong?"

She was still crying, tears flowing down her cheeks even while her skin boiled red with anger. "Why did you show up that day? That day of all days? Why did you come?"

Daniel stared at her, blinking.

"I can't take it anymore." Her look was angry, accusing.

"I don't know what you're talking about!"

"Why did you show up at the café?"

"I don't know. I was at the ocean with the whales, and then I was nearly run over by the train, across the street. I went to the café because it was the only place to go."

"Whales?" Her gaze floated to the ground. With one hand she clutched her other arm, and then looked from side to side. "Someone sent you." She shuffled closer to the pool's edge. "Someone sent you. Unless you knew, before . . ." She turned to look up at the mermaid and then walked toward the water.

She wasn't going to stop.

"Hey!" Daniel leaped forward but it was too late. She kept walking until there was no longer any stone under her feet, and she fell into the pool.

The original plan had involved a lecture on safety. Daniel had intended to explain the ins and outs of riding behind someone, the importance of balance and body position, how one rider needed to lean with the other to make sure the bike maintained the proper position through space.

They were going to take their first ride when the traffic was low and the visibility clear, some lazy afternoon when they could go about it with the proper approach.

But as Daniel stood by the dumpster where he'd thrown out the monster's stuff, the old pizza and the video game and the soda can and even the sheets and blankets that had been on the bunk bed, he ran through scenario after scenario, and none of them led to the right place. He could stay and tell his mother about what had happened, but that would embarrass Tony more and it wouldn't solve the problem. Valerie would be skeptical at first, but Tony was the favorite, and she'd be inclined to believe him. Then there would be apologies and tears but it wouldn't be enough to change anything. His brother would remain in the same danger the second Daniel returned to Reno. The monster might not return, but that was little consolation. Another could come along at any time, and then there was the trauma that should be dealt with, the type Valerie would try to shove under the rug, leaving Tony grappling with something he couldn't understand. Daniel could pack him away to a hotel for a few nights, but Valerie would worry and he'd have to let her know, and in the end he'd have to take him back to the trailer and that hot stuffy room with the bunk bed still up against the wall.

He retrieved the bloody bat and went inside to clean it off. Tony stood back, watching with dead eyes. As the water ran over the wood, Daniel thought he should have done more with it, should have finished the creep off. Someone like that didn't deserve to be alive. Most likely, he'd recover only to attack some other innocent kid. Worse, he could return, get back in Valerie's good graces. Daniel couldn't imagine that would be possible, but still, he didn't want to take the chance. His mother could weaken during one of her down periods. His only real option was to take Tony away that night. Whether they went back to his place, or he dropped him off at their Aunt Carrie's in Idaho.

It didn't matter.

What mattered was getting him up and out and on the road where Valerie couldn't find him. Would she call the police? Daniel had to believe she might, so he decided to leave her a note, make it sound like he'd taken his brother to spend a few weeks' quality time together, leave her a phone number to call. She wouldn't like it, but she wouldn't send the cops after him. That would give him time to figure out what to do next.

This plan felt right, completely doable and minimally destructive. He would tell Tony they were taking a little vacation. A spring break. They would go to Reno, and Daniel would show him around, get him out of Butte, let him see a little of the rest of the world. It was late, best to travel only across town that night and get a hotel. He couldn't stay with Gus. There would be too many questions. Valerie didn't need to know how far they'd gone, either, or when they'd left.

He applied some dish soap to the bat and washed the remaining traces of the monster's existence down the drain. When he finished, he turned to find the towel missing from the refrigerator door. Tony, standing behind him, handed it over. Daniel polished off the bat, inspected it, then took the towel to the laundry room. The bat he wasn't sure what to do with, especially considering they were leaving. He did a quick scan of the kitchen and living room, and then stashed it between the refrigerator and the cabinets, hidden but easily accessible, just in case Valerie needed it. Then he turned to look at his brother.

Tony stood in the middle of the kitchen with his hands at his sides, his eyelids heavy. He looked skinnier than Daniel remembered.

"You still got that helmet?"

Tony turned and walked through the living room, but when he got to the hallway that would lead to their bedroom, he stopped. Daniel mentally kicked himself. *Stupid stupid.* He put a clean towel on the refrigerator handle and hurried to Tony's side. "Tell me where you put it."

Tony stared at the bedroom door, his black hair too long in the front and covering his eyebrows. He was breathing more rapidly, his nostrils flaring. When he still didn't speak, Daniel went into the room. The bed was bare after he'd tossed the sheets, but there was still a putrid smell in the air. He crossed to the window and opened it wide, then turned on the air purifier. He considered tearing into the bunk bed and destroying the thing so he could take that out into the dumpster too. Instead he found Tony's backpack in the closet and filled it with extra shirts, underwear, socks, and jeans. All the while he scanned for the helmet but didn't find it. When the backpack was stuffed, he dropped down to check under the bed. No helmet. He toured the room, looking in and behind the dresser, behind the old desk where he used to do homework—now covered in Tony's makeshift ocean and sea creatures, the upgraded Dinotan, it seemed—and around the plastic storage bins behind the closet door. As he came back to the front of the room, he found Tony standing in the doorway. His brother pointed to the desk.

The ocean replica was more sophisticated than Dinotan had been, the base made of a wide piece of plywood that was nearly as long as the desk itself. On it, his brother had glued a thin layer of real dirt to represent the sand, whereas the water was a mix of paint and a frothy texture, the white-capped waves a material he didn't recognize. On top of the water Tony had placed a number of the toys Daniel had sent him, a couple of dolphins, several whales including the new killer whales, seagulls flying on toothpicks, jelly fish and a variety of other fish, all interspersed with tall pieces of seaweed, rocks, and coral. The effect was one of looking down into the ocean, the fish moving freely here and there in the currents. Tony had even placed a wrecked ship in the far corner with a human skull nearby.

"It's awesome," he said. "Even better than Dinotan. What do you call it?"

Tony only stared at the desk, his body turned toward it, blocking his view of the bed.

Daniel grabbed the backpack. "Take this." His brother obeyed, looping his fingers through the handle and then allowing the pack to settle on the floor beside him. "Put this on, and your shoes." He handed him a shirt. "Where is the helmet?" When Tony didn't answer he stopped to look at him again and found him pointing at the closet.

"I already looked there."

"In your orange shirt."

Daniel pawed at the clothes while Tony dressed, shuffling through old coats, pants, and then some of the clothes he'd left behind. Clear in the back, he found the orange shirt that Aunt Carrie had sent, the button-up one that was far too long and bunched up like a diaper when he tucked it in. It was tied at the bottom and bulging. He pulled it out, hung it on the door handle, and set to untying the ends.

The helmet fell out. It still looked new, the surface shiny and clean. He placed it on his brother's head, mentally crossing his fingers. The fit was better than when he'd given it to him, but still not ideal. There was too much space in the sides. He scowled, trying to fix it, adjusting the chinstrap below and near the ears, but no matter how he tightened it, it turned on Tony's crown, rotating near his temples.

"It's fine." Tony fiddled with the strap. "It will be fine." He glanced at the desk.

"We don't have room for that."

Tony stared at it a bit longer, then walked across the room, picked out one plastic animal from the makeshift ocean and stuffed it in his pants pocket. "My shoes."

Daniel spotted them by the foot of the bed. He scooped them up and swiped the backpack with his other hand. "Your coat," he said. "The leather one I gave you."

"In the closet."

Daniel got the coat, and then paused to look around. He was taken by a sudden feeling of nostalgia. So many memories they'd shared here. His gaze roamed to the window where they used to sit and stare up at the Big Dipper, trying to come up with a new name for it. Dinotan used to take up most of the floor, the Army men and reptile aliens co-existing in a perpetual war. He wondered where they all were now, if they were tucked into one of the plastic bins or resting under the clothes in a drawer. He found the leather jacket, and nearby, the blue and orange coat Tony had worn so many times when they'd escaped Valerie's wrath to wander down to Gus's house. Then he thought of Tony's money jar, the one he'd been using to save up for his guitar. He lifted the bunk bed and pulled it out, only to find it empty. Blood rushed to his head as he replaced the bed with a thump. Tony never would have spent that money. He kicked the wooden leg of the frame for good measure and strode out.

Toothbrush, toothpaste, a small black comb. He added these to the backpack, then checked his brother one more time, tightening the helmet as much as he could. It was too big, but they wouldn't go far. Not tonight. He looked down at Tony's red sneakers and wished he could replace them with something more substantial. "Ready?"

His brother nodded, his eyes nearly hidden by the hair the helmet pushed into them.

"Don't you want to know where?"

"Doesn't matter. We're going on the bike." Tony smiled a little then, and that's all Daniel needed. He rested his hand on his brother's shoulder and guided him out the door.

------·⊰⊱·—·—·⊰⊱·------

Jolene had dropped below the surface of the pool. Daniel tore off his shoes and jumped in after her. Within moments he found her, her eyes squeezed shut, her hands limp at her sides. Her hair flew above her like the mermaid's, her blouse billowing around her small body. When she started to float back up she used her arms to keep herself down, pushing upward with her palms to direct her body under. Daniel looped one arm around her waist and pushed to the surface. She fought him, trying to pull his arm away, and when that didn't work, thrashed more violently, but she was too light to create any real resistance. They broke through to the night air above.

Daniel inhaled sharply but Jolene resisted until she no longer could, then she too opened her mouth and breathed. Almost immediately she started arguing with him, telling him he needed to let her be, that it wasn't his place to interfere. He swam to the edge with her in tow. Keeping hold of one of her wrists, he lifted himself out and then pulled her up behind him. She struggled then too, trying to remain in the water, but soon he had her sitting on the stone tiles, and then he drew her back and away, setting her up where they had been before, against the nearest flowerbed wall.

When he finally let her go, she sat, defeated, her hair streaming water droplets down her face and onto her neck and chest. The blouse clung to her body like plastic wrap, her jeans dark and heavy. Daniel wrung out his own T-shirt and socks, then went back to retrieve his high-tops. When he'd done all he could to dry off, he remained in only his jeans. He sat down next to her and leaning his arms on his bent knees, waited.

She wasn't crying anymore. Her head down, legs bent, she'd curled in toward the wall, her cheek pressed against the stone. For several minutes they sat that way until finally Daniel turned and said, "Jolene, whatever it is. You have to tell me."

Small hands clung to Daniel's ribs, Tony's thin body pressed against his back. The sky over the city of Butte had darkened, much darker than Daniel had planned for their first ride. Plus it was cold, not the bright, warm sunny day he had always envisioned. "Ready?" he shouted.

"Yeah!" Tony hollered back over the din of the motorcycle engine.

"Hold on tight. Don't let go!"

"I got it."

"I mean it! You hold on tight, okay?"

"Okay!"

Daniel cast a glance up the hill and felt a moment's hesitation. He was pretty sure what he was about to do could be interpreted as kidnapping, but when he looked back at the trailer all he could see was the bedroom and the monster and no one around to do anything about it.

He squeezed the handlebars, cast another look up the hill, and gradually pulled the throttle. "Hang on!"

"Whoo-hoo!"

He turned the bike to the right at first. He wasn't going up that hill until Tony had a better feel for what they were doing. At the end of the gravel road lay a wide swath of bare ground where everyone turned their cars around. Over time, they'd worn, a safe place to make a gentle turn without having to lean too much, as long as one avoided the muddy grooves. Back and forth, he went from the trailer to the rounded circle until Tony shouted, "Aren't we going to go anywhere?"

After the fourth trip, Daniel came back about halfway and then stopped, pulled his helmet off and turned around. "Going up this hill, the bike is going to tip back. You need to cling to me like snot."

"Gross!"

"I mean it. You hold on tight." He grabbed Tony's hands at his middle and pressed down. "Gravity is going to pull on you, and you don't want to fall off the back. Got it?"

"I'm not stupid!"

"That's up for debate."

"At least I know which way we have to go. You're just going in circles."

Daniel put his helmet back on and eyed the hill. He'd take it as easy as he could, but he needed enough power to make it to the top. He exhaled, gripped the throttle, checked Tony's hold, and leaned forward.

His brother went with him, a warm presence against his back. Encouraged, Daniel eased into first gear, then second, a little more power, third, and then the pitch up. He drew his shoulders toward the handlebars, counteracting the backward pull, feeling Tony do the same, and within a few seconds, they reached the top. He coasted a ways and then stopped. "Okay?"

"Cool!" Tony grinned. Daniel could see his teeth even in the dark. "Can we do that again?"

Daniel turned and looked over the city. The lights were all on now, the sky black except for a bit of gray above the horizon. He would go to Jay's house. Jay's mom was great about allowing them to stay over without questions, and it would be good for Tony to be somewhere safe with a normal family. The Green Mile puttered evenly, awaiting his command.

Daniel glanced once more behind him, but the darkness had nearly obliterated the homes down in the hellhole, only a few of the porch lights on.

His mother's wasn't one of them.

"Are we going?"

"Downhill this time." Daniel pitched his flattened hand to demonstrate. "It's just the opposite. You need to lean back a little." He moved his body. "Got it?"

"Duh!"

Daniel grinned. How long had he imagined doing this, taking Tony for a ride? How long had he wanted to give him a taste of the freedom the bike gave him, show him how much more there was to this world? As he started down the hill, his heart felt light. His brother needed this.

He had to show him that he wasn't trapped and didn't have to do anything he didn't want to do. When they leveled out on the flat road, Tony's arms tight around him, Daniel felt a new sensation rise in his breast.

Finally, he was doing the right thing.

The Peppermill pools lay still around them, the air hanging quietly over the water as the lights cast their shimmering yellow streaks across the surface. Jolene had started crying again, quieter this time, her tears flowing gently down her cheeks.

Daniel took one of her hands in his. "I'm sorry. Whatever it is, let me help."

She shook her head, her eyes red and swollen. "You can't." She spoke in a whisper, the deep wrinkles returning to her brow. "It's why you can't remember."

"But I did remember. I remembered what happened. That it was me. That I . . ." He still couldn't say it. *Committed suicide? Took my own life?* "That I left the way I did."

She withdrew her hand from his. "You don't remember why."

He didn't know what to say to that. It was true, he didn't remember. He'd been riding for the Diamond Xtreme, something that had been his dream for years. He'd broken away from a destructive home. He'd shared an apartment with his best friend. It seemed like a good life, and part of him wanted to return and let it all be as it was. But when he thought about it, a familiar black hole opened inside him, and he closed his mind until it covered over again. "It doesn't matter now," he said.

"It's why you're here instead of up there." She pointed absently to the sky. "It's why you came to find me."

"But I didn't—"

She raised a palm. "You did. I'm sure of it now. It's the only explanation for . . . everything." She exhaled heavily and sat up straighter, wiping more wetness off her cheeks. Running her hands through her hair, she slicked it back, pulling water that ran down her neck, then looked up at the sculpture. The same pain flashed across her features, but gradually her face softened and when she returned her gaze to his, she looked resigned.

"I'm sorry, Daniel. That's one thing I never got to tell you." She looked down at her hands. "Not that it means much now, but . . . I'm sorry. I'm going to fix this, and then you can let go." Her eyes glistened as she looked into his, and he grabbed her hand, sensing something breaking in the space between them. She leaned in and kissed him, lightly brushing her lips against his and then pressing deeply into him, her arms around his shoulders, clinging.

He reached his hand behind her head, but then she broke away and stood up, steadying herself by holding onto the wall behind her. "I think I'm ready now."

* * *

It was an easy ride through old town Butte, the streets quieter than they were in the daytime, though the occasional vehicle still shined its headlights their way. Making his escape with Tony behind him, Daniel could see the beauty in the town, the simple nature of it, the way life here proceeded without the rush of the city, a slower and more relaxed pace to the days and nights. Yet he couldn't deny the deliciousness of the freedom at their fingertips, a chilly spring breeze feathering their faces, the road beckoning them on.

His arms ached as he gripped the handlebars, sore from his attack on the the monster, his rage over what had happened still simmering in his chest, his thoughts focused on how he might be able to get Tony the help he needed once they arrived in Reno. That may have been why he didn't notice the Toyota 4Runner approaching from the side street on the right. Dark and eyeless, it appeared more like a dead vehicle parked instead of a live one moving. Daniel had the green light. He watched it for nearly a block as he approached, wondering if it would change, shifting down in case it did, but it stayed green. They had the right of way.

As he drew closer, he pulled the throttle again, easing them back into a comfortable speed, and then something from the right came on fast and dark, the engine deceivingly quiet. Over there, the light was red, but the dark demon rolled on anyway, even though it was late and a vehicle shouldn't be on the road without working headlights at that hour.

Closing in on them, it made its stealth approach until Daniel discovered too late that it was coming and it wasn't going to stop, that it would keep advancing at a speed that made it impossible to avoid, driving straight into the green motorcycle that had the legal right of way.

He felt the shadow upon him before he saw it, and then the boxy shape appeared. He swerved in a last-minute attempt to avoid the collision, but the Toyota slammed hard into the front tire and then hit his right shoulder and knee. The bike scraped the doors, the rear tire skidding out from underneath him. He was still trying to maneuver when he felt two small hands leave his waist as easily as if the wind had lifted them away, the warmth at his back suddenly cold. His body rebounded and fell with the bike to the pavement.

Jolene's pale face stood out stark against the night sky. Daniel looked up at her from his seated position on the stones, frightened at the expression she wore, because it made it clear she had walled herself off from him and he had no way to break through.

"Looks like you two fell in."

They both turned to see Brent approaching, hands still in his pockets as if it had been his intention all along to take his time and arrive right at that moment. He came from behind them, perhaps having witnessed some of what had gone on in the pool. Daniel jumped to his feet and stood beside Jolene. The water clung to his soles, the air taking on a new charge around them.

"Not the best outfits for a swim." Brent's gaze lingered hungrily on Jolene's breasts until she crossed her arms over them, then rose to her face, where he seemed to admire the defeat he now saw etched around her eyes, his own expression growing eager as he studied her.

"I think we've all played nice long enough," Daniel said. "Why don't you tell us who you really are?"

Brent walked around to Daniel's left, forcing him to turn to maintain eye contact. Jolene stayed with Daniel, hovering slightly behind him, one hand in the crook of his arm. Her movements emboldened him, and he stood a little taller. Perhaps she was finally starting to see past Brent's cool façade. Brent stopped with his back to the mermaid, her body towering over his head as the water splashed down underneath her.

The image was unnerving, the way he'd positioned himself so they couldn't look at him without looking at her too, as if the two of them went together. The effect wasn't lost on Jolene.

Daniel glanced at her and saw her taking it in, the one and then the other.

"Took me a while to find you," Brent said. "One might have thought you were trying to ditch me on purpose."

"Surprised you caught on," Daniel said.

Brent's eyes flashed, but he kept the pleasant look on his face. Hands still in his pockets, he turned and examined the mermaid. "Beautiful, isn't she?" He caught Jolene's eye. "The way she's hanging like that, captured in the very moment when she's diving toward whatever's waiting for her in the depths."

"She's seen it." Daniel placed his arm around Jolene's shoulders. "She doesn't need a class on it."

"But you were the one who brought her here. I've been trying to get her mind off this sort of thing, this diving into the depths to disappear idea, but you marched her right down here as if you hoped to remind her. You'll be leaving soon, after all, and you don't want to go alone, do you?"

Daniel glanced at the mermaid. *Diving into the depths to disappear.* It's what Jolene had tried to do after seeing it, why she had jumped into the pool.

He remembered the slim scars on her wrist. "Why don't you tell us why you're really here?" he asked Brent.

"To protect her. She knows that."

Jolene stared at Brent, her shoulders hunched, hair dripping water by her ear.

"Don't worry, biker girl. I'm not going to break your confidence, but I did figure it out. Daniel and I took a brief trip down memory lane back in Cheyenne. It flipped open a few files, you might say."

He tapped his temple.

"Come on." Daniel tried to steer Jolene away. "We don't have to listen to this." But she was rooted to the stones.

"There's no reason to ruin this nice little reunion," Brent said to Jolene. "As long as you come back with me, everything will be fine. Just as it was before."

Jolene shook her head, but she still wouldn't go with Daniel. He tried moving her more forcefully, but she slid out from under his hold and took a step toward Brent.

"That's it." Brent smiled at her. "It's been a long night. We should get a room and get some rest. Everything will look better in the morning."

Jolene took another step toward him.

"Don't listen to him!" Daniel stepped between them, facing her. "He's not your friend. He's not even . . . I don't know what he is, but he's been manipulating you. We need to go. Come on." He took her hand and pulled but she resisted, her gaze on Brent.

"You made fun of me when I said I could see ghosts," she said.

The question seemed to catch Brent off guard. "It just causes you pain. No sense in focusing on it."

"Jolene," Daniel said, but she ignored him, walking on until she stood directly in front of Brent. With her right hand she took hold of his wrist and pressed her finger down on the pulse point.

Brent chuckled nervously. "What are you doing?" He stepped back, but she kept hold of his wrist, and after about a minute, let it drop. Daniel couldn't see her face any longer, but she seemed to stand taller as she continued to study the man in front of her.

"All this time . . ." She dropped her gaze to the ground and raised one hand to her mouth. "All the signs . . . It never occurred to me. They told me about you, but I thought you'd look different."

"Who told you about me?"

The water flowed steadily off the mermaid's perch, the splashing a constant sound in the background. "And people can *see* you."

"Of course they can see me." Brent opened his hands at his sides. "Can we go now?"

Jolene stood silent, watching him, then turned back to Daniel, her features softening as she gazed on his face. "Did you bring him here?" she asked Brent.

"What? You're the one who wanted him to come with us. If you hadn't decided to bleed for him back in Iowa, you wouldn't be feeling this way now."

The sculpture rose high over Jolene's head, the yellow lights beaming a halo around her wet hair.

She looked at Daniel and then Brent, not as if she were trying to choose, but as if she were finally putting together the pieces of a complex puzzle. "It's because of him that you remembered?" she asked Daniel.

He narrowed his eyes. He hadn't told her that. "He took my hand and I felt it, my last jump, rising into the air, the explosion and then the fire." He grimaced and clamped his teeth together.

"You restored this memory?" Jolene asked Brent.

Daniel watched Brent struggle for the right words. "I was there when he needed someone," he said.

Jolene focused on him, her gaze intense. "Were you there when it happened?"

Brent returned her gaze, the air seeming to crackle between them. "He'd been tortured for more than a year over ... you know what." He gestured toward her. "He was a total wreck. He'd even started drinking, and you know how much he abhors that."

Jolene shifted her gaze to Daniel. "Did you see him? Before?"

Daniel shook his head. "I heard him. His voice in my head. I didn't remember that until he showed me."

"Saying what? What was he saying?"

"You can't believe—" Brent began.

"It will be all over now," Daniel said. "Be at peace. You're doing the right thing. It's okay now. Peace is coming."

Jolene turned an angry gaze on Brent. "You lured him to his death."

"I didn't lure him anywhere!" Brent scoffed at the absurdity of the suggestion. "He was already there. I just helped him relax about it."

Jolene stepped back, staring at him.

"Don't look at me like that. I'm the one who saved you. I stopped you."

"All those people." She tented her fingers over her mouth. "The girl at the Perkins. The boy at the café. And William, at the library. It wasn't *his* fault." She pointed at Daniel. "You were whispering to them. All of them. Just like those three girls."

"What three girls?" Brent searched Jolene's face. "He brought those people around! Him and his suicidal energy! I had nothing to do with them."

"I'm such an idiot. I should have known." She ran her hand over her wet hair. "But I know what you are now." She glanced back at Daniel, then squared her shoulders and faced Brent straight on. "You're a Walking Sam, aren't you? The one who whispers despair into their ears."

Daniel thought back to their conversation in the Wyoming hotel. *He's a demon that lures those in despair to come over to the other side.*

"They told me about you, but I never thought you'd come to me. I guess I should have. I mean, it makes sense, right?" She wiped her face with the back of her hand and turned away from him.

Brent watched her, his posture stiffening, tendons standing out on his neck.

"So what was the plan for me? You just wanted to draw it out?"

"He's feeding off you, like a parasite." Daniel stepped closer. "Wells said so. It's how he manages to operate in the world. Otherwise, he'd be like me. Invisible. Isn't that right?"

Brent didn't answer.

"How much weight have you lost since you've known him?" Daniel asked.

Jolene touched her belly and then looked down at her thin body.

"He would drain you dry if you let him." Daniel looked on her face, hopeful. She'd figured it out. She had figured it all out, and now she was free to go with him.

"No." Brent shook his head. "She's not going with you."

Daniel looked at him, startled.

"You think this is perfect, don't you?" Brent turned an angry gaze on him. "She realizes who I am and goes off into the sunset with you. The two of you to San Francisco and then who knows? Whatever future exists for a fucking fading ghost!" He spat the words, taking a more aggressive stance now, bracing against them both. "Well, that's not happening, Danny." He glanced at Jolene and winked. "I think maybe it's time I changed my mind about our little secret, Biker Girl."

Fire erupted in Jolene's eyes.

She took a step toward him.

"No, no, don't try to stop me. It's clear that things have changed between us. Too much truth if you ask me. I prefer a little ignorant bliss, but no matter. It's out there now." He seemed to be hissing his "s" sounds, his posture stiff as he walked back and forth in front of the pool. "I think Danny here deserves to know the *whole* truth, not just the little pieces you want him to know. And it's obvious you don't have the courage to tell him, for if you did, what then? Clearly this little plan you two have to run off together wouldn't be quite so adorable." He *tsk-tsked* and looked from one to the other.

Daniel swore he saw a pointed tooth emerging from under Brent's upper lip, his dark eyes wider in their sockets.

"So where shall we start?" Brent continued. "That dark night in Butte, Montana, I think, when two boys were out for a motorcycle ride."

Jolene emitted a sound like a growl and rushed him, slamming into his body in an effort to knock him off his feet, but she was no match for him. He took a couple of steps back and then turned. She lost her hold and fell down hard.

Brent laughed. "Oh my, if I'd known this is what would happen, I might have decided to reveal everything much sooner!" His lips parted in a wide smile. This time, Daniel was certain he saw pointed teeth. There were new wrinkles on his forehead, too, and at the sides of his mouth. "Don't you want to know the secret?" Brent walked toward him. "The reason why you came back for her? All the pieces have come together now." He brought his hands in front of his face, his newly angled features taking on a melodramatic expression. "She was mourning a horrible tragedy. And how delicious, her despair. It's the reason I've lasted so long this time around. She has so *much* of it!"

Daniel retreated, his gaze never leaving Brent's face.

"Ooozing out of every attractive pore, and such a steady supply. I've never been so full in all my life, or had so much fun living among you humans." He opened long hands and grinned over pointed teeth, even as his skin seemed to turn a sickly shade of gray. "Your part in that was a mystery to me, but then I had a look inside that spirit of yours." He pointed at Daniel's forehead and then placed one finger on his tongue, reminding Daniel of when he'd tasted his blood.

Daniel glanced behind him. He was nearing the pool.

Another few steps and he'd fall into it. He looked around, seeking an alternative escape, for the creature coming at him was no longer human. Jolene's word—demon—described it best, something he would never have believed existed before that moment. And yet the voice—the voice was so familiar, soft and soothing and alluring even, the same voice that had comforted him before, sent him to a place where the only real answer was to walk away from it all.

"Now." Brent paused and stroked his chin. "Where to begin the story? You remember how you and little brother were riding away on the bike that night, when you vowed to rescue him from that horrible little trailer house?"

"Stop it!" Jolene screamed. The demon fell forward, having been hit in the back, but quickly recovered his footing. He whirled, and Jolene came at him again, running full speed with her head down and her fists clenched. She looked like she might ram into him until he reached out and placed a gnarled hand on her head. The touch arrested her advance and she stopped, still stooped over, a glowing light emanating from where his gray flesh touched her red hair. She cried out in pain and flailed her fists, but he stood just out of her reach, his arm longer now, allowing him to hold her there while he watched her squirm, a pleased smile on his wrinkled face.

Daniel watched them wrangle, his body held hostage as his mind shifted between the past and the present, He saw again the monster in Tony's bed, felt the reverberation in the bat as he laid down the blows. They had left that night on The Green Mile. He envisioned himself driving through the old town of Butte, the familiar blackness seeping into his gut as he saw the green traffic light approaching and, from the right, the dark shadow. *Stop,* he thought, but the bike kept going and the shadow came on and then right in the center of the intersection the two collided. Daniel buckled at the waist as he remembered the impact, the pain gripping his shoulder even as he watched the driver's side window break and rain glass all over the pavement. The Toyota had continued on its forward trajectory, but the bike rebounded off its side. It was then that the small hands left his ribs, and the warmth at his back disappeared.

"Daniel!"

Jolene's scream jerked him out of his reverie. She was writhing in the demon's hold, the glow of firelight having swept down around her shoulders, neck, and chest, pulsing like a living thing, delivering what could only be construed as searing pain. Watching her and then Brent's gleeful expression, Daniel felt a wave of rage roll over his body. Setting his jaw, he stormed toward the demon, running full out, his own hands poised to fold around the thing's scrawny neck. He had just about reached him when he felt a powerful force slam against his body, as if he had run straight into a brick wall.

What happened next, Daniel would never be able to fully describe or understand. Reeling, he stumbled back. The fiery glow disappeared, and Jolene fell onto the stones. Daniel called to her, but then the demon grabbed him by the arm. As they came face-to-face Daniel saw what Brent had become, or apparently what Brent had always been, and he shrank back in horror.

The demon was old, heavy wrinkles on his skin, his ears too long in the lobes, his hair practically non-existent. His teeth were yellowed, lips thin and gray. The head sat atop a neck too thin to hold it, the arms longer than a person's arms ought to be.

"Leave her alone," Daniel managed to say. The demon only laughed and placed an old hand on Daniel's chest, just over his heart, the other on his right shoulder. The face may have changed, but the dark eyes were the same, and now they looked into Daniel's with all the hatred one could muster in a pair of eyes. The hand pushed harder into Daniel's chest and his body lit up in pain, every nerve on fire as he felt himself lifted off the ground, the pool and the stone tiles receding as he was propelled up and back against the wall of the building behind them.

His body hit the stones with a dull thud, the force taking his breath away as he fell. His vision blurred, but he could see the demon coming toward him. He tried to get up, but his legs refused to work and then the thing was on him again, both hands on his chest holding him down, the eyes black as oil and the face locked in an angry grimace bent on destruction. Daniel couldn't breathe, the hot pain making it difficult to move, but he tried again and again, kicking out with legs that finally worked and catching the demon a time or two on the thighs, but it hardly seemed to notice. Instead, its grip grew stronger as it brought its face closer to Daniel's until their noses were almost touching, "It was her, you imbecile," the demon hissed. "It was her fault!" Daniel felt his breath leaving him, his vision swirling in a spiral of colors. "She took him away from you. She ruined it all, and yet you chase after her like some lovelorn puppy. I told you. She is *mine*. She will be mine, and you will leave her now to the fate she deserves."

Daniel wriggled, trying desperately to move and failing, his strength leaving him, draining as if sucked away by a vacuum. He registered the demon's words, and the vision of the Toyota appeared in his mind, the exhaust swirling out of the tailpipe as it sat just beyond the intersection, the Iowa license plate glowing under the red traffic light. His vision near gone, he reached a desperate hand to his pocket and wriggled his fingers inside, aching for the feel of the plane once more against his skin, the undeniable reality of its hard edges and points the only thing he could cling to. With the other hand he tried to reach the demon's neck and get his grip around it, but the limb moved only halfway up the body to the prominent ribs. He punched from there, but his blows landed softly and the demon smiled and pushed harder against Daniel's chest. Daniel sucked in one more difficult breath and finally felt the toy in his palm. Gripping it tightly, he pulled his hand out of his pocket and slammed it against the demon's throat.

"My brother is alive," he managed to say, "and I'm going to pick him up!" With all the strength he had left in his body, he pushed the plane hard into the wrinkled skin. Through blurry eyes he saw the demon's expression change to one of surprise. The pain lessened and Daniel felt a slight relief. Confused but encouraged, he pushed harder while moving his other hand up to support the first. Suddenly the pressure on his chest released. The demon tried to break his hold, the gray flesh throbbing yellow where the plane had embedded its wing. Emboldened, Daniel forced it as deeply as he could. The creature that once was Brent lifted a startled gaze to Daniel's face, the dark eyes seared in pain.

Locked in the embrace, Daniel pursued, gradually getting on his feet as the demon yielded ground, first a little and then more as Daniel moved with it toward the pool, pushing it in front of him, the pain nearly gone now and only the rage left, back back back, the demon growing weaker by the step. Daniel glanced away only once to gauge the distance to the water. Sparse eyebrows rose in response, and then the thing turned its gaze to where Jolene lay on the stones.

"Remember," the demon whispered, his mouth moving as if in slow motion. "Then leave her to me." In a thick cloud of smoke it vanished, leaving Daniel with nothing to push against. He stumbled forward and fell headlong into the pool, the plane still clutched in his fist.

"Son. Are you all right? Can you hear me?" A man looked down over dark-rimmed glasses, hooded eyes searching Daniel's face. "Can you tell me what happened?"

Hipbone married to the pavement, Daniel lifted his head. The single traffic light hung quietly on the pole, illuminated red. Above that, the night remained dark and quiet. He looked for the vehicle that had been there before, but it was gone. The man staring at him wore a long-sleeved shirt with a badge. A policeman. Daniel sat up slowly, his ribs and shoulder erupting in pain. Nearby, the Kawasaki lay on its side, wheels up, broken glass surrounding it. A shame. He'd had a few tumbles in the practice area, but that was soft dirt, much more forgiving than the hard pavement with its biting teeth. Had it ruined the paint, dug marks into the Kawasaki label? He kept looking at it, as if by staring he might develop the ability to see the underside. His eyes watered. A cave opened up in his belly. Something else was wrong.

"The Toyota," he said. "You've got to go after them."

"Who hit you?"

"We had the green light. They rammed me from the side. A silver SUV." Daniel tried to lift himself up and felt a sharp pain in his side. He grimaced and the officer guided him back down.

"Stay still, now. The medical team is on its way. Did you catch the license plate number?"

Daniel shook his head. "The headlights were off, or broken. I didn't see it until it was there."

"But you know it was a Toyota?"

He'd recognized the body style, the grill, the shape of the windows. He'd worked on enough of them in the shop. When the officer scratched more notes on his pad, Daniel added, "Aren't you going to go after them?"

"Do you remember the color?"

"I told you. Silver. Or gray. A dull gray." He waved his hand in frustration. "If you go now, you could track them down."

The man paused his writing. "We're taking care of you boys, first."

Boys. Daniel frowned, then looked left and right. He saw nothing but pavement and sparkling glass. He'd been riding The Green Mile. Heading home, or heading back? He couldn't remember. He turned a bit more to his right, twisting to look behind him as much as he could without experiencing the sharp pain. Shifting his gaze he saw a still form lying near the curb, shadowed in darkness until the streetlight changed to yellow and for a moment held the figure in a soft golden glow. It was wearing red shoes. *Tony.*

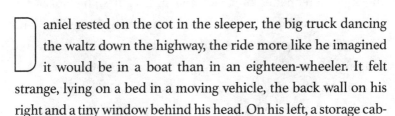

CHAPTER EIGHTEEN

Daniel rested on the cot in the sleeper, the big truck dancing the waltz down the highway, the ride more like he imagined it would be in a boat than in an eighteen-wheeler. It felt strange, lying on a bed in a moving vehicle, the back wall on his right and a tiny window behind his head. On his left, a storage cabinet and miniature refrigerator stood between him and the driver, a welcome separation even though he knew he was invisible.

He closed his eyes against the nausea threatening his stomach and once again, went over the events from the night before. He'd emerged from the mermaid's pool cold and dripping wet, the plane still clutched in his fist, and searched for Jolene all over the casino, but when he'd checked the parking lot, he'd found the white truck gone. Brent hadn't returned, he was sure. Not after everything, and not without Jolene to supply his energy. No, Jolene had taken the truck. She was already on the road. And she'd left him behind.

A well-dressed couple walked by, laughing. He thought of sneaking a ride with them, but there was no way to tell which direction they'd be headed. He watched a few more cars leave the parking lot, one after the other backing out while his time ticked away. Growing desperate, he thought he may have to steal one but then remembered the big trucks he'd seen parked behind the building. After a bit of eavesdropping, he stole onto the first one he found with a driver who was headed for San Francisco. When the semi pulled onto the highway, Daniel took the bed in the back.

Unsuccessful at preventing the nausea, he got up, crouched low, and moved to where he could see the dashboard. It was nearly nine in the morning, it read, Friday, August 29th. Tony would be waiting for him at three o'clock. Might be waiting for him. Thinking about it reopened the black hole in his gut, so he looked out the front windshield over the long stretch of highway. The land was unfamiliar, green trees and dry hills and a wide expanse of blue sky. He watched for road signs, eager to discover where they were and how far they had to go. He could see his brother waiting for him at the pier, the sea breeze blowing his hair back from his face, but then he remembered the dark shape resting against the curb, the red shoes faded orange in the glow of the yellow light.

The semi danced along, the driver a middle-aged man with graying hair and a plaid long-sleeved shirt. Country music played over the speakers. Daniel rolled the plane over his palm and then held it up in front of him. When playing with it, he could see

Tony's face as clearly as if his brother were with him, his fleshy young toddler features and then his more refined little boy cheeks and later his maturing jawline, each time with the plane going from one to the other and back.

In his other pocket was the phone he'd lifted from the well-dressed man in the Reno parking lot. The screen read nine-twelve. The battery was low, maybe enough for one more call. Jolene didn't have a cell phone, so he tried Jay's number for old time's sake. There was no answer.

Another country song came on, a woman singing about a burning house. He looked down at the phone. It was a good time. Odds were she would be home. He argued back and forth with himself. Did it really matter, especially now? But he had the phone and he had the time and it was likely he never would again. He backed up, sat on the edge of the bunk, punched up the numbers and pressed the phone to his ear.

She answered after the third ring. "Yeah?"

It took him a moment to remember to speak. "It's me. Daniel."

Silence.

"Don't hang up. I know it sounds weird but it's really me. I just wanted to talk to you for a minute, before . . . well, this will probably be my last chance." He heard rustling. Had she been sleeping? It was going on nine-thirty, about the time she usually had breakfast. He pictured the kitchen, the heaves in the linoleum over which he and Tony used to jump the toy plane. "Valerie, can you hear—"

"You son of a bitch," his mother said. "I don't know what kind of game you think—"

"Not a game." At least she was talking to him this time. That was something.

He leaned forward, feeling a powerful urge to keep her from hanging up. "I'm not trying to freak you out. It's me. I'm back, sort of. For a little while."

"People don't come back from the dead."

The word dropped in his ear. *Dead.* "I did." More rustling, and then the sound of a dish on the counter, a coffee cup maybe. "Look, I'm on my way to the coast. San Francisco." Water running from the sink. "I've got to go pick up . . ." He paused. "I don't think I have much time left."

"Which knee did you hurt when you got into that fight?"

Daniel paused. *Knee?* "You mean at the party?"

"When John beat the pulp out of you."

She was testing him. "The left one."

The beep of the microwave went off. "Your favorite place to go camping with Gus."

"Twin Lakes." The name brought back more painful memories, and Daniel wished more than anything his old friend was still alive, that it might have been him he called with the last of his battery power.

Valerie rattled plastic and paper, a cigarette box. "Where'd you keep the baseball bat?"

"In the corner of my room, until . . ." Daniel hesitated, images of the monster's face flashing in front of his eyes. "I put it in the kitchen later, by the refrigerator."

She exhaled. He could almost smell the smoke. "What was your father's name?"

"I don't know. You never told me." Silence. "You said he—"

"I gotta go to work soon."

He shifted on the cot and pressed the phone to his other ear. "You work at night."

"You telling me you didn't die in that explosion?"

"Were you there?" A cruel question, maybe. "Did you come?"

A ragged inhale followed by a cough. "They made me identify you . . . him. Imagine putting a mother through that, his face all burned up."

Daniel touched his face.

"He did that on purpose. I couldn't believe it. I told him to stay away from those things and then he goes and does that." She choked on her last words. Ran some water. Gulped it down.

"I was in a bad place."

"I'm playing violins." Exhale, another raspy cough. She was coughing more than usual.

The semi rocked back and forth. Daniel shut his eyes.

"We buried you. Him."

"We?"

"The whole town. As if they gave a damn."

Daniel tried to imagine it, the townspeople gathered in the cemetery. Or was it in Gus' church? "Who?"

"How was I supposed to know? People from work. Mike. Your friend's parents, and he came too."

Jay.

"All gathered around like you belonged to them." *You.* "He didn't belong to them."

"Not like you wanted to claim me."

"I raised you! Broke my back working for both you boys, and what do I get? I get to bury you both, that's what. That's the way this shitty world works. I get to bury both of my sons and then I'm just supposed to go on working, for what the hell I don't know."

The black hole spread like an oil spill over Daniel's gut, seeping into his ribs and underneath his heart with a sickening,

nauseating flow. *I get to bury you both . . . I get to bury both my sons.*
Tony had never gotten up from that dark curb at the edge of the
intersection. When his small hands had lifted away from Daniel's
ribs they'd never returned. It was too much to hope that the flight
through the air and down to the hard pavement would have been
survivable for a 10-year-old boy with a loose helmet on his head.
Daniel pressed his fingers between his brows, his eyes burning.

A raspy cough on the other end of the line. "What do you
want?"

Daniel clutched the plane in his fist. "I was supposed to pick
him up."

"Who?"

The name would trigger more pain and despite everything,
he didn't wish to do that. But he had to know. "Remember the
summer camp Tony used to talk about?"

"You want to reminisce now?"

"The one in San Francisco. Where they learn about the marine animals. Work with seals. He was saving money for it."

She was silent for a long time. "He wanted to see the whales
was what he wanted to do. I didn't get that San Francisco was the
place for that. Alaska or Hawaii maybe. But he was set on that
museum. Saw something on the computer about it."

"I'm supposed to pick him up." His head throbbed, the blood
pressing against his sinuses. "At the museum."

He steeled himself for the click in his ear, but finally she said,
"Today?"

Daniel stared at the cushioned ceiling above him. It looked
like a giant gray quilt with square-shaped stitching and but-
ton-like centerpieces. Out the front windshield, only a long
stretch of highway. "You think he'll be there?"

She took a drink of something. Coffee. Or water. The earpiece amplified the sounds of her swallowing.

"It's been in my head this whole time. I have to pick him up today at three o'clock."

She took another drag. "You know what this is about." It was her mother tone, the one she'd rarely used but when she had, it had made them both pay attention. "You want him to forgive you." The semi driver moved the big truck into the passing lane to get around another semi. "It's why you called me, too," she said.

Daniel longed for water. Inside the miniature refrigerator he found a six-pack of Coke. He pulled out a bottle, opened it, and took a long swallow. The bubbles sizzled in his throat. "You won't," he said.

"Hell no. You took him away and then you left, too. I'm here with nothing because of you."

Another swig of Coke. "I gotta go. The battery's going to die."

She didn't hang up. For a time it was quiet with only the sound of her labored breathing. "I'm afraid you won't be going to the good place."

"To hell, then?" He almost dared her to say it. Could a mother really tell her son that?

"God forgives, they say," she said finally.

"I'm going." He wiped his cheek with the back of his hand.

"Wait." Another raspy cough. "If you do see him."

"I know. You love him."

Daniel eyed the pillow on the bed beside him. The semi was still headed the right way, and there was nothing more he could do. "Goodbye, Mom."

"Danny—"

But his finger was already on the "end" button.

CHAPTER NINETEEN

hen the truck driver finally reached his destination, the clouds had dimmed the sun's rays and there was a gray pallor about the air. Daniel waited until he was alone inside the vehicle, then peeked out the windows. His gaze passed over a row of gas pumps nearby, snippets of his conversation with Valerie replaying in his mind. All this time, he'd been on a fool's errand. Tony was gone. His brother had died before he'd ever gotten on a plane, before he'd ever seen a whale. Sitting inside the truck that smelled like diesel fuel and nacho chips, Daniel felt gravity rooting his body to the floor and longed for it to push down even more heavily, to flatten him and cover him like a blanket, for now there was truly nowhere left to go. After a time, during which the driver didn't return, he reached into his pocket and pulled out the plane. There it was, solid in his hand, the little pilot still intent on his mission, his gaze directed straight out the front of the plastic window. Daniel sat looking at it for several minutes, remembering when he'd first found it on the beach, sensing again the smell of the ocean on the air, the calls of the whales below him, and then seeing the surprised look on Brent's face when he'd placed the toy against the demon's throat.

Standing up, he slid the plane back in his pocket and checked the time. A little before one. He had a couple of hours. He nearly fell out the door on his exit, catching himself with the handrail before landing on the gravel ground. Industrial buildings surrounded him, single-story gray with metal roofs. Behind him, traffic beat a steady pulse on the highway, the truck parked among others that were all sitting idle, one next to the other like soldiers. He guessed the driver was now inside one of those buildings. A broad swath of pavement stretched between where Daniel stood and the buildings began, two sets of towering power lines overhead, half-dead trees rising in a greener area beyond the lot. In the distance, a group of brown hills marked the edge of San Francisco, the sky textured with wispy gray clouds that all seemed to be streaming eastward.

Walking felt good after being cooped up for so long. He crossed the lot and stepped inside the metal door of the closest building. Fluorescent lights stretched across a broad ceiling. On his right sat a gray counter, a man in his twenties typing on a computer. Behind him was another workstation with another young man typing, and beyond that, a third with a middle-aged woman on the phone. Up ahead, he spotted his driver standing in the hallway. The guy was chatting with a heavyset woman, his thumbs hanging from his belt loops. Daniel got close enough to listen. The driver had finished his run and was preparing to go home, he said. That meant he had to have his own vehicle nearby. Daniel scanned the guy's pockets, but couldn't tell where he might be keeping his keys. The driver kept talking. Now he and the woman were complaining about their pay and musing about when they might quit and find easier work. Daniel got the time from a plastic clock on the wall. "Come on, blabbermouth, let's get moving," he said.

The two paid no attention, continuing their conversation as if they had all day to discuss not much of anything. Daniel shifted from one foot to the other, his toes squishing on some unseen layer between him and the linoleum floor, his body lighter than he remembered it.

He needed to go, before he ran out of time.

Finally the driver reached into his pocket and pulled out his keys. Daniel stared at the black fob, then snatched it from the driver's hand. The guy seemed not to notice and kept talking to the woman. Daniel saw a door at the end of the long hallway and figured that's where the driver was headed. He bolted, running until he burst through. Another parking lot lay in front of him filled with passenger cars and pickups. Lifting the fob, he pushed the unlock button and spotted a navy-blue Dodge truck flashing its parking lights. A turn of the key, and the engine sprang to life. A screen came up similar to the one he'd seen on Brent's dashboard, the navigation application waiting for input. He punched in Bay Area Museum. The directions came up along with a time estimate: sixty-seven minutes. In the corner of the screen, the clock read one-ten.

A spark of hope burned in Daniel's chest. He tamped it down with a firm clench of his jaw and backed the truck out of the lot. The last thing he saw was the driver coming out of the doorway pointing his key fob Daniel's way.

After about a half-hour, he could tell he was getting closer to the city. The other vehicles pressed in against his, all of them moving faster now, as if they were being swept along a river headed toward a narrow ravine. Daniel joined the flow of hurried drivers, following the navigation screen toward the Golden Gate Bridge. Ten after two. He would get there early, which was perfect. If Tony didn't come, he could fade away into nothingness and that would be that. As to why he thought the fading would return just then, he couldn't be sure. Mostly it was a feeling, as if his very cells and tissues itched to float up into the clouds.

Gradually, the scenery around him changed. More trees appeared near the road, the houses and business buildings closer at times, granting him a glimpse into wide swaths of lawn adorned with flowerbeds and painted fences, the road turning this way and that, the traffic still heavy, still encroaching, but when he finally rounded the corner and came into view of the bridge for the first time, he slowed down, traffic be damned.

The sun gleamed off the elegant red towers standing powerfully against the blue sky, their beams wreathed in cottony clouds, evergreen bushes clumped underneath like devoted groupies. Imposing but welcoming, majestic but friendly, the bridge seemed almost to have a face and smiled at him briefly before casting its sweeping gaze back to the horizon. It was the sentinel watching over it all, the little people and the rolling hills and the traffic and the buildings and the endless expanse of water into which it had driven its feet. Then the road curved, and it was gone.

Daniel searched frantically for it, bobbing his head and craning his neck. After another few curves the bridge reappeared, this time directly in front of him, rising up as if eager to reveal its full height. The windblown trees below bowed in reverence, and Daniel felt a lifting off his seat that frightened him, but he wasn't fading, only coming up on the structure now, entering it, the other vehicles going much too fast as he longed to stop and look and turn and gawk. They pressed and bustled around him, carrying him along while pedestrians and cyclists explored the bridge's generous sidewalks. Beyond, the beckoning bay danced with sailboats and barges and windsurfers and fishing boats. He could only snatch a quick look here and there, steal a glimpse as the traffic forced him under the first tower, where he couldn't help but look up just once, the pickup wobbling in response to the movement of the steering wheel, and then the second one, the two like majestic entry gates to a medieval castle. When he came to the end and left the red railing behind, he awoke as if from a daydream and focused on finding the road that would take him down to the Bay Area Museum.

The navigation screen guided him toward exit 442, then right again on Bunker Road. He was close now, and it was only two-twenty-four. He slowed as the dashboard guide took him around Fort Baker. All the buildings looked the same, barrack-style white with red roofs that matched the color of the bridge, the grounds trim and well-kept, trees providing a homey feel even among the rigid sameness of the buildings. When he saw the sign pointing him to the Bay Area Discovery Museum, his heart quickened. He slowed the truck again, taking the right turn as directed. On his left rested more of the barracks lined up one after the other, but straight ahead sat a large parking lot already filled with vehicles. He wiped sweaty hands on his jeans, his gaze seeking a familiar face, the boy who would be looking for him. The parking lot stretched for a long way on his right, but the building had to be on the left. He looked back once through the passenger window and saw the bridge there, the clouds covering the uppermost part of the towers, the water playing happily underneath.

He had to get out. He slid into the first open space available, pocketed the key and walked toward the buildings. He soon found signs and colorful miniature flags leading him to the entrance of one, which looked like all the others but was designated the museum. A crisp white three-foot fence enclosed the green lawn in front, other parents with their children in tow going the same way. He waved his hands at the ticket agent but she turned her attention to the next family in line, so he walked on through.

At the entrance, he stopped to take it all in, but the artifacts were of no interest to him. His gaze passed them over in favor of scanning every child's face he could find, his feet floating from one room to the next, on a mission that allowed for no diversions. Fifteen minutes later, he emerged again into the bright sunshine, having failed to find his brother. Two-forty-one. He still had time, plenty of time. He made his way back to the parking lot, scanning all of the areas in between, but saw no evidence of a group of camp kids. The dark hole ate at his belly, its greedy tongue licking his sides. He still had another fifteen minutes at least. After casting his gaze about once more, he drifted toward the water.

Beyond, the bridge stood a work of art under the sunshine, the suspension wires the arms of a ballet dancer, the long stretch of road a slim and sleek belt line. When he heard children's voices, he paused, searching, and twice walked toward them, but they were all much too young, five- and six-year-olds, he would have guessed, some even younger, darting about the grounds shouting at one another, all of them going the same way he was—toward the bay.

Leaving the museum and parking lot areas behind he soon reached the dark, rocky sand, his gaze on the bridge as a group of noisy seagulls argued over a dead crab. A Coast Guard boat rested at the pier ahead, the breeze stronger now that he had left the sheltered area, its breath edged in ice. A group of four children explored the rocks ahead, picking up shells and bones and feathers, none of them familiar, one drawing in a notebook like Jolene might have done.

His gaze jerked to the bridge. *Jolene.*

The wind hit his face with a fistful of sand, the ground shifting underneath him. He squeezed his eyes shut, his head coming back with a jerk as his body fell. For a moment he was aware of nothing but a sudden darkness and an anticipation of an impact against the ground. But then no impact came. When he opened his eyes again, he could see nothing but a white-gray fog around him. His feet dangled in the air, no ground underneath. It was the fading again, he thought, but it was worse this time. He couldn't see anything, the fog suffocating in its density. He twisted and turned, his feet pedaling at the air, his heart racing. This was it. This had to be it. He was leaving the Earth now, going to wherever it was he was going, and he hadn't been able to see Tony.

He waved his hands as if trying to dissipate smoke. At one point he called Tony's name. Suddenly the air cleared and as it did, he screamed, for just below him appeared one of the massive bridge towers. He was floating above it, the clouds surrounding him, the traffic moving along in miniature far below, boats like ornaments on top of the bay. He thrashed his arms, trying to find something to hold on to, his belly in his throat.

He dropped. The wind buffeted his body. Eyes watering, he could see that he would pass the tower by on his descent. The long line of cars grew larger by the second, the tower soon right across from him, and then he was falling in front of it, too far away to touch it but near enough to see the details in the steel, the box-like cells and round rivets placed in rows. With only seconds now before a very painful death—or second death—he struggled to direct his fall somehow, finally getting it into his head to angle his body and take advantage of the air around him. Forcing his arms to his sides he pointed himself like an arrow toward the vertical suspender cables, seeing in them something he could hold onto, perhaps stop his fall before he splatted like a bug on the road below or broke his spine against the railing. His body shook and he had to tense his muscles to hold himself together, but it started to work, his trajectory changing a bit to the right, and for a moment he thought he might have done it, but then he went too far and drifted out over the water, leaving the bridge behind.

The bay opened its vast mouth below, a windsurfer crossing his path, and Daniel pushed his arms and legs as if swimming, willing himself back to the left, left, please left! He squinted his eyes shut, expecting the worst, but then opened them again and saw the main cable coming up fast in front of him, the thick one that dipped like a dancer's arm. He reached out too late and collided, his head smacking hard and then his chest. Despite the pain, he managed to wrap his body around one of the smaller vertical cables, arms and legs clinging until he was sliding down the woven steel like a pole, only to slam hard into the red railing bottom first, the impact ramming his sitting bones and reverberating up his spine. He grimaced but held on until finally, everything stopped.

Opening his eyes, he found himself sitting on top of the railing, clinging for dear life to the cable, facing the road beyond. In front of him, the sidewalk buzzed with pedestrians, some walking along with purpose as if intending to get to the other side, others pointing out items of interest in the bay below. Faces of every color and nationality blended together in a heady blur, but none of them saw him, their gazes passing over him as if he were part of the cable he clung to.

His heart slamming against the steel, Daniel remained where he was, unwilling to let go and feel that dreadful nothingness again. As he began to calm down, he thought to check the time but there was no clock nearby. Tony could have arrived in his absence. Daniel touched his pocket and felt the familiar bulge of the plane's form.

He needed to move. Struggling to control his trembling, he forced himself around the railing, both hands on the cable, until his back was to the sidewalk. Slowly, he lowered one leg and then the other until he could feel the cement pressing under his high-tops. For a moment he could only stand there, panting, but eventually he cast his gaze down and north, where the museum was. He had to get back.

He wrested both hands off the cable, allowing one to grab the top of the railing. Then, while keeping the steel under his palm, he began to walk north. Within a few steps he realized he had traveled all the way back to the first tower, putting him a good distance away from the pier and the museum. He needed to move quickly to get back to the water's edge. It seemed so far away now, the white buildings much smaller, the wide swath of sandy beach no longer revealing any telling details. Daniel walked and then jogged, focused on feeling the cement with each step, using the steel against his hand to keep himself anchored.

As he moved, he started to feel stronger, the Earth's energy returning to him in a mysterious downward push, as if gravity had decided once again to bless him with its presence. The others on the sidewalk were now mere obstacles. He didn't look at their faces but only pushed past them, an arm, a shoulder, a hat, a baby stroller, all of them like cones through a construction zone. He even let go of the railing at times to get by but then quickly recovered it, grasping the steel as if it were life itself. But whether the steel or the cement under his feet, something was changing. With every step north he felt more substantial, like the fading was over and he'd be okay now, though he dared not trust that notion.

He ran a little faster, passing the streetlamps with their square lights and red overarching beams, the cars rushing alongside him spewing exhaust, but when he turned his head only the fresh bay air greeted his sinuses. He was unable to look up for fear he'd rise again, but he could cast a glance down now and then, spotting a sailboat and then a slow-moving barge and soon a tourist boat packed with people, their multi-colored clothing bright and cheery in the sun. Far out, the shadow of Alcatraz waited under the haze. He ran faster, panicking now that Tony would leave, that somehow he'd miss seeing him, all the while knowing he might not be there at all. He pushed his legs to go, go, even though after every ten steps or so he had to slow down again to get around more people. As soon as he made it by, he picked up his pace, his throat burning, eyes watering from the constant wind in his face. It had to be three o'clock by now. Again he sought out the shoreline, searching for one dark-headed boy, the one solitary figure who had to be waiting there.

⸺ ❦❦ ⸺ ⸺ ❦❦ ⸺

He had made it to the point about halfway between the two towers when he spotted a clump of people gathered at the railing's edge. He planned to plow through them, but they were packed too tightly, their faces pointed toward the bay. He slowed, trying to spot a hole through which he could maneuver, but they had formed an impenetrable mass, a humming, buzzing group all agitated over something, the ones in the back standing on their tiptoes trying to see, as if there were some attraction uniquely notable at that spot.

He gritted his teeth and moved away from the railing, then set to squeezing through the tightly packed bodies, men and women and children talking in hurried tones, some of them dialing on their cell phones, others pointing the phones forward trying to catch video footage of whatever it was. Daniel cared only about getting to the other side and dashing as quickly as he could across the rest of the bridge. He caught the time on one of the elevated phones: 3:07. He ducked and wriggled, side-stepped and zigzagged, his shoulders at times passing through other shoulders with a sickening sensation that made him want to vomit. Avoiding that unpleasantness as much as possible, he stuck to the small empty spaces and finally broke through to the other side.

As he prepared to run again, an uncontrollable curiosity took hold of him, and he turned and went to the railing to look.

A solitary figure stood on the wrong side. Daniel had to blink and look again to be sure. Her slim body was exposed to the bay, her black boots resting on the track-like beam that formed the deck of the bridge, her hands gripping the steel bars behind her. It was a shocking sight, this waif-like figure standing where she clearly wasn't supposed to be standing, wavering over the deadly drop below. Daniel stared at her and then the water and felt a surge of adrenaline shoot through him, the drop too vast to contemplate, fear clutching his throat even at the thought of it.

The wind blew hard against her as if compelling her to return to safety, blasting her hair back from her face, her rich, red hair. At first Daniel stood frozen in place, bewildered, the sight so alarming he couldn't quite comprehend it, a person willingly facing that dreadful drop he'd just escaped, tempting it to take her, to compel her forward with just one misstep. But then, as he pressed against the railing, staring like all the others, it gradually dawned on him what he was really seeing, the figure so familiar, the hair he'd held in his hands, the small neck he'd stared at from the back of the Ford truck. She'd hardly moved the whole time, the only sign she was even real the occasional shift of her fingers as she loosened and then tightened her grip on the same rails that kept everyone else safe on the other side.

Daniel turned his gaze to the museum, the white buildings, and the rocky beach where Tony would be. He tried to see if he could pick out a small boy wandering about on his own, but he was too far away to identify any one person, his gaze catching only the sand and the water's edge and something dark here and there, but whether they were children or rocks he couldn't be sure. He imagined his brother standing in front of him, and his heart squeezed so hard his chest hurt. He started walking again, two and then three steps, but then stopped and turned back to the small figure balancing on the beam.

Jolene leaned out over the water. The crowd behind her continued to grow. It wouldn't be long before the authorities would be there too. Daniel could leave it in their capable hands, but his throat tightened every time he looked at her, the fear retaking him, the bald-faced fear that she was avoiding so calmly. Below, the seaweed drifted by like snakes, coiled and threatening on the surface, the waves short and hard in the afternoon chop. He took another step and another, but then paused, remembering her hands on his face, the soft touch of her skin. No, this couldn't happen now.

He whirled on his toe and stormed back. The closer he got the angrier he became, the demon's words whispering in his head: *She took him away from you. She ruined it all.* He pushed through the crowd, maneuvering between them with clenched teeth, and arrived just in time to see the small bones in her wrists change with the contraction of her arm muscles, her knees bent. Two hands reached through the bars to take hold of hers.

"Don't!" the bystander shouted. "We can help you!"

Daniel couldn't see who it was that had yelled the words, for it was necessary to yell over the power of the strong wind. Jolene whirled around, her face in full panic, and jerked her hands away. Her body wobbled precariously, boots unsteady on the narrow beam. A collective gasp went up from the crowd. Daniel stopped, his throat closed, until she grabbed the railing again to stop her fall.

"Stay back!" she demanded. The crowd responded, all of them retreating just a little, clearing the railing by about half a foot. Jolene remained with only one hand on the bar, the other at her side now. That hand was trembling but her face looked angry, not afraid, frustrated that she'd been interrupted.

Daniel stared at her, then glanced toward the pier. He felt a powerful urge to run. Three-fifteen on a neighbor's phone. In his pocket, the hard shape of the plane remained. He shut his eyes against the wind. *You need to hold on, okay? Lean forward when I do, and back when I do. You have to pay attention.*

Will you just go? I'm not a baby.

It's a hill we have to crest first thing, so you need to hold on.

I am holding on! Geesh!

Another collective gasp went up from the crowd. Daniel looked to see Jolene had moved closer to the edge of the beam, her hands on one of the cables. In the distance, sirens rang out. Help was coming. Daniel hesitated, his heart racing. She couldn't do it, wouldn't do it. It was too frightening. Completely against any kind of human nature to leap into that vast open air from so high a perch.

On his left, a small sailboat exited the pier by the museum, unusual in that it had one bright white and one smaller blue sail, the blue a brilliant shade like the lakes of Montana on a warm summer day. The craft's little body wavered back and forth as it sought to balance itself, a fragile vessel setting out on a mighty adventure. The sirens grew louder. Jolene looked back over her right shoulder, then out and down. She bent her knees again. Clenched her left fist. Let go of the cable.

"No! Jolene. Wait!"

She turned back just as two officers came onto the scene. They directed the crowd away, clear the way. "Miss? Hold on there." One of them began talking to her, but she wasn't looking at him. Her green eyes focused on Daniel's face. Daniel felt a surge of strength, the bond between them like gravity itself. "Come back," he said. Her eyes were red, the wind having beaten them to death, or was that from tears? Her cheeks burned a bright red too, and Daniel realized she was cold, frighteningly cold. "Come back where it's warm," he said.

The first officer, a stout man with thick wavy hair, urged her to rethink what she was doing, the other taller officer on his phone. Jolene stared at Daniel. "Did you find him? Did you find Tony?"

Daniel couldn't help but glance toward the pier.

"Did you find him?" she asked. The wind buffeted her body and whipped her jacket with a loud flapping sound. "It was me, you know. In the car that night. It was all my fault." She took her lower lip in under her teeth. "I had hoped he would come. You were so sure, I thought maybe . . . you'd have better luck than I did. With Mom."He stared at her face, her skin blotched with welts.

"What about your mom?" the first officer said, picking up on her last words. "Tell me about her."

Jolene's face changed, her features hardening. "I was drunk. Mom was gone. I wanted to see you, but I chickened out and went to the bar. It was my car. The Toyota. I'm the one who did it. I'm the reason you're here." She gestured at the air around them. "That's why you came back. That's why you found me."

Daniel stared at her. The truth lay between them a dead thing. The wind buffeted them both, pushing hard against them as if to discourage them from lingering any longer. The officers continued their efforts to get Jolene back over the railing. Daniel knew he should say something. She was waiting for it. She watched him, longing perhaps for him to condemn her. Or forgive her. When she got only silence, the lines disappeared from her forehead and the calm returned, the deadly, numb calm. She raised her head in acceptance, then pressed her lips together. In one smooth movement, she bent her knees, leaned forward, let loose of the railing, and jumped.

Reality split down the middle. Jolene entered the deadly void and suddenly Daniel knew nothing but the icy cast of fear. Every nerve in his body recoiled. Time stretched into an unnatural thinness, the microseconds like minutes. Robbing him of breath and argument, it suddenly made one thing abundantly clear: he had failed.

This wasn't about being reunited with his brother. Or having a chance to find forgiveness in those brilliant blue eyes. He glanced one more time at the pier below, longing for the way Tony's face would light up when he saw him, the stories he would tell about his week at camp, his chatter an endless joyful stream of excitement.

Danny, you should have seen it. It was so cool!

Perhaps that had been the carrot, the motivation to pull him here, but it was not the reason death had regurgitated him back onto the beach where the dying whales lay. Death wasn't consoling or comforting. It didn't defy every law of nature to assuage his guilt.

It had another reason altogether, a reason that had much more to do with serving its partner, life, than making itself any different than what it had ever been.

You're here for a reason, Wells had said.

The wind tore at her leather jacket, the fall a hard stepping-stone to the punishment she felt she deserved. He cast a final glance toward the museum but saw only the little boat with the one blue sail. It entered the bay a happy adventurer, both sails unfurled to their full majesty. Watching it begin its journey, he said a sad goodbye, a release of all he'd hoped might have happened, an acknowledgement of the finality of death and how his brother could have never returned here. He reached into his pocket. Feeling the toy plane solid against his skin, he understood. His only fear now was that he was too late.

Jolene's body tipped forward. The air took her. Defying every instinct, Daniel leaped off after her.

He was unprepared for the sheer force of the wind, the strength with which it pushed against him as if it might reverse his momentum and return him to the bridge. But then gravity reached up from the depths of the Earth to grasp him with an easy encircling of its invisible hand. With glee it yanked him down to deliver what was left of his body into the mouth of the hungry bay, the wind slicing his skin with its icy breath, the water a dark and devastating grave into which he would land with a crack, all his bones and muscles yielding to its superior strength. At first it took his breath away, and he could do nothing but fall. Then it occurred to him he wasn't going to reach her in time. Slamming his arms into his sides, he pointed his body toward the very grave that horrified him below.

Time stretched, pulling his bones thin while his thoughts sharpened with heightened focus. She still had her back to him, her arms and legs out as she fell, the jacket fringe flying behind her as if her mother had given her wings. When he reached her, he grabbed for the leather and, feeling it in his hands, experienced a momentary rush of relief, but the water still came, a speeding wall no less forgiving than one made of brick or stone. He pulled hard up and back and then, reaching around with his left hand, placed the plane up against Jolene's chest just under the hollow of her throat.

She had squinted her eyes closed but at his touch opened them wide. Her face expanded in alarm. The wind pushed hard at Daniel's back. He focused his thoughts up, up, up, concentrating on reversing their trajectory, dreading the impact of the water below. With everything that was in him he bent himself to this last effort, dreading the realization that he'd waited too long, that again he'd arrived on the scene after the worst had happened and any of his efforts now would fail to create any meaningful change. But then another nanosecond passed and he was still alive, still falling through the air, and when he looked up Jolene was looking back at him, the fear on her face having given way to wonder, her eyes questioning as they looked into his. Her skin remained pale and cold as it had been on the bridge, but her face was deliciously alive. Feasting his gaze upon it, Daniel hoped perhaps it had worked, that they were flying back up from the water, and in that moment he grabbed her hand and placed it over the one he held to her chest.

"For you," he said, "from Tony." Just before gravity reasserted itself with a savoring lick of its lips, Daniel transferred the plane from his hand to Jolene's, closing her fingers around it. He nodded, encouraging her to take it, to hold onto it as firmly as she could, and then squeezing the back of her hand, he began to let go. When he sensed her fingers responding, her arm close to her body as she accepted the gift, he hit hard, the impact shattering his spine, his organs slammed against muscles and bone, his head falling back and then smacking like a rock on the water's surface. Eyes bulging, he opened his mouth to scream but there was no sound, as the air had been forced out of his lungs. Fire shot from his lower spine to his neck and then circled around to consume his ribs. Something tore inside his gut, his stomach and liver lifting away from their nests and then settling again with a mushy thud, sharp knives all over his body stabbing, both legs breaking as they fell against the stone-hard surface of the water, his lungs like eggs dropped on cement and spilling new blood into his body. The metallic taste rose to his throat, his right shoulder separated from the joint to dangle aimlessly near. The only limb left intact was his left arm as he dropped low in the water, the light receding above him.

It hadn't worked. He'd failed again. In the midst of the pain and the blood rising into his mouth, this was all he could think, that it hadn't worked. He'd been too late. He tried to blink, to see clearly but couldn't, couldn't feel his legs anymore even as the pain knifed his shoulders and ribs. He was sinking, falling quickly into the depths of the bay. He needed to get back to the surface but couldn't move. He tried again to see through the depths, spot her figure above him. When his vision cleared, he saw only water. It filled the spaces between his fingers, the toy plane gone, in Jolene's hands now, if she had managed to hold onto it.

Blood swelled under his skin. His stomach bloated. He tried moving his arms and cried out in pain. Water rushed in, encroaching on his throat, threatening to sink into his lungs. He flapped his good arm and though his body moved a little, it wasn't enough. Looking up, he finally saw the sunlight on the bay, and there, straight above him, a shadowed figure lying on the surface. He went still and stared, a spark of hope in his breast, and for what seemed the longest time, his throat pressing in against itself as if a vice had clamped around his neck, he watched, squirming, suffocating, dying, hoping, and then finally, he saw it move, the arms and legs gently swimming, keeping the body afloat.

Daniel brought his good arm down next to him but the plane was no longer there. He pictured Tony sitting across from him on the tile floor, his eager gaze on the toy, his hands in front of him ready to catch it, his tongue poised at the corner of his mouth, making a little bulge just at the edge of his lips.

"Make it a good one, Danny. Make it fly."

The Coast Guard rescue boat skimmed across the water, its target the spot where the jumper had entered the bay. The craft had previously darted out from the north pier at top speed, the officers in blue uniforms having been alerted by the security personnel on the bridge. They'd prepared for the worst, for it was extremely rare for anyone to survive the deadly fall, their gazes trained toward the beam where the girl wavered, and then all of them with their hearts in their mouths when she jumped, the shadow of her fate darkening the sky over their heads. A negligible splash and the captain throttled forward, rushing them all toward the landing, their gazes searching but not finding, the surface having hidden the evidence among all the other waves.

Three people stood at the railing, dreading the inevitable nothingness they usually found, but then one of them called out and pointed and the captain responded. They soon pulled up alongside the girl to discover not only that had she survived but she seemed relatively intact, as if she had simply jumped into a swimming pool. They shook their heads as they lifted her onboard and draped her with a wool blanket, their expressions awestruck as they examined her, checking for injuries, each of them looking at her and then at one another with questioning gazes, the captain communicating with the emergency technicians waiting back at the pier.

"I don't know how it happened." A slim gentleman with pure white hair, he spoke in a coarse voice weathered by the sea. "Looks like she's got a sprained wrist and a bruised arm, but otherwise she seems fine."

He directed the craft back to the shore, puzzling over the miracle he'd just witnessed, for it wasn't what they usually found when retrieving the lost souls who had so naively taken that deadly step off the bridge. The typical find, if anything was retrieved at all, was a broken, bleeding mass of near-unrecognizable tissue and bone, the necks often twisted, the eyes reflecting the pain and shock that had come in the last moments. None of the victims expected the drop could be so brutal. Certainly nothing like the flight into blissful escape it seemed.

The girl sat by the railing, her small body shivering even in the heavy wool blanket, her gaze out on the water, and it wasn't until the boat had made it halfway back across the bay that one of the officers spotted what she was looking at. He pointed then, and they all gathered to see that something was following alongside, swimming quickly enough to keep pace. A long, angled fin popped out of the water and they guessed it was a dolphin but then noticed the bulbous head, lengthy body, and tucked tail at the end. A pilot whale, one said, eyebrows raised, and the others bent over to observe the unusual speed with which the creature swam.

The girl moved close to the edge of the bow. One officer darted after her, fearing she'd leap over, but she only grasped the railing to get a closer look. He stood nearby, ready to act. She watched the whale swimming alongside, her gaze focused somewhere in the middle of its back. At one point, she raised her hand and the officer saw that inside her palm she held a toy plane, something a boy might like to play with. He cocked his head, curious that a young woman would cling to such a thing, and even more puzzled as to why she'd be showing it to the whale.

The creature stayed with them until they got close enough to the pier that the shrinking depths became dangerous. Then it turned and made its way back out to sea. The girl waved, a long, sad wave with a bent arm and curved fingers, and the officer stared into the light over the water, wondering what it was she thought she saw. When he noticed the tears falling down her cheeks, he gently guided her back to the middle of the boat, but she kept looking over her shoulder, watching for the whale spout, and at one point she spoke.

"I'll try," she said, her gaze on the distant plume. "I promise."

After the boat was secured to the pier, the girl went willingly with the medical technicians in the emergency vehicle, the officer who'd watched over her standing by until the taillights were no longer visible on the road beyond. Then he turned to find the whale again, but it had gone too far out and he could no longer see its spout. For a long while he remained, searching, for never had he seen a pilot whale swim alongside a boat like that in San Francisco Bay. He knew as sure as he stood there that he'd never see one do it again.

Past the Golden Gate Bridge out on the Pacific side, the whale swam close to the surface. It followed a wave-like pattern up and down, going only so deep as to keep its momentum constant. To anyone who might have spotted it from the bridge, it was simply heading out to the ocean, but a trained eye would have noticed that it was following a very specific course, one that would eventually lead to the sailboat with the one blue sail. The craft had made good progress since leaving the pier, its bow bravely pointed toward the horizon. With a pair of powerful binoculars, an observer could have zoomed in on the passengers and seen one young boy around ten years old with dark hair and brilliant blue eyes. Next to him stood an older gentleman wearing a cowboy hat that somehow managed to stay on even as the ocean breezes whipped by, filling the sails full to taut. Both stood at the railing scanning the sea, and strangely, both were soon waving at the whale, whom it was now clear was headed straight for them. They waved with eager hands and arms, bright smiles on their faces. As the whale continued its journey, coming ever nearer, the boy's smile seemed to take up the entirety of his face. He began to jump up and down, shouting something that must have been a name, but the breeze whipped the sound away, sending it out over the waves and beyond, where only the seabirds would hear.

THE END

If you have thoughts of suicide or self-harm,
or if you have been affected by suicide, contact:

National Suicide Prevention Hotline:
1-800-273-8255

Suicide Prevention Resource Center:
https://www.sprc.org/

American Foundation for Suicide Prevention:
https://afsp.org/

ACKNOWLEDGMENTS

After I completed the first draft of *The Beached Ones*, I wanted to experience for myself the journey Daniel and his companions took. It seemed an indulgent idea at the time, but I am fortunate to have a supportive mom who loves to travel and encouraged me to go by gamely offering to go with me.

We enjoyed a once-in-a-lifetime trip, and I'm deeply grateful for her support, as well as to all the friendly people we met along the way. Many of the locations in the book are based on real places: Harlan, Iowa, is a beautiful little town with a picturesque central square; the Salt Lake City public library is an incredible feat of architecture joyful to experience; and I highly recommend the food and good service at the Diamond Horseshoe Café in Cheyenne, Wyoming, the inspiration for the café where Daniel and Jolene meet Ronny and Hank. (I assure you—the real location is peaceful and violence-free.)

I reserve a special place in my heart for the Golden Gate Bridge Patrol officer I met while visiting San Francisco. It was after dark when we stopped on the north side of the great bridge to gaze at it once more in its lit-up splendor. When the officer approached, I felt nervous, afraid he was coming to tell me to move along. The bridge was soon to close to pedestrians, after all. Instead he kindly took his time to chat with me about the structure, its history, and his work there, and without any prompting from me, soon began sharing some of his experiences with individuals who had either committed suicide or had intended to do so while on the bridge. His real-life stories informed the final scene between Daniel and Jolene, and gave me a much richer understanding of the tragedies that occur there on a regular basis. I was awed by this man's compassion and by the work he and his colleagues do to save lives every day.

This book was a nine-year project between first draft and publishing contract. My mom and I took the journey in 2014. I had hoped to find the officer's name in my notes, but I think I was too nervous and overwhelmed that night to work up the courage to ask for it. (To me, it felt like the universe had dropped an angel in my path to help me finish the book, and I didn't want to do anything to disrupt the flow of the conversation.) It is my hope that somehow *The Beached Ones* makes its way to that officer, so that he will know the impact he made on me and this story.

As for the book production, I am grateful to the insightful and wise Helga Schier for her thoughtful feedback during editorial development. I have no doubt her expertise helped improve the work, and her reassuring manner at every step of the way was a blessing. I thank editor Elana Gibson as well for her careful review and input, and for catching those important details a writer can sometimes miss.

My gratitude to the entire CamCat team, including publisher Sue Arroyo, outstanding cover designer Maryann Appel, copyeditor Cassandra Farrin, and marketing manager Laura Wooffitt, for their enthusiastic support and efforts in creating the best book possible and getting it out to readers.

My thanks to my family and friends for their enduring support of my writing career. Much love to my brothers, who taught me what sibling bonds are all about. A huge thanks to my stepdad Gerald for holding down the fort at the Swan View Goat Ranch while Mom explored Daniel's journey with me.

And finally, to anyone who may be experiencing the despair that can push one to consider leaving this life prematurely, I pray that this book will help you see that there is always hope to be found somewhere, in a friend's heart, a wild creature's eyes, or even in an innocent toy leftover from the happy moments of childhood.

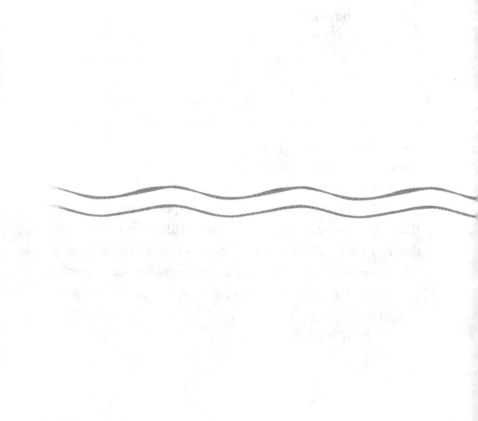

FOR FURTHER DISCUSSION

1. Has your life been touched by suicide? How did it affect you?

2. How close are you with your siblings? Would you spend the last hours of your life trying to get back to one of them?

3. What did you think of the character Brent Leary? What did he represent for you?

4. Jolene resorted to cutting to try to deal with her emotions. Have you known other people who went to great lengths to cope with painful emotions?

5. Do you think Daniel made the right choice in saving Jolene? Why or why not?

6. Talk about the significance of the toy plane. What role did it play in the story? Did you think that it was effective?

7. What would you say was the theme of the story? Why?

8. Daniel was dealing with a horrible, traumatic loss. In the face of something that difficult, what do you think is a way to heal?

9. What role did Gus play in the boys' lives? How important was that role? Do you have anyone in your life like that?

10. Talk about the boy's mother and their relationship to her. How did you feel about her? Did you condemn her for how she treated them, or did you feel compassion for her? Why or why not?

ABOUT THE AUTHOR

Colleen M. Story has worked in the creative writing industry for over twenty years. Her previous novel *Loreena's Gift* was a *Foreword Reviews'* INDIES Book of the Year Awards winner. She also writes nonfiction books for writers, including her most recent release, *Your Writing Matters*, as well as *Writer Get Noticed!*, a gold-medal winner in the Reader's Favorite Book Awards, and *Overwhelmed Writer Rescue*, Book by Book Publicity's Best Writing/Publishing Book of 2018.

As a full-time freelance health writer, Colleen has authored thousands of articles for publications like *Healthline* and *Women's Health*, worked with high-profile clients in the healthcare industry, and ghostwritten wellness books. She frequently serves as a workshop leader and motivational speaker, where she helps attendees remove mental and emotional blocks and tap into their unique creative powers.

A lifelong musician, Colleen plays the French horn in her local symphony and pit orchestras. When not writing or playing music, she's walking, reading, and exploring the beautiful Northwest with her four-legged pal, Storm. To learn more, see her website (colleenmstory.com), motivational blog (writingandwellness.com), and mystical blog (lifeandeverythingafter.com), and connect with her on Twitter (@colleen_m_story).

Q: What inspired this book?

A: The idea for this book came to me after watching the movie, "Sarah's Key," which was based on the book of the same title by Tatiana de Rosnay. The movie had a profound effect on me. Without giving too much away, the main character is haunted by the death of her little brother, for which she blames herself. At the end of the movie (spoiler alert), unable to shake her guilt, she commits suicide. Close curtain. That movie haunted me for months. It seemed so unfair, what happened to the main character. And I kept feeling like her story was left unfinished. What happened *after* the suicide? *The Beached Ones* gave me a chance to explore that general question, although of course, within an entirely different story.

Q: **Are there real-life models to your characters?**

A: The characters are all fictitious. I was affected by the suicide of someone dear to me early in my life, though, so the subject is close to my heart. I also have two brothers who are seven and eleven years younger than me, so the relationship between Daniel and Tony is familiar.

Q: **What do you want your readers to take away from this story?**

A: I hope readers may come away from *The Beached Ones* with compassion for those who are at the end of their ropes, and more so, with the understanding of the theme—that we help ourselves by helping others.

I'll never forget an experience I had a short time after my father died. I was feeling pretty down, understandably, and absorbed in my pain. I had to conduct a business meeting that day with a professional in the printing industry whom I had known for years. He was as congenial as always during our meeting, and revealed only afterwards that he had also lost someone special only a few days before.

My eyes were opened. I realized that at any one time, the people around us may be struggling just as much or more than we are. Being able to offer a shoulder that day helped lift my spirits. In my life it has never failed—when I can leave a smile on someone else's face, improve someone's day, or even just offer a listening ear, my load gets a little bit lighter.

Q: What would you consider to be the key theme of this book?

A: I feel that the main theme of this book is this: In order to heal ourselves, we must reach out and try to heal others. Often when we're consumed with pain, we can't see beyond our own experience. It's when we come face-to-face with someone else's struggles and feel compelled to help that we find relief.

Q: What was the greatest challenge when writing this book?

A: This book was very difficult to write. Not only was it painful, but it was hard to figure out logistically. What was the best way to tell it? In what order? How much did Daniel know, and how much did he not know? I started and stopped numerous times over a period of many years before I finally experienced a breakthrough. I'm so glad I stayed with it, as the struggle was worth it. I now feel at peace with Daniel's story.

If you enjoyed

The Beached Ones by Colleen M. Story,

you will also enjoy

The Secret Garden of Yanagi Inn by Amber A. Logan.

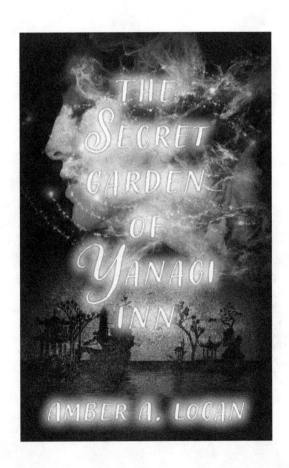

CHAPTER ONE

December 24th—Chicago, Illinois

⎪) d always been told hospitals were a place to heal and rest, but
⎪ my mother's hospital room was an assault on the senses. The
⎪ stench of decaying flowers and cloying cherry disinfectant
clung to my skin, invaded my nose. A wave of nausea swept over
me. I couldn't breathe, couldn't think.

"I need to get some air."

I rose to my feet before Risa could object, although I knew she
wouldn't. My sister had been trying to convince me all day to leave
Mom's hospital room, to go get some real food or take a walk.

"Sure, Mari, go ahead. I'll stay with Mom." Risa nodded without looking up, her short blond curls bobbing. She leaned back

in her bedside chair, still absorbed in her book. I glanced at Mom, now a papery, skeletal version of the woman she once was. But at least she was peaceful, sleeping.

As soon as I stepped through the hospital's sliding glass doors, the blast of cold air sent an involuntary shiver through my body. I pulled my shoulder-length hair back into a ponytail, knowing the chill wouldn't last, that five minutes in I'd be sweating, my muscles warmed.

Maybe the fact I already wore running shoes was fate, or maybe I'd just gotten lazy—too exhausted after so many long days split between the gallery and the hospital to care about my appearance. Either way, I'd dressed in sweats that morning and I was going for a run, damn it.

I turned north and ran down the nearly deserted sidewalk. Streetlights were wrapped with faux greenery and twinkling lights, and last week's snowstorm had left lingering mountains of gray snow on the edge of parking lots. The morning air stung my throat, but the cold was a welcome change from the stifling hospital room.

I ran for most of an hour, my pace too fast to fall into a comfortable groove. But the burn in my muscles and the emptiness of my mind renewed me. No worrying about the doctor's cryptic prognoses, about visits from the counselor who peeked in occasionally to "see how we were doing." I could just run—it was me and the cold air and the thud-thud-thud of my feet on the pavement, and all was right in the world.

But it wasn't.

This was a dream, and reality waited for me back in that suffocating room. Risa would be wanting her mid-morning coffee and I, being the good big sister that I was, ordered two drinks from the Starbucks around the corner so she didn't have to settle for the unbranded kiosk in the hospital's lobby.

I expected to return a hero, sweaty but triumphant, brandishing two grande peppermint lattes as I opened Mom's door. But as I carried the drinks down the hospital corridor, I saw Mom's door was already open. My hands trembled.

I sped up.

Sounds of movement and talking inside the room. And crying—Risa was crying. I broke into a run, burning my hands as peppermint latte sloshed onto the pristine polished floor.

Risa was still in her chair, sobbing behind both hands, her book dropped at her feet. Two hospice nurses stood at the foot of Mom's bed, speaking in quiet, respectful tones.

Mom didn't look any different, looked for all the world like she was still sleeping.

But the whirring, dripping sounds had stopped. They'd turned off all the machines. Only Frank Sinatra's crooning "Silent Night" drifted down the hall from a distant room.

Mom had died.

And I'd missed it.

CHAPTER TWO

Two Months Later—En Route to Kyoto, Japan

The dimmed cabin lights brightened to a rosy glow, mimicking a sunrise though it was late evening in Kyoto. I wiped the drool off my lip with the back of my hand, glanced at the passengers on either side of me. The elderly woman to my right was awake, watching *Roman Holiday* on her seatback screen—Mom's favorite movie, one I'd watched with her three times in the hospital alone.

The smartly dressed blond woman on my left had her laptop out on her tray table, her stockinged feet resting on a carry-on bag with the same floral print as Mom's weekender bag. Something Mom had picked up in England, an optimistically small bag for her hospital stay. The woman was probably working. Her nails on the keys tick-tick-ticked away, knocking on the door to my brain, reminding me I should check my work email. I reached for the bag between my feet. And Risa would need to know where I'd left Mochi's pills. She needed to know he wouldn't take them without sticking the pills inside butter. She needed to know—

STOP IT, Mari. I pictured my little sister smirking at me, arms crossed, standing next to my white puffball of a dog. Relax—*I've got this.*

I leaned back in my seat, rhythmically twisting the too-loose ring on my middle finger.

The flight attendant pushed a drink cart down the aisle. She wore a fitted top and pencil skirt, a jaunty kerchief with the Japan Airlines red crane logo tied around her neck. "Green tea, coffee?" Her voice was quiet, soothing.

I raised my hand. "Coffee would be amazing, thank you."

She smiled a practiced smile, set a small cup on a metal tray, and poured the coffee from a carafe. The two women on either side of me asked for green tea.

Even over the aroma of my coffee, I could smell their tea. I'd missed it, the slightly bitter scent, the warmth of it. A scent from my childhood.

Japan. *I'm really going back. This is real. This is NOW.*

I took a sip of the coffee, hissing as it stung my tongue. A sharp, cheap flavor like the instant crap Thad used to buy when he'd finished off my good stuff.

I should've asked for tea.

"*Ladies and gentlemen, we will be landing at Kansai International Airport in approximately half an hour. We anticipate a slightly early arrival. Local time is 7:14pm.*"

My cardigan was damp with sleep sweat. I'd take it off, but I was afraid of elbowing the ladies next to me, so I made do with pulling my hair back into a ponytail and hitting the button for my personal fan. It whirred to life, but its clicking annoyed me and I turned it back off. In the row behind me, someone sneezed.

What the hell was I doing running away like this—abandoning my sister, my newly-ex-boyfriend, maybe even my job? Tears welled in my eyes and I fought them back, staring at the screen in front of me, at the image of the tiny airplane and the dashed-line trek it'd made across the Pacific Ocean. Even if Risa had made all the arrangements and basically shoved me out the door, it felt wrong to just leave. Even if it was for only four weeks.

Deep breaths, Mari, deep breaths.

At first the timing of the grant had seemed fortuitous, if a bit rushed. But the closer I got to Japan, the more reality set in and the vague details of the NASJ grant paperwork felt more and more inadequate. Photograph an old Japanese inn "for posterity's sake?" It wasn't much to go on. Had I brought the right camera lenses? Would four weeks even be enough time? It seemed an eternity to me right now, but I'd never been asked to document an entire estate, never even received a grant before. I was an artist, not a documentarian. At least, I used to be an artist.

Maybe I should've splurged for the upgraded camera bag with better padding. I pictured the *Roman Holiday* woman next to me opening the overhead compartment and my camera bag tumbling out onto the floor. Contents may have shifted during flight.

Could she even reach the overhead compartment? She was a tiny Japanese woman—70 at least. I snuck a glance at her.

But Mom was sitting next to me.

I froze, my entire body turning numb.

Mom, leaning back in her seat, was watching the movie with a slight smile on her lips. Her platinum blond hair was tied back in a loose ponytail, but tuffs had fallen out and were dusting her shoulders, her blouse, like dead leaves. She sipped her green tea.

I struggled for air. The sweat dotting my skin turned cold, clammy. *No, no, no. I'm just tired, didn't get enough sleep.* I closed my eyes, inhaled deep, gasping breaths. Oranges, I smelled freshly peeled oranges.

"Are you all right, honey?"

My eyes flew open. CEO woman on my left, with her slim laptop and flowered bag, stared at me. Her eyes were wide with concern. I shot a glance to my right. The little grandmother had returned and was happily watching her movie, oblivious to my distress. *Am I all right?* The dreaded question.

Did she mean "do I need medical attention?" Or was it more of the existential "all right" we all seem to strive for but never quite manage? I smiled at the woman, responded with the only reasonable lie one can give to that question: "I'm fine."

Deep breaths, Mari. Deep breaths.

The flight attendant in her perfect pillbox hat and red bandana came by again with white gloves and a plastic trash bag. I handed her my half-empty cup of coffee with an apologetic smile.

I should've asked for tea.

Like an orderly river, we flowed off the plane and down the jet bridge, then spilled out into the brightly lit airport. I squinted, one hand carrying my camera bag, the other pulling my square under-the-seat luggage.

The stop at the bathroom with its private floor-to-ceiling stall doors, the polite customs workers, the wait for baggage—it was all a blur. A foggy-headed, clips-and-phrases of Japanese and English blurring together kind of chaos. But I was a dumb American, the tall, brown-haired white lady looking like a confused tourist, so of course I was funneled through with utter politeness and a tolerance I was grateful for, yet also resented. I didn't need their help. I say that, but when I finally stepped out into the arrivals area and scanned the crowd for a sign or a screen or a hand-scrawled note featuring "Marissa Lennox," I found none. My heart leapt into my throat for a moment, but I swallowed it back down. No worries, the plane had landed a few minutes early. Maybe my ride was running late. Maybe there was a miscommunication about the terminal.

Maybe...

I scanned the line of men in suits and white gloves again, watching for a glimmer of recognition in their alert faces, but each one's eyes slid past me to the next arriving passenger. I didn't match their profiles. Of course I didn't.

I found a bench nearby where I could keep one eye on the sliding glass doors and the other on my oversized suitcase and assorted bags. But no drivers came rushing in, embarrassingly late to pick up the unfortunate foreign woman. I considered buying a coffee at the kiosk or indulging in my love of Japanese vending machines, but decided against it. I didn't relish shoving all my luggage into a tiny bathroom stall if I had to pee before I left.

And so, I waited.

A handful of older businessmen passed by, glanced surreptitiously my way, chattering amongst themselves with the self-assuredness of men who assume I can't understand them. One laughed and nodded. I caught a few of their words in passing: foreigner, tall, Chelsea Clinton. I chuckled and raised an eyebrow. Maybe Chelsea Clinton on her worst day—my frizzy brown hair with graying roots was already sneaking out of its scrunchie to spill across my oily face.

I tucked a strand of hair behind my ear and turned on my phone, careful to keep it in airplane mode. Damn it, I hadn't thought I'd need an international plan. I pulled up the email from Ogara-san at the Yanagi Inn—no phone number, not even in the email signature. I leaned my head back against the hard wall, practiced the breathing technique Risa had taught me in the hospital months ago. *Breathe in, one-two-three, breath out, one-two-three.*

I double-checked the email, noted the inn's street address. If no one came to pick me up, I could just step outside, find a cab, and give them Yanagi Inn's address. I wasn't helpless, after all.

But still, having no one to meet me . . . it wasn't a good omen.

A half hour passed before I thought to check the print-out of the grant paperwork Risa had sent me. I spent long minutes digging through bags until I found it slid in the pocket beside my laptop. I balanced the computer on my lap and smoothed the sheet of printer paper across its flat top.

I hadn't bothered printing the front page, only a few paragraphs from the middle, with highlighted parts I'd thought relevant. No contact info.

. . . for the purpose of documenting, via artistic photography and for the sake of posterity, the property known hereafter as YANAGI INN . . .

"Lennox-san?"

I glanced up sharply, nearly toppling the laptop. A 60-something woman with greying, short-cropped hair stood over me. She wore a simple indigo kimono with a wide cream-colored obi belt, and a grandmotherly air of silent disapproval.

"Ogara-san?"

She gave a barely discernable nod and turned toward the glass doors. I scrambled, shoving the printout and my laptop back into their bag. I didn't even have time to pull out my jacket.

"Wait!" I called after her, frustration creeping into my voice as I grabbed the handles of my various bags and rolling luggage.

It felt like every one of the airport's many patrons turned and stared at me. I flushed and scrambled after Ogara-san, the only person in the building who hadn't bothered acknowledging my cry.

I tripped out of the automatic doors, following the old woman into the brisk night air. She was surprisingly quick in her traditional wooden sandals, weaving between travelers toward a slick black sedan waiting at the curb, its lights flashing. A driver in a black suit and white gloves hopped out of the car and started loading my bags into the spacious trunk. I thanked him, my cramping arms lightening with every bag removed from my care.

Ogara-san climbed into the passenger's seat before we had the final bag in the trunk, so the driver opened the door to the back and I slipped inside, grateful to sink into the soft leather interior.

It's dark, I thought vaguely, for both the car's tinted windows and the sky outside were inky, seductive, and as soon as I set down my camera bag, clicked my seatbelt, and rested my head against the cold window beside me, I was out.

MORE SPINE TINGLING STORIES FROM CAMCAT BOOKS

CamCat Books

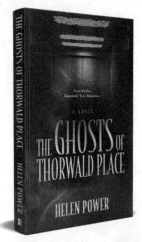

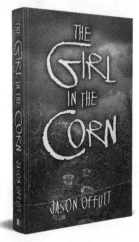

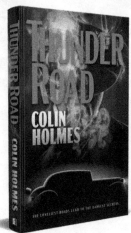

Available now, wherever books are sold.

CamCat Books

VISIT US ONLINE FOR
MORE BOOKS TO LIVE IN:
CAMCATBOOKS.COM

FOLLOW US

CamCatBooks   @CamCatBooks   @CamCat_Books